NOT MARY SHELLEY'S
THE LAST MAN

A Novel of 1826 Refashioned
for Modern Readers
by
LIZ MACKIE

• NOSTALGISTUDIO : NEW YORK •

2024

Published by Nostalgistudio

ISBN 978-1-7323931-6-5

Visit nostalgistudio.com to learn more.

Not Mary Shelley's
THE LAST MAN

A futuristic account of a global pandemic that wipes out the entire human race, Mary Wollstonecraft Shelley's second novel was published in 1826 to poor reviews and long oblivion. The haste in which she wrote The Last Man shows, and to this day the writing style elicits harsh complaints. Now, word-by-word renovation by novelist Liz Mackie reveals a text that stands comfortably alongside Frankenstein as a masterwork of speculative horror. This showcase for Mary Shelley's epic imagination and rich talents as a travel writer, social critic, and psychologist, also succeeds in bringing readers into the room with literary history, as poets Percy Shelley and Lord Byron, heroes of the Romantic era, both appear in detailed fictionalized portraits. And in a remarkable departure from its best-selling predecessor, the book abounds in closely observed female characters, women and girls of strong opinions and strong passions, articulate, dynamic, confronting tragedy with memorable valor. Likewise their creator—who, through them, explored her young widowhood and memorialized her grief.

In this Nostalgistudio edition, originally presented online as a pandemic project, The Last Man emerges as the heartbreaking, gripping, well-tuned Mary Shelley novel that 200 years of readers have been hoping for.

Liz Mackie launched Nostalgistudio, her independent publishing company, with the epic historical novel LAMENT: A Soviet Woman and Her True Story. Three volumes deep into FAMEPUNK, her picaresque historical-fantasy series set in the world of women's tennis, Liz has also published a poetry collection (Dug for Victory: Poems from RIP-TV), a travel novella called The Happy Valley, and many on-line writings. A long ago graduate of Swarthmore College, she lives and works in New York City.

Dedicated to a fellow writer
Robert Bevan Dunphy
with gratitude for his encouragement

CONTENTS

Reunions in Scotland end in recovery. Adrian salutes creation and resolves to live for others.

Adrian's sister has captured Lionel's heart. Her mother the Ex-Queen has other ideas. "Attend, O reader! while I narrate this tale of wonders!"

Idyllic years for a circle of friends conclude with an experiment in politics. Who wants to run England?

Psychological torture enters the story, as Lionel's sister Perdita begins to experience the world of a politician's wife.

In the midst of his term as head of state, Lord Raymond stumbles on extramarital love in a poor artist's garret.

With his wife holding proof of his adultery, Lord Raymond puts on a show and then loses his mind.

A brave and determined Perdita plays hostess at an elaborate gala; the guest of honor fails to arrive.

Two letters to one man.

After a musical evening, Perdita tells her brother Lionel that he cannot understand what woman's love is.

Lord Raymond seeks a remedy for what his passions have done to him.

War in Greece returns one character to Windsor, and takes two more away.

ACKNOWLEDGEMENTS

In May 2021, at thelastman.blog, I began offering the present work online in serialized .pdf form, each installment accompanied by images, essays, and historical background; I posted the fifty-third and final one in September 2023. Much revised, the text that follows is essentially the same as can be found there on Wordpress. The "for sale" aspect of a public "for free" literary project by Nostalgistudio, my small independent publishing company, this book is to be bought for the sake of convenience and style.

Mary Shelley's original is already in the public domain, of course. The online project offers links and readers are encouraged there and now to compare our two writings of the novel. The digital copy I used came from Project Gutenberg, one of the very greatest public resources. Another is Internet Archive, whose boundless treasures include a scanned copy from Brandeis University Libraries of The Last Man in its original second and final edition, complete with marbled endpapers and a letter in Mary Shelley's own hand, preserved there by a collector; Internet Archive also allowed me to consult her published letters, collected in three volumes and edited by the late, great Betty T. Bennett. And a free account at JSTOR supplied essays with key information on Baiæ, just for starters.

Throughout the project I referred to an annotated on-line edition of The Last Man created in the late 1990s and housed, along with many helpful supplemental materials, on a U.S. university website called Romantic Circles; I'm deeply indebted to all the scholars involved in that work, which I am sad to report appears to have been taken down in a revamp.

The Last Man is full of travels by land, sea, and air. In attempting to update and clarify its geographies for today's readership, my reliance on Google Maps cannot be overstated.

My project eventually involved many nighttime visits to museums and libraries near home and out of town—to antiquarian societies and historic sites across Britain and Europe and beyond. That is, along with the rest of the world that found itself shut in by the COVID pandemic, I owe another debt of lasting gratitude to the talented, principled people who've worked to build and maintain fine institutional digital collections along with fair public use of them. More thanks go to the dozens of professors and students, researchers, historians, natural scientists, private scholars and smart bloggers whose websites—many of them passion projects like mine—supplied insights and images that brought The Last Man alive online, and so often made their way from the screen into the fabric of the text.

Near the end of the project, I reached out to Ian Coulling, creator of the beautiful website Images of Venice, for permission to include some of his work in an installment of the blog. His generosity at that time, has extended to the use of one of his photographs for the cover image of this book. I thank you from my heart, Mr Coulling.

For his simply transformative advice, all praise to my title man Ragland Watkins.

To my sister Claudia Mackie, infinite thanks. Our mother, Myrna Mackie, as well as our dear friend Lynne Mazza, both died while I was working on this project. I feel their loss, maybe not least in the way it's deprived me of two invaluably enthusiastic and very fast early readers. So I'm all the more grateful for Claudia. When she finished reading the eventual manuscript and called it "a good yarn," I felt I had my reward.

Summer 2024

INTRODUCTION

LIKE most people who've read and enjoyed Frankenstein, up until the pandemic year of 2020 I'd never heard of Mary Wollstonecraft Shelley's futuristic second novel, The Last Man. Since it concerns a plague that wipes out the entire human race, leaving just one survivor, it was inevitably written up in online outlets at the time. Project Gutenberg offers downloads. Prepared to be highly entertained, I was perplexed to find a rather meandering story of British ruling class politics and infidelity, set mostly at Windsor Castle of all places; after the action moved to the Mediterranean came what felt like an endless bog of battle scenes. With swords, amid cannon fire, Greeks fight "Mahometan" Turks on horseback and foot—this though the year is supposed to be about 2090. There was no sign of a plague yet when I shut the file and set The Last Man aside. Weeks passed before my curiosity got the better of me. How, I asked myself, could a book by Mary Shelley not be worth taking the time to finish?

Published at the end of 1826, as a new work by "The Author of Frankenstein," it received bad reviews and only went to two editions: a disappointment to its author, who needed money. Though not yet thirty years old, she was four years widowed, the mother of four children all but one of whom had died in infancy. Her remaining son's aristocratic grandfather was her central financial support; her own father, also a writer, constantly in debt, also relied on what she could extract from the rich father-in-law. She was sitting on a potential gold mine, for she had all her husband's papers, the last known drafts of essays and poems that would add to his legacy as one of the great Romantic poets, prose artists, thinkers, revolutionaries, visionaries, untamed spirits—Percy Bysshe Shelley was all those things. He was also an extremely difficult person to be married to, one who threw away his life for a whimsical trip in a badly-designed boat. Never less than notorious, he had fame in life and in death; a memoir

4

would sell, the last poems and essays would sell. But the Baronet, Percy's unforgiving father, would not allow one word of it onto the market. His son had been a source of shame to him for years: the old man thought enough was enough. He'd relent eventually, but his long hostility and sporadic mean intransigence made Mary Shelley a writer in need of a follow-up best-seller.

To create the story, she drew heavily on her own past and present life. The battle scenes that almost defeated me derive from letters she was getting from a close male friend and eyewitness in Greece, where the people's fight for independence from Turkish rule had just claimed the life of their superstar partisan: George Gordon, Lord Byron. Poet, idol, anti-hero, restless soul, Byron, a man Mary Shelley knew well (he did not seduce her), is easily recognized as the model for Lord Raymond, a major character in The Last Man; likewise the royal-born Adrian, her narrator's closest friend, stands as a portrait of Percy Shelley. Though she never published a thing under her own name, contemporary readers knew very well who "The Author of Frankenstein" was before one of The Last Man's more hostile reviewers also revealed her identity (this occurrence prompting the Baronet to once again cut off her funds). For its roman à clef aspects alone, the book should have drawn a big audience. Instead, it went out of print for over a hundred years.

Why, even now, read The Last Man? Why, for that matter, spend hours and hours on the editing job one has made of it? A major reason has to be for how close it brings the reader to Shelley and Byron and Mary Shelley herself, brilliant young people, as they were when they were living and breathing; as it felt to be in the same room with them (not always comfortable); even as it felt to love them; and finally as it felt when the great poets were gone, taking the spells they'd cast with them—though their fascination proves enduring.

While admirers of Frankenstein might miss its inspired plot and charismatic Creature, they'll find its author at work on a larger, even more prophetic scale here. Enduring stubborn irksome inequality, compromised leaders, warring religions, fractured politics, climate change, a global pandemic, mass migration—one after another, our real-life current dilemmas make their sometimes uncanny appearance among the pages that follow. And in a revelatory departure from

Frankenstein, we're given an abundance of closely-observed female characters, women and girls of strong opinions and strong passions, articulate, dynamic, memorable, much like their creator.

Then there's the last half of the book, where humanity slips through an hourglass and Mary Shelley's strengths as a writer really come into play. Rest assured: The Last Man is a very challenging and complicated novel, and also extremely frightening. It delivers on its promises.

But in its day the story's idea was attacked and called unoriginal. The writing style was savaged. Could it be more difficult, as well, for "a female writer," as one critic called her, to build up a reputation strong enough to carry two major works into posterity? While Frankenstein's popularity has never waned, The Last Man fizzled. Which did not stop Mary Wollstonecraft Shelly, whose admirably, infinitely fearless self-respect marked her as her mother's daughter. She wrote other now-forgotten novels. She continued to live a rich though often financially insecure life, full of friends and interests and relocations and greatness; her biographical notes to Shelley's poems are great—as a document of their age, essential. Her boy, Percy Florence Shelley, would live and grow up to inherit and marry and, with his wife, be his mother's support until the end of her life; brain cancer claimed her at 53.

Overall, and today, the critical consensus is that the book could have been better edited. Considering that Volume 1 has two fourth chapters, reproduced ever since as 4/I and 4/II, the publisher's attention to the text was questionable. For such a long novel, it was turned out quickly, in only sixteen months. And for the first time in her writing career, Mary Shelley didn't have her brilliant husband there to edit the manuscript: she was on her own. Redundancies abound in Volume 1 and internal inconsistencies aren't absent. Long passages seem repurposed from old letters and journals dating from her marriage. As mentioned, those battle scenes in Volume 2 don't help. Online, a one-star review of The Last Man runs:

"Horrible. . . .Frankenstein is my fav novel of all time. The last man is the worst book i ever read. Waste of time".

This says a lot, and speaks directly to why I undertook to re-write it.

Advocating for The Last Man before me was the wonderful British writer Muriel Spark, who published her first book, Mary Shelley: Child of Light, in 1956. At that time, the novel was long out of print and only available on the antiquarian market. In Child of Light, she describes it as "not. . .a Gothic novel entirely;"

> nor is it realist fiction, for the whole work is a fantasy; and neither is it a domestic tale, for the work deals with society at large as well as family life; moreover, it is not a sociological novel, since the disintegration of the social scene leaves a large part of the book to a study of individual man. The Last Man, in fact, defies classification in any known fictional genre. . . a group of three futuristic pictures, associated with, yet distinct from, each other.

Really, then, a very modern novel, she might have added; otherwise I could not improve upon Child of Light's discussion of the book and where it came from. After quoting one of Mary's letters from 1824, when she'd just begun writing it: "'The last man! Yes I may well describe that solitary being's feelings, feeling myself as the last relic of a beloved race, my companions extinct before me,'" Spark concludes:

> Evidence of the physical analogy between the novel and its author occurs throughout; she depicted, in terms of enormously wide invention, the narrow and individual process that led to her own isolated situation in the years immediately following Shelley's death.

Muriel Spark's estimation of The Last Man was high enough, that in the hope "that wide recognition of its merits may lead to its being reprinted," she included an abridged "utilitarian" version as an appendix to Child of Light's first edition. (After 1965, when the novel itself was finally reissued, this appendix was dropped; it appears, though, in the Carcanet Press edition currently available for Kindle.) Here, she intersperses a detailed plot synopsis with key passages of text. No word processors, no scanners, not even a copier—this was a massive job at the time, undertaken freely, all for the sake of a worthy cause, the increase of a good writer's reputation and readership. As an act between writers, novelists, it inspires emulation.

In revising and editing The Last Man for modern readers, I've sought to make its many strengths shine forth—so that it might be easier to see, for instance, the book's affinities with Frankenstein, another tale of adventures in philosophical horror. Taking the comprehensive line-by-line approach enabled by digital technology, I've moved some passages around to heighten the action of the plot, pared back redundancies, and generally "fixed" how things sound: updating old locutions that might act as stumbling blocks to present-day ears; adding contractions and possessives; rendering Mankind and the like more inclusive. True to its era, the original text is packed with poetic quotations and references to myth and ancient history; I've given context, translated, or cut as seemed best. I've worked to sharpen visual details for readers raised on camera images: Mary Shelley has a different eye from ours, one trained in a world dominated by the printing press. I've made a handful of additions and outright transformations. I've also left countless passages of wonderful writing unchanged. Though each chapter wound up some hundreds of words shorter than in the original, it's all here. My goal has been to offer The Last Man to the public in the form of the gripping, well-tuned nineteenth-century novel it always had the potential to be.

> Doubtless the leaves of the Cumæan Sibyl have suffered distortion and diminution of interest and excellence in my hands. My only excuse for thus transforming them, is that they were unintelligible in their pristine condition.

These words of Mary Shelley's, preserved verbatim from the novel's opening pages, overstate the present case but capture the elements of mission and transmission at work here. This book is the culmination of a literary project begun during the latest pandemic, which seeks to honor a writer who was writing on the subject almost two hundred years ago—to honor her and the enormous grief her work memorializes. It takes its place beside the countless thousand theatrical, film, and literary projects she and her writing constantly inspire. Why Mary Wollstonecraft Shelley? Maybe because her mother died when she was born; maybe because of all that befell her; maybe because she was a prophetess; maybe because by nature she wrote scary things. Somehow, across the centuries, she enlists us to her side.

Mary Shelley's

THE LAST MAN

(1)   I VISITED the Bay of Naples in the year 1818. On the 8th of December, my companion and I went to see the antiquities which are scattered on the shores of Baiæ. We took a boat there from Naples.

Nearing Baiæ, the translucent waters of a calm sea disclosed fragments of old Roman villas, interlaced by seaweed and touched with diamond tints by the flash of sunbeams on the shining surface overhead. Though it was winter, the genial warmth on sea and land seemed more appropriate to early spring, and it was with sensations of placid delight that we disembarked on that volcanic shore and wandered through various ruined temples, baths, and classic spots renowned from myth and ancient poetry.

At length, through a gash in a rocky hillside, we entered the gloomy realm of the Cumæan Sibyl, legendary priestess and prophetess of Apollo. The red flames of our guides' flaring torches dimmed duskily in the murky subterranean passages, whose darkness seemed eager to swallow any light. At one natural archway, we asked whether we could enter and continue; but the guides pointed to the reflection of their torches on the water that paved the floor there, leaving us to form our own conclusions. It was a pity, they added, for it led to the Sibyl's Cave. Excited and curious now, we insisted upon attempting the passage. Sure enough, we found the edges dry and passable. Reaching a large, dark, empty cavern, which the guides assured us was the Sibyl's Cave, we were disappointed, but examined everything closely, seeking traces of the wonders it had witnessed.

All we found was a small opening on one side. The guides said it led nowhere. My companion and I decided to try it anyhow, guessing it might be the way to the real cavern. But our guides protested, loudly, in their native Neapolitan dialect, with which we were not very familiar. We gathered that there were ghosts ahead—that the roof would fall in—that the passage was too narrow to admit us—also, that a deep hole further on was filled with water and might drown us. My friend shortened the harangue by taking the man's torch from him. We proceeded alone.

The passage did indeed grow narrower and lower. Bent almost double, we kept on until we reached a spot where we could stand upright. Our self-congratulations and relief were extinguished by a current of air that blew out our torch and left us in utter darkness. We'd brought no matches. All we could do was go back—but where was the passage? We groped around the walls until we found an opening that led, however, to a second, ascending passage which terminated like the first in a wider space. Here, though, a very doubtful twilight made it just possible to see around us. A dim cavern; up high on one side we spotted a narrow arch from which the little light seemed to be issuing. With considerable difficulty we scrambled through and found another, slightly less dim passage to another narrow ascent. Several more such followed, which our resolution alone permitted us to surmount.

At last we beheld the source of the light we'd been following: an aperture in an arched dome-like roof, overgrown with brush and brambles which acted as a veil, obscuring the day, and giving a solemn religious hue to the cavern below. This was spacious and nearly circular, with a raised seat or small couch of stone at one end. In the middle lay the perfect snow-white skeleton of a goat. The animal must have missed its footing as it grazed on the hill above and fallen headlong. Ages perhaps had elapsed since this catastrophe; and the brief rip it had made above had been repaired by vegetative growth many dozen summers past.

Otherwise the cavern contained nothing but piles of leaves, fragments of bark, and some pale filmy stuff that resembled husks from unripe Indian corn. Fatigued by our climb through the caverns, we seated ourselves on the rocky couch. The sounds of tinkling sheep-bells and the shout of a shepherd-boy reached us from above.

At length my friend, who had taken up some of the leaves from the floor, exclaimed, "This is the Sibyl's cave! Look—these are Sibylline leaves, the written prophecies, here." On examination, we found that all the leaves, bark, and other substances were traced with written characters. What appeared to us more astonishing, was that these writings were expressed in a variety of languages. Some— ancient Chaldean, and Egyptian hieroglyphics, old as the Pyramids— were unknown to us. Stranger still, some we recognized, including

English and Italian. We could make out little by the dim light, but they did seem to contain prophecies; and often exclamations of exultation or woe, of victory or defeat, were traced on their thin scant pages. There were detailed relations of events not long past, and names we knew, of modern date.

This was certainly the Sibyl's Cave; not indeed exactly as Virgil describes it, with a hundred entrances; but the whole of this land had been so convulsed by earthquakes and volcanic activity that the change was not wonderful. For the preservation of its contents we could probably thank the accident which had closed the cavern mouth, and the swift-growing vegetation overhead which had sealed it against storms. Between us, we made a hasty selection of those leaves we could understand; laden with our treasure, we then retraced our steps and after much difficulty succeeded in rejoining our guides.

During our stay at Naples, we often returned to this cave, skimming the sunlit sea on our way, and each time added to our store. Since then, whenever possible, I've been employed in deciphering these sacred remains. Their meaning, wondrous and eloquent, has often repaid my toil, soothing me in sorrow and exciting my imagination to the most daring flights. For awhile, my labors were not solitary; but that time is gone; and, along with the chosen and matchless companion of my toils, their dearest reward is also lost to me.

Di mie tenere frondi altro lavoro
Credea mostrarte; e qual fero pianeta
Ne' nvidio insieme, o mio nobil tesoro?

wrote Petrarch. ("I thought to show you further labors from my tender leaves: but what cruel planet envied us being together, O my noble treasure?")

In the chapters that follow, I present the public with my latest discoveries among the slight Sibylline pages. Scattered and un-connected as they were, I have been obliged to add links and model the work into a consistent form. But the main substance rests on the truths contained in the original poetic rhapsodies, and on the divine intuition which their ancient authoress obtained from heaven.

I have often wondered at the subject of her verses. Sometimes I have thought that, obscure and chaotic as they are, they owe their present form to me, their decipherer. As if we should hand another painter the fragments of a masterpiece, say Raphael's Transfiguration, from the Vatican Collections, to put back together; in the resulting mosaic we'd find expressed the second artist's own peculiar mind and talent. Doubtless the leaves of the Cumæan Sibyl have suffered distortion and diminution of interest and excellence in my hands. My only excuse for thus transforming them, is that they were unintelligible in their pristine condition.

My labors have cheered long hours of solitude, and taken me out of a cheerless world whose once-smiling face has turned from me, to another one glowing with imagination and power. Will my readers ask how I could find solace in the narration of misery and woeful change? This is one of the mysteries of our nature, which holds full sway over me, and from whose influence I cannot escape. I confess: I have not been unmoved by the development of the tale; I have been depressed, even agonized, by some of what I've faithfully transcribed from my materials. Yet such is human nature, that the excitement of mind was also dear to me. Imagination—painter of tempest, earthquake, and the stormy, ruin-fraught passions of humanity—softened my real sorrows and endless regrets, by clothing these fictitious ones in that ideality which takes the mortal sting from pain.

I hardly know whether this apology is necessary. The merits of the adaptation and translation which follows must decide how well I have bestowed my time and imperfect powers, in giving form and substance to the frail attenuated Leaves of the Sibyl.

(2)   I AM the native of a sea-surrounded nook, a cloud-caped land. Only a speck in relation to the immensity that makes the surface of the globe and yet, when balanced in the scale of mental power, far outweighing bigger, more populous countries: England, seated in its northern sea, now visits my dreams in the semblance of a vast and well-manned ship, which mastered the winds and rode proudly over the waves. In my boyish days she was the universe to

me. When I stood on my native hills and saw plain and mountain stretch out to the utmost limits of my vision, girdled by the dwellings of my compatriots and subdued to fertility by their labors, the earth's very centre was fixed for me in that spot, and the rest of it like nothing but a fable.

My father was one of those men gifted with neither reason nor judgment to guide their very enviable wit and imagination. His roots were obscure; but circumstances brought him early into public notice, and a small inheritance was soon dissipated in the splendid scene of fashion and luxury he came to inhabit. During the short years of thoughtless youth, he was adored by the high-bred triflers of the day—including a youthful sovereign, who would escape from party intrigues and arduous kingly duties to find never-failing amusement and exhilaration in his society. My father's impulses, never under his own control, perpetually led him into difficulties. He met his accumulating debts of honor and of trade, which would have broken another man, with a light spirit and irrepressible hilarity; while his company was so necessary at the tables and assemblies of the rich that he found his derelictions considered venial, and himself received with intoxicating flattery.

This kind of popularity, like every other, is evanescent. The difficulties, of every kind, with which he had to contend increased in a frightful ratio to his small means of extricating himself. At such times the King would come to his relief, and then kindly take his friend to task. My father would promise to mend his ways but his social disposition, his craving for the usual diet of admiration, and more than all, the fiend of gambling, which fully possessed him, made his good resolutions fleeting, his promises vain. Then the King married; and the haughty European princess who became, as Queen of England, the head of fashion, looked with harsh eyes on the favorite's defects, and cast contempt on the affection her husband entertained for him. My father realized his fall was near. Far from profiting by a final calm before the storm to save himself, however, he sought out new rounds of senseless pleasures.

The King was a fine man, but easily led. His imperious consort now induced him to look with extreme disapprobation, and at last with distaste, on his favorite's imprudence and follies. True, my father's presence lifted many clouds; his warm-hearted frankness, brilliant repartee, and confiding demeanor were irresistible; but at a distance, while tales of his errors were being poured into his royal friend's ear, he lost his influence. The Queen worked dexterously to prolong these absences. She collected accusations. The King, who'd begun to see in him a source of perpetual disquiet, resolved to make one more attempt to reclaim my father, and in case of failure cast him off once and for all.

The scene was set. A powerful king, conspicuous for goodness, with alternate entreaty and reproof, besought his friend to attend to his real interests, and to spend his great powers on some worthy field in which he, his sovereign, would be his prop and advocate. My father felt this kindness. With new and ambitious dreams floating before him, he determined to exchange his present pursuits for nobler duties; sincerely, he gave the required promise. As a pledge of continued favor, he received from his royal master a sum of money to defray pressing debts and set him up well in his new career. That very night, while yet full of gratitude and good resolutions, my father lost the whole sum at the gaming-table, tried to repair the loss by risking double stakes, lost that, and thus incurred a debt of honor he was wholly unable to pay. Ashamed to apply again to the King, he turned his back upon London's false delights and clinging miseries; and, with poverty for his sole companion, buried himself in solitude among the hills and lakes of Cumberland. His wit, his *bon mots*, his personal attractions, fascinating manners, and social graces, were long remembered and recounted. Those who asked his whereabouts heard he was under a cloud, a lost man. His long reign of brilliant wit earned him no pension on retiring. The King lamented his absence; he loved to repeat his sayings, relate the adventures they'd had together, and exalt his talents—but here ended the remembrance.

My father, forgotten, could neither forget nor recover from the loss of what was more necessary to him than air or food—the excitements of pleasure, the admiration of the noble, the luxurious and polished living of the great—and a nervous fever was the consequence. His nurse during this crisis was the daughter of the poor cottager under whose roof he lodged. She was lovely, gentle, and, above all, kind to him; nor is it surprising that the late idol of high-bred beauty should, even in a fallen state, appear a being of an elevated and wondrous nature to the lowly Lake District girl. The attachment between them led to the ill-fated marriage of which I was one offspring. For all my mother's tenderness and sweetness, her husband still deplored his degraded state. Unaccustomed to work, he lacked any notion of how to support his growing family. He thought of applying to the King; but pride and shame withheld him. At last, before his necessities grew so imperious as to compel him to some kind of exertion, he came to his deathbed. There he surveyed the future, and contemplated with anguish the desolate situation in which his wife and children would be left. His last effort was a letter to the King, full of touching eloquence and occasional flashes of that brilliant spirit which was inimitably his own. Bequeathing his widow and orphans to the friendship of his royal master, he felt satisfied that, by this means, their prosperity was better assured in his death than in his life. The letter was given into the care of a nobleman whom my father trusted would place it for him in the King's own hand.

He died in debt, and his little property was seized immediately by his creditors. My mother, penniless and burdened with two children, waited week after week, month after month, in sickening hope of a reply that never came. She had no experience beyond her father's cottage; a large manor house was the highest type of grandeur she could conceive. From my father she'd learned the names of royalty and court; but if, under any circumstances, she could have acquired sufficient courage to address them, the ill success of his own application caused her to banish the idea. Perpetual care and hard unceasing labor, joined to sorrow for the loss of the wondrous being with whom she was still in love, and her naturally delicate health, at length combined to release her from the sad prospect of more want and misery.

The condition of her orphan children was especially desolate. Her own father, an emigrant from the north, was recently dead; there was not a single relation to take them by the hand. They were outcasts, paupers, friendless beings left to the close-handed charity of the families around them.

I, the elder child, was five years old when my mother died. Memories of my parents' talk, stories of my father's past, his royal friends, floated like an indistinct dream through my brain. I conceived that I was different and superior to the people around me, though how or wherefore, I had no idea; and a sense of injury, associated with the names of king and nobles, clung to me. But I could draw no conclusions from such feelings to serve as a guide to action. My first real knowledge of myself was as an unprotected orphan among the valleys and fells of Cumberland. I was in the service of a farmer. With crook in hand, my dog at my side, I shepherded a numerous flock on the near uplands.

I cannot say much in praise of such a life. Its pains far exceeded its pleasures. There was freedom in it, a companionship with nature, and a reckless loneliness; but these, romantic as they were, clashed with a young person's love of action and desire for human sympathy. Neither the care of my flock, nor the change of seasons, were enough to tame my eager spirit; my outdoor life and unfilled time became temptations that led me early into lawless habits. When I found others friendless like myself, I formed them into a band, became their chief and captain. All shepherd boys alike, while our flocks were spread over the pastures we schemed and executed mischievous pranks that drew on us the anger and revenge of the country folk. As my comrades' leader and protector, their misdeeds were usually blamed on me. I endured punishment and pain in their defense with heroic spirit, but claimed their praise and obedience as my reward.

In such a school my disposition became rugged and firm. Nursed by adversity, the appetite for admiration and incapacity for self-control which I inherited from my father, made me daring and reckless. I was rough as the elements, empty-headed as the animals I tended and to whom I often compared myself. Finding that my chief superiority consisted in power, I soon decided that it was power only, and its lack, that distinguished me from any ruling potentate. Ignorant, untaught, pursued by a restless feeling of degradation from my true place in society, I wandered among the hills of civilized England as uncouth a savage as the wolf-bred founder of old Rome. My one law was that of the strongest, and what I deemed the greatest act of virtue was never to submit.

Yet let me a little retract this sentence I've passed on myself. With her dying words, my mother had committed her other child, a girl three years younger, to my guardianship; and this one duty I performed with all the zeal and affection of which my nature was capable. When the difference of our sexes, reflected in the occupations we were given, in great measure divided us, the sister I'd nursed as an infant remained the object of my careful love.

She was a singular being, and, like me, inherited much of our father's peculiar character. Her face was wholly expressive. Her eyes were not dark, but impenetrably deep; you seemed to discover space after space in their glance, and to feel an universe of thought being comprehended by the soul therein. Her golden hair clustered on her temples, contrasting its rich hue with the pale living marble beneath. The coarse cast-off she wore for a dress little matched the refinement of feeling her face displayed, yet strangely accorded with it. She was like one of the painter Guido Reni's saints, with heaven in her heart and in her look; when you saw her, all thoughts turned inward. Her costume, even her features were secondary to the mind that beamed through her countenance.

Lovely and full of noble stuff, my poor, fancifully-named Perdita was yet not altogether saintly in her disposition, and her manners were cold. If she'd been nurtured by affectionate people, she might have been different; but unloved save by me, and neglected, she repaid want of kindness with distrust and silence. She was submissive to those who held authority over her, but a perpetual cloud dwelt on her brow; her look said that she expected enmity from everyone who approached her, and her actions sprang from the same feeling. She spent all the time she could in solitude, rambling to the most unvisited places, scaling dangerous heights, seeking spots where she might wrap herself in the loneliness she prized.

Often she passed whole hours walking in the woods or weaving garlands of flowers and ivy. Sometimes she sat tossing pebbles into a stream; or she'd set afloat crafts made of tree bark or leaves, with feathers for sails, and study their navigation among the rapids and shallows. Meanwhile her active fancy wove a thousand stories. She'd lose herself delightedly in these self-created wanderings and return with unwilling spirit to a dull daily laboring life. Poverty veiled her most excellent qualities, and all that was good in her seemed about to perish from want of affection. Lacking even my advantage of being able to remember our parents, she clung to me as her only friend. But her alliance with such a brother compounded the distaste in which her protectors held her—then every error was magnified by them into crimes. Orphans, in the fullest sense of the term, we were poorest among the poor, and despised by all. If my daring and courage obtained for me a kind of respectful aversion, her youth and sex caused her constant troubles; and her own disposition was not so constituted as to diminish the evil effects of a lowly station.

Though almost equally cut off from the usual forms of social life, my sister and I made a strong contrast to each other. I always required the stimulants of companionship and applause. Perdita was sufficient to herself. For all my lawless habits, my disposition was sociable, hers reclusive. My life was spent among tangible realities, hers was a dream. I might be said even to love my enemies, since by exciting me they in a way bestowed happiness upon me; Perdita almost disliked her friends, for they interfered with her visionary moods. All my feelings, even of exultation and triumph, were changed to bitterness by solitude; Perdita, even in joy, fled to loneliness, and could go on from day to day neither expressing her emotions nor seeking fellow feeling in another mind. Like a fruitful soil that first imbibes the airs and dews of heaven, then gives them forth again to daylight in loveliest forms of fruits and flowers, she was often dark and rugged, raked up for the unseen seed.

She dwelt in a cottage whose trim grass lawn overlooked the lake called Ullswater. From the beech wood that stretched up the hill behind, issued a purling brook that ran close by and down through poplar-shaded banks into the lake. I lived with a farmer whose house was built higher up among the hills. A dark crag rose behind it, with snow year-round in the crevices of its northern exposure. Before dawn I led my flock to the sheep-walks and guarded them all day. It was a life of toil. Rain and cold were more frequent than sunshine; but it was my pride to disdain the elements. My trusty dog watched the sheep as I slipped away to rendezvous with my comrades; at noon we'd toss aside our meager daily fare and build a blazing fire to cook the game we'd just stolen from the neighboring preserves. After lunch we'd sit around the pot trading tales of hairsbreadth escapes, combats with dogs, flights, ambushes. The search after a stray lamb might fill up the hours of afternoon, when we weren't attempting to elude punishment for our crimes. In the evening my flock went to its fold, and I to see my sister.

It was seldom indeed that my band of poachers and I escaped, to use an old-fashioned term, scot free. Our tasty fare was often exchanged for blows and imprisonment. At thirteen, I was sent for a month to the county juvenile hall and rejoined society with my morals unimproved, my hatred of my oppressors increased tenfold. Bread and water hadn't tamed my blood, nor had solitary confinement inspired me with gentle thoughts. I was angry, impatient, miserable; my only happy hours were those during which I devised schemes of revenge. These I perfected in my forced solitude, with the result that during the whole of the following season, and I was freed early in September, I never failed to provide excellent and plenteous fare for myself and my comrades. This was a glorious winter. The sharp frost and heavy snows tamed the animals and kept the country gentlemen by their firesides; we got more game than we could eat, and my faithful dog grew sleek upon our refuse.

The next years only added fresh love of freedom, and contempt for all that was not as wild and rude as myself. At sixteen I was tall and athletic, adept at feats of strength and inured to any weather. Browned by the sun, my step firm with conscious power, I feared no man, and loved none. My life was almost an animal's, and my mind was in danger of degenerating to match it. Up to this point, my savage habits had done me no deep harm; in fact, while my physical powers had grown and flourished under their influence, they'd taught me all the hardy virtues, too. Now my unbridled strength was daily instigating me to acts of tyranny over my companions. And freedom was becoming licentiousness. On the brink of manhood, my passions, strong as the trees of a forest, had already taken root within me, and threatened to shadow with their noxious overgrowth my path of life.

Longing for enterprises beyond my childish exploits, I began to avoid the other shepherds. I'd soon have lost them anyhow. We reached the age when boys are lifted from the pastures and sent to fulfill their destined situations in life; but I, an outcast, with none to lead or drive me forward, paused, a shepherd still. Old people began to point at me as an example, and the young to wonder at my difference from themselves. I hated all of them and began, last and worst degradation, to hate myself. I clung to my ferocious habits, yet half despised them; I continued my war against civilization, yet wished I could belong to it.

Time again and again I reviewed all my mother ever told me of my father's former life, and took out the few relics I possessed of his to hold. Here was greater refinement than could be found among the mountain cottages, but no guide to lead me to another and pleasanter way of life. My father had been connected with nobles, but all I knew of that was his subsequent neglect. The name of the king to whom my dying father had addressed his final prayers, and who had barbarously slighted them, was synonymous in my mind with unkindness, injustice, and consequent resentment. I told myself that I was born for something greater than I was, and greater I determined to become; but greatness, at least to my distorted perceptions, had nothing to do with goodness. Wild thoughts unchecked by moral considerations rioted through my mind in dreams of distinction. Thus I stood upon a pinnacle, a sea of evil boiling at my feet. I was just about to jump—when a strange new influence came over the current of my fortunes, and changed their tumultuous course to what was in comparison like the gentle meanderings of a streamlet around a meadow.

(3)   I LIVED far from the busy haunts of civilization. Rumors of wars or political changes, by the time they reached our mountain abode, would be worn to mere sounds. But England had been the scene of momentous struggles during my boyhood. In the year 2073, the last of its kings—my father's friend—had abdicated in compliance with his subjects' will, and a republic was instituted. Large estates were secured to the dethroned monarch and his family; he received the title of Earl of Windsor, and Windsor Castle with its extensive land and natural surroundings made a part of his allotted wealth. He died soon after, leaving two children, a son and a daughter.

The Ex-Queen, former princess of a royal house of Austria, had long urged her husband to resist the changing times. Haughty and fearless, she cherished a love of power, and nursed a bitter contempt for the husband who'd lowered himself to surrender a kingdom. For her children's sake alone she accepted her new non-regal status as a member of the English republic. Well before widowhood, she'd turned all her thoughts to raising her son Adrian to accomplish her ambitious ends once he inherited the earldom; he must grow up educated in the steady purpose of re-acquiring his lost crown. Adrian was now fifteen.

He was said to be a boy addicted to study, imbued beyond his years with learning and talent. Rumor was he'd turned against his mother's views and taken up republican principles. No one knew for sure, for the haughty Countess had bred up Adrian in solitude and kept him apart from the natural companions of his age and rank. Some unknown circumstance now induced her to send him from home, and we heard that he was about to visit Cumberland. The local air was rife with a thousand explanations for the Countess of Windsor's conduct, none true probably; but each day it became more certain that we should have the noble scion of the late regal house of England among us.

This family owned an estate at Ullswater. With the large park attached to the mansion and grounds I was well familiar through my poaching habits, the neglected state of the property having facilitated my incursions among its plentiful stock of game. When it was decided that the young Earl of Windsor should visit Cumberland, workmen arrived to put the house and grounds in order for his reception. The apartments were brought back to pristine splendor, and the park, cleared of overgrowth, its paths restored, was guarded with unusual care.

The news of Windsor's coming disturbed me beyond measure, rousing all my dormant recollections and suspended sentiments of injury. I seemed about to begin the worst chapter yet in a bad life. Every other scheme forgotten, I thought ceaselessly of my future meeting with this titled stripling, the son of my father's friend. He'd be hedged in by servants and noble companions, the sons of nobles. All England rang with his name, and his coming, like a thunderstorm, was heard from far away; while I was a miserable pauper, uneducated, unfashionable—a degraded being. In the eyes of his courtly followers, my very impoverishment would be proof that I and my family merited his family's continued neglect.

As if fascinated, I began to haunt the young Earl's destined abode. I watched the progress of the improvements, and stood by the mansion drive as luxurious contents from London were unloaded from wagons and conveyed indoors. It was part of the Ex-Queen's plan to surround her son with princely magnificence. Rich carpets, silken hangings, ornaments of gold, embossed metals, emblazoned furniture: nothing but what was regal in splendor should meet his eye. Doubtless he'd been taught to repeat my father's name with disdain, and to scoff at my just claims to protection. So what was all this grandeur but the glare of infamy? Yet I envied him. His stud of beautiful horses, his arms of costly workmanship, the praise that attended him, the adoration, the ready servants, high place and high esteem—I considered them as having been forcibly wrenched from me, and envied them all with novel and tormenting bitterness.

I began to want revenge.

To crown my vexation, Perdita, the visionary Perdita, seemed transported with excitement when she told me that the Earl of Windsor was about to arrive.

"And this pleases you?" I observed moodily.

"Yes, indeed, Lionel," she replied. "I'm longing to see him. He's the descendant of our kings, the first noble of the land. Everyone admires and loves him, and they say his rank is his least merit; that he is generous, brave, and affable."

"You have learnt a pretty lesson, Perdita," said I, "and repeat it so literally, that you forget all those actual proofs we have of the Earl's virtues. His generosity is manifest in our plenty—his bravery in the protection he affords us—his affability in the notice he takes of us. His rank his least merit, you say? But all his virtues are derived from his station. Because he is rich, people call him generous; because he is powerful, brave; because he is well served, he is affable. Let them call him so, let all England believe it. We know him better. He is our enemy—our dastardly, arrogant enemy. If he had one particle of the virtues you say he does, he would do justly by us. His father injured our father—unassailable on his throne, daring to despise one who'd only stooped beneath himself when he deigned to associate with the royal ingrate. We must be enemies, this Earl and I. He'll find that I can feel my injuries; he shall learn to dread my revenge!"

A few days later, he arrived. Even the most miserable cottage emptied as every inhabitant, Perdita too, went to swell the sea of folk that poured forth to behold and meet this idol of all hearts. I, driven half mad as I met party after party of the country people descending the hills in their holiday best, escaped to the cloud-veiled heights. Here, the sterile rocks never cried, "Long live the Earl!" Night fell, accompanied by drizzling rain and cold, but I stayed where I was. I knew my home and every cottage like it would be ringing with Adrian's praises. As my limbs grew numb and chill, the discomfort fed my insane aversion; I almost reveled in it, since it seemed to justify my hatred for my unheeding adversary. Everything was his fault: for I confounded so entirely the idea of father and son, that I forgot how the latter might be wholly unconscious of the king's neglect of us. Pounding my aching head with both hands, I cried, "He'll hear of this! I will be revenged! I won't suffer like a whipped spaniel! He's going to know, beggar and friendless as I am, that I won't put up with it!"

Each day, each hour increased my sense of wrong. If I saw the Earl at a distance, riding a beautiful horse, my blood boiled with rage. The air I breathed seemed poisoned by his presence; his praises, which I heard everywhere, were so many snakebites to my bruised heart. I panted for the relief of doing some misdeed that should rouse him to a sense of my hatred. For his greatest offense was that he should cause me such intolerable sensations yet appear to be unaware that I was alive to feel them.

It soon became known that Adrian took great delight in his park and preserves. He never hunted, but spent hours watching the tribes of lovely and almost tame animals with which the woods were stocked, and had ordered them put under even greater care than usual. Here I recognized my chance to offend him. My few remaining comrades all shrank from the peril, though they were the most determined and lawless of the crew, when I proposed a poaching raid on the young Earl's estate; so I was left to achieve my revenge alone.

When I wasn't caught at first, I increased in daring. My footsteps on the dewy grass, the torn boughs and marks of slaughter I left, at length betrayed me to the gamekeepers. They kept better watch; I was taken and sent to jail—not a youth facility this time.

I entered those gloomy walls in a fit of triumphant ecstasy. "He feels me now," I cried, "and he will again—and again!" I passed one day's confinement; that evening I was freed, as I was told, by order of the Earl himself. This news cast me down from my pinnacle. *He despises me,* I thought. Never mind: he'd learn that I despised him, too, and held in equal contempt his punishments and his clemency. On the second night after my release, I was again taken by the gamekeepers—again imprisoned, and again released. The very next night, I made a third expedition.

A late-setting moon, and the extreme caution I'd been obliged to use, put me behind time; signs of dawn appeared while I was still inside the forbidden park. I crept along through its fern banks on my hands and knees, seeking deeper shadows, while birds awoke with unwelcome song above my head, and the fresh morning wind, playing among the boughs, made me hear footfalls all around. My heart raced as I reached the fence and readied for the leap that would take me to the other side. Just then, two keepers sprang out—an ambush.

The gamekeepers were more enraged than their lord by my obstinacy. They'd received orders that if they took me again, I should be brought directly to the Earl, whose lenience so far made them expect an outcome which they considered ill befitting my crime. The head among them had resolved to satisfy his own resentment before he made me over to the higher powers. The pair who'd surprised me knocked me down, and one delivered me a few severe blows with a whip. I leapt up, armed with my knife, and managed to inflict a deep, wide wound in his hand. Our three voices, loud with rage, pain, bitterness and fury, echoed through the dell; morning broke more and more, its celestial beauty unsuited to our brute and noisy contest. In the midst of our struggle, the wounded man exclaimed, "The Earl!" At this I broke away from my persecutors and, panting from the effort, stood with my back to a tree, resolved to defend myself to the last. My garments were torn and stained like my hands with the blood of the man I'd wounded. In one hand I grasped some dead birds—my hard-earned prey—the other held the dripping knife. My hair was matted; my filthy face was bloodied. Though tall and muscular of form, my whole appearance was haggard and squalid. I must have looked like, for I was, the merest ruffian that ever trod the earth.

At the name of the Earl, all the indignant blood that warmed my heart had rushed into my cheeks. I'd never seen him before, and was expecting a haughty, assuming youth who'd show—if he even deigned to speak to me—all the arrogance of superiority. I was ready with a reproach calculated to sting his very heart. He came near; and what I saw blew aside, with gentle western breath, my cloudy wrath. A tall, slim, fair boy, his face somewhat overflowing with sensibility and refinement, stood before me; the morning sunbeams tinged with gold his silken hair, and spread light and glory over his beaming countenance.

"What is this?" he cried. The men eagerly began to excuse themselves; he put them aside, saying, "Two of you at once against a mere lad—for shame!" He came up to me and spoke. "Verney— Lionel Verney, do we meet thus for the first time? We were born to be friends to each other. Ill fortune has divided us, but will you not acknowledge the hereditary bond of friendship which I trust will unite us from now on?"

As he spoke, his frank eyes seemed to read my very soul: and my heart, my savage revengeful heart, felt the influence of sweet benignity sink upon it. His thrilling voice, like sweetest melody, awoke a mute echo within me that stirred to its depths the lifeblood in my frame. I wanted to reply, to acknowledge his goodness, accept his offer of friendship; but words, fitting words, failed the rough mountaineer. I would have held out my hand, but there was too much blood on it. Adrian took pity on my hesitation.

"Come with me," he said. "I have so much to say to you; come home with me—but, you know who I am?"

"Yes," I exclaimed, "I know you now, and I believe that you will pardon my mistakes—my crime."

Adrian smiled gently; and after giving his orders to the gamekeepers, he came up and put his arm in mine. Together we walked to the mansion.

It was not his rank—after all I've said, surely it will not be suspected that it was Adrian's rank that, from the first, left my heart subdued and laid my entire spirit prostrate before him. I wasn't the only one who felt this way. His sensibility and courtesy fascinated everybody; while his vivacity, intelligence, and active spirit of benevolence, completed the conquest. Even at fifteen, he was deeply read and imbued with the spirit of high philosophy, which gave a tone of irresistible persuasion to his every word; like an inspired musician, he could strike with unerring skill the "lyre of mind" to produce divine harmonies. In person, he appeared not quite of this world. His slight frame was too small for the soul that dwelt within; he was all mind. In Othello's words, "Man but a rush against" his breast, and you'd conquer his strength; but the might of his smile would have tamed a hungry lion, or caused a legion of armed men to lay their weapons at his feet.

I spent the day with him. He never mentioned the past, at first, nor indeed any personal matters; instead he talked of general subjects, wishing probably to gain my confidence, and give me time to gather my scattered wits. We sat in his library. The room was decorated with the busts of many old Greek sages. He described their characters and told me of the power they'd acquired over the minds of men through the sheer force of love and wisdom alone. As he spoke, I felt all my boasted pride and strength being subdued by the honeyed accents of this blue-eyed boy. To the trim and fenced domain of civilization, which had looked so inaccessible from my wild jungle, he opened the gate for me; I stepped inside, and felt, as I entered, that I trod my native soil.

"I have something to tell you," he said towards evening, "and much, too much, to explain about the past. Maybe you can help. Do you remember your father? Though I never had the happiness of seeing him, his name is one of my earliest recollections. For me he's always been the male ideal of all that's gallant, amiable, fascinating. His great wit was matched by the overflowing goodness of his heart, which he poured in such full measure on his friends as to leave, alas!

too little for himself." Encouraged by this encomium, I told what I remembered of my parent. In answer, Adrian told me what had happened to cause the neglect of my father's testamentary letter.

When his father, then King of England, had felt his situation becoming more perilous, his options fewer, his line of conduct more embarrassed, again and again he wished for his early friend, who could at once have shielded him against the impetuous anger of his queen and served as a mediator with the parliament. After the fatal night of loss at the gaming-table, when he quitted London, the King received no news of my father; by the time he tried to find him, too many years had passed, every trace was lost. With fonder regret than ever, the King, soon the Ex-King, clung to his memory; and charged his son, if ever he should meet this valued friend, to bestow every help and reward, and to assure the old favorite that their attachment survived separation and silence.

A short time before Adrian's visit to Cumberland, the heir of the nobleman to whom my father had confided his last appeal to his royal master, put this letter, its seal unbroken, into the young Earl's hands. It had been found tossed among a mass of old papers, accident alone brought it to light. As soon as he began reading, Adrian recognized the living spirit of genius and wit he'd heard so much about. He also discovered the name of the spot to which my father had retreated and where he died, leaving children. Ever since his arrival at Ullswater he'd been making inquiries about us; learning that we still lived here, he'd been arranging a variety of plans for our benefit, preliminary to meeting us.

The way he talked about my father was gratifying to my vanity; the delicate way he veiled his benevolence to me behind the filial oath he told of was soothing to my pride. Unusual respect, admiration, love: other feelings, less ambiguous than pride, were provoked by his disarming manner. All his words and looks were generous, open, warm. Before I knew it, he had touched my rocky heart with his magic power, and the stream of affection gushed forth, imperishable and pure. In the evening we parted. He reached to shake hands. "We'll meet again; come back tomorrow," he said. I clasped that kind hand; I tried to answer; a fervent "God bless you!"

was all my ignorance could manage, and I darted away, oppressed by my new emotions.

I could not rest. I sought the hills; a west wind swept them, and the stars glittered above. I ran on and on, carelessly, trying to wear out the struggling spirit within me along with my body. *This*, I thought, *is power! Not to be strong of limb, hard of heart, ferocious, daring; but kind. Compassionate. Soft.* Stopping short, I put my hands together and with the fervor of a new convert cried, "Adrian! Adrian, I am going to become wise and good too!" and then quite overcome, I wept aloud.

After this gust of passion, when I'd begun to feel more composed, I lay on the ground and let my thoughts go where they liked. My former life passed before me; fold by fold the many errors of my heart fell open and showed me to have been brutish, savage, worthless. I was without remorse, though; for I'd been born again—my soul threw off the burden of past sin for a new career in innocence and love. Nothing harsh or rough remained to jar with the soft feelings this day had inspired; I was a child lisping its prayers after its mother. My plastic soul had been remolded by a master hand, which I neither wanted to nor was able to resist.

This was the beginning of my friendship with Adrian—and the most fortunate day of my life. I now began to be human. I was admitted within that sacred boundary which divides the intellectual and moral nature of our species from that of animals. My best feelings were called into play as I sought to respond to his generosity, wisdom, and simple friendliness.

(4)   WITH A noble goodness all his own, Adrian took infinite delight in bestowing to prodigality the treasures of his mind and fortune on the long-neglected son of his father's friend. As I was to learn, after the abdication his father had retreated from politics into an unhappy private life. The Ex-Queen possessed none of the domestic virtues, while her attractive courage and daring had been rendered null by her husband's secession. She despised him, and did not care to conceal it. To please her the King had cast off his old

friends, but acquired no new ones by her help. In this dearth of sympathy, he turned to his almost infant son, whose early signs of talent and sensibility were to prove well worthy of the father's confidence they inspired. Adrian never wearied of the stories about old times in which my own father had played a distinguished part; the man's triumphs, reversals, escapades, and keenest witticisms he'd committed to memory from childhood. Even the Ex-Queen's enduring dislike—bitter, sarcastic, contemptuous—failed to touch the boy's admiration for the one-time favorite, whom he held as the epitome of male gallantry, amiability, and fascination. So it was natural that when he learned of our existence, he immediately formed the plan of bestowing on this celebrated person's offspring all the advantages procurable by one of his own wealth and rank. When he found me a vagabond shepherd of the hills, a poacher, an unlettered savage, still his kindness did not fail. He believed that his father was to a degree culpable of neglect towards us, and that he was bound to every possible reparation. At the same time, he was pleased to say that under all my ruggedness there glimmered forth an elevation of spirit, beyond mere animal courage, which—combined with what I'd inherited of my father's looks—gave proof that all his virtues and talents had not died with him. Whatever was in there, my noble young friend resolved should not be lost for want of culture.

I became an eager participant in an ambitious plan to cultivate my intellect. At first, my great object was to match my father's merits and render myself worthy of Adrian's friendship. But curiosity soon awoke, followed by an earnest love of knowledge for its own sake which made me pass days and nights in reading and study. Already well acquainted with what I may term the panorama of nature—the night stars, the cycles of animal life, the change of seasons—I was at once startled and enchanted by my sudden extension of vision when the curtain was drawn back to reveal the intellectual world, and I saw the universe, not only as it presented itself to my outward senses, but as it had appeared to the wisest across time. Poetry and its creations, philosophy and its researches and classifications, alike roused sleeping ideas in my mind, and gave me new ones.

I felt as the sailor, who from the top-mast first sighted the shore of America, and like him I rushed to tell my companions of my discoveries in unknown regions. But I was unable to excite in any breast the same craving appetite for knowledge that existed in mine. Not even Perdita could understand me. Her own visionary relationship with the world was sufficiently inexhaustible to content her. She listened as ever to my latest adventures, and sometimes took an interest in this new species of information; but she did not, as I did, look on it as an integral part of her being, which once obtained could no more be shed than the sense of touch, or something equally basic. We both agreed in loving Adrian; though Perdita, still a child, couldn't appreciate as I did the extent of his merits, or feel the same sympathy with his pursuits and opinions.

I was forever with him. A sensibility and sweetness in his disposition gave a tender and unearthly tone to our conversations. Then he was so various: merry as a lark caroling on high, soaring in thought as an eagle, innocent as the mild-eyed dove. He could lighten Perdita's too-deep seriousness or take the sting from my typical self-tortures. I looked back to my restless desires and painful struggles with my fellow beings as to a troubled dream, and felt myself as much changed as if I had transmigrated into another form. But it was not so: I was the same in strength, in earnest craving for sympathy, in my yearning for active exertion; only all was softened and humanized. Nor was Adrian's instruction limited to the cold truths of history and philosophy. For while he taught me by their means to subdue my own reckless and uncultured spirit, he also opened to my view the living page of his own heart, and gave me to feel and understand its wondrous character.

The Ex-Queen of England had, even during his infancy, endeavored to implant daring and ambitious designs in the mind of her son. She recognized his genius and surpassing talent; these she cultivated for the sake of afterwards using them for the furtherance of her own views. She encouraged his craving for knowledge and his impetuous courage; she even tolerated his irrepressible love of freedom, hoping it might, as is too often the case, lead to a passion for command. She tried to raise him with a sense of resentment towards, and a desire to revenge himself upon, those who had been instrumental in bringing about his father's abdication. In this she did not succeed. The accounts furnished him, however distorted, of a great and wise nation asserting its right to govern itself, excited his admiration. The rumors about him were true: early on, he'd become a republican from principle. Still his mother did not despair. To the love of rule and haughty pride of birth she added determined ambition, patience, and self-control. She devoted herself to the study of her son's disposition. By the application of praise, censure, and exhortation, she tried to seek and strike the fitting chords; and though the first melodies that followed her touch played out of tune, she built her hopes on his talents, and felt sure that she would at last win him. The kind of banishment he now experienced, in Cumberland, arose from other causes.

She had also a daughter, now twelve years old—his fairy sister, Adrian was wont to call her; a lovely, animated little thing, all sensibility and truth. With these, her children, the noble widow lived at Windsor, admitting no visitors save her own partisans, native German-speaking travelers, and a few of the foreign ministers. Among these, and highly favored by her, was the ambassador to England from the free States of Greece, Prince Zaimi, whose daughter, the young Princess Evadne, passed much of her time at Windsor Castle. This sprightly, clever Greek girl was a sort of plaything for the Countess, who found alleviation from the monotony of a retired life in her talents and vivacity; around Evadne, her usual stiff, stately attitudes relaxed as they never did around her own children.

Evadne was now eighteen. For all the time they'd spent together at Windsor, Adrian's relative youth prevented any suspicion as to the nature of their relationship. But he, uncommonly ardent and tender of heart, had already learned to love; while the beauteous Greek smiled encouragingly on the boy. It was strange to me, who, though older than Adrian, had never loved, to witness my friend's sacrifice of his whole heart. There was neither jealousy, disquiet, or mistrust in his sentiment, only devotion and faith. His life was swallowed up in the existence of his beloved; his heart beat only in unison with hers. This was the secret law of his life. Neither human efforts nor events could bring him happiness or misery, for the universe was no more than a dwelling for him and his chosen one. Say life and society were a wilderness, a tiger-haunted jungle: through the midst of its worst errors and thickest excesses, there was a disentangled and flowery pathway along which they might journey in safety and delight. Their track would be like the passage of the Red Sea, dry, between two seawater walls of destruction.

Alas! why must I record the hapless delusion of this matchless specimen of humanity? What was it in our nature that kept urging us forever on towards pain and misery? Were we not formed for enjoyment? Though we set our sails to fill with pleasure, disappointment—the ruthless pilot of our life's bark—never failed to carry us onto the shoals. Who was better framed than this highly gifted youth to love and be beloved, and to reap unalienable joy from a first and blameless passion? If his heart had slept but a few years longer, he might have been saved; but it awoke in its infancy; it had power, but no knowledge; and it was ruined, even as a too early-formed bud is nipped by the killing frost.

I did not accuse Evadne of hypocrisy nor of wishing to deceive her lover; but the first letter that I saw of hers convinced me that she did not love him. It was written with elegance, and, foreigner as she was, with great command of English. The handwriting itself was exquisitely beautiful; there was something in her very paper and its folds which even I, impartial and unskilled in such matters as I was, could discern as being tasteful. There was much kindness, gratitude, and sweetness in her expression, but no love. Evadne was three years older than Adrian; and who, at eighteen, ever loved someone so much their junior? I compared her placid epistles with the burning ones that Adrian had shown me. His soul seemed to distil itself into the words he wrote; they breathed on the paper, bearing with them a portion of the life of love, which was his life. The very writing used to exhaust him, and he'd weep over these letters of his merely from the excess of emotion they awakened in his heart.

Evadne had made Adrian promise not to let his mother find out about the two of them. For a while he contested the point but finally yielded. A vain concession; for Adrian's soul was painted in his countenance, and concealment or deceit were completely alien to the trusting frankness of his nature. His demeanor quickly betrayed his secret to the quick eyes of the Ex-Queen. With characteristic wary prudence, she concealed her discovery, but hastened to remove her son from the sphere of the attractive Greek. He was sent to

Cumberland; but an active correspondence between the lovers, arranged by Evadne, was kept hidden from his mother. Thus Adrian's absence, designed to separate, united them in firmer bonds than ever. To me my friend discoursed ceaselessly of his beloved Ionian. Her country, its ancient greatness, its late memorable struggles, found their culmination in her glory and excellence. He only submitted to being away from her because she continued to command it; if she'd let him, he would have declared his love before all England, and resisted, with unshaken constancy, his mother's opposition. But Evadne, with feminine prudence, perceived how useless it would be to assert himself like that at fifteen; more years would give weight to his power. Perhaps there was besides a lurking dislike to bind herself in the face of the world to one whom she did not love—not love, at least, with that passionate enthusiasm which her heart told her she might one day feel towards another. He obeyed her injunctions, and passed a year of exile in Cumberland.

(5)   WHAT HAPPINESS is so true, so unclouded, as the overflowing and talkative delight of young people? Enthusiasm for knowledge, and boundless affection for Adrian, combined to keep my once empty heart and head joyfully occupied that happy year. In our boat, upon my native lake, beside the streams and the pale bordering poplars—in walks through valley and over hill, my crook thrown aside, a nobler flock to tend than silly sheep, being flocks of newborn ideas—I read or listened to Adrian. His discourse, whether it concerned his love or his theories for the improvement of human-kind, alike entranced me. Sometimes my lawless mood would return, my love of peril, my resistance to authority; but this was in his absence. Under the mild sway of his dear eyes, I was obedient and good as a boy of five who does his mother's bidding.

After he'd been at Ullswater for about a year, Adrian visited London, and came back full of plans for our benefit. "You must begin life," he said. I was seventeen, a ripe age for the apprenticeship he'd planned. He foresaw that his own life would be one of struggle. We agreed I must partake his labors with him. But I needed training for the job, so we must now separate and I begin my political career. He'd procured me a place as private secretary to the Ambassador at Vienna. In two years, I should return to England with a name and reputation already established.

And Perdita? Perdita was to become the pupil, friend and younger sister of Adrian's adored Evadne—though not her dependent. With his usual thoughtfulness, Adrian had provided the younger girl a private income. How could I refuse such generosity? Though it could never be repaid, I did not wish to refuse; but a short while later, on my way to Austria, I made a vow of devotion and gratitude. All my knowledge and present power, my actual life, only existed or had any value because my friend had given it to me—and so all, all my capacities and hopes, to him alone I would devote.

Thus I promised in my heart of hearts, on a journey—my first—full of roused feelings and ardent expectation. Told of the dangers of the world by the wisest philosophers, who with perfect accuracy described human deceit and showed us our own treasonous hearts: not the less fearlessly did each of us put off in a frail bark from the port, spread the sail, and strain the oar to reach deep water.

Life is before me and I rush to take possession. Hope, glory, love, and blameless ambition are my guides, and my soul knows no dread. What's past, though sweet, is gone; the present is good because of its potential; and the future is all mine. Vienna draws nearer. High aspirations raise my pulse, and my eyes seem to penetrate the cloudy midnight of time. Within the depths of its darkness, I discern the fruition of all my soul's desires.

Behold me in a new capacity. A diplomatist: one among the pleasure-seeking society of a lively and fashionable city, a youth of promise, favorite of the Ambassador. With breathless amazement I entered a scene whose actors appeared like the lilies of parable, neither toiling nor usefully spinning. All was strange and admirable to the shepherd of Cumberland. Soon, too soon, forgetting my studious hours, forgetting Adrian's companionship and example, I entered the giddy whirl. My character remained the same: passionately desiring human sympathy, ardent in pursuit of what I wanted. The sight of beauty entranced me, and attractive manners in man or woman won my entire confidence. I called it rapture, when a smile made my heart beat; and I felt the life's blood tingle in my frame when I approached the idol whom for a while I worshipped. When it was time to go home, I only wanted to come back again. The mere flow of animal spirits was Paradise. Dazzling light-filled ornamented rooms; lovely forms arrayed in splendid dress; the motions of a dance, the voluptuous tones of exquisite music—*this dear work of youthful revelry*—cradled my senses in one intoxicating delusion, the ecstasy of a freshman in the school of pleasure.

But sharp rocks lurked beneath the smiling ripples of such shallow waters. Caught in the heartless company of those who made amusement their sole aim, starving on their vacant kindness, my flagging spirits asked for something genuine, that really spoke to my affections; and, not finding it, disappointed, weary, I drooped. All told, notwithstanding the thoughtless delight that marked its opening, the impression I have of my life at Vienna is melancholy. Goethe said, that in youth we cannot be happy unless we love. I did not love; but I was devoured by a restless wish to be something to others. Made the victim of ingratitude and cold coquetry, I felt so injured that I was sure my discontent entitled me to hate the world. I receded from my career into solitude; I had recourse to my books, and my desire to be with Adrian again became a burning thirst.

Not only embassy society had stung my feelings in Vienna, but something like envy, almost venomous. At this period the name and exploits of one of my countrymen filled the world with admiration. Stories of what he had done, conjectures concerning his next move, were the never-failing topics of the hour. I was not angry on my own account; but I felt as if the praises which this idol received were leaves torn from laurels which by right belonged to Adrian, my friend. But I must enter into some account of this darling of fame—this favorite of the wonder-loving world.

Lord Raymond was the sole remnant of a noble but impoverished family. From early youth he had admired his own pedigree and bitterly lamented not having wealth. His character was self-aggrandizing and not overly scrupulous. Haughty, yet trembling to receive every demonstration of respect; ambitious, but too proud to show ambition; seeking to be honored while yet a votary of pleasure—he entered upon life. Some insult, real or imaginary, met him on the threshold; some repulse, where he least expected it; some disappointment, hard for his pride to bear. Details were missing. He writhed beneath an unspecified injury he was unable to revenge; and so he left England with a vow not to return until the time had come that his country might feel the power of him she now despised.

He became an adventurer in the Greek wars of independence against the Turkish empire. His reckless courage and military genius brought him acclaim; in Athens he soon became the darling hero of the people. His foreign birth and citizenship were all that prevented him from filling high office. Even so, while others might rank above him in title and ceremony, Lord Raymond held a higher place; he was on another level. He led the Greek armies to victory, to him belonged their triumphs. When he appeared, towns poured forth their entire populations to meet him; Athens made him an honorary citizen; the old national songs got new lyrics whose themes were his glory, valor, and munificence.

At length a truce was concluded. Around the same time Lord Raymond, by some unlooked-for chance, came into an immense fortune in England. So to London he returned, crowned with glory, and offered every courtesy and mark of distinction that had once been denied to his pretensions. As I was to learn, his proud heart rebelled against this change: for was he not the same? The same despised Raymond? Yes, only this time with power, in the shape of wealth, to impose like an iron yoke on his cynical flatterers, to start with; power that he made it his aim to increase. In open ambition or close intrigue, he was after one thing—to become England's head of state.

Among his other advantages, Lord Raymond was supremely handsome; everyone admired him; he was an idol to women. Courteous, honey-tongued, adept at fascinating: what could not this man achieve in the busy English world? Far away, I was left to wonder. The whole story never reached me. Adrian had ceased to write, and Perdita wrote laconically. She had withdrawn from the protection of the Princess Evadne, but didn't say why. Then came rumors that Adrian had become—incredible!—mad, insane; and that Lord Raymond was now both the Ex-Queen's favorite and her daughter's destined husband. Nay, more, he was said to have revived the claim of the House of Windsor to the crown. If the Earl's disorder were incurable, and Raymond's marriage with the sister took place, the aspiring noble's brow might wind up encircled with the magic ring—crowned, so said speculation.

When I heard that, I couldn't stay at Vienna, away from the friend of my youth, any longer. *Farewell to courtly pleasure—to political intrigue—to the maze of passion and folly! All hail, England! Native England, the scene of all my hopes, receive your child!* It was time to fulfill my vow, range myself at Adrian's side, and become his ally and support till death.

I landed, after a nearly two-year absence, and dared make no inquiries, fearful what I might hear. I decided to go straight to my sister. She'd moved from the Lake District to a little cottage, part of Adrian's gift, on the borders of Windsor Forest. I'd never been in that part of the country before; its fertility and beauty now struck me with admiration which increased as I approached its woods.

The trees that had been planted during Queen Victoria's reign now stood in the pride of maturity; while the ruins of majestic oaks which had grown, flourished, and decayed during the progress of earlier centuries, marked where the limits of the Forest once reached. Perdita's humble dwelling lay on the edge of the most ancient portion. Bishopsgate Heath stretched before it, interminably, it seemed, towards the east; Chapel Wood and the grove of Virginia Water marked the western boundary. Behind, where the deer came to graze, the cottage was shadowed by the venerable fathers of the forest, for the most part hollow and decayed, whose fantastic groups contrasted with the regular beauty of the younger trees. These stood erect and seemed ready to advance fearlessly into coming time; while those out-worn stragglers, blasted and broken, clung to each other, their weak boughs sighing as the wind buffeted them—a weather-beaten crew.

Modest, simple, small, the low-roofed cottage seemed to submit to nature's majesty and cower amidst the remains of forgotten time. The graceful taste of its inmate was revealed by an air of elegance all about. Flowers, the children of the spring, adorned her garden and windowsills. A light railing surrounded the yard. With pounding heart

I entered; as I stood at the entrance, I heard her voice, melodious as it had ever been, and knew that she was well.

Perdita appeared; she stood before me in the fresh bloom of youthful womanhood, the same yet somehow different from the mountain girl I'd left. Her former life had given freedom to her motions, and her light step was almost soundless as her lovely figure came across the hall to meet me. At our earlier parting, I'd clasped her to my bosom with unrestrained warmth; we met again, and at first I only stared, as I understood something new. Had she had been bred in that sphere of life to which, perhaps by inheritance, her mind and body's fine framework were best adapted, my sister would have been the object almost of adoration. All the genius that ennobled the blood of our father tinged hers, too; a generous tide flowed in her veins; artifice, envy, or meanness were antithetical to her nature; when aglow with amiable feeling, her countenance might have belonged to a queen of nations; her eyes were bright; her look fearless.

A moment more and childhood passed away, and Perdita and I became full grown actors on this changeful scene. Then an unchecked flood of association and natural feeling rushed in full tide upon our hearts. With tenderest emotion we embraced.

Over tea, we sat together more calmly, talking of the past and present. I told about my work and life in Vienna, and alluded to the coldness of her letters—the cause of which was already obvious. New feelings had arisen within her, which she'd been unable to express in writing to someone she'd known only in childhood; but our intimacy was renewed now that we sat face to face. I asked about the changes that had taken place at home, and especially in Adrian. The tears that filled my sister's eyes when I mentioned our friend seemed to vouch for the truth of the reports that had reached me. But I could hardly believe it. Was there indeed anarchy and madness in the sublime universe of Adrian's thoughts? Was he no longer the lord of his own soul? Had those gentle eyes lost the meaning from them—did that voice no longer, with Hamlet's flute, discourse excellent music? Horrible, most horrible! I veiled my eyes in terror of the change, and gushing tears bore witness to my sympathy and grief at this unimaginable ruin.

Perdita detailed the melancholy circumstances that had led to the event.

Adrian's frank and unsuspicious mind, gifted by every natural grace, endowed with transcendent powers of intellect, unblemished by any shadow of defect (unless his fearless independence of thought were construed as one), was devoted to his love for Evadne. He entrusted to her keeping the treasures of his soul, his aspirations after excellence, and his plans for the improvement of humanity. His schemes and theories, far from being changed by personal and prudential motives, acquired new strength from the powers he felt arise within him as manhood dawned; and his love for Evadne became deep-rooted, as every day his certainty grew that the path he chose was full of difficulty, and that he must seek his reward, not in the applause or gratitude of his fellow creatures, not even in the success of his plans, but in the approbation of his own heart, and in her love and sympathy—Evadne's—which was to lighten every toil and recompense every sacrifice.

Alone, in solitude, he matured his views for the reform of the English government and the improvement of the people. He should have concealed his sentiments until he'd gained the power to secure their practical development. But he was impatient, frank of heart, fearless. Openly opposing his mother's schemes, he published his intention to use his influence to diminish the power of the aristocracy, mitigate the effects and advantages of wealth and privilege, and introduce a perfect system of republican government into England. His mother, the Ex-Queen, treated his theories as the wild ravings of inexperience, at first. But they were so systematically arranged, and his arguments so well supported, that behind her appearance of incredulity, she began to fear her son. She tried to reason with him, and finding him inflexible, learned to hate him.

Strange to say, this feeling was infectious. His enthusiasm for abstract good, his contempt for the sacredness of authority, his ardor and imprudence were all opposed to the usual routine of life. The worldly-wise feared him; the young and inexperienced, who found the lofty severity of his moral views incomprehensible, disliked him for being so different from themselves.

And Evadne turned a cold eye on his systems. She was glad to see him assert his own will, but she wished he might have made it more intelligible to the multitude. No martyr in spirit, neither did she incline to share the shame and defeat of a fallen patriot. Towards Adrian in person she remained affectionate, aware of the purity of his motives, the generosity of his disposition, his true and ardent attachment to her; and she entertained a great affection for him. He repaid this spirit of kindness with the fondest gratitude, and made her the treasure house of all his hopes.

At this time Lord Raymond returned from Greece. No two persons could be starker opposites than Adrian and he. Raymond was emphatically a man of the world. Since his passions, which were violent, often mastered him, he could not always square his conduct to the obvious line of self-interest; for Raymond's paramount object remained self-gratification. For him, the structure of society was there to support him and his life—the earth was spread out as a highway for him, the heavens built up as his personal canopy. Adrian, by contrast, felt that he made one part of a great whole. He felt an affinity not only with the rest of humanity, but with all of Nature. The mountains and sky were his friends; the winds of heaven and the animal kingdom his playmates; his life, as he felt it, was mingled with the universe of existence. His soul was sympathy, and dedicated to the worship of beauty and excellence.

Adrian and Raymond met, and they disliked each other. Adrian despised the narrow views of the politician, and Raymond held in supreme contempt the benevolent visions of the philanthropist.

Meanwhile, a storm was about to destroy at one fell blow everything Adrian thought he'd secured to himself of delight and refuge from the defeats to come. Raymond, the deliverer of Greece, the graceful soldier, brown from the battlefields of her native clime— Evadne fell in love with Raymond. Overpowered by her new sensations, unthinking, with nothing left to regulate her conduct except the tyrannical sentiment which had suddenly usurped the empire of her heart, she yielded to its influence. The too-natural consequence, in a mind as basically unsentimental as hers, was that Adrian's attentions became distasteful to her. She grew capricious; her gentle conduct towards him turned to asperity and repulsive coldness. At times she perceived a wild or pathetic appeal in his expression; then she'd relent, and for a while resume her former kindness. But these fluctuations shook to its depths the soul of the sensitive youth. How could Adrian change the world if he no longer possessed Evadne's love? He felt in every nerve that the dire storms of madness were about to attack his fragile being, which quivered waiting.

Perdita, who was living with Evadne at the time, saw the torture that Adrian endured. She adored his virtues and loved him as a kind, elder brother—someone to guide, protect, and instruct her without a parent's too frequent tyranny. She watched with mixed contempt and indignation as Evadne piled sorrow on his head for the sake of Raymond who hardly noticed her. In his solitary despair Adrian would often seek out my sister, hoping to relieve his misery in talk while fortitude and agony split his mind in two. Soon, alas! one antagonist would conquer. Anger played no part in his emotion. With whom should he be angry? Not with Raymond, a man unconscious of the misery he caused; not with Evadne, for whom Adrian's soul wept tears of blood—poor, mistaken girl, not a tyrant but a slave. Amidst his own anguish he grieved for her future destiny. Once, Perdita found something he'd written; it was blotted with tears:

Life—it began—is not the thing romance writers describe, as going through the measures of a dance, and after various turns arriving at a conclusion, when the dancers may sit down and rest. While there is life, there is ceaseless action and change. We go on, each thought linked to the one which spawned it, each act to a previous act. No joy or sorrow dies barren of offspring. Thus is woven the chain that makes our life. Calderon wrote: Un dia llama à otro dia y asi llama, y encadena llanto à llanto, y pena à pena. *'One day calls to another day; and so it calls again and links cry to cry, pain to pain.' Truly, Disappointment is the guardian deity of human life; she sits at the threshold of unborn time, marshalling events as they come forth. Once my heart sat lightly in my bosom; all the beauty of the world was doubly beautiful, irradiated by the sunlight shed from my own soul. O, why are love and ruin forever joined in this, our mortal dream? So that when we make our hearts a lair for that seemingly gentle beast, its companion enters with it, and pitilessly lays waste what might have been both home and shelter.*

By degrees his health was shaken, and then his intellect yielded to the same tyrannous misery. His manners grew wild; he was sometimes ferocious, sometimes absorbed in speechless melancholy. Suddenly Evadne decided to move to Paris. Adrian overtook her just as she was about to depart. No one knew what passed between them, but Perdita had never seen him since. He lived in seclusion, no one knew where, attended by such persons as his mother selected for that purpose.

(6)   THE next day Lord Raymond called at Perdita's cottage, on his way to Windsor Castle. My sister's blush and her sparkling eyes half revealed her secret to me. He was perfectly self-possessed, his complexion colorless. After a courteous greeting, he seemed immediately to enter into our feelings and become one with us. I scanned his features, which varied as he spoke, yet were beautiful in every change. The usual expression of his eyes was soft, though at times he could make them glare with ferocity; his smile was pleasing, though disdain too often curled his lips—lips which to female eyes were the very throne of beauty and love. His voice, low and pleasant, often startled you by a sharp discordant note, which showed that its usual tone was rather the work of study than nature. Thus full of contradictions—sociable yet haughty, gentle yet fierce, tender then negligent—he by some strange art found easy entrance to the admiration and affection of women; now caressing, now tyrannizing over them according to his mood, but always a despot.

At the present time Raymond evidently wished to appear amiable. Wit, hilarity, and deep observation were mingled in his talk, turning every sentence he uttered into a flash of light. Watching him with Perdita, I tried to keep in mind everything I'd heard to his disadvantage. But all appeared so harmless, and all was so fascinating, that I soon forgot everything except the pleasure of his society.

Under the idea of initiating me into the scene of English politics and society, of which I was soon to become a part, he narrated a number of anecdotes and sketched many characters; his discourse, rich and varied, flowed on, pervading all my senses with pleasure. But for one thing he would have been completely triumphant. When he mentioned Adrian, he spoke with that disparagement the worldly wise always bestowed on enthusiasm. I stopped him:

"Permit me to remark that I am devotedly attached to the Earl of Windsor. He is my best friend and benefactor. I reverence his goodness, I accord with his opinions, and bitterly lament his present, and I trust temporary, illness. I cannot hear him mentioned unless in terms of respect and affection."

Raymond replied; but there was nothing conciliatory in his reply. "Everyone," he said, "dreams about something—love, honor, pleasure. You dream of friendship, and devote yourself to a maniac; well, if that be your vocation, doubtless you are right to follow it." I saw that in his heart he despised people who dedicated themselves to any except worldly idols. But then some reflection seemed to sting him, and the pain behind his sudden wince caused me to check my indignation. "Happy are dreamers." His voice was no longer derisive. "As long as they're not awakened. I wish could dream! But I live by broad, garish daylight, in the dazzling glare of reality. Even the ghost of friendship is gone. And love—" He broke off; nor could I guess whether the disdain that curled his lip was directed against the passion, or against himself for being its slave.

My conversations with Lord Raymond often ran this way. But we became close, and each day afforded new occasion to admire the powerful and versatile talents which, together with his eloquence (graceful and witty) and his wealth (now immense), caused him to be at the same time the most feared, loved, and hated man in England.

I had entered public life. My father's name claimed interest, if not respect. When added to my long connection with Adrian, and the Austrian ambassador's known favor, and now my intimacy with Lord Raymond, it gave me easy access to the fashionable and political circles of England. At first sight, we appeared to be on the eve of civil war. Each party was violent, acrimonious, unyielding. Parliament was divided by three factions—aristocrats, democratic popular reformers, and royalists. The last had nearly died out after Adrian's defection to the republican ideal became widely known. Then Lord Raymond stepped forward as a royalist partisan, and they revived with redoubled force. Some were royalists from prejudice and ancient affection for the House of Windsor; many were moderates who lived in equal fear of the popular party's capricious tyranny and the old aristocrats' unbending despotism. Ranged under Raymond, the royalist faction was growing every day. Between the other two, the aristocrats built their hopes on their own outsized share of wealth and influence, the reformers on the force of the majority—the people. The debates in government were violent, but the committee meetings were worse. Assembled in knots at closer quarters to arrange their measures, politicians bandied opprobrious epithets and slung vows of resistance to the death. Such strife spilled over into the populace, whose mob unrest disturbed the quiet order of the country. Except in civil war, how could all this end?

Then, just as the really destructive flames were ready to break forth, I saw them shrink back. Another crisis in government had passed. Because no faction had an army, and no one wanted any violence (save of speech), and cordial politeness and even friendship were always maintained between the hostile leaders when they met in private society. After this, I watched events ever more closely.

My sister was my chief solace and delight, and my spirits always rose at the thought of seeing her. Perdita's conversation was full of pointed remark and discernment. In her pleasant rooms, their alcoves redolent with the sweetest fresh flowers, adorned by antique vases and magnificent casts, and hung with brilliant art—skillful copies she'd painted herself of the best works by Raphael, Correggio, Claude—I fancied myself in a fairy retreat untainted by and inaccessible to the noisy, flashy worlds of politics or fashion.

In my hours with Perdita, I could not but perceive that she loved Raymond; methought also that he regarded my fair sister with admiration and tenderness. Yet I knew that he planned to marry the presumptive heiress of the Earldom of Windsor, and had keen expectations of the advantages he'd gain thereby. It seemed certain. All the Ex-Queen's friends were his friends; not a week passed that he didn't hold consultations with her at Windsor.

I had never seen Adrian's sister. I'd heard that she was lovely, amiable, fascinating. Yet any discussion concerning her union with

Lord Raymond was real agony to me. Given Adrian's withdrawal from active life, this beauteous Idris had probably fallen victim to her mother's ambitious schemes; in my friend's place, I ought to come forward and protect her from undue influence, guard against her unhappiness, and secure to her the freedom of choice that is the right of every human being. Yet how? She'd be bound to reject my interference, that of a stranger, an object of indifference or contempt to her. Far better to keep apart and not risk self-exposure and scorn. Something else held me back, though—a premonition that for better or for worse, our meeting would change things; as often happened with people in such cases, fearing the change, I shunned the event, and avoided this high-born damsel whose plight wrung my heart.

Yet. . .on one occasion when I quitted London to visit the cottage by Windsor Forest, my sister was not alone; nor could I fail to recognize her companion. It was Idris, the till now unseen object of my slightly mad idolatry.

In what fitting terms of wonder and delight, in what choice expression and soft flow of language, can I usher in the loveliest, wisest, best? How in mere words convey the halo of glory that surrounded her, the thousand graces that waited tirelessly on her? The first thing that struck you on beholding that charming countenance was its perfect goodness and frankness; candor sat upon her brow, simplicity in her eyes, heavenly kindness in her smile. Her figure was tall, slim, graceful; her gait, goddess-like, was also that of a winged angel; and her voice resembled the low, subdued tone of a tenor flute. It is easiest perhaps to describe by way of Wordsworth, who in one poem compared a beloved woman to both a flower and a star; but his lines always described to me two contrasting characters:

> *A violet by a mossy stone*
> *Half hidden from the eye,*
> *Fair as a star when only one*
> *Is shining in the sky.*

Such a violet was my sister, sweet Perdita, reconciled to solitude, reserved and timid even where she loved; trembling to entrust herself to the very air, cowering from observation, yet betrayed by her excellences; and repaying with a thousand graces the labor of those who sought her in her lonely by-way. Fearless, open-hearted Idris was that fair star, set in single splendor in the diadem of balmy evening; ready to enlighten and delight the subject world, shielded from every taint by her unimagined distance from all that was not, like herself, akin to heaven.

I found this vision of beauty seated in an alcove, wrapped in earnest conversation with my sister. Perdita, seeing me, rose and took my hand, and told her companion, "He's here—our wish is granted! This is Lionel, my brother."

Idris stood at the same time. Her eyes were a celestial blue. With peculiar grace she said, "You hardly need an introduction. We have a picture, highly valued by my father, which declares at once who you are. Yes, a Verney. I hope you'll acknowledge this family tie—and as my brother's friend, I feel that I may trust you." Tears filmed her eyes and her voice trembled as she continued: "Dear friends, please don't think it strange that now, when I'm visiting you for the first time, I confide in you completely and then ask your assistance. You're the only ones I dare speak to—both of you so good—and as my brother's friends, you must be mine—oh, what can I say? If you refuse to help me, I am lost indeed!"

Neither Perdita nor I could answer a word. Idris gazed upward, while wonder held us mute, and cried, "My brother! Beloved, ill-fated Adrian! How speak of your misfortunes? My friends, doubtless you've both heard the current tale. Perhaps you've even believed the slander—but he is not mad! Were an angel from the foot of God's throne to assert it, never, never would I believe it. He is wronged, betrayed, imprisoned—save him! Verney, you must do this; seek him out in whatever part of the island they've hidden him; find Adrian, rescue him from his persecutors, restore him to himself, to me—on the wide earth I have none to love but only him!"

This earnest appeal, so sweetly and passionately expressed, filled me with wonder and sympathy; and, when Idris added, with thrilling voice and look, "Do you consent to undertake this enterprise?" I vowed, with energy and truth, to devote myself in life and death to Adrian's restoration and welfare.

At once we began laying out the plan I must pursue. We were strategizing over the fastest way to determine Adrian's whereabouts, when Lord Raymond entered the room without knocking. I saw Perdita tremble and grow deadly pale, and Idris's cheeks glow with the purest blushes. He must have been astonished at our conclave, and considerably disturbed by it I should have thought; but nothing of this showed. He saluted my companions and gave me a cordial greeting. Idris froze for a moment. Then, in the sweetest tones, she said, "Lord Raymond, I confide in your goodness and honor."

Smiling haughtily, he tipped his head. "Do you indeed confide, Lady Idris?"

She studied him, then answered with dignity. "As you please. It is certainly best not to compromise oneself by any concealment."

"Pardon me," he replied, "if I have offended. Whether you trust me or not, rely on my doing my utmost to further your wishes, whatever they may be."

Smiling her thanks, Idris stood up to take leave. Lord Raymond asked permission to accompany her to Windsor Castle; she consented, and they quitted the cottage together. My sister and I were left—truly like two fools, who fancied they'd obtained a golden treasure, till daylight showed it to be painted lead—a pair of silly, luckless flies, caught in a glistening spider's web that we mistook for sunbeams. I leaned by the window and watched those two glorious creatures till they disappeared among the forest glades; and then I turned. Perdita had not moved. Her eyes fixed on the ground, her cheeks pale, her very lips white, every feature stamped by woe, she sat motionless and rigid. Alarmed, I went to take her hand; but she shudderingly withdrew it and strove to collect herself. I entreated her to speak to me.

"Not now," she replied, rising. "And don't you speak either, my dear Lionel. There is nothing you can say, for you know nothing. I'll see you tomorrow; in the meantime, adieu!" She paused at the parlor door, leaning there as if the havoc in her mind made her need the support; and added, in a faltering voice, "Lord Raymond will probably return. Please tell him that he must excuse me today. I am not well. I'll see him tomorrow if he wishes it. You'd better return to London with him; you can start making those inquiries about Adrian. Visit me again tomorrow, before you leave to go find him." I agreed to everything. "Till then, farewell," she concluded with a heavy sigh.

(7)   I FELT as if, from an orderly and systematic world, I'd plunged into chaos. That Raymond should marry Idris seemed more intolerable than ever; yet even through my passion, a giant from its birth, strange, wild, and impracticable, I could perceive Perdita's misery. How should I act? How could I help her? She hadn't confided in me. I could demand no explanation from Raymond without risking the betrayal of what was perhaps her most treasured secret. Could I get the truth from her tomorrow? My reflections were multiplying when Lord Raymond returned. He asked for my sister, and I delivered her message. After musing on it for a moment, he asked me if I were about to return to London—if so, would I accompany him?

I consented. Full of thought, he remained silent during a considerable part of our ride. At length he said, "I must apologize for my abstraction. The truth is, Ryland's motion comes on tonight, and I'm considering my reply." Ryland was the leader of the populist party, a hard-headed man, and in his way eloquent; the bill he was poised to offer made it treason to attempt to change the present state of the English government and the standing laws of the republic. This attack was directed against Raymond and his machinations for the restoration of the monarchy.

Raymond asked me if I'd accompany him to the House that evening. With my inquiries to make, I excused myself. "Don't worry," said my companion, "I can free your time for you. The plan I think was to spend it asking after the Earl of Windsor. I can tell you at once: he's in Scotland, at the Duke of Athol's seat at Dunkeld. At the onset of his disorder he began traveling about from place to place; but once he got to Dunkeld, he refused to leave. We've made arrangements with the Duke for his continuing there—in romantic seclusion."

I was hurt by the careless tone with which he conveyed this intelligence, and replied coldly, thanking him, that I would make use of it. He nodded.

"Yes, you shall, Verney—but first, come witness, I beseech you, the triumph I'm about to achieve tonight in the House. If I can call it triumph, when I fear it means my defeat. But what can I do? My dearest hopes appear to be on the verge of fulfillment. The Ex-Queen gives me Idris; Adrian is totally unfitted for the earldom of Windsor, and that paltry earldom in my hands becomes a kingdom. By the reigning God it's true! The Countess can never forget that she has been a queen, and she hates the thought of leaving her children a diminished inheritance; her power and my wit will rebuild the throne, and this brow will be clasped by a kingly diadem. I can do this—I can marry Idris."

He stopped abruptly. His face darkened and twitched, as passion drove one expression after another across it. I asked, "Does Lady Idris love you?"

Raymond laughed. "What a question! She will of course, as I shall her, when we are married."

"You begin late," said I, ironically. "Marriage is usually considered the grave, and not the cradle of love. So you are about to love her, but do not already?"

"Don't cross-examine me, Lionel; I will do my duty by her, I assure you. Love! I must steel my heart against love, expel it from its bastion, barricade it out—shut off its fountains and let my desire for a passionate love dry up and die of thirst—I mean, the love I'm trying to handle, not the one I can, with ease. Idris is a gentle, pretty, sweet little girl; it's impossible not to have an affection for her, and I have a very sincere one; only do not speak of love—Love, the tyrant and the tyrant-slayer, the hungry fire, the tameless beast, the fanged snake—no—no—I will have nothing to do with that love." He bent his keen eyes upon me. "Tell me, Lionel, do you consent that I should marry this young lady?"

My uncontrollable heart swelled in my bosom. I replied in a calm voice—but how far from calm were my thoughts: "Never! I can never consent that Lady Idris should be united to a man who doesn't love her."

"Because you love her yourself."

"Your Lordship might have withheld that taunt. I do not—dare not love her."

"At least," he continued haughtily, "she does not love you. I wouldn't even marry a reigning sovereign if I weren't certain that her heart was free. But, O, Lionel! A kingdom! What a word of might. I love those gentle sounds and styles of royalty. Weren't the mightiest men of the olden times kings? Alexander was a king; Solomon, the wisest of men, was a king; Napoleon was a king; Caesar died trying to become one, and puritan Cromwell, the king-killer, aspired to regality. The scepter of England that Adrian's father yielded up was already broken; but I will raise it, restore it, and exalt it again above all others.

"Don't be surprised that I tell you where to find Adrian. Don't suppose me wicked or foolish enough to found my kingdom on a fraud, especially one so easy to investigate as the Earl's insanity. I've just come from him. Before deciding on my marriage with Idris, I wanted to see for myself again, and judge the probability that he might recover. He's incurably mad."

I gasped for breath.

"I will not burden you," continued Raymond, "with the melancholy details. You'll see him, and judge for yourself; though I fear this visit, useless to him, will be insufferably painful to you. Excellent and gentle as he is even in the downfall of his reason, seeing him this last time has weighed on my spirits ever since. I don't worship him as you do, but I would give all my hopes of a crown and my right hand to boot, to see him restored to himself." Raymond's voice expressed the deepest compassion.

"You most unaccountable being," I cried, "where will your actions take you, when you're so lost in the maze of your own purposes?"

"Where indeed? To a crown, a golden gem-studded crown, I hope. Yet a busy devil never stops whispering to me, that I only chase a dunce's cap—and that if I were wise, I'd trample on my chance at a crown and take in its place, something worth more than all the thrones of the East and the presidencies of the West put together."

"And what is that?"

"If I make that choice, you'll know; at present I dare not speak, nor even think of it."

After a pause he turned to me, laughing. When his mirth wasn't inspired by scorn, and genuine gaiety painted his features with a joyous expression, his beauty became supreme, divine. "Verney," said he, "my first act when I become King of England, will be to unite with the Greeks, take Istanbul, restore its name, and from the new Byzantium subdue the whole of Asia. I intend to be a warrior, a conqueror; Napoleon's name will be forgotten for mine. No one will visit his rocky grave when they have my majesty to adore, my achievements to exalt."

I listened absorbedly. How could I not, to one who seemed to govern the whole earth in his grasping imagination, and who only quailed at the attempt to rule himself—when on his word and will depended not just my own happiness, but the fate of all who were dear to me? Perdita's name wasn't mentioned; yet love for her lay behind his vacillation of purpose, I was sure. And who was so worthy of love as my noble-minded sister? Who deserved the hand of this self-exalted king more than she whose glance belonged to a queen of nations? She who loved him, as he did her; though disappointment quelled her passion, and ambition held his in strong combat.

We went together to the House that evening. A hum as of ten thousand hives of swarming bees stunned us as we entered the coffee-room. Knots of politicians stood about, all taking at once; we saw many anxious brows. The aristocrats' party, comprising England's richest and most influential citizens, appeared less agitated than the rest, for the question was to be debated without their interference. Raymond, whose plans and prospects all depended on the outcome, wore a carefree air. Nearest the fireplace, Ryland and his supporters had gathered. A man of obscure birth and immense wealth, inherited from his manufacturer father, Ryland had witnessed, as a young man, the king's abdication and the amalgamation of the two houses of Lords and Commons; sympathizing with these popular developments (some called them encroachments), he'd made it the business of his life to consolidate and increase them. Since then, however, the influence of the landed proprietors had grown; and at first Ryland wasn't sorry to observe Lord Raymond's machinations, which drew off many of his aristocratic opponents' partisans. But the thing was now going too far. The poorer nobility hailed the monarchy's return, as an event which would restore them to their lost power and rights. The half-extinct spirit of royalty roused itself in people's minds; willing slaves and so-called subjects, they were ready to bend their necks to the yoke. Some proud and virtuous spirits still remained, the pillars of the state. But the word "republic" had grown stale to the vulgar ear; and many—we'd learn tonight whether it was a majority—pined for a royal family's tinsel and show. Ryland was bent on resistance. Claiming that he'd been the one who'd allowed Raymond's numbers to increase, he said the time for indulgence had passed. With one motion of his arm—he raised a copy of his bill—he'd sweep away the cobwebs that blinded the rest of the country.

Raymond's entrance had been hailed by his friends almost with a shout. They gathered round him in the coffee-room, counted their numbers, and started tallying new and still undeclared votes. Then it was time for the leaders to take their seats in the House chamber, where the clamor of voices continued until Ryland rose to speak. Now the slightest whisper was audible. All eyes were fixed upon him as he stood—a man with a ponderous frame and a sonorous voice, whose manner, though not graceful, was impressive. I turned from his marked, iron countenance to Raymond's face, veiled by a smile, betraying not a care; yet his lips quivered somewhat, and the muscles in his arm were starting through his coat sleeve at the convulsive strength with which he gripped the bench we sat on.

Ryland began by praising the present state of the British empire. He recalled his listeners' memory to the miserable contentions which in the time of our fathers arose almost to civil war; then the abdication of the late king, and the foundation of the republic. He described this republic, demonstrated how it privileged each individual in the state equally, so that any one of them could rise to consequence, even—for a span—to the highest office. Comparing the royalist with the republican spirit, he showed how the one tended to enslave the mind, while the other through its institutions could serve to raise even the lowliest among us to something great and good. Britain, in Ryland's telling, had become powerful, and its inhabitants valiant and wise, by means of the freedom they enjoyed. As he spoke, every heart swelled with pride, and every cheek glowed with delight to remember that each one there was British, each one a supporter and contributor to the happy state of things the orator described. Ryland's fervor increased—his eyes lit up—his voice grew passionate.

One man, he said, was out to change all this, and return us to our days of impotence and contention—one man, who would dare to arrogate the honor which was due to all British citizens, and set his name and style above the name and style of his country.

Here I saw Raymond change color and direct his gaze at the ground. Other listeners turned to look at one another; but Ryland's voice went on filling their ears, the thunder of his denunciations influencing their senses. The very boldness of his language gave it weight; each of us knew he was speaking the truth—a truth we'd kept unacknowledged. Raymond's purposes had been stealthy, seductive; but this speech tore the mask from reality, to show the ensnarer as a hunted stag—even one at bay, as appeared from the look of him. Ryland ended by moving, that any attempt to reestablish the monarchy should be declared treason, and anyone a traitor who should endeavor to change the present form of government. Loud cheers and acclamations followed.

After the motion had been seconded, Lord Raymond rose. His countenance bland, his voice softly melodious, his manner soothing, his grace and sweetness came like the mild breathing of a flute after the loud, church organ-like voice of his adversary. He rose, he said, to speak in favor of the honorable member's motion—yes, in favor, if one slight amendment could be made. He was ready to go back to olden times, and commemorate the contests of our fathers, and the monarch's abdication. Nobly and greatly, he said, had our illustrious last sovereign sacrificed himself to the apparent good of his country, and divested himself of a power which could only be maintained by the blood of his subjects. These same subjects, no longer subjects, but now his friends and equals, had in gratitude conferred certain favors and distinctions on him and his family—forever. An ample estate was allotted to them, and they took the first rank among Britain's peers. Could it be right, Raymond asked, that an heir of this king should be charged and suffer the same punishment as any other pretender, if he attempted to regain what by ancient right and inheritance belonged to him? He did not say that he should favor such an attempt; but he did say that such an attempt would be understandable; and, if the aspirant did not go so far as to declare war, and erect a standard declaring his kingdom, the fault ought to be regarded with an indulgent eye. With the amendment he proposed, the bill would exempt any person who claimed the sovereign power in right of the House of Windsor.

Nor did Raymond end there. He began to draw, in vivid and glowing colors, the splendor of a kingdom, as opposed to the commercial spirit of republicanism. Under the British monarchy, he asserted, each individual was just as capable as now of attaining high rank and power—higher and nobler to be sure than a bartering, timorous commonwealth could afford. One title alone would be lost, as the king resumed the function of Chief Magistrate. As to which, Raymond asked, so what? Now, every three years brought a struggle for the seat. The nature of wealth and influence forcibly confined the list of candidates to a few rich ones; and an impartial observer might question whether the advantages of holding these elections outweighed the public harm caused by their wasteful contentiousness. And so on: I can't do justice to the flow of language and graceful turns of expression, the wit and easy raillery that gave vigor and influence to Raymond's speech. His manner, almost timid at first, became firm; his changeful face was lit up to superhuman brilliancy; his voice, various as music, was alike enchanting.

I won't record the debate that followed. Party speeches were delivered which clothed the question in cant and left its simple meaning veiled in a woven wind of words. The motion was lost; Ryland withdrew in rage and despair; and Raymond, gay and exulting, retired to dream of his future kingdom.

(8)   WAS there ever such a feeling as love at first sight? And if yes, what made it different from love based on long observation and slow growth? Which one was more often permanent—which one's effects while they lasted were more violent and intense?

We walked the pathless mazes of society, vacant of joy; suddenly we held this clue, leading us through that labyrinth to paradise. Our nature dim, formless, an unlit match asleep until the fire attained it: then Love—light—this life of life. At no moment then or in time to come did I feel the same as I had before. In the deepest fountain of my heart the pulses were stirred; and like a cloak, around, above, beneath, clinging Memory enwrapped me. The spirit of Idris hovered in the air I breathed; her eyes were constantly bent on mine; her remembered smile blinded my faint gaze, and caused me to walk as if through dark and vacant space—but my steps were slowed by a new and brilliant light, too novel, too dazzling for my human senses. On every leaf, on every atom, I saw imprinted the talisman of my existence: SHE LIVES! SHE IS! With no time yet to analyze, much less leash, a tameless passion, I had but this one idea, one feeling, one thing I knew. It was my life!

But the die was cast—Raymond would marry Idris. The merry marriage bells rang in my ears; I heard the nation's cheers greet this wedding. With the swiftness of an eagle in flight, the poor but ambitious noble had risen to regal supremacy and won Idris's love. Yet, not so! She did not love him; she had called me her friend; she had smiled on me; to me she had entrusted her heart's dearest hope, Adrian's welfare. This idea kept returning to cheer me before being swept away by my busy thoughts.

The debate had ended at three in the morning. My soul in tumult, I sped, directionless, through London's streets. Truly, I was mad that night, when the love which I have called a giant from its birth, wrestled with despair! Day, hateful to me, dawned; I retreated to my lodgings—I threw myself on a bed—I slept—was it sleep? Thought was still alive—love and despair kept up their struggle, and I writhed with unendurable pain. I awoke half stupefied, unable to place the cause of the heavy oppression I could feel lying upon me. I had to enter, as it were, the council chamber of my brain, and question the various ministers of thought therein assembled. Too soon I remembered all; too soon my limbs quivered beneath the tormenting power; soon, too soon, I knew myself a slave!

Suddenly, unannounced, Lord Raymond entered my room. He came in gaily, singing the Tyrolese song of liberty; noticed me with a gracious nod, and threw himself on a sofa. Just opposite stood a copy of the Apollo Belvedere. After one or two trivial remarks, to which I replied sullenly, he burst out, all smiles, and pointed at the wall.

"I've been said to resemble him! My face, that is. Here's an idea: Apollo's head on my new coinage—to stand as an omen to all dutiful subjects of my future success. I must contact the Vatican Collections for the rights."

His playful self-mockery passed all of a sudden and left his features troubled. In that shrill tone peculiar to himself, he cried, "I fought a good battle last night! Higher conquest, the plains of Greece never saw me achieve. Now I am the first man in the state, topic of every popular ballad, the object of old women's mumbled devotions. What are you thinking about it all? Verney, a man who imagines he can read the human soul, as your native lake reads each crevice and fold of its surrounding hills—say what you think of me. King-to-be? Angel or devil, which do you think?"

Irked to my depths by his ironical tone and his insolence, I replied with bitterness: "There is a spirit, neither angel or devil, damned to limbo merely." I saw his cheeks become pale, and his lips whiten and quiver; his anger served but to feed mine, and I answered his glare with a determined look. Suddenly his eyes were withdrawn, cast down; a tear, I thought, wetted the dark lashes. I was softened, and with involuntary emotion added, "Not that you are such, my dear lord."

His agitation silenced us both for a few moments. "Yes," he said at length, rising and biting his lip, as he strove to curb his passion. "I am such! You don't know me, Verney; neither you, nor our audience last night, nor anyone in the whole of England knows anything about me. I stand here, it would seem, an elected king; this hand is about to grasp a scepter; these brows feel in each nerve the coming crown. I appear to have strength, power, victory; to stand as the foremost column which supports the dome; and I am—a reed! I have ambition which attains its aim; my nightly dreams are realized, my waking hopes fulfilled; a kingdom awaits my acceptance, my enemies are overthrown. But here," and he struck his heart with violence, "*here* is the rebel, here the stumbling block! This overruling heart, which I could drain of its living blood and yet while one fluttering pulsation remained, I would be its slave."

He spoke with a broken voice, then bowed his head, and, hiding his face in his hands, wept. I was still smarting from my own disappointment; yet this brought me to the point of terror. I couldn't speak as I watched Raymond throw himself on the couch. There he remained silent and motionless, save that a strong internal conflict kept his features changeful. At last he rose, and said in his usual tone of voice, "The time flies, Verney. I've got to go—but don't let me forget my main errand here. Will you accompany me to Windsor this afternoon? There will be nothing dishonorable for you involved, and as this is probably the last service, or disservice, you can do me, will you say yes?"

He held out his hand with almost a bashful air. Swiftly I thought, *Yes, I will witness the last scene of the drama.* Besides, his manner conquered me. With affection towards him filling my heart again, I bade him command me. He laughed. "Aye, that I will—that's my cue now. Be with me as the clock strikes four; be ye secret and faithful, and ye shall be Groom of the Stole ere long!"

So saying, he hastened away, vaulted onto his horse, and with a gesture as if he gave me his hand to kiss from my window, bade me another laughing adieu. Left to myself, I spent the next several hours striving with painful intensity to figure out Raymond's motives and predict the events of the coming day. In the end, my head ached with thought, the nerves teeming from overwork; I clasped my burning brow, as if a fevered hand could medicine its pain. Later, punctual to the appointed hour, I found Lord Raymond waiting for me. We got into his carriage and proceeded towards Windsor. I'd told myself to show no outward sign of my internal agitation.

"What a mistake Ryland made," began Raymond, "when he thought to overpower me on the floor. He spoke well, very well; such an harangue would have succeeded better addressed to me singly, than to those fools and knaves assembled yonder. Had I been alone, I'd have listened to him and tried to hear reason; but when he tried to vanquish me on my own territory, with my own weapons, he put me on my mettle, and the outcome might have been expected."

I smiled incredulously and replied, "I'm of Ryland's way of thinking. I'd be happy to repeat all his arguments; let's see how far you'll be induced by them to change the royal for the patriotic style."

"The repetition would be useless," said Raymond. "I remember them; and I've come up with many arguments of my own, on the same side, which are even more persuasive."

He didn't explain himself, nor did I remark on his reply. Our silence endured for some miles. Countryside with open fields, shady wood, parks, had begun to present pleasant objects to our view, which soon gave rise to conversation. Raymond said, "The philosophers who call the human being a microcosm of nature, find some correspondence inside the mind for every bit of this" (he gestured at trees, grasses, sky) "this machinery visibly at work around us. Their theory has been a frequent source of amusement to me; and many an idle hour have I spent, exercising my ingenuity in identifying so-called resemblances."

His gaze at the passing view grew more distant, as he continued, "What a sea is the tide of passion, whose fountains are in our own nature! Our virtues are the quick sands, which show themselves at calm low water; but let the waves rise and the winds come up, and the poor devil whose hope was in their solidity, finds them sink from underfoot. The fashions of the world, its laws, educations and pursuits, are winds to drive our wills, like clouds, all one way; but let a thunderstorm in the shape of love, hate, or ambition blow up, and the rack goes backward—our progress is stemmed by the triumph of the opposing air."

"Yet," replied I, "nature is essentially passive. We human beings possess an active principle, capable of mastering and ruling fortune—or at least of tacking against the gale, until beating it somehow."

"Your distinction is specious," said my companion. "Active? Did we form ourselves, then? Choose our dispositions? Our powers? I find myself, for one, to be like a stringed instrument. Here are all the chords and stops—but I have no power to turn the pegs, or pitch my thoughts to a higher or lower key."

"Other people," I observed, "may be better musicians."

"I talk not of others, but myself," Raymond said, "and I am as fair an example to go by as another. I cannot set my heart to a particular tune, or perform voluntary changes on my will. We are born; we choose neither our parents, nor our station; we are educated by others, or by the world's circumstance, and this cultivation, mingling with our innate disposition, is the soil in which our desires, passions, and motives grow."

"There's a great deal of truth in what you say," said I, "and yet no one ever acts upon your theory. Who, in the midst of choosing, ever says, *Thus I choose, because I have no choice?* Don't we all, on the contrary, experience an inner freedom of will, which, though you may call it fallacious, still actuates our decisions?"

"Exactly," replied Raymond. "Here's another link in the unbreakable chain. Tell me, were I now to commit an act which would annihilate my hopes, sweep the royal robes from my shoulders, and leave me in a set of ordinary clothes for life—would this, think you, be an act of free will on my part?"

While we'd been talking, I'd noticed that we weren't taking the ordinary road to Windsor, but instead one through Englefield Green, towards Bishopsgate Heath. I began to realize that Idris was not the object of our journey. I had indeed been brought to witness the scene that was to decide Raymond's fate—his fate, and Perdita's. Clearly, he was still vacillating. Irresolution marked his every gesture as we entered my sister's cottage. I had my eyes trained on him. If Raymond kept hesitating, I was determined to intervene; I'd help Perdita to overcome herself, and teach her to disdain a love that wavered over someone's wish to wear a crown, when her own excellence and affection transcended the worth of any kingdom.

We found her among the flowers in her alcove; she was reading a newspaper report of last night's parliamentary debate which had apparently sunk her heart and doomed her to hopelessness. We were in time to hear a sigh. Her eyes circled with shadowy distress, her attitude spiritless; a cloud was on her beauty. The effect on Raymond was instantaneous. His eyes beamed with tenderness; remorse clothed his manners with earnestness and truth. He sat beside her and took the paper from her hand. "Not a word more shall my sweet Perdita read of this contention of madmen and fools. I must not permit you to become acquainted with the extent of my delusion, lest you despise me; although, believe me, a wish to appear before you, not vanquished, but as a conqueror, inspired me during my wordy war."

Perdita's amazement blazed into joy; tenderness shone in her countenance; to see him was happiness. But bitter thoughts swooped in and bent her. Eyes fixed on the ground, she tried to master the passion of tears that threatened to overwhelm her.

Raymond continued, "I won't act a part with you, dear girl, or let you think me other than what I am, weak and unworthy, more fit to excite your disdain than your love. Yet you do love me; I feel and know that you do, and thence I draw my most cherished hopes. If pride guided you, or even reason, you might well reject me. Do so; if your high heart, incapable of my infirmity of purpose, refuses to bend to the lowness of mine. Turn from me if you will—if you can. If your whole soul does not urge you to forgive me—if your entire heart does not open wide its door to admit me to its very center—then forsake me, never speak to me again. I, though sinning against you almost beyond remission, I also am proud; there must be no reserve in your pardon—no drawback to the gift of your affection."

Perdita looked down, confused, yet pleased. A blush mantled her cheek. My presence embarrassed her so that she dared neither turn to meet her lover's eye, nor trust her voice to assure him of her affection; but her disconsolate air had been entirely replaced by one of deep-felt joy. Raymond, putting an arm around her waist, continued:

"I do not deny that I have balanced between you and the highest hope that mortal men can entertain; but I do so no longer. Take me— mould me to your will, possess my heart and soul to all eternity. If you refuse to contribute to my happiness, I quit England tonight, and will never set foot in it again." He turned. "Lionel, you've heard everything. Witness for me. Persuade your sister to forgive the injury I have done her—persuade her to be mine."

"There needs no persuasion," said the blushing Perdita, "except your own dear promises, and my ready heart, which whispers to me that they are true."

That same evening we all three walked together in the forest, and, with the talkativeness which happiness inspires, they told me the history of their romance. It was pleasant to see the haughty Raymond and reserved Perdita changed through happy love into prattling, playful children, both losing their characteristic dignity in the fullness of mutual contentment. A night ago Lord Raymond, with a brow of care, and a heart oppressed with thought, had bent all his energies to silence or persuade the legislators of England that a scepter was not too weighty for his hand, while visions of dominion, war, and triumph floated before him; now, frolicsome as a lively boy sporting under his mother's approving eye, the hopes of his ambition were complete, when he pressed Perdita's small fair hand to his lips; while she, radiant with delight, looked on the still pool, not truly admiring herself, but drinking in with rapture the reflection its surface made of herself and her lover—their first appearance as a couple.

I rambled away from them. If theirs was a rapture of assured sympathy, mine was one of restored hope. At length, I looked on the regal towers of Windsor. My thoughts at twenty, as I was then:

High is the wall and strong the barrier that separate me from my Star of Beauty. But not impassible. She will not be his. Spend a few more years in your native garden, sweet flower, till I by toil and time acquire the right to deserve you and gather you to me. Don't despair— and don't give me cause to!

What must I do now? First, find Idris's brother and restore him to her. Patience, gentleness, and untiring affection will cure Adrian if he's mad as Raymond say he is. Energy and courage will rescue him if he's been unjustly imprisoned.

(9)   THE LOVERS and I joined up again and returned together to dine in Perdita's cottage. It might have been a fairies' supper, the air perfumed by scents of fruits and wine, and none of us eating or drinking a thing. Even the beauty of the night went unobserved: their ecstasy could no longer be increased by outward objects, and I was wrapped in reverie. At about midnight Raymond and I took leave of my sister and headed back towards town. He was all gaiety; scraps of songs fell from his lips; every thought in his mind—every object about us—gleamed under the sunshine of his mirth. He accused me of melancholy, of ill-humor and envy.

"Not so," said I, "though I confess that my thoughts are not occupied so pleasantly as yours. You promised to facilitate my visit to Adrian—I call upon you to fulfill your promise. I can't linger here. I have one thing I want to do and that's comfort—perhaps help to cure—my first and best friend in his hour of sickness and need. I want to leave for Dunkeld immediately."

"You bird of night," replied Raymond, "what an eclipse do you throw across my bright thoughts, forcing me to call to mind that melancholy ruin, which stands in mental desolation, more irreparable than a fragment of a carved column in a weed-grown field. You dream that you can restore your friend? Daedalus in Crete never wound so inextricable an error round Minotaur, as madness has woven about his imprisoned reason. You can't thread that labyrinth, nor could any other would-be Theseus—though perhaps some unkind Ariadne has the clue."

"You mean Evadne Zaimi—but she's not in England."

"And if she were," said Raymond, "I would not advise her seeing him. Better to decay in absolute delirium, than to suffer the methodical insanity of loving the wrong person. He's been sick long enough to have forgotten any vestige of Evadne; and it would be just as well not to let her get imprinted again. You will find him at Dunkeld, gentle, tractable. Weed and wild flowers stuck in his hair. He wanders up and down the hills, through the woods; he sits listening beside a waterfall. You may see him—his eyes full of untraceable meaning—his voice broken—his body wasted to a shadow. He plucks grasses and things and weaves them into garlands. He sails yellow leaves and bits of bark on a stream, rejoicing if they float safely—but when they wreck, he weeps! By Heaven, I swear, the first tears I've shed since boyhood rushed scalding into my eyes at the sight—the memory by itself almost brings them back."

I didn't need to hear this account to want to be on my way as soon as possible. I was debating whether to try to see Idris again, before leaving, when the question was decided for me. Early the next morning, Raymond reappeared, this time bringing news that Adrian had fallen dangerously ill. Given his failing strength, his survival looked impossible. His mother and sister would travel to Scotland, in order to see him one last time. "They go tomorrow," said Raymond.

"I go today," I told him. "This very hour. I'll hire a sailing balloon and be there in forty-eight hours at most—less, if the wind is fair. Farewell, Raymond. Be happy in having chosen the better part in life. For Adrian I like this turn of events—not madness as feared, but sickness. I have a feeling he won't die; that this illness marks a crisis, and he could recover."

Everything favored my journey, including the wind. Half a mile above the earth, the balloon hurried through the air, its feathered wings cleaving an unresisting atmosphere. Despite the melancholy object of my journey, my spirits were exhilarated—by hope, by speed, by motion. The slender mechanism of the extended wings gave forth a murmuring noise, soothing to the ear. Plain and hill, stream and cornfield, passed below; on we sped, secure and unimpeded as a wild swan in springtide flight. The pilot hardly moved the controls, the machine obeying the slightest motion of the helm. With the wind blowing steadily, our course faced no obstacle.

I landed at Perth. Though much fatigued by many hours' constant exposure to the high-altitude air, I would not rest, but kept going, only by land now, to Dunkeld. The sun was rising as I neared this ancient seat of Scotland's kings. Many ages after the one Shakespeare chronicled, Birnam Hill was again covered with pine woods. The most aged trees, planted by a previous Duke of Athol in the very early 19th century, gave solemnity and beauty to the scene. Sunrise tinged the top branches; and in its beams my mountain-educated mind read good omens for Adrian, on whose life my happiness depended.

Poor fellow! Stretched on a sickbed, fever burning his cheeks, he lay with half-closed eyes, his breathing irregular, difficult. Yet it was less painful to see him thus, than to find him in apparent physical health, his mind only sickened. I established myself at his bedside and never left it, day or night. Bitter task, to behold his spirit waver between death and life; to see fever on his cheek, and know that inside, its fire was consuming the vital fuel of Adrian's life; to hear inarticulate moaning in a voice which might never again speak words of love and wisdom; to witness the ineffectual motions of his limbs, and picture how soon they were to be wrapped in a burial shroud. Such, for three days and nights, appeared to be the outcome decreed. I became haggard and almost spectral through anxiety and watching.

At last his eyes unclosed, faintly, yet with a look of returning life. The fever's passage left him pale and weak, but more relaxed; his features were softened by approaching convalescence. He knew me. What a brimming cup of joyful agony it was, when his face first gleamed with a look of recognition—when he pressed my hand, now more fevered than his own, and when he pronounced my name! No trace of his past insanity remained, to dash my joy with sorrow.

That same evening his mother and sister arrived. The Countess of Windsor was highly emotional by nature, but she had very seldom in her life permitted the contents of her heart to show themselves on her face. Its studied immovability, together with her slow, equable manner, and soft but unmelodious voice, were a mask which hid a fiery, passionate, and impatient disposition. She did not in the least resemble either Adrian or Idris; the sparkling black of her eyes, lit up by pride, was totally unlike the blue luster and kind, frank expression of her children's. There was something grand and majestic in her motions, but nothing persuasive, nothing amiable. Tall, athletic—she was a champion cyclist—thin, erect, her face still handsome, her raven hair hardly tinged with grey, her forehead arched and beautiful (save for the eyebrows being somewhat scattered); it was impossible not to be struck by the Ex-Queen, almost to fear her. Idris appeared to be the only being alive who could resist her mother. Her own character was extremely mild; but there was a fearlessness and frankness about her, which proclaimed that she would never encroach on another's liberty, but likewise held her own to be sacred and unassailable.

The Countess cast no look of kindness on my worn-out frame, though afterwards she thanked me coldly for my attentions. Not so Idris. Though her first care was for her brother, whom she kissed and showered with looks of compassion and love, her eyes glistened with tears when she stood and came to thank me; the grace of her expressions was enhanced, not diminished, by the fervor which caused her almost to falter as she spoke. Her mother, all eyes and ears, soon interrupted us. I saw that she wished to dismiss me quietly, as one whose services were of no further use to her son now that his relatives had arrived. Harassed and ill, I was resolved not to give up my post, yet wondering how to assert it, when Adrian called to me, clasped my hand, and told me not to leave him. His mother yielded the point to us.

The days that followed were so difficult that I sometimes regretted not yielding first and at once to the haughty lady, who watched my every move and turned my beloved task of nursing my friend into a work of pain and irritation. Never did any woman appear so entirely made of pure mind as the Countess of Windsor. Her passions had subdued her appetites, even her natural wants; she slept little, ate almost nothing; her body evidently considered by her as a mere machine, whose health was necessary for the accomplishment of her schemes, but whose senses formed no part of her enjoyment. It was with a kind of fear that I beheld the figure of the Countess awake, when others slept; fasting when I, abstemious naturally, and rendered more so by the fever that preyed on me, was forced to take a few bites of food. She had also resolved to prevent or diminish my opportunities of acquiring influence over her children, opposing a hard, quiet, stubborn will that seemed not to belong to flesh and blood. War was at last tacitly acknowledged between us. We had many pitched battles, during which not a single word was spoken and barely one look exchanged, but in which each resolved not to submit to the other. The Countess had the advantage of position; so I was vanquished, though I would not yield.

Sick at heart, and wearing a face of ill health and vexation, I found my best medicine in the tender concern shown me by Adrian and Idris—there, and in the sure recovery of my friend that was each day more apparent. The faint rosiness again touched his cheek; his brow and lips lost the ashy paleness of threatened dissolution; so much I'd won by my unremitting attention—and bounteous heaven added overflowing rewards when it gave me also words of thanks and smiles from Idris.

A few more weeks passed before our party quitted Dunkeld. While Idris and her mother returned immediately to Windsor, his continued weakness made it necessary that Adrian and I follow by slow, brief stages, making frequent stops. So, north to south, we traversed the various counties of a fertile isle. My companion, so long secluded by disease from the enjoyments of weather and scenery, was exhilarated by the sight of everything: busy towns, cultivated plains; plenteous harvests; rustic family groups of happy, healthful women, men and children, the very sight of whom sent cheerfulness directly to the heart.

At one stop, leaving our inn for some air, we strolled down a shady lane that took us to an eminence commanding an extensive view of hill and dale; of meandering rivers, dark woods, and bright, prosperous villages. Harmonized by distance, the busy hum of evening reached us. The sun was setting, and the clouds that strayed like new-shorn sheep through the vast fields of sky received the gold dye of its parting beams; the distant uplands shone out. Adrian, all fresh spirit infused by returning health, clasped his hands in delight, and exclaimed, transported:

"O happy Earth, and happy inhabitants of Earth! A stately palace has God built for you, O humanity! and worthy are you of your dwelling! Behold the carpet of greenery spread at our feet, and the azure canopy above—behold the earth which generates and nurtures all things, and the circumference of heaven, which contains and clasps all things. Now, at this hour of repose and reflection, methinks all hearts breathe one hymn of love and thanksgiving, and you and I, Lionel, like priests of old on the mountaintops, give a voice to their sentiment.

"To be sure, a most beneficent power built up the majestic reality we inhabit, and framed the laws by which it endures. If mere existence, and not happiness, were the point of our being, what would we need with all the luxuries that we enjoy instead? We need houses to protect us from the seasons, and behold what provides the wood and stone for them: the growth of trees with their adornment of leaves and the glory of forests; cliffs of rock piled above plains, adding their pleasant irregularity and interest to our prospects. Why make this planet so lovely, and our natural instincts so often pleasurable to satisfy? The very upkeep of the body is made delightful by delicious food—fruits, say, painted with transcendent hues, breathing attractive scents, uniquely palatable. Our senses feast. Why should this be, if the DIVINITY were not good?

"Nor do outward objects alone receive the Spirit of Good. Look into a human mind where Wisdom reigns enthroned; or where Imagination sits re-painting life with a brush dipped in celestial colors. What a noble boon, a gift worthy the giver, is Imagination! She takes the grey out of reality, envelopes every thought and sensation in a radiant veil, and with her beautiful hand beckons us from the sterile seas of life, to her gardens, and bowers, and glades of bliss. And is not Love a gift of the divinity? Love, and her child,

Hope, which can bestow wealth on poverty, strength on the weak, and happiness on the sorrowing.

"My lot has not been fortunate. I have long known grief. I've known madness, and been near death. Yet I thank God that I have lived! I give thanks, that I have beheld God's throne, the heavens, and earth, God's footstool. I am glad to have beheld the sun, fountain of light, and the gentle pilgrim moon; and seen the fiery flowers of the sky, and the flowery stars of earth; and witnessed the sowing and the harvest. I am glad that I have loved and have experienced sympathetic joy and sorrow with my fellow creatures. I'm glad now to feel the current of thought flow through my mind, as the blood circulates through my frame. Mere existence is pleasure, and I thank God that I live!

"And all you happy nurslings of Mother Earth, do you not echo my words? You who are linked by the affectionate ties of nature to companions, friends, lovers! Fathers, who toil with joy for their offspring; women, who while gazing on the living forms of their children, forget the pains of maternity; children, who neither toil nor spin, but love and are loved!

"Oh, that death and sickness were banished from our earthly home! that hatred, tyranny, and fear could no longer make their lair in the human heart! that each person might find a brother or a sister in his fellow man or woman, and all a nest of repose amid the wide plains of their inheritance! that the source of tears were dry, and that lips might no longer speak the language of sorrow! The choice is with us; let us will it, and our habitation becomes a paradise. For the human will is omnipotent: it blunts the arrows of death, soothes the bed of disease, and wipes away the tears of agony. And what is any of us worth, if we don't exert ourselves to help other people? My soul is a fading spark, my nature frail as a spent wave; but I dedicate all the intellect and strength that remains to me, to that one work—I take upon me the task, as far as I am able, of bestowing blessings on my fellow human beings!"

His voice trembled, his eyes and hands were prayerful, and his fragile person was bent, as it were, with excess of emotion. The spirit of life seemed to linger in his form, as a dying flame on an altar flickers on the embers of an accepted sacrifice.

(10)   WHEN we arrived at Windsor, I found that Raymond and Perdita, now married, had left for the Continent. I took possession of my sister's cottage, and blessed myself that I lived within view of Windsor Castle. It was a curious fact, that at this period, when I was allied by marriage to one of England's richest individuals and bound by the most intimate friendship to its foremost noble, I experienced the greatest excess of poverty I'd ever known. My knowledge of Lord Raymond and his worldly principles would have prevented me from applying to him under any circumstances. As to Adrian, I told myself in vain that his purse was open to me; that one in soul, as we were, our fortunes ought also to be common—for I could never, while with him, think of asking his bounty, and even his offers of supplies I was quick to put aside, assuring him (falsely) that I didn't need them. How could I say to this generous being, *Maintain me in idleness,* or expect one who'd dedicated every power of mind and fortune to the benefit of his species, to so misdirect his efforts and exertions as to support in uselessness those, like me, who were strong and healthy and capable?

And yet I dared not ask him to use his influence to help me find work so I could provide for myself—for then I'd have had to leave Windsor. This way I could hover constantly around its Castle, haunting the shadowy thickets piled beneath its walls, my books and my loving thoughts as my sole companions. I studied the wisdom of the ancients, and gazed on the happy stones that sheltered the beloved of my soul. I pored over the poetry of old times; I studied the metaphysics of Plato and Berkeley; I read the histories of Greece and Rome, and of England's kings and queens, and I watched the lady of my heart's every movement. At night I could see her shadow on the walls of her suite; by day I'd spot her and her usual companions in her flower garden, or riding in the park. Mad though I was with passionate devotion, my nature's own unquenchable pride—along with a wish, I think, to prolong the charm—made me keep myself unseen by her, and my feelings hidden from all; but I heard the music of her voice and was happy. Then every heroine of whom I read, took on her beauty and matchless excellences. In the Antigone of

Sophocles, guiding the blind Oedipus to the grove of the Eumenides; Shakespeare's Miranda in her father Prospero's unvisited cave, listening to his Tempest roar; Don Juan's Haidee, child of Lord Byron's Ionian island sands—in three paragons I saw Idris tripled.

While my mind fed richly, my daily fare sometimes consisted of what I could rob from the forest squirrels. I admit, I was often tempted to revive my lawless boyhood long enough to knock down the almost tame pheasants that bent their bright eyes on me from their perches in the trees. But they were Adrian's property, raised by Idris from the egg; and so, as my hunger-sharpened imagination had pheasants roasting on spits in my kitchen, I dined upon acorns and sentiment.

But the whole scheme of my existence was about to change. Very soon, the orphaned and neglected son of Verney would enter into all the duties and affections of common existence, bound to them by chains of gold. Miracles were to be wrought in my favor—the juggernaut of social life opposed and pushed with vast effort backward. Attend, O reader! while I narrate this tale of wonders!

One day, the Countess and her household were on a riding party in the forest, when Idris drew her brother aside from the rest of the cavalcade and asked him what had become of me, his friend, Lionel Verney? "Look," Adrian replied, pointing through the old trees to my sister's cottage. "You can see where he's living." Idris exclaimed, and asked why, if I were so near, I never came to see them. Adrian spent many hours at my place, he said, and added, "But you can easily guess what prevents Verney from coming where his presence may annoy any person among us."

"I do guess his motives," said Idris, "and I wouldn't venture to argue. Tell me, though, how he passes his time—what he's doing and thinking in his cottage retreat."

"Nay, my sweet sister," Adrian laughed, "you ask me to tell too much. If you feel interested, why not visit him? He'll feel highly honored, which will help repay the obligation I owe him, not to mention compensate for the injuries done him by Fortune."

"I will most readily accompany you to his abode," said she, as a lady. "But without wishing that either of us could ever pay that debt— which, being no less than your life, must remain ever unpayable. But let's go; tomorrow we'll arrange to ride out together towards that part of the forest, and call upon him."

The next evening, therefore, though the autumnal equinox had brought on cold and rain, Adrian and Idris entered my cottage. They found me at a sorry supper, this angelic pair that brought invaluable stores of friendship and delight to my lowly dwelling and grateful heart. We sat like one family round my fireside. Disconnected from the emotions that preoccupied us, our talk touched on various things, indifferent matters; our voices spoke while our eyes, in mute language, told a thousand things no tongue could have uttered.

They left me in an hour's time. They left me happy—how unspeakably happy. Idris had visited me; Idris whom I should see again and again see, in my presence—my imagination did not wander beyond the completeness of this knowledge. In my ecstasy I seemed to levitate. No doubt, no fear, no hope even, disturbed me; I clasped with my soul the fullness of contentment, satisfied, undesiring, beatified.

Adrian and Idris continued their visits for many days. Gradually, omnipotent Love, in the guise of enthusiastic friendship, infused more and more of them. Idris felt it. Yes, Divinity of the world, I read your characters in her looks and gestures; in her melodious voice I heard yours echoed—you prepared for us a soft and flowery path, all gentle thoughts adorned it—your name, O Love, remained unspoken; only time, not mortal hand, might raise that veil. No word or sound proclaimed the union of our hearts; happenstance still presented no opportunity to express what hovered on our lips. Oh my pen! quickly, write what was, before the thought of what is, arrests the hand that guides you. If I look up and see the desert earth, and feel what comes from knowing that those dear and starry eyes have spent their mortal luster—that those beauteous lips are silent, their crimson faded like a leaf's—forever I am mute!

But you live, my Idris, even now you move before me! There was a glade, O reader! A grassy opening in the wood; the retiring trees left its velvet expanse as a temple for love. The silver Thames bounded it on one side, where the wind's invisible fingers disheveled the water-dipped Naiad's hair of a bending willow. The oaks around were the home of a tribe of nightingales—

—there's me now. And Idris, in youth's dear prime, is by my side— remember, I am just twenty-two, and seventeen summers have scarcely passed over the beloved of my heart. The river, swollen by autumnal rains, has deluged the low lands, and Adrian in his favorite boat is employed in the dangerous pastime of plucking the highest bough from a submerged oak. Are you weary of life, O Adrian, that you thus play with danger? He obtains his prize, and begins to pilot his boat through the flood; the stream carries him past us. We watch anxiously until, some distance away, we see him land, leap onto shore, and wave the bough over his head in token of success.

"He's safe!" said Idris. "We'll wait for him here."

We were alone together. The sun had set; the song of the nightingales began; the evening star shone distinct in the flood of light still high in the west. The blue eyes of my angelic girl were fixed on this sweet emblem of herself. "How the light palpitates," she said. "That star's life. The way it twinkles seems to say that its state, even like ours here on Earth, is wavering and inconstant; it fears, methinks, and it loves."

"Gaze not on the star, dear, generous friend," I cried, "read not love in its trembling rays; look not upon distant worlds; speak not of the mere imagination of a sentiment. I have long been silent; long even to sickness have I desired to speak to you, and submit my soul, my life, my entire being to you. Look not on the star, dear love, or do, and let that eternal spark plead for me; let it be my witness and my advocate, silent as it shines—love is to me as light to the star; even so long as the light of heaven lasts, so long shall I love you."

Veiled forever against the world's callous eye must be the transport of that moment. Still do I feel her graceful form press against my full-fraught heart—still does sight, and pulse, and breath sicken and fail, at the remembrance of that first kiss. Slowly and silently we went to meet Adrian, whom we heard approaching.

I entreated him to return to me after he'd conducted his sister home. And that same evening, walking among the moonlit forest paths, I poured forth my whole heart, its transport and its hope, to my friend. Adrian was disturbed at first.

"I might have foreseen this," he said. "What strife will now ensue! Pardon me, Lionel, but please don't wonder that the expectation of a conflict with my mother should jar me—when otherwise I should delightedly confess that my own best hopes are fulfilled, in confiding my sister to your protection. If you don't already know it, you are soon to learn the deep hate my mother bears to the name of Verney. I'll talk with Idris; after that, all that a friend can do, I will do. Idris, I'll leave to play the lover's part, as well as she's able."

The brother and sister were still hesitating over how to overcome their mother's opposition when she, suspecting our meetings, accused her children outright. Her fair daughter she taxed with deceit, and called unbecoming an attachment to someone whose only merit was being the son of her imprudent father's profligate favorite; a boy no doubt as worthless as the man from whom he boasted his descent. Her eyes flashing at this accusation, Idris replied, "I do not deny that I love Verney. Prove to me that he is worthless; and I will never see him again."

"Dear Madam," said Adrian, "let me entreat you to see him, to cultivate his friendship. You will be amazed and wonder then, as I do, at the extent of his accomplishments, the brilliancy of his talents." (Pardon me, gentle reader, this is not futile vanity—not futile, since to know that Adrian felt thus, brings joy even now to my lone heart).

But the angry lady exclaimed, "Mad and foolish boy! You have chosen with dreams and theories to overthrow my plans for your greatness; I won't let you do it again, not to my plans for your sister. I but too well understand the fascination you both labor under, since I had the same struggle with your father, to make him cast off the parent of this youth, who hid his evil propensities with the smoothness and subtlety of a viper. In those days how often did I hear of his attractions, his wide-spread conquests, his wit, his refined manners! Who minds when flies get caught by such spiders' webs? But for the high-born and powerful to succumb to the flimsy yokes of these unmeaning pretensions, this is wrong. Were your sister indeed the insignificant person she deserves to be, I would willingly leave her to the fate, the wretched fate, of the wife of a man whose very person, resembling as it does his wretched father, ought to remind you of the folly and vice it typifies—but remember, Lady Idris, you have not only the once-royal blood of England in your veins, you're also Princess of Austria, blood kin to emperors and kings. Are you then a fit mate for an uneducated shepherd-boy, whose only inheritance is his father's tarnished name?"

"I can make but one defense," replied Idris, "the same offered by my brother. See Lionel, converse with my shepherd-boy—"

"Yours!" The Countess interrupted her indignantly. Then she smoothed her impassioned features to a disdainful smile. "We'll talk of this another time. All I now ask—all your mother, Idris, requests—is that you will not see this upstart for a time—say, for a month."

"I dare not comply," said Idris, "it would pain him too much. I have no right to play with his feelings, to accept his proffered love and then sting him with neglect."

Anger sparked in the Ex-Queen's eyes. Her lips quivered. "This is going too far," she declared.

Adrian interposed, "Nay, Madam, unless my sister consent never to see him again, it is surely a pointless torment to separate them for a month."

"Certainly," the mother replied, with bitter scorn, "his love, and her love, and both their childish flutterings, are fit to weigh against my years of hope and anxiety—yes, their little love can stand comparison with the duties of the offspring of kings, and the high and dignified conduct which one of your sister's descent ought to pursue. But it is unworthy of me to argue and complain. Perhaps you will have the goodness to promise me not to marry during that same month's interval?" This was asked half ironically; and Idris wondered why her mother should extort from her a solemn vow not to do something she'd never dreamed of doing—but the promise required was given.

All went on cheerfully now; with Adrian playing chaperone we met as usual, and talked without dread of our future plans. The Countess was so gentle, so amiable with them, that her children began to entertain hopes of her ultimate consent. She was too unlike them, too utterly alien to their tastes, for them to find delight in her society, or in the prospect of continuing very long with her; but it gave them pleasure to see her conciliating and kind. Yet when Adrian ventured to propose her receiving me, she refused with a smile, reminding him that for the present his sister had promised to be patient.

Nearly a month passed. Then Adrian received a letter from a friend in London, requesting his immediate presence for some important cause. Guileless by nature, he feared no deceit. I rode with him part of the way. Since I could not see Idris during his absence, he promised a speedy return. He was in high spirits, which had the strange effect of awakening in me quite contrary feelings; a presentiment of evil hung over me as I returned to count the hours that must elapse before I saw Idris again. Soon I began to question my own patience. What evil might not happen in the meantime? Her mother might take advantage of Adrian's absence to harass her beyond her endurance, perhaps to entrap her. I resolved, come what may, to see and talk with Idris the following morning. This determination soothed me. *Tomorrow, loveliest and best, hope and joy of my life, tomorrow I'll see thee*—Fool, to dream of a moment's delay!

I went to bed. It was now deep winter; it had snowed and was still snowing; the wind whistled in the leafless trees and its dreary moaning, and a violent knocking, mingled wildly in my dreams until at length I woke—well past midnight. The knocking continued. I dressed myself hastily and hurried to open my door to the unexpected visitor. Pale as the snow that showered about her, hands clasped to pray, there stood Idris. She spoke:

"Save me!"

She would have sunk to the ground had I not caught and supported her. Moments later she'd revived and with almost violent energy was entreating me to saddle horses and take her away, away to London—to her brother—I had to do this to save her. I had no horses. She wrung her hands and cried, "Then I've lost—we've both lost everything, forever! But come—come with me, Lionel; here I must not stay. We can get a carriage at Englefield Green, we may still have time! Come, O come with me to save and protect me!" Her dress disordered, hair disheveled, looks aghast: while I took in her person and heard her piteous demands, the idea shot across my mind—*Is she also mad?*

"Sweet one," and I folded her to my heart, "better rest than wander further—relax, my beloved. I'll make a fire—you're chilled through."

"Rest!" she cried. "Relax! You're out of your mind, Lionel! If you delay we're doomed; come, I beg you, unless you want to lose me forever."

I remained bewildered. That Idris, born a princess, nursed in wealth and luxury, should have descended all alone from her castle and come nearly five kilometers, at midnight, on foot through heavy snow to stand at my lowly door and conjure me to fly with her through darkness and storm—I must still be dreaming—but no. Her voice was too plaintive, and the sight of her too lovely, to be anything but real. She gave a timid look around, as if she feared being overheard, and whispered:

"I have discovered that tomorrow—that is, today—tomorrow has come—before dawn, some foreigners, Austrians, hired by my mother, are going to abduct me and take me to Europe, to prison, to marriage—to anything, except you and my brother. Do you understand now? Take me away, they'll be here soon!"

Alarmed, though still slightly doubtful, I no longer hesitated to obey her. The ground she'd already covered on this tempestuous winter night had used all her strength; we now had two more kilometers to go, and Idris could hardly walk, even with my best support. After many points where she was near fainting, she slipped from my grasp onto the snow, and sobbed, "You'll have to carry me— I can't go another step." I lifted her up in my arms; her light form rested near my heart. I was conscious of no burden except the internal one of my contrary and contending emotions—brimming delight, for one. While I shuddered in sympathy with her pain and fright, her chill limbs set off torpedoes where they touched me. Her head lay on my shoulder, her breath waved my hair, her heart beat near mine; transport, ecstasy made me tremble, blinded me, annihilated me; until a groan she couldn't suppress burst from her lips. Then all the signs of her suffering—like the chattering of her teeth that she tried to but couldn't subdue—recalled me to the necessity of speed and succor.

At last the lights of Englefield Green and its inn were before us. But if Idris were to be seen there like this, so strangely circumstanced, word of her flight might be broadcast and her enemies learn of it too soon. She agreed: better that I go alone to hire the carriage. Seeking for a place to put her in safety, I spotted the door of a small empty shed standing ajar. The interior was strewn with hay that I piled into a couch; there I placed her exhausted frame and covered her with my cloak. I felt afraid to leave her, she looked so wan and faint—but she came to herself in a moment. At once her fear returned; again she implored me to hurry. To rouse people at the inn, and obtain a conveyance and horses, though I harnessed them myself, was the work of many minutes; minutes, each freighted with the weight of ages. Finally I had the driver go a little distance, and watched until the inn went back to bed. Then I ordered us to the spot where Idris, impatient, and now somewhat recovered, stood waiting for me. I lifted her inside. With our four horses we should arrive in London before five o'clock, the hour when she would be sought and missed, I assured her of this, and besought her to calm herself. Some tears relieved her, and by degrees Idris shared her tale of fear and peril.

That same night, after Adrian's departure, her mother had attacked her on the subject of her attachment to me. Every angle, every threat, every angry taunt was tried. The Countess seemed to consider me the reason why her daughter had lost Raymond; called me the evil influence of her life; I, with all I'd done to increase and confirm Adrian's mad, base apostasy from destined grandeur—I, this miserable mountaineer, was out to steal her daughter now. Luckily, said Idris, the angry lady had dropped any pretence at gentleness and persuasion, or else it might have been more painful to resist her. As it was, the sweet girl's generous nature was roused to defend, and ally herself to, my despised cause. The look her mother answered with, awoke her first suspicions; it held contempt and covert triumph.

They were parting for the night, when the Countess said, "Tomorrow I trust your tone will be different. Try to compose yourself; I can see I've upset you. Go to bed, I'll send you up something I always take when I cannot sleep—it will give you a quiet night."

Sure enough, she'd no sooner laid her uneasy head on her pillow when a servant of her mother's came in with sleeping tablets. Taken aback at the novelty of this offering, Idris almost refused; but almost instinctively, and in contradiction to her usual frankness, she pretended to swallow the medicine. Now, at least, she'd discover whether she had any just foundation for her suspicions. Agitated first by her mother's violence, and now by strange fears, she lay wakeful and tense, startling at every sound. Then her bedroom door opened softly. She sat bolt upright and heard a woman whisper, "Not asleep yet." The door closed again.

Idris waited with a pounding heart for the next visit. When it arrived, she lay back, composed her limbs, and pretended to be in a drugged sleep; for she'd recognized the intruders. One came closer; and now she had to struggle to conceal and calm the violence of her palpitations, as she heard the Ex-Queen muttering over her, "Pretty little idiot. You have no idea that your game is already finished. Forever." The daughter understood the German perfectly. For a moment the poor girl fancied that her mother believed she'd taken poison—that those hadn't been sleeping tablets at all. She almost jumped out of bed; but now the Countess, back across the room, was speaking in a low voice. Idris calmed herself and listened:

"Hurry—there's no time to lose. It's almost midnight and they'll be here at five. Take merely the clothes necessary for her journey, and her jewel-casket." The other, a trusted attendant, murmured obedience. Few words were spoken on either side; but those were caught at with avidity by the intended victim. She heard the name of her own maid mentioned. "No, no," came her mother's voice. "She does not go with us; Lady Idris must forget England, and all belonging to it." Her mother again: "She won't wake up till late to-morrow, and by then we'll be at sea." At length the attendant announced that all was ready. The Countess returned to her daughter's bedside. "In Austria at least," she said, "you will obey. Yes, in Austria, where obedience can be enforced, and no choice left but between an honorable prison and a fitting marriage."

The two women began to withdraw. From the doorway, once more, came the voice of the Countess to her companion: "Softly; the whole Castle is sleeping—but they haven't all been sent to sleep, like her. I want no one to suspect what is happening and possibly try to stop it. Come wait with me in my room." They went.

Idris, panic-struck, but driven and even strengthened by her terror, dressed herself hurriedly. By avoiding her mother's suite and taking a back staircase, she managed to escape from the castle; through snow, wind, darkness, she'd made her way to my cottage;

never losing her courage until the minute she arrived, put her fate in my hands, and gave herself up to the desperation and weariness that overwhelmed her.

I gave what comfort I could. Joy and exultation, meanwhile, were mine—I possessed, I had saved her. Yet to keep from disquieting her, or as Petrarch writes, "*per non turbar quel bel viso sereno*"—so as not to raise the color in her calm face—I tried to curb my delight and conceal the eager dancing of my heart. I turned my eyes from her, and beamed with too much tenderness, too proudly, on the dark night and inclement skies; to them I murmured my exhilaration. We reached London, methought, all too soon; and yet I could not regret our speedy arrival, witnessing the ecstasy with which my beloved girl found herself in her brother's arms, safe from every evil, under his unimpeachable protection.

Adrian wrote a brief note to his mother, informing her that Idris was under his care and guardianship. Several days later an answer finally came, dated from Salzburg. It was useless (wrote the haughty, disappointed lady) for the Earl of Windsor and his sister to address one whose only expectation of tranquility must be derived from oblivion of their existence. Her desires had been blasted, her schemes overthrown. She did not complain, she said; in her brother's court she would find, not compensation for their disobedience—for filial unkindness was uniquely devastating—but such conditions and mode of life as might best reconcile her to an injured parent's fate. Under the circumstances, she positively declined any communication with them.

Such were the strange and incredible events that brought about my union with the sister of my best friend, with my adored Idris. With such simplicity and courage did she set aside the prejudices and opposition which were obstacles to my happiness, and never scrupled to give her hand, where she had given her heart. To be worthy of her, to raise myself to her height through the exertion of talents and virtue, to repay her love with devoted, unwearied tenderness, were the only thanks I could offer for the matchless gift.

(11)   AND NOW, reader, observe our happy circle.

Some time has passed. Adrian, Idris, and I are established at Windsor Castle. Lord Raymond has built a house near Perdita's cottage, as everyone still calls it, near the border of the great park, and he and my sister live there. The five of us have our separate occupations and our common amusements. In England's rare sunlight, we pass whole days in the canopying forest with our books and music. Darker, windy weather might find us on a higher spot, watching the clouds that veil the sky be torn and blown and scattered here and there. Frequent rains shut us indoors, where we spend our day in study; then music and song commence evening's fun. Idris has a natural musical talent and her well-trained voice is full and sweet. We're all as gleeful as summer insects, playful as children; we always smile when we meet one another; we can read contentment and joy in each other's countenances.

We travel, occasionally for days on end; we'll cross the country to visit any spot noted for beauty or historical interest. Sometimes we go up to London and join the amusements of the busy throng; sometimes our retreat is invaded by visitors from town. These changes only make us more sensitive to the delights of our own intimate circle, the peace of our divine forest, and our happy evenings in the halls of our beloved Castle. Our prime festivals we still hold, sentimentally, in Perdita's cottage; we never tire of talking about the past. Jealousy and disquiet are unknown among us. Neither fear nor hope of change disturbs our tranquility. Others say, We might be happy—*we say*—We are.

Idris. . .she had a peculiarly frank, soft, and affectionate disposition. Her temper was always sweet; and although firm and resolute on any point that touched her heart, she was yielding to those she loved. Perdita's nature was less perfect; but tenderness and happiness improved her temper and softened her natural reserve. Her intelligence was keen and comprehensive, her imagination vivid; she was sincere, generous, a good reasoner. Adrian, the matchless brother of my soul, the sensitive and excellent Adrian, loving all, and beloved by all, yet seemed destined not to find his own missing half to complete his happiness. He'd leave us, and wander alone in the woods, or sail his little skiff, his books his only companions. Often the gayest of our party, he was also the only one visited by fits of despondency. His slender frame seemed overcharged with the weight of life, and his soul appeared rather to inhabit his body than unite with it. I was hardly more devoted to my Idris than to her brother, and she loved him as her teacher, her friend, the benefactor who had secured to her the fulfillment of her dearest wishes.

And Raymond, the ambitious, restless Raymond, whose love of action found its best outlet now in conversational exchanges about national affairs and moral philosophy: Adrian had the superiority in learning and eloquence; but Raymond possessed a quick penetration and a practical knowledge of life to counter with, and keep a subject in lively play. Lord Raymond, marked for greatness, was content to give up all his schemes of sovereignty and fame, to make one of us, the idling flowers of the field. His kingdom was Perdita's heart, his subjects her thoughts; by her he was loved, respected as a superior being, obeyed, waited on. No task or office, no devotion could be irksome to her, when it came to him. She would sit apart from us and watch him; she would weep for joy to think that Raymond was hers. She erected a temple for him in the depths of her being, and made every aspect of her personality a priestess vowed to his service. Perdita might be wayward, capricious; but her repentance was always bitter, her return entire, and even these discords suited him who was not formed by nature to float idly down the stream of life.

During the first year of their marriage, Perdita presented Raymond with a lovely baby girl. It was curious to trace the development in this miniature model of its father's traits. The same half-disdainful lips and smile of triumph, the same intelligent eyes, the same brow; she had his hands' tapered fingers and his chestnut hair. How very dear she was to Perdita! In the course of time, I too became a father, and our little darlings, our playthings and delights, called forth a thousand new and delicious emotions.

Truly, our lives were living proof of Plutarch's beautiful remark, that "our souls have a natural inclination to love, being born as much to love, as to feel, to reason, to understand and remember."

Years passed like this—five full ones. Orderly months succeeded one another, each dozen like the last. We talked of adopting more active pursuits, but still remained at Windsor, incapable of violating the charm that attached us to our secluded life. We found excuses for our idleness in our children, with whom we occupied ourselves in ways of bringing them up to more splendid careers. But the course of events, having flowed so long in hushed tranquility, finally struck obstacles; whitewater and breakers disturbed and woke us from our pleasant dream.

A new Lord Protector of England was to be chosen. Raymond, eager to witness and even take part in the election, wanted us to go to London with him. As usual, he got his way.

On our journey up to town by carriage I watched him but could make little of him. If Raymond had united himself to Idris, this Protectorship was the post that would have been his stepping-stone to his nation's pinnacle. With his desire for power and fame so nearly crowned to the fullest measure, he'd exchanged a scepter for a lute, a kingdom for Perdita. Did he think of this as we rode along? He was particularly gay, playing with his child, and making jokes over every word anyone uttered. Perhaps he'd spotted the cloud upon Perdita's brow. She kept trying to fight it, but as she looked at Raymond and her girl, her gaze would grow wistful and then her eyes fill with tears, as if she feared some evil would betide them.

And so she did. A presentiment of the worst kind hung over her. She leaned from the window looking on the forest, and the turrets of the Castle, and as these were lost behind the intervening landscape, she exclaimed in a passionate voice: "Scenes of happiness! Scenes sacred to devoted love, when shall I see you again? And when I do, shall I be still the beloved and joyous Perdita I am—or more like the ghost of myself, a lost, heart-broken wanderer among your groves?"

"Silliness!" cried Raymond. "My dear, what is going on in your little head that you should have become so sublimely dismal all of a sudden? Cheer up!" he ordered her.

The following morning Lord Raymond visited us early; our London places were all in the same part of town, near Hyde Park.

"I come to you with a project, only half certain that you'll agree to help me, but resolved to go through with it, whether you do or not. Promise me secrecy, though, before I describe it. You don't need to contribute to my success, but at least let me pursue it my way." He finished with a glower. I looked at Idris.

"Well, we promise," she said quietly. "And so?"

"And so, my dear friends, tell me—why have we come to London? To be present at the election of a Protector, and to give our yea or nay for a shuffling Sir So-and-So? Or for that noisy Ryland? Do you honestly believe that I brought us all to town for that? No, we will have a Protector of our own. We will set up a candidate, and ensure his success. We will nominate Adrian, and do our best to bestow on him the power to which he is entitled by his birth, and which he merits through his virtues.

"Don't answer; I know all your objections and will reply to them in order. First, whether he will or will not consent to become a great man—leave the task of persuasion on that point to me; I do not ask you to assist me there. Secondly, whether he ought to exchange his daytime job of plucking blackberries, and nursing wounded partridges, for the command of a nation? My dear Lionel, we are married men, we're happy just amusing our wives and dancing around with our children. But Adrian is alone, wifeless, childless, unoccupied. I have long observed him. He pines for want of some interest in life. His heart, exhausted by his early sufferings, is like a recovering invalid who shrinks from all excitement. But his understanding, his charity, his virtues, want a field for exercise and display; and we will procure it for him.

"Besides, is it not a shame, Idris, that your brother's genius should pass from the earth without having borne fruit? Nature bestowed on him every gift in prodigality—birth, wealth, talent, goodness. Do you think She composed the best of men for no purpose? Believe me, he was destined to be the author of infinite good to his country. Doesn't everyone love and admire him? and does he not delight in any chance to show his love to all? Come, I see that you're already persuaded, and will second me when I propose him tonight in Parliament."

"You've got your arguments in excellent order," I replied. "And, if Adrian consents, they are unanswerable. I'd add only one condition—that you do nothing unless he does consent."

Raymond paused. "I'd planned differently; but you may be right. So be it. I'll go instantly to Adrian—and Idris, if he inclines to consent, I hope you won't destroy my labor by persuading him to return to his circle of squirrel friends in Windsor Forest, will you?"

"Trust me," she replied, "to preserve a strict neutrality."

"For my part," said I, "I'm too well convinced of our friend's worth, and the rich harvest of benefits that all England would reap from his Protectorship, to deprive my fellow citizens of such a blessing—if he'll consent to bestow it on them."

In the evening came Adrian's visit; he entered laughing.

"Do you two cabal against me? You plan to help Raymond pull a poor visionary from the clouds, away from his heavenly rays and airs, and surround him with the artillery fire of earthly grandeur, instead? I thought you knew me better."

"I do know you better," I replied, "than to think that becoming Lord Protector would make you happy. But the good you'd do for others must appear as some inducement. If the time is ripe, indeed, what better chance to put your theories into practice, and bring about the reforms needed to establish that perfect system of government you love to talk about."

"You speak of an almost-forgotten dream," said Adrian, sadness growing in his look. "The visions of my boyhood have long since faded in the light of reality; I know now that I am not a man fitted to govern nations. It's enough for me, if I can keep in wholesome rule the little kingdom of my own mortality.

"But don't you catch, Lionel, our noble friend's drift? He might have missed it himself. Lord Raymond was never born to be a drone in the hive and find contentment in our pastoral life. He believes he ought to be satisfied; he imagines his present state and situation to be fixed; even in his own heart, he plans no change for himself. But don't you see? Under the idea of exalting me, he's chalking out a new path for himself, one that gives scope to his tremendous mental powers— the path of action from which he has long wandered.

"Let *us* be the ones pushing *him*. Raymond, the noble, the warlike, the great in every quality that can adorn a mind and person; he is fitted to be the Protector of England. If I—that is, if *we* propose him, he's certain to be elected. As for Perdita, the ambition she fulfilled by marrying Raymond has remained a covered fire; Verney, your sister will rejoice in the glory and advancement of her lord—and, coyly and prettily, be not too discontented with her share. And we, the wise of the land, will return to our Castle, and like Cincinnatus and George Washington, take to our commonplace labors, until our friend shall require our help again."

For many reasons, Adrian's scheme was by far the more feasible. His determination never to enter into public life could not be shaken, and the delicacy of his health was a sufficient argument against trying. So—could we induce Raymond to confess his secret wishes for honors and fame? Adrian had already primed him. He entered while we were speaking, with a look and manner that betrayed irresolution and anxiety; but a few words from us decided him. Now hope and joy sparkled in his eyes; the idea of re-embarking on a cherished career made him energetic and bold. Immediately we started to discuss his chances, the merits of the other candidates, and the voters' dispositions.

(12)   AFTER ALL, we miscalculated.

A prominent Duchess, and Mr. Ryland, Lord Raymond's old antagonist, were the other two candidates. Ryland led the populists. The Duchess was supported by all the aristocrats of the republic, who considered her their proper representative. Lord Raymond was added to the list of candidates. Various people still admired his transcendent talents and the electric effect of his presence, his eloquence, his address, his imposing beauty; but he'd lost much of his popularity and was deserted by some former partisans. Absence from the busy stage had caused him to be forgotten by the people. The royalists formerly in his camp had been willing to make an idol of him when he appeared as the heir of the Earldom of Windsor; they were indifferent to him now, when he offered nothing they didn't have themselves. Adrian, despite his reclusive habits and his well-known opposition to party spirit, had many friends, and though they were easily induced to vote for the candidate of his choice, to judge from the debate that followed our chances of success were small.

We retired to Hyde Park, where Raymond sat dispirited while Perdita reproached us, his mortified nominators, bitterly. She'd favored our project but its apparent failure changed the current of her thoughts. After this, Raymond could never be happy again at

Windsor, she said. His habits were unhinged, his restless mind aroused and coupled for life to ambition; if he didn't succeed in his present attempt, she foresaw unhappiness and incurable discontent to follow. Her personal disappointment doubtless adding sting to her remarks, she did not spare us, and our own reflections compounded our disquietude.

The next stage in the nomination required us to present our candidate to the electors. This was to occur on the following evening; but for the moment, Raymond was obstinate. He'd embark in a balloon instead, or sail for a distant quarter of the world, where his name and humiliation were unknown. But as we quickly convinced him, this was useless. His attempt was registered, his purpose published to the world; his shame could never be erased from people's memory. Better to struggle and fail than to run away at the start of his enterprise.

From the moment he adopted this idea, he was changed. His depression and anxiety seemed to vanish. Now he was all life, activity, determination. Capped by a smile of triumph, his whole bearing seemed a predictor of his success. But his high spirits alarmed Perdita, for she feared a worse counter-reaction—and if his appearance inspired us with hope, it only rendered the state of her mind more painful. She didn't want to let him out of her sight, yet she couldn't stand seeing him optimistic; not daring to be present when he debated at Parliament, she let herself be prey to twice the anxiety at home, where she wept over her little girl. She looked and spoke as if she dreaded the occurrence of some frightful calamity, and was so uncontrollably agitated as to be half mad at times.

Striding through the House, waving, shaking hands, pausing to speak into ears, Lord Raymond presented himself with fearless confidence and insinuating address. The Duchess and Mr. Ryland made their speeches first, then he commenced. At first he hesitated, as if his memory were faulty, pausing in his ideas and his choice of words. By degrees he warmed until the words flowed with ease; his language was full of vigor, and his voice of persuasion. He talked of his past life, his successes in Greece, his favor at home. Shouldn't his added years and the prudence they brought, along with the pledge which his marriage gave to his country, all serve to increase, rather than diminish, his claims to confidence? He drew a glowing picture of Britain's present situation and enumerated the necessary measures to be taken to ensure its security and confirm its prosperity. As he spoke, every sound was hushed, every thought suspended by intense attention. His grace of speech enchained his listeners' senses. In some degree, he was fitted to reconcile all parties. His birth pleased the aristocracy; and his being the candidate recommended by Adrian, a man intimately allied to the popular party, also swayed a number of voters to his side.

The contest was keen and doubtful. Night after night passed in debates for which we spent our days preparing, and still offered no conclusion. At last the crisis came: Parliament could delay its choice no longer. When the great clock struck twelve, and the morrow began, the nation's government, by virtue of the constitution, was dissolved, its power extinct. It must decide tonight.

At half past five, we and our partisans left Raymond's house. Idris stayed behind to try and calm Perdita, who'd lost all self-control; later she told me the poor girl, desperate for the arrival of news, had stopped her wild pacing only to retreat to her chamber in a storm of tears. I'd seen her state myself: as we were leaving, Perdita had seized my hand and drawn me into an empty room, where she threw herself into my arms and wept violently.

I did justice to my sweet sister, in being sure it was not for herself that she thus agonized. She alone knew what weight her husband attached to his success. To us Raymond put on a show of gaiety and hope, acting them so well that we never spotted the secret workings of his mind. Yet sometimes a nervous trembling, a sharp dissonance of voice, his momentary fits of absence, hinted at the truth. Perdita, closest to him, saw the violence he did himself. While we, intent on our plans, observed only his ready laugh, his constant jokes, his endlessly high spirits, she was there for the moodiness that succeeded to this forced hilarity; and for his disturbed sleep, his painful irritability—even, once, when he couldn't repress them, tears; since seeing which, her own had scarcely ceased to flow. What wonder then, I told myself, that her feelings were wrought to this pitch! But there was more to it, as we were to learn.

At the time, I tried to soothe her. I encouraged her to hope, but also asked how much our failure would really matter—she was exaggerating the damage a loss could do us, I said. She couldn't be comforted.

"My brother," she cried, "protector of my childhood, dear, most dear Lionel, my fate hangs by a thread. I have all of you around me now—you; and Adrian, practically another brother; Idris, the sister of my heart, and her lovely children. O, to think, tonight could be the last time you surround me like this—*ah!*" She drew back. "What have I said? Foolish, false me!" I caught a wild look, then watched my sister calm herself, though she still wept. She said, "Forgive me. I must be insane. As long as Raymond is alive, I am a happy woman."

She was nearly tranquil at our departure; when Raymond only took her hand as he went, and looked at her; Perdita's look answered his, and she nodded. Poor girl! What she then suffered! I could never entirely forgive Raymond for what he put her through then, out of his own selfishness. He had decided, if he lost that night's election, to leave for Greece, without saying goodbye to any of us, and never return to England. Perdita had agreed, wanting only his happiness; but to face leaving all her beloved companions, while keeping this frightful plan from us in the interim, was a task that almost conquered her strength of mind. Their departure was arranged, and she'd promised Raymond to make the first stage of the journey that evening, while the house was empty. Once his defeat was certain, he'd slip away from us and join her.

Though I was bitterly offended at the time by the small attention Raymond paid my sister's feelings, my eventual knowledge of this scheme led me to conclude that he'd been overpowered by an excitement strong enough to take from him the consciousness, and, consequently, the guilt of wrongdoing. If he'd let us see his agitation, it might have made him more open to reason; but his struggles to show composure acted with such violence on his nerves as to warp his judgment. I am convinced that, at the worst, he would have come back to take leave of us; we'd have been the partners of his council again. But that probability made Perdita's task no less painful. He'd extorted her vow of secrecy; and her part in the drama, since it was to be performed alone, was the most agonizing that could be devised.

But to return to the events at Parliament.

The latest British constitution had been designed for the better preservation of peace foreign and domestic. Only two candidates for the Protectorship were allowed to remain on the election's last day; and to forestall, if possible, a final struggle between them, a bribe was offered to the one who should voluntarily resign the contest: first, a ceremonial position of great emolument and honor, followed by advantageous placement in a future election. Strange to say, however, no candidate had ever chosen this expedient; by now, no one even discussed it.

Long, loud, often protracted merely for the sake of delay: such had been the debates so far. But now, with the fatal moment looming, a strange silence reigned; the members of the House spoke in whispers as their ordinary business was transacted with quiet speed. Then came the election. The Duchess was already out of the running; the contest featured two old antagonists. Mr. Ryland had felt his victory secure until Lord Raymond's appearance; ever since, he'd canvassed incessantly, and had scowled at us from the opposite side of the hall each evening, as if his mere frown would cast eclipse on our hopes.

So it was to our extreme surprise, upon its being moved that we should resolve ourselves into a committee for the election of the Lord Protector, that the member who had nominated Ryland rose and informed us that the candidate had resigned the contest.

Silence greeted this information. A confused murmur followed; but when the house chair declared Lord Raymond duly chosen, the noise mounted to a unanimous shout of applause and victory. With the contest and crisis averted, all hearts returned to their former respectful admiration of our accomplished friend. It was agreed: England had never seen a Protector so capable of fulfilling the arduous duties of that high office. One voice rose and drew many in unison, resounding through the chamber, one name:

Raymond.

He entered. I was on one of the highest seats, and could see him walk all the way up the passage to the speaker's table. His native modesty kept the joy out of his triumph. He looked around timidly; a mist seemed before his eyes. Adrian, who was beside me, hastened to jump down the benches and stood at his side in a moment. This reanimated our friend; and, when he came to speak and act, his hesitation vanished, and he shone out supreme in majesty and victory. The former Protector tendered him the oaths, and presented him with the insignia of office. The ceremonies of installation were performed and duly concluded. The crowds began to break up.

At some point, Adrian vanished; he returned leading Idris to congratulate her friend on his success.

"But where is Perdita?" asked Raymond, forgetful at first. A few words, which told of her mysterious disappearance, recalled him. Guessing her anxiety might have led her in the direction of events, Adrian wanted us to look around the streets outside in case some sinister event had detained her. But Raymond, with no explanation, rushed out, and in another moment we heard him gallop down the street, in spite of the wind and rain that scattered tempest over the earth. We didn't know how far he had to go, and soon separated, supposing that he'd shortly be at his new palace with Perdita, and that they would not be sorry to find themselves alone.

In assuring the secrecy of his retreat in case of failure, Raymond had neglected to provide any way for Perdita to hear of his success. Never expecting it, she'd slipped unseen from the Hyde Park house to the waiting carriage, and alighted with her child at Dartford, weeping and inconsolable. When all had been prepared for the continuance of their journey to Greece, and her lovely charge was asleep on a bed, my sister passed several hours in acute suffering. Rain pattered at the window: the elements at war outside seemed to have declared against her, too. Perdita hung over her child where she slept, and traced the little girl's resemblance to the father—a fearful one. What if she should grow up to display the same passions and uncontrollable impulses that made him so unhappy? But then again, with a gush of pride and delight, she marked in Clara's features the same smile of beauty that often irradiated Raymond's own. Seeing it soothed her. She thought of the treasure she possessed in the affections of her lord; of his accomplishments, surpassing those of his contemporaries; of his genius, and his devotion to her. It occurred to her that all she possessed in the world, except him, might well be spared—nay, given with delight, a propitiatory offering—to secure the supreme good she retained in him. Perhaps fate demanded this sacrifice from her, as a mark of her devotion to Raymond, a sacrifice that must be made cheerfully. She began to picture their life on the Greek island he'd selected for their retreat; pictured soothing him; pictured them raising their beauteous child; pictured rides in her husband's company, her life dedicated to his consolation. The scenes as they occurred to her came in such glowing colors, that their reverse became fearful. What if he actually won? How little she wished for a life of magnificence and power in London, where Raymond would no longer be hers only, nor she the sole source of happiness to him.

So far her thoughts had brought her when she heard him gallop into the courtyard of the inn. That he should come to her alone, soaked by the storm, careless of everything except speed—what else could it mean? Vanquished and solitary, they were to take their way from native England, the scene of shame, and hide themselves away in the myrtle groves of the Grecian isles.

In a moment she was in his arms. A wordless embrace: the knowledge of his success had become so much a part of himself, Raymond forgot he had still to impart it to his companion. She only felt in his arms a dear assurance that while he possessed her, he would not despair.

"This is kind," she cried, "this is noble, my own beloved! O fear not disgrace or lowly fortune, while you have your Perdita; fear not sorrow, while our child lives and smiles. Let us go even where you will; the love that goes with us will prevent our regrets."

Locked in his embrace, she cast back her head when she'd spoken; she looked for assent to her words in his eyes—but they were sparkling with ineffable delight. He spoke playfully. "Why, my little Lady Protectress, what is this you say? And what pretty scheme have you been weaving out of exile and obscurity, when you have a brighter web to contemplate, all laced with gold?"

He kissed her brow—but the wayward girl, agitated by the timing and its shock to her thoughts, half sorry at his triumph, hid her face in his bosom and wept. He comforted her; he instilled into her his own hopes and desires; and soon her countenance beamed with sympathy. How very happy they were that night! How full even to bursting was their sense of joy!

(13)   THEIR NEW London home, in the Protectoral Palace, was near enough to Windsor to remove the pain from separation when we left Raymond and Perdita installed there. I'd been glad to see my sister enter, as it were, into the spirit of the drama, and fill her station with becoming dignity. Her shy and humble manner was not artificial but arose from that fear of not being properly appreciated, that nagging expectation of the world's neglect, which Raymond shared. But then Perdita thought more constantly of others than he did. Still, whereas for Idris, with her princess's birth, education, and lifetime of habit, the very ease of a life so based on ceremony would have rendered it tedious, for Perdita even its drawbacks were evidently enjoyable. She was too full of new ideas to be very sorry to see us go. As for Raymond, his spirits were unbounded. What to do with his new-got power? His head was full of plans. He'd made no decisions yet—but he promised himself, his friends, and the world, that the era of his Protectorship should be marked by some act of surpassing glory.

We talked of the couple, and moralized, but as our pared down troupe returned to Windsor Castle, we felt extreme delight at our escape from political turmoil, and sought our solitude with redoubled zest. There was plenty to do. I turned my active, eager disposition to pure intellectual exertion, and found in hard study an excellent medicine to keep off the feverish spirits that indolence might have bred. What's more, Perdita had permitted us to take her little girl back with us to Windsor. Clara and my two lovely infants were perpetual sources of interest and amusement.

The only circumstance that disturbed our peace was Adrian's health. Its decline was clear, the diagnosis less so; his symptoms uncertain, only his brightened eyes, animated look, and strange blushes made us dread tuberculosis—once called consumption; but if tubercular, he was without pain or fear. He betook himself to books with ardor, and reposed from his studies in the company he loved best, his sister's and mine. Sometimes he went up to London to visit Raymond and watch the progress of events. Clara often accompanied him in these excursions; partly that she might see her parents, partly because Adrian delighted in this lovely child's intelligent prattle.

Meanwhile all went on well in London. Parliament was meeting again, and Raymond was occupied in a thousand beneficial schemes. Canals, aqueducts, bridges, stately buildings, public works: he was continually surrounded by designers and project managers, whose brief was to render England an unbroken scene of fertility and magnificence. Poverty was to be abolished—disease, banished—hard labor lightened of its heaviest burdens. People would ride mass transportation from place to place almost with the same ease as Houssain, Ali, and Ahmed of the Arabian Nights rode their magic carpet—indeed, the physical state of humankind would soon rival the beatitude of angels. This didn't seem extravagant. The arts of life, and the discoveries of science, had without question progressed at immeasurable rates; so that food appeared, so to say, spontaneously. Convenient machines existed to supply every want of the population. An evil tendency still survived, and people weren't happy—but that was only because they made too little effort to vanquish the obstacles they'd raised against themselves. Raymond was out to inspire them with his beneficial will. Once systematized according to faultless rules, the mechanism of society would never again swerve into disorder. For these hopes, he abandoned his long-cherished ambition of becoming known to world history as a successful warrior; laying aside his sword, he made peace and its enduring glories his aim instead. Benefactor of His Country was the title he coveted.

One of his pet projects was a new national gallery for statues and pictures. He owned a large collection, which he intended to give to the Republic; and, as the building was to be the great ornament of his Protectorship, he was very fastidious in his choice of architect. Hundreds of proposals were brought to him and rejected. He sent even to Italy and Greece. The plan must combine originality with perfect beauty, and he searched to no avail. At length a drawing came, with a post office box return address and no artist's name attached. The design was new and elegant, but faulty; so faulty, that although drawn with skill and taste, it was evidently not the work of an architect. Raymond contemplated it with delight; the more he gazed, the more pleased he was; and yet the errors multiplied under inspection. He wrote to the address given and asked to meet, suggesting that some alterations might be made.

A Greek came; a middle-aged man, somewhat intelligent but so commonplace-looking, Raymond could scarcely believe he'd produced such a novel design. He was not an architect, the stranger admitted; but the idea of the building had struck him. He'd sent it without the smallest hope of its being accepted. He was a man of few words. Raymond questioned him, but the limited answers soon made him turn from the man to the drawing. He pointed out the errors, and the alterations that he wished to be made; he offered the Greek a pencil that he might correct the sketch on the spot; the visitor declined and said he'd understood perfectly, and would take the work home.

When he returned the next day, the design had been re-drawn but many defects still remained. Raymond could see that some of his instructions had been misunderstood. "Here," he said, "I yielded to you yesterday, now it's your turn to comply—take the pencil."

The Greek did, but he handled it as no artist would have. Finally he said, "I must confess to you, my Lord, that I did not make this drawing. It is impossible for you to see the real designer; your instructions must pass through me. Condescend therefore to have patience with my ignorance, and to explain your wishes to me; in time I am certain that you will be satisfied." Raymond questioned vainly; the mysterious Greek would say no more. Would an architect be permitted to see the artist? Another refusal. The visitor went off with a second set of instructions.

Our friend had resolved, however, to find out what lay behind the mystery. He suspected that the artist had fallen into unfamiliar poverty and refused to be seen under its conditions. All the more excited by the possibility of having discovered an obscure talent, Raymond had ordered a skilled member of his security detail to follow the Greek this time and see where he went. Sure enough, he was traced to one of the poorest streets in the city.

That same evening, Raymond went alone to the address. Poverty, dirt, and squalid misery: *Alas!* he thought, *I have much to do before England becomes a Paradise.* He knocked; the front door was unlatched by a string from above. A broken, wretched, unlit staircase confronted him. No one appeared; he knocked again, then started climbing up through the darkness to the artist's garret. His main wish, particularly now that he'd seen how abject the dwelling, was to bring relief to one possessed of talent but depressed by want. He was picturing a young man whose eyes sparkled with genius, whose person was attenuated by famine. Raymond half feared to displease him; but he trusted that his generous kindness would be administered so delicately as not to excite repulse and refusal. What human heart is shut to kindness? Encouraged by this thought, he finally stood at the top of the house. One door was ajar. He could see a pair of small Turkish slippers lying next to the threshold; but all was silent within. Guessing he'd found the right person, who wasn't at home, our adventurous Protector decided to enter, leave a sum of money on the table, and go away again. He pushed open the door—but found the room inhabited.

Raymond had never visited the dwellings of want, and the scene that now presented itself struck him to the heart. The floor had holes and sunken places, the walls were ragged and bare, the ceiling weather-stained. A tattered bed stood in one corner; the other furniture consisted of two chairs and a rough table, where stood a light in a tin candlestick. Yet in the midst of such dreary and heart-sickening poverty, there was an air of order and cleanliness that surprised him. The thought was fleeting; for his attention was instantly monopolized by the inhabitant of this wretched abode. It was a female. She sat at the table. One small hand shaded her eyes from the candle; the other held a pencil; her looks were fixed on a drawing before her, which Raymond recognized as the design. Her whole appearance awakened his deepest interest. Her dark hair was braided and twined in thick knots like the headdress of a Grecian statue; in her run-down clothes, she sat like someone modeling the height of grace. Raymond had a confused idea that he'd seen a form like hers before. He walked across the room. Without raising her eyes, she asked who was there.

"A friend," replied Raymond, in the same Romaic dialect. She looked up wondering, and he saw that it was Evadne Zaimi. Once the idol of Adrian's affections: Evadne, who, for the sake of her present visitor, had disdained that noble youth, and then, neglected by him she loved, devastated when he wed another, with crushed hopes and a stinging sense of misery had returned to her native Greece—what revolution of fortune could have brought her back to England, and housed her thus?

From the moment of recognition, Raymond's manner changed. The sight of her, in her present situation, passed like an arrow into his soul. Dropping all airs of polite beneficence, he sat by her, took her hand, said a thousand things which breathed the deepest spirit of compassion and affection. Evadne did not answer. She kept her large dark eyes cast down; at length a tear glimmered on the lashes.

"Look," she cried, "what kindness can do, that no want, no misery ever could; I weep." She shed indeed many tears; her head sank unconsciously onto Raymond's shoulder; he held her hand; he kissed her sunken tear-stained cheek. He told her that her sufferings were over.

No one possessed the art of consoling like Raymond. He didn't reason or declaim, but his look shone with sympathy, and all he said brought pleasant images before the unfortunate sufferer. His caresses excited no distrust, for they arose purely from the feeling which leads a mother to kiss her wounded child; a desire to demonstrate in every possible way his caring's sincerity, and the keenness of his wish to pour balm into a lacerated mind. As Evadne regained her composure, his manner even turned playful; he called her his Princess in disguise. Something told him that it was not her poverty's present evils that lay heavily at her heart, but the debasement and disgrace it signified. He found her too much preoccupied by more engrossing thoughts to answer his warm offers of service. At length he left her with his promise to return the next day, and went home, full of mingled feelings—pain excited by Evadne's wretchedness, pleasure at the prospect of relieving it. Some motive for which he did not account, even to himself, prevented him from relating his adventure to Perdita.

The next day he disguised himself in a cloak and headed back to Evadne. Along the way, he bought a basket of costly Mediterranean fruits and piled it with various beautiful flowers. "Behold," cried he, as he entered the miserable garret of his friend, "what bird's food I have brought for my sparrow on the housetop."

Evadne now related the tale of her misfortunes. Her father, a man of high rank, had run through his fortune by the time a course of dissolute self-indulgence destroyed his reputation and influence as well. With his health impaired beyond hope of cure, it became his earnest wish, before he died, to save his daughter from the orphaned poverty in which he'd leave her. He accepted on her behalf, and persuaded Evadne to agree to, a proposal of marriage from a wealthy Greek merchant settled at Istanbul. She left her native Greece; her father died; by degrees she was cut off from all the companions and ties of her youth.

The renewal of war between Greece and Turkey brought more reverses of fortune. Her husband went bankrupt. Soon after, the Turks threatened a massacre of the city's Greek inhabitants. Obliged to flee in an open boat, the couple reached a British vessel, which had brought them to England. The few jewels they'd saved supported them awhile. Evadne put all her energy into bolstering her husband's spirits. To no avail: his losses, his lack of occupation, and his hopelessness about the future, combined to reduce him to a state bordering on insanity. After five months in London, he committed suicide.

"You will ask me," continued Evadne, "what I've done since. Why haven't I gone back to Greece? Of course, I couldn't afford to. Why haven't I gone to any of the rich Greeks who live in London, and asked them for money? All I can tell you is that I've had reasons enough to keep me going, day after day, enduring every wretchedness, rather than seek that kind of help. Shall the daughter of the noble, though prodigal, Zaimi, a man without superiors, lower herself to appear a beggar in front of—at best—her peers? Shall I bow my head before them, and with servile gestures sell my nobility for mere life? Had I a child, or any tie to bind me to existence, I might descend to this. But, as it is, the world has been to me a harsh stepmother; I feel ready to leave this place she seems to grudge me, and in the grave forget my pride, my struggles, my despair. The time will soon come; grief and starvation have already undermined my being; a very short time, and I shall have passed away. Unstained by the crime of self-destruction, unstung by the memory of degradation, my spirit will throw aside the miserable world, and find such reward as fortitude and resignation may deserve. This may seem like madness to you—yet you also have pride and resolution. Do not wonder then at mine."

Raymond was immediately eloquent and full of eager plans to restore his lovely friend to her rank in society, and to her lost prosperity. But Evadne checked him. No one, especially not her former friends, should know of her presence in England. She explained haughtily, "The Earl of Windsor's relatives doubtless think that I injured him. Perhaps the Earl himself would be the first to acquit me, but probably I do not deserve acquittal. I acted then, as I ever must, from impulse. My present abode may at least prove the disinterestedness of my conduct. No matter: I don't wish to plead my cause before any of them, not even before your Lordship, if you hadn't discovered me first. My conduct will prove that I had rather die, than be held up to scorn. Behold the proud Evadne in her tatters! See the beggar-princess! There is snakebite in the thought. Promise me to keep my life here secret."

He promised; but argued against Evadne's next request, that he neither enter into any project for her benefit, nor himself offer relief. "Do not degrade me in my own eyes," she said. "Poverty has long been my nurse; hard-featured she is, but honest." She feared being disgraced in her own eyes. Stubborn against Raymond's fervent persuasions to overcome her feelings, she finally grew agitated into making a wild, passionate, solemn vow to run and hide herself where he never could find her, someplace where hunger would soon bring death to end her woes, if he persisted in his offers. She could support herself, she said, and showed him how, by executing various designs and paintings, she actually earned a pittance. Raymond yielded for the present. He was sure, if he humored her properly, that friendship and reason would gain the day.

But the feelings that drove Evadne were rooted in the depths of her being, and grew in ways he had no means of understanding. Evadne loved Raymond. He was the hero of her imagination, the single image carved by love in the unchanged texture of her heart. He had served her country against the Turks, in her own land acquired that military glory peculiarly dear to the Greeks. Seven years ago, in her youthful prime, she'd fallen for him with everything she had. Yet her love did not purchase his, her love was unreturned. While

Raymond's heart was vacillating between Perdita and a crown, Evadne left England; the news of his marriage reached her, and her hopes, frost-struck blossoms, withered and fell. The glory of life was gone for her; the roseate halo of love, which had imbued every object with its own color, faded; she was content to take life as it was, and to make the best of a leaden reality.

She married, and new scenes awoke her restless energy of character. Her thoughts turned to gaining a title and power. She chose the Danube principality of Wallachia, where her efforts to set her husband at the head of state brought her close to her goal of becoming a princess again. But she lived to find Ambition as unreal a delusion as Love. Her partnership of intrigue with Russia provoked the animosity of the Turkish and Greek governments; both accused her of treason. Her husband's financial ruin followed. The threatened massacre she'd mentioned to Raymond was a fable: her crimes being capital, Evadne had avoided death by a timely flight. Nor had she confessed the truth about her fellow Greeks in London: for she had indeed sought their help and had been repulsed and denied as the worst kind of criminal, a traitor to her country's battle against foreign despotism.

She knew herself to be the cause of her husband's utter ruin, and set herself to bear the consequences, along with the reproaches which his agony extorted from him; or worse, the cureless, uncomplaining depression, when his mind was sunk in a torpor no less painful for being inert. Later she reproached herself with the crime of his death. Guilt and its punishments appeared to surround her. In vain she endeavored to allay remorse by thinking of her real integrity; the rest of the world, and she among them, judged her actions by their consequences. She prayed for her husband's soul; she conjured the Supreme to place on her head the crime of his self-destruction—she vowed to live to expiate his fault.

Sunk in such wretchedness as must soon have destroyed her, one thought alone brought consolation. She lived in the same country, breathed the same air as Raymond. His name as new Lord Protector was on every tongue; his achievements, projects, and magnificence, monopolized the public mind. Nothing is so precious to a woman's heart as the glory and excellence of the one she loves; in the midst of every horror Evadne reveled in Raymond's fame and prosperity. While her husband lived, she'd treated this feeling as a crime to be repressed, repented of. At his death the tide of love resumed its ancient flow, and she gave herself up to the deluge, a prey to the uncontrollable power of its tumultuous waves.

But never, O, never, should Raymond see her in her degraded state! never behold her fallen from her pride of beauty, poverty-stricken, inhabiting the meanest garret, with a name which had become a reproach, and a weight of guilt on her soul.

Though impenetrably veiled from each other, his public office permitted Evadne into all his actions, his daily course of life, even his conversation. She allowed herself one luxury, and bought the newspapers every day to feast on praise and news of the Protector. Not that this indulgence was painless. She read Perdita's name forever joined with his and saw countless images of this faithful companion of all his labors and pleasures. They were continually together, and all reports vouched for their conjugal felicity. They, their Excellencies, met her eyes everywhere, the sight brewing an evil potion that poisoned her very blood.

It was in a paper that she'd seen the call for the national gallery design. The one she sent to the Protector combined and unified, by an effort of genius, her flawless taste with her remembrance of the great buildings she'd known in the east—the massive synagogues and mosques, the Acropolis and Delphi, the Hagia Sophia. Knowing her work chosen, she felt her triumph in the idea of bestowing, unknown and forgotten as she was, a benefit upon him she loved; and with enthusiastic pride looked forward to her efforts' being immortalized in stone, knowing they'd go down to posterity stamped with Raymond's name. Drinking in her messenger's account of the Protector, insatiably, demanding each word, each look, she felt bliss in this communication with her beloved, one-sided as it was. The drawing itself became ineffably dear to her. He had seen it, and praised it; as she retouched it, each stroke of her pencil was like a chord of thrilling music; the work of her hand made a symphonic wave that bore to her the idea of a temple, raised to celebrate the deepest and most unutterable emotions of her soul. And there she had been when Raymond's unforgettable voice came out of nowhere.

Somehow she'd mastered her gush of feelings, to welcome him with quiet gentleness.

Pride and desire had struggled inside Evadne to an uneasy compromise. She would see Raymond, since destiny had led him to her, and her constancy and devotion really did merit his friendship. But she refused to let him make her in any way financially dependent. Her mind was of uncommon strength; she could subdue her body to it, and suffer cold, hunger, misery, rather than concede to fortune a contested point. Alas! that in human nature such a high pitch of mental discipline, and disdainful negligence of nature itself, should not have been allied to the extreme of moral excellence! But the resolution that made her able to resist the pains of privation, sprang from her excessive passions; and the concentrated self-will this signified was destined to destroy even the idol, the dazzling Protector himself, to preserve whose respect she submitted to an ongoing wretchedness.

Their meetings continued, and over time Evadne gave a more honest account of her story, admitting the stain of treason her name had received, and her share of guilt in her husband's death. When Raymond answered with offers to clear her reputation, and demonstrate to the world her real patriotism, she told him that it was only through her present sufferings that she hoped for any relief to the stings of conscience; that, in her state of mind, diseased as he might think it, the need to work was the best medicine; and she got another promise from him, this time to avoid discussing her interests for one month—at the end of which, she might yield in part to his wishes.

She could not disguise from herself that she wanted Time to pause where it was. Any change from the present would separate her from Raymond. She saw him daily. His connection with Adrian and Perdita was never mentioned. He was to her a meteor, a companion-less star, whose appearance at its appointed hour brought her felicity, and which, though it set, was never eclipsed. He came each day to her impoverished room and his presence transformed it to a temple redolent with incense and sweetness, radiant with heaven's own light; he partook of her delirium, its reckless blindness and delusive joy. Like the lovers in many a tragedy, they built a wall between them and the world. Outside, a thousand harpies raved, the forces of remorse and misery, waiting for their signal to descend. Inside, Peace, almost like the peace of innocence, lay anchored in still but treacherous waters.

Thus, while Raymond remained wrapped up in visions of power and fame, while he looked forward to entire dominion over the elements and the culture, the territory of his own heart escaped his notice. And from that unthought-of source arose the mighty torrent that would overwhelm his will, and carry to the oblivious sea his fame, hope, and happiness.

(14)   PERDITA in the meantime…

During the first months of his Protectorate, Raymond and she had been inseparable; they'd discussed and she'd approved all his projects. I never beheld anyone so perfectly happy as my sweet sister then. Her expressive eyes were two stars whose beams were love. Hope and light-heartedness sat on her cloudless brow. Her joy fed even to the point of tears on her Lord's almost divine celebrity. She lived for him and through him; and if she ever stopped to think highly of herself, it was only to reflect that she had won and wed the distinguished hero of the age, and had for years kept him, even after the passage of time had seen his love exchange some heat for warm familiarity. Her own feeling was as entire as at its birth. Five years had failed to dim the dazzling unreality of passion. Most men ruthlessly destroy the sacred veil, with which the female heart is wont to adorn the idol of its affections. Not so Raymond. He was an enchanter, whose reign was forever supreme; a king whose power never was suspended. Follow him through the ups and downs of common daily life, still the same charm of grace and majesty adorned him. Like a deity, he invested his votaries with his own nature. In Perdita's manner, a graceful air of decision had replaced the timidity almost amounting to awkwardness; her expression was frank, instead of reserved. Under his eye, her beauty and excellence had multiplied to the point that it was hard to recognize my reserved, abstracted sister in the fascinating and open-hearted young woman, her voice attuned to thrilling softness, who was Raymond's consort.

In Perdita, he possessed all that his heart could desire. She was now in the pride of womanhood, fulfilling the precious duties of wife and mother, possessed of all her heart had ever coveted. Raymond was ten years older. His famous good looks maintained their noble and commanding aspect; but gentlest benevolence, winning tenderness, graceful and unwearied attention to the wishes of another—marriage and its exercises had further beautified him, too. Watching her wild girl's willful temperament gradually give way to an ideal and changeless serenity, he'd grown to respect my sister as much as he loved her. Five years that had given the couple a child and strengthened their union, had also added sober certainty to their yet ethereal emotions. They no longer had to guess their way and totter on the path, trying to divine how to please one another, hoping for more bliss yet fearing it could never last. Perdita's warmth of affection, the depth of her understanding, the brilliancy of her imagination, and also that gentle compliance the years had added to her other wifely qualities, made her beyond words dear to Raymond.

Happiness is in its highest degree the sister of goodness. Suffering and amiability may have existed together, as writers loved to show us; there is a human and touching harmony in the picture. But perfect happiness is an attribute of angels, and those who possessed it, appeared angelic. Fear has been called the parent of religion—as it is, for such religion as demands victims and human sacrifice at its altars. But the religion which springs from happiness is a lovelier growth; the religion which makes the heart breathe forth fervent thanksgiving, and causes us to pour out our overflowing souls to the author of our being; the wellspring of imagination and the nurse of poetry; a religion that looks at the visible mechanism of the world and sees a benevolent intelligence, making earth a temple with heaven for its cloak. Such happiness, goodness, and religion inhabited Perdita's mind.

While our knot of happy human beings had lived together at Windsor Castle, my sister often rhapsodized to me about her state. I was her confidante. I remember our sunset walks among the shadowy forest paths, when I listened with joyful sympathy. Security gave dignity to our two passions, and the certainty of a full return left us with no wish unfulfilled. The birth of Clara, her Raymond's tiny replica, which produced a sacred and indissoluble tie between them, brought Perdita to perfect contentment. Sometimes she felt proud that he had preferred her to the hopes of a crown. Sometimes she remembered that she had suffered keen anguish when he hesitated in his choice. But this unhappy memory only served to enhance her present joy. What had been hard won was doubly dear. Spotting him in the distance, she'd look at Raymond with the same rapture (O, far more exuberant rapture!) as someone who, after surviving a tempest at sea, arrives in the destined port; she'd hasten towards him to feel his arms confirm the reality of her bliss.

If she ever worried, it was that he was not perfectly happy. Desire for fame, restless and presumptuous ambition, had characterized his youth. Renown he had acquired in Greece; ambition he had sacrificed to love. In a domestic circle so literary, adorned by refinement, touched by genius, his intellect found sufficient field for exercise. Yet his virtues thrived best in an active life. Sometimes he suffered tedium from the monotonous succession of events in our retirement. We all observed this, none with more regret than Perdita, whose life was consecrated to him. Did he need any gratification that she was unable to bestow? This was the only cloud in the azure of her happiness.

His journey to power had been full of pain to both of them. He'd attained his wish, however, and at present filled the situation for which nature seemed to have molded him, with his exceptional energy, taste, genius, and the goodness of heart which made him never weary of conducing to the well-being of his fellow creatures. His magnificent spirit, along with his aspirations for the respect and love of humankind, were achieving fruition. True, his exaltation was temporary, for our laws prohibited him from being elected for a second term; perhaps it was better that way. Habit wouldn't dull his sense of the enjoyment of power, nor disappointing struggles and defeats have time to wear him down. No: he was determined to extract and condense all the glory, power, and achievement he might have drawn from a long reign, into the three years of his Protectorate.

Raymond was eminently social. All that he now enjoyed would have been devoid of pleasure to him, had it been unshared. He'd made Perdita, until now, his partner in everything. Her love made her sympathetic; her intelligence made her understand him at a word; then she could assist and guide him. He felt her worth.

His visits to Evadne's garret made the first secret that had ever existed between them.

He had been struck by the fortitude and beauty of the ill-fated Greek; and, when her unaltered tenderness towards him unfolded itself, Raymond asked with some astonishment, what he'd ever done to merit this passionate and unrequited feeling. But soon they were lovers. She for a while monopolized his reveries; and Perdita became aware that his thoughts and time were bestowed on a subject kept from her.

My sister was by nature destitute of ordinary, anxious, petulant jealousy. She did not suspect any alienation of affection but guessed at first some circumstance connected with his high place as the mystery's cause. Startled and pained, she began to count the long days—months and years of them—which must elapse before he'd be restored to a private station, and once more hers alone. She wasn't happy that, even for a time, he should practice concealment with her. She was sad; but her trust in his love and fidelity was undisturbed. When they were together, she still opened her heart without fear to the fullest delight.

Time went on. Then Raymond, stopping mid-way in his wild career, paused to think of consequences. Two possible futures faced him. A third could not be; for Evadne's destitute condition and her highly nervous state combined to prevent him from even trying to part from her. So, either his involvement with Evadne should continue a secret to Perdita, or she would finally discover it. In the first case, he had bidden an eternal farewell to open-hearted talk and entire sympathy with his life's companion—an intolerably painful idea. Frankness was an essence of Raymond's nature; without it, his qualities became commonplace. If honesty and trust weren't there to spread glory over their marriage, his vaunted exchange of a throne for Perdita's love became a thing as weak and empty as the rainbow hues which vanish when the sun goes down. Too, the veil must be impenetrable, the wall unscalable and high enough to scrape the sky, which should conceal from her the workings of his heart and hide from her view the secret of his actions.

But this was the question's better side. What if circumstance should lead Perdita to suspect, and from there to know? The idea made all the fibers of his frame slip loose. Cold sweat rose on his brow. Many men may scoff at his dread; but Perdita's peace of mind was too dear to him, and her speechless agony too certain, too fearful, not to unman him. It didn't take long to decide his course. If the worst befell, if she learned the truth, then he would stand neither his wife's reproaches nor the anguish of her altered looks. He would forsake her; leave England, his friends, the scenes of his youth and of his present hopes. He would seek another country, and in other scenes begin life again. As at times before, resolving this made him calmer. His course from now on must be a prudent one. He'd endeavor to guide the steeds of destiny along the devious road he'd chosen, bending all his efforts the better to conceal what he could not change. For there was no remedy, and no return. Genius, devotion, courage, the adornments of his mind, the energies of his soul, all exerted to their utmost stretch, could not roll time's chariot wheels one hair's breadth backward. What he'd done was written with Reality's adamantine pen on the everlasting volume of the past; nor could agony and tears suffice to wash out one iota from his adultery.

Always, perfect confidence had existed between the couple. They even opened each other's letters, exactly as they disclosed their hearts' inmost thoughts and folds to one other. For Perdita, the treasure she possessed in Raymond's affections was more necessary to her being than the lifeblood in her veins.

An unexpected letter was delivered. Perdita read it. Had it contained more explicit proof, she would have been annihilated. As it was, trembling, cold, deathly pale, she didn't hesitate to seek out Raymond. He was alone, reviewing the latest petitions. She entered silently, sat down on the sofa opposite and gazed at him, exhibiting a look of such despair that the wildest shrieks and direst moans of misery would have seemed tame and underplayed by comparison to her living incarnation of the thing itself.

He kept his eyes on his papers. When he did raise them, her manifest wretchedness struck Raymond hard enough that he forgot his own acts and fears in a rush of consternation:

"Dearest girl, what's the matter—what has happened?"

"Nothing!" she began. "And yet not so." A hesitant pause; then words began to rush from her. "You have secrets, Raymond! Where have you been lately, whom have you seen, what do you conceal from me? Why am I banished from your confidence? Yet that's not it—I don't intend to entrap you with questions. One will suffice. Am I completely a wretch?"

With trembling hand she gave him the letter. He recognized Evadne's handwriting and blushed crimson. While Perdita sat looking at him, he appeared to read the message which in fact he'd absorbed with lightning speed. It was all coming down to one throw of the dice. Either he'd entirely dispel Perdita's suspicions, or he'd quit her forever. The moment had come. Raymond looked at impending ruin, and judged falsehood and artifice as trifles by comparison.

So, he cheated.

"My dear girl!" he said. "I have been to blame but you must pardon me. I was wrong to conceal this from you in the first place. But I did it for the sake of sparing you pain—and every day that's passed has made it harder to change course. Besides, I was constrained by delicacy towards the unhappy writer of these few lines."

Perdita gasped. "Well," she said. "Well, go on!"

"That is all—this paper tells all. I'm placed in the most difficult position. I have done my best, though perhaps I've done wrong. Of course my love for you is inviolate."

Perdita shook her head. "False!" she cried, "I know it. You would deceive me, but I will not be deceived. I have lost you—myself—my life!"

Raymond took a haughty tone. "You don't believe me?"

"Believe you!" she exclaimed, "I would give up everything and die with joy this minute if it meant I'd die feeling you were true—believing you—but that cannot be!"

"Perdita!" he warned her. "You do not see the precipice on which you stand. Believe me, I did not enter on my present line of conduct without reluctance and pain. I knew you might begin to have suspicions, but I trusted that my simple word would be enough to allay them. I built my hope on your confidence. Do you think that I will be questioned, and hear my replies disdainfully set aside? Do you think I'll be suspected, even watched, cross-examined, disbelieved? I am not yet fallen so low; my honor is not yet so tarnished. You have loved me. I adored you. But all human sentiments reach their end. Let our affection expire—but without exchanging it for distrust and recrimination. We've always been friends—lovers—let's not become enemies, mutual spies. I cannot live the object of suspicion—you cannot believe me—enough! Let us part."

"Exactly so!" cried Perdita, "I knew it would come to this! Aren't we already parted? Doesn't a gulf, deep as vacuum, yawn between us?"

Raymond rose, his features convulsed, his manner similar in calm to an earthquake-cradling atmosphere. "I am rejoiced that you take my decision so philosophically," he said, his voice breaking. "Doubtless you will play the part of the injured wife to admirable perfection. Sometimes you might have a momentary stinging feeling that you've wronged me; but your relatives' condolences, the world's pity, and all the complacency that consciousness of your own immaculate innocence will bestow, must combine to make excellent balm. Me—you will never see more!"

He moved towards the exit. He'd forgotten that every word he spoke was false—his impersonation of innocence had passed into self-deception. Didn't actors sometimes weep from the imagined passions they portrayed? Fiction's own heightened feeling of reality had Raymond in its spell. The pride he'd spoken with was genuine; he felt injured. Perdita looked up and saw the anger in his glance. He was reaching for the door handle. She sprang up and threw herself on his neck, gasping and sobbing. He took her hand, led her to the sofa, sat beside her. Her drooping head fell on his shoulder; he felt her tremble, as fire raced ice around and through her limbs. He spoke to her emotion with softened accents:

"The blow is given. I will not live the mark of suspicion, the object of jealousy. Nor will I part from you in anger—I love you too well and owe you too much. I owe you six years of unalloyed happiness. But they are passed. Faith and devotion have always been the essence of our relationship. Now that they're gone, let's not cling to an empty husk. We shall not be degraded from our true characters if we separate forever now. You'll have your child, your brother, Idris, Adrian—"

"And you!" Perdita exclaimed. "You'll have the writer of that letter."

Uncontrollable indignation flashed in Raymond's eyes. He knew that this accusation at least was false; for his plan was to quit Evadne, too. "Embrace this belief!" he cried. "Hug it to your heart, pillow your head on it, make it a cool compress for your eyes—I don't mind. But, by the God that made me, hell is not more full of lies than what you've just said!"

Much struck by his impassioned seriousness, Perdita replied, "I do not refuse to believe you, Raymond; on the contrary I promise to put implicit faith in your simple word. Only assure me, please, that your love and faith towards me have never been violated; and my suspicion, and doubt, and jealousy will vanish at once. We shall continue as we have ever done—one heart, one hope, one life."

"I have already assured you of my fidelity!" Raymond's voice turned cold. "Triple assertions will avail nothing. I'll say no more; for I can add nothing to what you've already ignored in your contempt. This dispute is unworthy of both of us; and I confess, I'm tired of answering charges equally unfounded and unkind."

Perdita tried to read his angrily averted face. His resentment was so obviously genuine that her doubts fell away. Her countenance, which for years had not expressed a feeling unallied to love, resumed again its radiant satisfaction. She found it, however, no easy task to soften and reconcile Raymond. First she must persuade him to stay and hear her. Then she must endure his haughty silence before her assurances of boundless confidence in him, and more: she enumerated their years of happiness; she brought before him past scenes of intimacy and happiness; she pictured their future life; she mentioned their child. Now tears unbidden filled her eyes. They wouldn't stop, and her utterance was choked.

She had not wept before. Raymond—who felt perhaps somewhat ashamed of the part he'd acted as the injured man, who was in truth the injurer—couldn't resist a sign of distress. And then he devoutly loved Perdita. The bend of her head, her glossy golden ringlets, her supple form were to him subjects of deep tenderness and admiration.

As she'd spoken, her melodious tones entered his soul; he was already softened. Now he comforted and caressed her while trying to deceive himself into the belief that he had never wronged her.

But he staggered forth from this scene as if from a torture chamber; a victim unliberated, sent to wait in a cell, knowing the worst would be resumed before too long. Raymond had sinned against his own honor, by affirming, swearing to, a direct falsehood; true, one he had palmed off on a woman, which therefore might be deemed less base—by others—not by him. For whom had he deceived? His own trusting, devoted, affectionate Perdita, whose generous belief, next to the pretence of innocence with which he'd extorted it, felt doubly galling. He heartily despised himself; at the same time, he was angry with Perdita. The mere idea of his Greek friend, meanwhile, evoked all that was hideous and cruel. The sense of remorse, that worst and fiercest of miseries, goaded and tormented him. The clinging weight of destiny bent him down. Raymond was all nerve; his spirit a pure fire which fades and shrinks from every foul, contaminated atmosphere. But how painful the change, as the contagion had become incorporated with the essence! Truth and falsehood, love and hate, lost their eternal boundaries; heaven rushed in to mingle with hell. Raymond's sensitive mind, one neither rough-cast nor calloused by life's rude handling, was stung to madness by being made such a battlefield. And now his passions, always his masters, woke refreshed from the long sleep in which love had cradled them.

(15) OUTWARDLY, Raymond's troubled and disturbing state yielded, by degrees, to sullen animosity. People accustomed to his suavity and benevolence of manner were startled to be met with anger, derision, bitterness. He transacted public business with distaste, and hastened from it to a solitude which was at once bane and relief. Mounting the same fiery horse he'd ridden to victory in Greece, he sought fatigue in deadening exercise.

His full recovery of himself was slow. But he emerged at last, as if from a fog of poison vapors. His thoughts were clear and calm. He was struck by how much time had elapsed since he'd acted through any impulse other than madness. A month had gone by—a month without sight of Evadne. Her power, so secondary to his heart's enduring emotions, had greatly decayed. He was no longer her slave, no longer her lover. He'd never see Evadne again; returning to Perdita completely, he'd once more deserve her confidence.

Yet even as he decided this, Raymond's imagination showed him the Greek girl's miserable abode—which, from noble and lofty principles, she'd refused to exchange for one of greater luxury. What a contrast to the splendor of her situation and appearance when they'd first met! To her life at Istanbul, one of riches and magnificence, he compared her present penury, her daily toil, her forlorn state, her faded famine-struck cheek. Compassion swelled his breast. No, he would see her, and he'd devise some plan for restoring her to society and the enjoyment of her rank—after which, as a matter of course, they'd separate.

Dimly Raymond recalled how during this long month, he'd avoided Perdita, flying from her as from the stings of his own conscience. But he was awake now; all would be remedied, and future devotion erase the memory of this single blot on the serenity of their lives. Having resolved this, he became cheerful. Suddenly it struck him: today was October 19th, the anniversary of his election as Protector. This very evening, he and Perdita were to host the gala festival event in his honor; a good omen of an auspicious future, he thought. First, briefly, he'd look in on Evadne—he owed her some account, some compensation for his long and unexplained absence— and then, to Perdita; to the forgotten world; to the duties of society, the splendor of rank, the enjoyment of power.

He set off. Autumn was far advanced and dreary. A chill late afternoon wind howled and tore from the trees what leaves they'd kept. Perfumed with decayed vegetation, the city's air was hostile to cheerfulness or hope. Raymond's spirits, just exulting from his latest pledge, were in decline before he reached the wretched streets of Evadne's neighborhood. There his heart smote him for the whole course of his conduct towards the luckless Greek. First, ever agreeing to let her remain in such degradation; then their short wild dream; and finally leaving her to drear solitude, anxious conjecture, and, most bitter! disappointed hope. He must be still awaited. What had she done for a month, how had she endured his absence and neglect?

Dusk dimmed the narrow streets leading to the well-known door, which stood ajar. The staircase was shrouded in perfect night. Raymond groped his way up and entered the garret. He found Evadne stretched speechless, almost lifeless on her wretched bed.

He called for the people of the house, but could learn nothing from them, except that they knew nothing. Her story was plain to him, plain and distinct as the remorse and horror that darted their fangs into him. When she found herself forsaken by him, she'd lost the heart to work at her designs and support herself as usual; pride forbade her to contact him; at last she'd welcomed kind starvation to provide her with this sinless solitary death. No creature came near her, as her strength failed.

And Perdita—how had she passed that month?

After the terrible scene in his office, she'd expected her former life with Raymond to resume, all those affectionate habits that were the delight of her life, along with their natural freedom of communication. But it didn't happen. Raymond transacted the business of each day apart from her. He went out without telling her where. Perdita loved him so greatly and so far with such happy returns, that her keen disappointment came as a painful torment. There was neither submission, patience, nor self-abandonment in my sister's grief; she fought with it, struggled beneath it, rendered every pang sharper by resistance. Again and again the idea recurred, that he loved another. She did him justice; she believed that he felt a tender affection for her. But give a paltry prize to someone who's counted on the winnings from the year's richest lottery, and watch it disappoint worse than a dud ticket. Raymond's love was an indivisible treasure. Of its sum total, no arithmetic could calculate its price; but take away the smallest portion, name its parts and separate them into degrees and sections, and like the magician's coin, it turned from gold to trash. There is a meaning in the eye of love, a cadence in its voice, an irradiation in its smile; its spirit is elemental, its essence singular, its divinity a unit. The very heart and soul of Raymond and Perdita had mingled, two mountain brooks joined in their descent to flow murmuring and sparkling over shining pebbles, beside starry flowers;

but let one rivulet desert its course, or be dammed up by some obstruction, and the other shrinks to a trickle down its altered banks. All month long, Perdita sensed the failing of the tide that fed her life.

As for the cause of this change, she located it squarely in her husband's exaltation to the office of Protector. A variety of feelings had urged her, as the annual event's organizer-in-chief, to bring double magnificence to this year's festival; yet on October 19th, as she arrayed herself for the evening gala, she was wondering why she took such pains to put on a sumptuous anniversary celebration of the day her sufferings started.

Woe befall that day instead, she thought. *Better woe, tears, and mourning betide the hour that gave Raymond another hope than love, another wish than my devotion. And thrice joyful the moment when he shall be restored to me. Two years more in this palace! God knows, I put my trust in his vows, I do believe him—if I didn't, I wouldn't want him for myself again. But can we spend two more years like this, each day adding to our alienation, each act piling another stone onto the wall between us?*

No, my Raymond, my only beloved, sole possession of Perdita! This night, this splendid assembly, these sumptuous apartments, this adornment of your tearful girl, are all united to celebrate—your abdication. Once, for me, you relinquished the prospect of a crown. That was in days of early love, when I could only hold out the hope, not the assurance of happiness. Now you have the experience of all that I can give: the heart's devotion, taintless love, and unhesitating subjection to you. You must choose, so she would tell him, *between these and your Protectorate. This, proud noble, is your last night in office! Perdita has bestowed on it everything magnificent and dazzling that your heart best loves—but from these gorgeous rooms, from this princely attendance, from power and elevation, you and I must return with tomorrow's sun to our home in the country; for I wouldn't put up with another week like this last one even if it guaranteed me an immortality of joy.*

Devising these powerful arguments and resolutions left Perdita's heart exalted and her course very clear. She'd cast her fate on a throw of the dice. She felt secure of winning. Her cheek was flushed by the expectation of struggle; her eyes sparkled with her coming triumph;

she rose like some queen of nations, and in the nobility of her bearing there seemed power enough to stop the wheel of destiny with a fingertip. She had never before looked so supremely lovely. Or so I must imagine. We, the Arcadian shepherds of the tale, had intended to be present; but Perdita, then suffering, had told us not to come this year. Better so, she thought now. It meant we'd be home at Windsor next morning to greet her and Raymond on their return to our dear circle, where they'd renew a course of life in which she had found entire felicity.

Her thoughts were absorbing and it was late when Perdita descended from her rooms and made her entrance at the sparkling gala. Raymond who'd promised to grace the assembly was still awaited. She had no doubt he'd arrive very late. The wider the breach between them might appear at this crisis, somehow the more secure she was of closing it forever. Thus the warmth and brilliance with which she set about entertaining her guests, and with heartfelt smiles excusing her tardy lord.

Evadne's crisis peaked a few hours before midnight. It was then, with his suspense and fear at their height, that Raymond once more remembered the festival Perdita was giving in his honor this night— now. In his honor, exactly when misery and death were painting his name with indelible disgrace; honor to one whose crimes deserved a scaffold; this was the worst mockery. Still, Perdita would expect him. He called the landlady from the corner where she lurked and bade her take a note—he wrote one very hastily on a scrap of paper—and deliver it into the hands of the wife of the Lord Protector at their palace.

"Me?" The woman, who failed to recognize him, answered contemptuously. "Get in there? To see her? On festival night? That's a laugh."

Raymond pulled off his ring. "Here—take this to show them at the gates. You'll get through. Now without delay, just go!"

He got back on his knees by the bedside of his starved, almost lifeless lover, and returned to berating himself. If Evadne died, where could a recorded murderer be found whose cruelty in the act could stand comparison with his? What fiend more wanton in his mischief, what damned soul more worthy of perdition! But he was not reserved for this agony of self-reproach, only conjecture's pangs. He'd sent for medical assistance. Hours would pass, spun by suspense into ages of dark autumnal night. Not before morning would the patient's survival be sure enough to allow her removal into larger rooms nearby, where he'd hover concernedly about her pillow.

Her thoughts in confusion, Perdita clutched Raymond's ring and followed her attendant out of the gala hall. The impoverished woman who'd shown it at the gates was claiming to have a note as well from the man who wore it. A fall from his horse, or some similar accident—this was what she was dreading until the woman started to talk; then other fears awoke. The old gossip's vanity was raised by her commission, which, after all, she did not understand, since even now she had no suspicion that Evadne's visitor was Lord Raymond himself. From blind if not malignant cunning, she avoided any mention of Evadne's alarming state; but she was garrulous over the great frequency of Raymond's visits to her young widowed tenant. Her narrative combined innuendo with enough circumstantial detail to convince Perdita of a truth somewhat worse than actuality. Worst of all, his absence tonight, his message wholly unaccounted for—except by the old crone's disgraceful hints—appeared the deadliest insult. Again she looked at the ring in her hand: a small ruby, almost heart-shaped, a gift from her. *Do not, I charge you, I entreat you, permit your guests to wonder at my absence.* She looked at the handwriting, hurried but unmistakable, and repeated the words of the note in an undertone. The messenger's strange medley of truth and falsehood went on filling her ears. All at once Perdita burst out, "Please—go!" and the woman found herself dismissed.

My sister returned to the assembly. The hubbub was near its peak and no one had missed her yet. Gliding over to an empty corner of the room, she leaned there, out of sight against an ornamental column, and tried to recover herself. Every part of her was shaking. Nearby stood a carved vase full of flowers she'd arranged herself, that morning. They were rare and lovely plants; even in her devastation, the poor girl remained alive to their brilliant colors and starry shapes. Divine infoliations of the spirit of beauty, which neither drooped nor mourned—the despair that clasped Perdita's heart had no power to spread contagion over them! Why, she wondered, could she not be insensible like the flowers? No, they had the calm she'd lost forever.

"To my task!" she told herself, remembering Raymond's note. "I obey; my guests shall not perceive reality—not his nor mine, anyhow. Though it kills me, as long as they're here tonight, they shall behold the antipodes of what is real—for I will appear to live—while I am— *dead.*" It took all her self-command to prevent the self-pity that flooded her from issuing in tears. After a struggle of some minutes, she was able to rejoin the company.

From this point on, the night was pleasureless acting. In the part of a courteous hostess, she attended to all while shining personally as the focus of enjoyment and grace. The show must go on; though in her depths she sighed for loneliness, and would gladly have traded her crowded palace rooms for the dark heart of a forest, or a dreary, night-blanketed heath. But she became gay, brittle, extra-bright. With her spontaneity she'd lost her even-tempered ease. Her exhilaration of spirits was noted; and if a sharpness in her laugh, or an abruptness in her sallies, might have betrayed her secret to an attentive observer, the greatest number of her guests surrounded her applaudingly. She carried on, careful not to pause lest her wrecked hopes find a way to raise their wailing voices from her misery-flooded soul, and make those who now echoed her mirth, and provoked her repartees, shrink in fear from her convulsive despair. Her only consolation during the violence which she did herself, was to watch the motions of an illuminated clock and count down the time which must elapse before she could be alone.

Finally, the rooms began to thin. She chided her guests on their early departures as, one by one, they left her. At length came the last handshake. "How cold and damp your hand is!" said her friend. "You're over-tired—please go straight to bed." Perdita smiled faintly in farewell and stayed to watch the final carriage roll away. Then, as if pursued by an enemy—as if her feet had wings—she sped to her own rooms, where she dismissed her attendants, locked the doors behind them, and with a wild heave of limbs, threw herself to the floor; to keep from shrieking aloud, she bit her lips until they bled. She lay there a long while, prey to the vulture of despair. Despite trying not to think, she felt overrun by ideas; horrid as furies, cruel as vipers, they seemed to jostle and wound each other in their haste to work her up into a state of madness.

At length she got to her feet, more composed, not less miserable, and made her way to her dressing room. She stood where she'd begun the night, before a large mirror. The light and graceful dress, the jewels that studded her hair and encircled her beauteous arms and neck, her small feet shod in satin, her profuse and glossy tresses, all these were identical to what she'd seen reflected earlier; against her present woebegone and troubled face, they seemed to make a gorgeous frame for a painting of a shipwreck.

Not a calm flower—no, I'm the vase! A carved vase, she thought, *brimful of despair's direst essence. Farewell, Perdita! Farewell, poor girl! You've seen yourself thus for the last time. No more luxury and wealth for you; in fact your poverty is so extreme, you could wind up envying a homeless beggar.*

Perdita shook her head and turned away.

Truly—I am without a home! I live instead on an interminably wide and barren desert which brings forth neither fruit or flower; in the midst is a solitary rock, to which poor Perdita is chained.

She threw open a window which overlooked the palace garden. Light and darkness were struggling together, and the eastern sky was streaked with gold and rosy rays. One star alone still trembled in the depths of the kindling atmosphere. Fresh morning air streamed over the dewy plants and rushed into the heated room.

Nothing lasts! thought Perdita. *All things go on, decay, and perish! The planet spins, the fires of heaven move in their accustomed paths, and the eyelids of day are opened. Birds and flowers, bedewed vegetation, fresh breezes awaken; at length the sun appears and starts its climb. Then comes noon, and then comes night again. Nothing lasts, except the misery in my bursting heart.*

Yes, all things go on and everything changes: what wonder, then, that love has gone and set? Why shouldn't the lord of my life have changed? The stars we call eternal wander all over the skies—if I look again where I looked an hour ago, the face of heaven is completely altered. The silly moon and the inconstant planets dance a different routine every night; ruler of them all, the sun is always deserting its throne. Dominion's in the hands of night and winter, eclipse and death. Nature grows old, and shakes in her decaying limbs; creation falls bankrupt. O Perdita! How does it come as such as surprise, that the light of your life has been led to destruction?

(16)

A Letter to Raymond from Evadne

At first, safe from famine and the grave, blanketed by Raymond's most tender care, lulled by that feeling of repose peculiar to convalescence, Evadne gave herself up to rapturous gratitude and love. But with health returned reflection. Where had he been, and why never with her, those nearly fatal weeks? With Greek subtlety did she begin to question him; but she formed her conclusions as to the motives for his absence in her own uncompromising way. Though unaware that the breach she'd occasioned between Raymond and Perdita was already irreparable, she judged the present situation to be widening it each day, and knew the result must be to destroy her lover's happiness. Remorse would have its fangs in his heart. There was only one thing she could do. She must—she would—part from him forever.

She left London immediately, keeping her destination unknown.

Her letter to Raymond offered no clues, only assurances. Yes, she was safe and in no danger of wanting the means of life; yes, she promised to preserve herself. He might find her someday in a station not unworthy of her father's daughter.

Then came, with the eloquence of despair and of unalterable love, a last farewell. It was impossible to guess at the whole of her plan.

≈≈≈≈≈

A Letter to Raymond from Perdita

By December, my sister was still unable to calm her mind or subdue her thoughts to any regular train; she careened among hours of suspicion, self-reproach and blind serenity. Raymond and she seldom addressed each other, shunning explanation, each fearing to know what the other might say. He'd been limiting his time at the palace to those public occasions when his duties prevented his remaining alone with her.

Suddenly, his manners to Perdita changed. He appeared to be looking for opportunities to bring about a return to kindness and intimacy between them. The tide of love towards her appeared to flow again; he spoke to her again and let her read his countenance. Which said, he could never forget how devoted he'd been to her once, nor how he'd made her the shrine and storehouse for his every thought and sentiment. He seemed to be holding back out of shame; yet he evidently wished to establish a renewal of confidence and affection.

Once Perdita recovered from her shock, she laid down an immediate plan of action for herself. Raymond's tokens of returning love she received with gentleness; she did not shun his company; but against easy familiarity and more intimate painful discussion alike, she placed careful barriers. These, a mix of pride and shame kept him from surmounting. He grew impatient and began to show it. Perdita realized she must explain herself to him; she could not summon courage to speak, and preferred to write as follows:

Read this letter with patience, I entreat you. It will contain no reproaches. For what should I reproach you? Just let me explain my feelings. If we misunderstand one another less, maybe we can stop groping around for a way out of our life of the last few weeks.

I loved you—I love you—

I believed that you read my heart, and knew its devotion, its unalienable fidelity towards you.

Neither anger nor pride dictates these lines; but a feeling beyond, deeper, and more unalterable than either. My affections are wounded;

it is impossible to heal them—cease then the vain endeavor, if indeed that way your endeavors tend. Forgiveness! Return! Idle words these! I forgive the pain I endure; but the trodden path cannot be retraced.

Common affection might have been satisfied with commonplace treatment. But I never loved anyone but you. You arrived in my life as the embodied image of my fondest dreams, with your success, your celebrity. Love for you invested the world for me in enchanted light. No more poverty, no more trite, stale repetition of old worn out days: I lived in a temple of the senses glorified by intensest devotion and rapture; I walked, a consecrated being, contemplating only your power, your excellence. Our beloved Schiller writes of this—oh happy hours, when you read to me from Coleridge's translation:

> For O, you stood beside me, like my youth,
> Transformed for me the real to a dream,
> Clothing the palpable and familiar with golden exhalations of
> the dawn.

The bloom has vanished from my life! There is no morning to this all-pervading night; no rising from love's sunset. In those days the rest of the world was nothing to me. All other men—I never considered nor felt what they were, nor did I look on you as one of them. Separated from them; exalted in my heart; sole possessor of my affections; single object of my hopes; the best half of myself, that was you.

Is not love a divinity, because it never dies? Did not I appear sanctified, even to myself, because this love had my heart for its temple? I have gazed on you as you slept, melted even to tears, as the idea filled my mind that all I possessed lay cradled in those lineaments before me, idolized but subject to death and decay. Then I'd check the fears that thronged forth; I would not fear dying, because the emotions that linked us must be immortal.

Ah, Raymond, weren't we happy? Did the sun ever shine on a couple that enjoyed its light with purer and more intense bliss? It was not—it is not a common infidelity at which I repine. It is the disunion of an indivisible whole; it is the carelessness with which you shook off the mantle of election that you alone wore for me, and made yourself one among the many. Dream not to alter this.

I still don't fear death. I'd be happy to close my eyes and never open them again. And yet there is one fear I have—because in any state of being linked by the chain of memory with this life, how could happiness return? Even in Paradise, I fear, I must feel that your love was less enduring than the mortal beatings of my fragile heart, every pulse of which knells audibly, like the poet Byron's words...

The funeral note of love, deep buried, without resurrection

No—no—to my misery: for love extinct there is no resurrection!

I love you yet. Even yet, and forever, would I contribute all I possess to your welfare. On account of a tattling world, for the sake of my child—of our child—I'm willing to remain by your side, Raymond, share your fortunes, counsel and be counseled by you as I can. Shall it be thus? We are no longer lovers; nor can I call myself a friend to you or anyone—lost as I am, I have no thought to spare from my own wretched, engrossing self. But it will please me to see you each day! Yes, and to listen to the public praising you; to keep up your paternal love for our girl; to hear your voice; to know that I am near you, though you are no longer mine.

If you wish to break the chains that bind us, say the word, and it shall be done—I will take all the blame on myself, of harshness or unkindness, in the world's eye.

But, as I have said, I'd most like, at least for the present, to live under the same roof with you. Who knows? When the fever of my young life is spent; when placid age shall tame the vulture that devours me, friendship may come, love and hope being dead. My soul, inextricably linked to this perishable frame, could become lethargic and cold, much as my aging body must lose its youthful elasticity. Though now the words sound hollow and meaningless—then, wrinkled, grey-headed, with lackluster eyes, a woman tottering on the grave's extreme edge, then I may be—your affectionate and true friend,

PERDITA.

This letter was found among his possessions; I kept it later.

(17)   AT WINDSOR, in our retirement, we remained long in ignorance of my sister's misfortune. Soon after the festival she'd sent for her child, and then seemed to have forgotten us. Adrian visited and observed a change, but neither its extent nor cause were clear. Suave Raymond was occasionally abrupt and had moments of haughtiness which startled his gentle friend; the Protector's brow was not exactly clouded, but his lips wore a disdainful set, and his voice was harsh. Perdita had grown thin and pale. She was all kindness and attention to her lord; but she was silent, and beyond words sad; her eyes were often tear-filled. But was she in despair? Or was this resignation? Clara was always with her, and she seemed most at ease when she could sit in an obscure corner, holding her daughter's hand. Still, the couple continued to live under the same roof and make public appearances together. Unable to guess at the truth, full of concern, Adrian entreated them to visit us at Windsor.

It was May before they did. Spring's height had decked the forest with leaves and its paths with a thousand flowers. With only a day's notice, Perdita made an early-morning arrival; she had the child along but Raymond had been detained by business—he'd follow soon, she said. After what Adrian had told us, I was surprised to find my sister in the highest spirits. True, she'd grown thin, even a bit hollow-eyed; though tinged by a bright glow, her cheeks had sunk. In delight to see us, I watched her caress our children; she praised their growth and improvement; she wanted the children all around us. A reunion for them, as Clara got to meet her old playmate Alfred again; a cause for celebration, Perdita called it, to be marked by all kinds of childish games in which she joined with whole-hearted hilarity. Her laughter was contagious. Watching us amuse ourselves on the Castle terrace, no one could have pictured a happier, less care-worn party.

At the height of the gaiety, little Clara looked at Perdita all aglow and said, "This is so much better, Mamma, than being in that dismal London, where you cry so much and never laugh like now."

"Quiet, now, silly baby," was the reply. "And remember the rule we agreed on—anyone who mentions London gets sent to Coventry for an hour." The little girl, who hated being left out of anything, giggled at her mother's old-time threat but said no more.

Arriving soon afterwards, Raymond refrained from joining the fun as he would have done usually. He was insistent to converse, instead, with Adrian and myself apart, and by degrees we followed him, leaving Idris and Perdita behind with the children. Raymond talked of his new buildings; of his plan for an establishment for the better education of the poor; as usual Adrian and he started to argue, and the time slipped away unnoticed. Only towards evening did the whole party assemble again—for music, Perdita insisted now. We must have a night of Mozart. She wanted, she said, to give us a specimen of her new accomplishment; for she'd been applying herself to music lessons in London, singing especially. (Though her voice lacked power, it had developed a great deal of sweetness.) She bade us limit the program to light-hearted melodies; and we combed our scores of Mozart's operas for his most exhilarating airs.

More than any other, Mozart's music possessed the transcendent attribute of appearing to come from the heart; you entered into the passions he expressed, and were transported with grief, joy, anger, or confusion, as he, our soul's master, had chosen to inspire. That night at Windsor, the spirit of hilarity was kept up for some time; but at length Perdita slipped away from the piano. Raymond had just joined in the trio of Don Giovanni's *Taci ingiusto core*. Idris sang next, at the harp, *Porgi, amor, qualche ristoro*, that passionate and sorrowful lament by the Marriage of Figaro's deserted Countess, over the ruin of her marriage to the faithless Almaviva. Tender sorrow's very soul was breathed forth in this aria, which had reached its final pathetic appeal when a stifled sob attracted our attention to my sister. She hastened from the music room at our notice.

I followed. Though she seemed to want to shun me, I was persistent. All at once, with a sob, she threw herself against me to cry on my shoulder. "His voice—his voice!" came through her weeping.

Later, I understood. Raymond's silken baritone, softening the seducer Don's arch entreaties into tenderness, had been the same as when he'd used to sing these same lines as his homage of love to her— even the same tone of voice—yet it was homage no longer; and this irony penetrated her with regret and despair.

"Once again," she sighed at length, "once again onto your friendly breast, my beloved brother, the lost Perdita pours forth her sorrows. But I can't talk about them. Let it be enough for you to know that I'm miserable—and that the painted veil of life is torn—that I sit shrouded in unrelieved darkness and gloom—that grief is my sister, everlasting lamentation my mate!"

Of course I did not question her. Instead I held and endeavored to console her, though I could offer nothing but assurances of my deepest affection and intensest wish that things should soon get better for her.

"Loving words!" she cried. "They sound in my ear like a piece of favorite music I'd somehow forgotten. They are vain, I know; how very vain in their attempt to soothe or comfort me. Dearest Lionel, you cannot guess what I've suffered during these past months. I remember reading about mourners in ancient days, who clothed themselves in sackcloth, scattered dust upon their heads, ate their bread mingled with ashes, and went to live on bleak mountain tops the better to cry creaseless reproaches against heaven and earth for their misfortunes. Compared to me, they lived in luxury! Day to day contriving new extravagances of sorrow, reveling in the paraphernalia of woe, equipped with every appurtenance of despair—I can only envy grief like that. I, alas, must conceal the wretchedness consuming me. I must weave a veil of dazzling falsehood to hide my grief from vulgar eyes; I must smooth my brow, and paint my lips in deceitful smiles—even in solitude I dare not think how lost I am, lest I become insane and rave!"

"My dear sister—"

"O, Lionel, I wrote Raymond a letter. It was—the best thing I ever wrote." Now Perdita dug through her bag and produced a much-handled envelope. "His reply," she said. "Read it." I extracted the single page inside. Raymond's answer, dashed off on a writing machine, was brief.

Notwithstanding your bitter letter, for bitter I must call it, you are the chief person in my estimation, and it is your happiness that I would principally consult. Do that which seems best to you: and if you can receive gratification from one mode of life in preference to another, do not let me be any obstacle. I foresee that the plan which you mark out in your letter will not endure long; but you are mistress of yourself, and it is my sincere wish to contribute as far as you will permit me to your happiness.

Still in no state to rejoin the others, my sister let me persuade her outdoors for an evening carriage drive around the park, where I hoped to get the story from her. Talking about her unhappiness would lighten the burden, I thought; nor did I doubt we'd find her a remedy, if there were one to be found. As I listened, it grew harder to feel hopeful on either count. Raymond had dealt her a death-blow, Perdita said. Nothing he could do now, not even by his best intentions, could change that. She wouldn't be the one to leave, but he was right—they must part soon.

"Cleopatra choosing her jewelry," she said, through sobs, "might as well have worn the vinegar she dissolved her famous pearl in, as I could be content with the love Raymond is able to offer me."

I was sorry to recognize these tear-storms and asperities of character; with other signs, they showed me that under the force of a mortal blow to her emotions, Perdita had in some degree regressed. That concentrated, self-lacerating hermit's pride of hers, dormant while her wedded bliss lasted, was awake, and with its "adder's sting" pierced a heart already sickened by humiliation. She'd been proud of having won and kept him—but if another had won Raymond from her, then all she'd possessed of worth was gone. Even her maternal tenderness borrowed half its force from the delight she found in tracing his features and expressions across Clara's development.

But I didn't see their case as such a hopeless one as Perdita did. No: the wound could be healed; and, if they stayed together, it would be. She heard my soothing attempts in this line with impatience, finally interrupting: "Do you think that any of your arguments are new to me? Or that my own burning wishes and intense anguish have not suggested them all a thousand times, with far more eagerness and subtlety than you can put into them? Lionel, you cannot understand what woman's love is.

"In days of happiness I've often repeated to myself, with a grateful heart and exulting spirit, the story of all that Raymond sacrificed for me. I was a poor, uneducated, solitary mountain girl, raised from nothingness by him. Along with the first luxuries of my life, he gave me an illustrious name and noble station; the world's respect came to me reflected from his glory: all this joined to his own undying love, inspired me with sensations towards him, akin to those with which we regard the Giver of life. I gave him love only. I devoted myself to him: imperfect creature that I was, I took myself to task, that I might become worthy of him. I watched over my hasty temper, subdued my burning impatience of character, curbed my self-involvement, educated myself to the best perfection I could attain, all for his happiness's sake. I took no merit to myself for this. He deserved it all—all labor, all devotion, all sacrifice. I would have toiled up a perpendicular Alp, to pluck a flower that would please him. At one time, I was ready to quit you all, my only family and beloved and gifted companions—we were near to going abroad, I to live alone with him, for him. I couldn't do otherwise, even if I'd wished; he was the better half of my soul, to which the other half was a perpetual slave. All he owed me was one return: Fidelity. I earned that; I deserved it. Because I was poor, and come from the mountains, does he think I wanted a great name and high station all along? He can take them back; without his love they are nothing to me. Their only merit in my eyes was that they were part of him."

Certain they were bound to separate, she acknowledged herself too big a coward to take the decisive step and end their imperfect companionship. "Our masquerade of union is strangely dear to me. Painful, I allow, and destructive, and impracticable. Living with Raymond keeps up a perpetual fever in my veins; I have a case of blood poisoning from my own fretted-at wound. Yet I must cling to it. I'll be thankful if it kills me soon, which it might." Thus passionately Perdita ran on.

Raymond had remained with Adrian and Idris back inside. Naturally frank, he was encouraged by our prolonged absence to seek relief from the constraint of months, by an almost unreserved confidence. He told his two friends of the situation in which he'd found Evadne Zaimi. Her name could not be concealed, even for Adrian's sake, and her former lover heard with the most acute agitation the history of her sufferings. Idris had shared Perdita's ill opinion of the Greek; but Raymond's account softened and interested her. Evadne's constancy, fortitude, even her ill-fated and ill-regulated love, inspired admiration and pity; especially the way she'd preferred suffering and death to what would have been in her own eyes a degrading application for his pity and assistance. Her subsequent conduct did not diminish this interest. They wondered where she might have gone.

Now Raymond spoke of what he called an incurable evil: his marriage. He lamented Perdita's harshness, her coldness. He loved her still, he declared, and had been ready not long since, with the humility of a penitent and the bearing of a vassal, to surrender himself to her, give up his very soul to her control; to become her pupil, her slave, her bondsman. She had rejected these advances. The time for such exuberant submission, along with the love that drove it, had passed. Still, everything he did was meant to promote her peace of mind—exertions, sadly, he appeared to make in vain. If she were to continue like this, so inflexible, they must part. What indeed could he reply to her complaints, to her griefs which she jealously marshaled and guarded, keeping out all thought of remedy? The frustrations and inconveniences of this senseless mode of married life were maddening to him. Yet he wouldn't propose separation. He was haunted by the fear of thereby causing either Perdita's death, or little Clara's; how, he couldn't say. But to take decisive action without knowing the next way forward, was to risk their ruin.

After a few hours, Raymond took his leave. Perdita and I still hadn't returned, but he didn't want to meet her in front of us, knowing all that had and must have been said. Perdita, in her turn, wanted to follow him to London with Clara. Idris tried to persuade her to remain—to at least stay the night. My poor sister looked at her fearfully. *Raymond must have talked to her; was this, keeping her at Windsor, his idea? Was this the beginning of their final separation?* As I've said, certain defects of her character had been revived by her dilemma. She declined Idris's invitation with suspicious looks; she embraced me, as if she were about to be deprived of my affection, too, calling me her more-than-brother, her only friend, her last hope. "Don't you stop loving me!" she cried, and with a heightened, panicked air, departed for London, the scene and cause of all her misery.

The weeks that followed convinced her that she had not yet

touched the bottom of the abyss into which she'd been plunged. Every day her unhappiness took a new shape; every day some unexpected event seemed to bring to a stop, then only lead onward, her private train of calamities.

(18)   A BORN leader, Raymond had all the ambition and talent of a successful hero; but he was neither calculating nor determined enough to become one. Other elements in his character intervened. He was obstinate, but not firm; benevolence itself at first contact, harsh and reckless if provoked. Above all, he was remorseless and unyielding in the pursuit of any object of desire, however lawless. Love of pleasure, of beauty, of luxury, were prominent in him, conquering the conqueror; obsessed with some acquisition, he'd forget all else and lay aside the toil of weeks for the sake of a stronger pull's indulgence. These were the impulses he'd been obeying in his decision to marry my sister; when they'd egged him on again, he wound up Evadne Zaimi's lover. He had now lost both women, and had nothing to console him: neither the self-congratulatory sense of personal nobility which marital constancy inspires; nor the voluptuous sense of abandonment to a forbidden but intoxicating passion. His heart was exhausted by recent events; his enjoyment of life was destroyed by Perdita's resentment piled on top of Evadne's flight. The former's inflexibility set the final touch upon the annihilation of his hopes. The idea of reunion was futile, since he couldn't get her to change; so he gave up and sought only to reconcile himself to the present state of things. He made a vow against love and its attendant struggles, failures, remorse. Mere sensual enjoyment was the only thing he pursued now, seeking in it a remedy for what his passions had done to him.

Debasement of character is the certain result of such choices. It might have been less immediately obvious in his case, had Raymond continued to apply himself to fulfilling his duties as Protector. But, extreme in all things and lost to the moment, he gave up everything to go pleasure-chasing. The council chamber was deserted; the execution of his plans for the public benefit were forgotten; the crowds which attended on him and those he employed on his various projects were disappointed to find themselves likewise neglected. Private festivity, and even libertinism, became the order of the day.

Perdita beheld with alarm the increasing disorder, the incongruous intimacies, the lack of reflection or foresight. At one point she believed she could stem the tide and induce Raymond to hear reason. Vain hope! The moment of her influence was past. He listened with haughtiness and replied disdainfully; she might in fact have succeeded in awakening his conscience, but the sole effect was that he sought an opiate for its pangs in oblivious riot. So, with the energy natural to her, Perdita endeavored as his wife to fill his place. She could do much; but in the end, no woman or man could make up for the increasing negligence of a Protector who, as if seized with a paroxysm of insanity, trampled on all ceremony, all order, all duty, and gave himself up to licentiousness.

Reports of these strange proceedings reached Windsor, of course. In the midst of one of our debates over what could be done to restore our friend to himself and his country, Perdita suddenly arrived from town. Questioned, she supplied details about the progress of the mournful change; she'd come today, she said, to entreat Adrian and myself to go up to London, where we must endeavor to stop the evil from increasing any further.

"Tell him," her voice rose, "tell Lord Raymond that my presence shall no longer annoy him. That he need not plunge into destructive dissipations for the sake of disgusting me and causing me to fly from nearness with him. This purpose is now accomplished; he will never see me anymore. But let me—this is the last thing I'll ask of him—only let me, in the renewed praises of his countrymen and the prosperity of England, find the choice of my youth justified."

During our ride up to town, Adrian and I discussed and argued about Raymond's conduct. Both of us perceived a falling off from the hopes of permanent excellence on his part that his rise had convinced us to entertain. My friend and I had been educated in one school, or rather I was his pupil in the opinion, that steady adherence to principle was the only road to honor; and a ceaseless observance of the laws of general utility, the only conscientious aim of human ambition. We differed, though, in our views of the present case.

Resentment on my sister's behalf adding sting to my censure, I reprobated Raymond's conduct in severe terms. Adrian was more benign, more considerate. Yes, he admitted, the principles that I'd laid down were the best; but he denied that they were the only ones. I should remember my New Testament, he told me, and quoted John's gospel: *There are many mansions in my father's house.* He insisted that the modes of becoming good or great, varied as much as people's dispositions—of which, as they said of the leaves of the forest, no two were alike.

We arrived in London an hour before midnight. Stopping by Parliament just in case Raymond had deigned to convene the session, we found the chamber at full attendance; the Protector's was the single empty chair. An austere discontent emanated from the party leaders awaiting him. We marked a no less ominous whispering and busy tattle among the underlings. We hastened to the palace of the Protectorate. There we found Raymond in his dining room with six merry companions. Bottles and various pipes being passed around had made considerable inroads on the general understanding. The guest who sat nearest Raymond was telling a story which convulsed the other five with laughter.

Only Raymond refrained. While he entered into the spirit of the hour, his natural dignity never forsook him. Though he was gay, playful, fascinating, never did he overstep the modesty of nature, or the respect due to himself, in his wildest sallies. Yet I own, that considering the task which Raymond had taken on himself as Protector of England, and the cares to which it behooved him to attend, I was exceedingly provoked to observe these jovial if not drunken spirits, and the worthless types on whom his time was wasted. I stood observing the scene, while Adrian stepped forward; no doubt he aimed to restore order in the assembly by the example of his own sobriety. Raymond gave a cry of delight upon seeing him.

"My dear Adrian, you must join the party!" Nodding at the invitation, Adrian took a seat.

This action provoked me. Indignant that he should sit at the same table with Raymond's companions—men and women of abandoned character, of no character, the refuse of high-bred luxury, the disgrace of their country—I cried, "Let me entreat you, Adrian, not to comply like this. Rather join with me in trying to get Lord Raymond away from this scene, and restoring him to more appropriate society."

"My good fellow," said Raymond, "this is neither the time nor place for a moral lecture. Take my word for it: my amusements and society are not so bad as you imagine. We're not hypocrites or fools. And we adore our country and its culture. *Tell me, Malvolio, dost thou think because thou art virtuous, there shall be no more cakes and ale?*" The guests, recognizing Shakespeare, raised applause.

I spun away and went to look at the contemporary artworks on the nearest wall. Though celebrated, they appeared worthless to me. At length I heard Adrian call me back. "You, Verney," he said, "Are very cynical. Sit down. Or if you won't, perhaps, as you're not a frequent visitor, Lord Raymond will humor your wish to see him in action at Parliament, and take us there now." Raymond glanced keenly at him, then turned from that benign and gentle expression to my own glowering demeanor, which he observed with scorn. "Please," Adrian continued. "I've promised you would, Raymond—don't let me down. Come with us."

The other made an uneasy movement, no more, then said, "I won't!"

The party had been breaking up around us. The guests had risen to look at the artworks, then strolled into the other apartments; some had talked of billiards; one by one they vanished. Fuming at the loss of his night's entertainment, Raymond sprang up from the table and began to pace the length of the long room. "This is infinitely ridiculous!" he cried. "Two schoolboys could not conduct themselves more unreasonably."

I stood to face him while Adrian, who'd finally risen, leaned against a wall. We didn't understand, Raymond told us, gesticulating. "This is all part of the system—an elaborate form of tyranny to which I will never submit—never! Because I am Protector of England, am I to be the only slave in the realm? My privacy invaded, my actions censured, my friends insulted? I've had enough, I say! Be you witnesses," and he took the insignia of office from his breast and threw it on the table. Pearls, diamond, gold: "I renounce my office, I abdicate my power—assume it who will!"

"Let the one assume it," Adrian answered him, "who can rightly claim to be your superior. There's no one in England with the adequate presumption. Know yourself, Raymond, and your sense of well-being will return. Three months ago, for the people of this country, you were our Protector in every way. Your hours were devoted to our benefit. Your ambition was to obtain the people's kudos. You built up and decorated our towns, gave us useful establishments, gifted the soil with abundant fertility. The powerful and unjust cowered at the steps of your law courts, and the poor and oppressed rose like night-folded flowers under the morning sunshine of your protection. Can you wonder that we are all aghast and mourn when so very much appears to have changed? But, come, this fit of spleen is already passed. Resume your functions. Your partisans will hail you; your enemies will be silenced; and your public and your friends will show you their love, honor, and duty once more. Master yourself, Raymond, and make the world your subject."

"No doubt excellent advice—for someone else," Raymond answered moodily. "Take it yourself, why don't you? Already the first peer of the land, why not its sovereign? You, Adrian, the good, the wise, the just, might rule all hearts. But I perceive, too soon for my own happiness, too late for England's good, that I undertook a task to which I am unequal. I cannot rule myself. My passions master me; my smallest impulse is my tyrant. You think that I renounce the Protectorate—and I have renounced it—in a fit of spleen? By the God that lives, I swear never to take up that bauble again—never again to burden myself with the weight of care and misery it signifies.

"Know myself? Once, in the heyday of youth, in the pride of boyish folly, I desired to be a king. A crown came within my grasp. I knew myself when I renounced it. I renounced it to gain—who cares? I've lost that as well. For too many months I have submitted to this mock majesty, this solemn farce. I am its dupe and joker no longer. I will be free."

But he'd stopped proclaiming; drained of its excessive character, his voice was now dead serious. "I have lost," he continued, "that which adorned and dignified my life, that which linked me to other men. Determined to believe the worst of my character, Perdita has renounced me. Again I am a solitary man; and I will become again, as in my early years, a wanderer, a soldier of fortune.

"My friends—for Verney, I feel you're my friend—please don't try to change my mind. This palace, this masquerade as one of the world's great ones: what I did to get here, I did more for your sister's sake than my own. Just as when we used to put on skits and masquerades outdoors, beneath the branches of your beloved forest, here in London I led Perdita behind the scenes of grandeur and acted a nice little high leader's part with her before the world. It was my explicit intention to vary the monotony of her life with a short segment of magnificence and power. This was to be the splash of color on the substance and canvas of our existence, an otherwise pure expanse of mutual affection, mutual confidence.

"But we must live, always, and not act our lives. Pursuing the shadow, I lost the reality. Now I renounce both.

"Adrian, I'm about to return to Greece, to become a soldier again, perhaps a conqueror. My old comrades are still obliged inch by inch to fight for their security. Will you join us? You'll behold new scenes—see a new people—witness the mighty struggle that's taking place there between civilization and barbarism—become part of, even help direct, the movement of a young and vigorous population seeking liberty and order. Come with me, Windsor. I've been expecting you since Perdita left, and I've prepared everything with your company in mind. We can leave at any moment. Will you come with me?"

"I will," replied Adrian. "Immediately, you mean?"

"Tomorrow, if you prefer."

"Reflect!" I cried.

"Why? On what?" asked Raymond. "My dear fellow, I've done nothing but reflect on this step all summer; and rest assured, Adrian has condensed a lifetime of reflection into his reply. Don't talk of reflection! I'll never reflect again, I swear; this is my first happy moment in ages. I must go, Lionel. The Gods will it—and I must. Don't make an effort to deprive me of my companion: Windsor, the outcast's friend!

"One word more concerning unkind, unjust Perdita. There was a time in spring, when I sought chances to rekindle the flame of your sister's love for me. I found it more cold within her than an abandoned campfire in winter, spent embers crowned by a pyramid of snow. If anything, I only succeeded in making the situation worse than before. Still, I believe that time—and absence—may restore her to me. Remember, I love her still. My dearest hope is for her to be mine again. I know, though she does not, how false a picture she's formed of reality. Don't disillusion her too quickly, let it happen by degrees. Hand her a mirror in which she may know herself, and give her time to learn to use it. When she's adept enough, she'll wonder at her present mistake, and hasten to restore to me what is rightfully mine: her forgiveness. Her kind thoughts. Her love."

(19)   AFTER these events, it took a long time for the ones our friends had left behind to regain our composure. A moral tempest had wrecked the richly freighted vessel bearing us through life together, and we, remnants of a shrunken crew, were aghast at the losses and changes we'd had to undergo.

To Idris his sister as to myself, Adrian's society was of the dearest and most necessary kind; we missed him constantly, as did all the children, whose regret over the loss of their kind playfellow was bitter. For myself, I'd been relying on his tutorship and help as I took my first serious steps towards a literary occupation. The delights of his mild philosophy, unerring reason, and enthusiastic friendship were not only the best ingredients in my progress, they were the exalted spirit of our circle itself. We needed him, and could never stop wondering when (not to mention, whether) he'd return.

Fairly quickly, Perdita became almost a shadow of herself. Bringing Clara she'd returned to us from London, her power and rank gone with her husband's Protectorate. She was furious, resentful, grief-stricken, all at once. Raymond she could not forgive, she blamed him for all her misery; at the same time, she obsessed over his welfare, consuming every account of his toils and dangers, worried day and night. Now that he was distant and exposed to peril, what happened to him was her foremost care—not that she would ever call him back from harm. She could never take him back; their union was former, irreparable; which made an anguish of its own. Before he and Adrian left, while there was still time, I'd tried everything to convince her that she must talk to Raymond and try at all costs to make him stay; but she had refused—not unless time could be reversed, she'd said, and the past erased along with his falsehood. Thus with stern pride she let him go, though her very heartstrings cracked and all sense that life was worth living seemed to go with him. Characteristically, she sought solitude over our happier family hours, and made lonely musings, interminable wanderings, and solemn music her only pastimes. Even Clara was neglected; while I, her first and always fast friend, saw reserve grow between us, as my sister shut her heart against all tenderness.

For the whole household's sake, it seemed best to get away from Windsor. My proposal for a long trip to the Lake District being accepted, we lingered for weeks at my native Ullswater, among scenes dear from a thousand associations. From the north of England we lengthened our tour into Scotland, saw Loch Katrine and Loch Lomond, then crossed to Ireland, where we spent several more weeks in the neighborhood of Killarney. The change of scene seemed to do my sister all the good I'd hoped; she was calmer, gentler, more sociable by the time we returned from our travels. But she couldn't forget. As soon as we returned, so did all the old associations; at the first sight of our Castle, she began to break down. Forest, ferns, lawns—breezes, bolts of sunlight—silvery-blue glimpses of the ancient Thames through trees that flashed like memory's very pathway—every atom of earth, air, and wave at Windsor greeted her in chorus and overwhelmed her with plaintive regret.

I was glad to be home again, for I'd begun to miss my study, my books, my writing machine. Since Adrian, in that first unforgettable summer, had drawn me from my all-encompassing wilderness to his own paradise of order and beauty, I had been wedded to literature. Books: with the world in its present state, no one, I felt, could call their faculties developed, their moral principles large enough or liberal, without an extensive acquaintance with books. To me, they took the place of an active career, of ambition, of involvement with those palpable excitements necessary to the multitude. The collation of philosophical opinions, the study of historical facts, the acquirement of languages—these were my recreation and the serious aim of my life, as well. As I've indicated, I turned author myself. My productions however were fairly minor; they were confined to biographies of favorite historical characters. I was drawn to those whom I believed to have been traduced, or about whom clung obscurity and doubt.

No one ever lived who enjoyed the pleasures of literary work more intensely than I. Music, my inspiration, was partly the cause. From the woods, the majestic temple of nature, where I sat and wrote to the solemn music of the waving branches, I'd take my way back to the Castle's vast halls and panoramic views of a fertile England spread beneath our regal mount; and there, in the musical household, inspiring strains were always to be heard. Whenever I felt my mental energies lagging, some melody would lift them, inspire them, and even permit them, methought, to penetrate the last veil of Nature and her God; at times the beauties I perceived lay at the limits of what human capacity could see or understand. On music's wings, my ideas seemed to quit their mortal dwelling in my head and fly outward to seek their own source in the skies of thought itself; I saw the creation filled with new glory, and rousing sublime imagery that would otherwise have slept unseen, voiceless, showed itself to me. Then I'd hasten to my desk, and try to weave the new-found webs with words to give them firmness, texture, brilliant colors. The fashioning of the material I'd leave to calmer moments.

As my authorship increased, I acquired new sympathies and pleasures. I had found another and a valuable link to enchain me to my fellow-creatures; my point of sight was extended, and the inclinations and capacities of all human beings became deeply interesting to me. I felt as it might to be a king: they were my people, and posterity my heirs. My thoughts were gems to enrich the universal treasure house of intellectual possessions; each sentiment was a precious gift I bestowed on the future. Let not these aspirations be attributed to vanity! Unarticulated even in my own mind, they filled my soul, exalted my thoughts, gave me an enthusiastic glow, and led me out of the obscure path I'd walked alone, into the noon-bright highway of common humanity. I was made a citizen of the world, a candidate for immortal honors, and, yes, an eager aspirant to other people's praise and sympathy.

I describe a time in my life so different from the present moment; yet often the feelings as I write are not so unlike. Then, it was the pleasure I took in literature, the discipline of mind I derived from it, that made me eager to recommend the same course to Perdita. Clearly, she needed something to fill her hours now that we were home again—something satisfying enough to make her half forget her sorrows. If not writing, then take up music again, or learn a language: she rejected all suggestions, saying she lacked the concentration. Her education had been minimal; though she'd managed, in her lonely cottage days, under the elegant and cultivated Evadne's tutelage, to develop a near-genius for painting. But now, returned to Windsor, at each attempt to paint her hand trembled, her eyes filled with tears; so she threw aside her palette and abandoned her easel. *Too many memories!* It was the same with everything she tried. Predictably, her too-idle mind preyed upon itself almost to madness.

Though she now took pleasure in being around me, Idris, Clara and the boys—her child especially enjoyed her tenderness and care in abundant measure—this was a kind of surface calm. Neither grief, philosophy, nor love could make Perdita think with mildness of Raymond's dereliction. In contrast to the weeks that had followed her arrival from London, she refused to read any communications from Greece. All she wanted was to be told when we'd had news, and whether our two wanderers were still alive and well; more than that, we weren't supposed to say. A more painful curb was the law she'd made among us never to mention Raymond's name in front of her. It was curious and sad to see that even little Clara obeyed, and never spoke of the father she dearly loved; more than sad, it was painful to watch untimely care turn a disposition from its born light-hearted mirthfulness to moods less natural and more reserved. This lovely child was nearly eight years old, graceful as one of the bounding fawns of the forest outside; her sweet complexion seemed the work of a celestial portraitist. All the troubled thought she wore on her young brow dated from her father's departure. Children, unadepts in language, seldom find words to express their thoughts; how recent events had impressed themselves on her mind, we couldn't tell. But certainly Clara had made deep observations, while noting in silence the changes happening around her. Never mentioning her father to

Perdita, she appeared half afraid to speak of him at all. I tried, unsuccessfully, to draw her out on the subject and perhaps dispel the gloom that hung about her ideas concerning him. Yet each foreign post-day the little girl watched for the arrival of letters; she knew the postmark; she watched me as I read. More than once I found her poring over illustrated articles on the Greek war in one of our newspapers.

For her beloved daughter's sake, along with her own, Perdita must take herself in hand—so I told her, exhorting, expostulating. Though never bookish, my sister had always been brainy, perceptive, creative. If she had something of interest to do, say a productive intellectual pursuit, it must soon become easier to reconcile with her present reality, and speak both openly and honestly again with her child. What's more, if she needed to forgive Raymond somewhat for this to happen, so be it: forgive him. But she rejected all such counsels. The loss of love had swallowed her whole. She grieved with an anguish that exiled all smiles from her lips; grief drew lines across her brow and down her beautiful cheeks.

But in human beings, the world had a strange animal. Forty-horsepower of forceful reasoning couldn't budge my sister from her fixed resentment; yet change she did. If the time for forgiveness wasn't yet, at least the grip in which she held her sense of injury began to loosen. Each day seemed to alter the nature of her suffering; from the unbroken black of mourning, her soul appeared to brighten its styles step by step. Music fed her starving intellect and aired out her melancholy thoughts with its variety. And in the books I'd pressed upon her, the productions of the wise, she discovered medicine for her sorrow. Reading not, as many did, for the mere sake of filling up time, Perdita read in search of truth, to improve her understanding. The gentle discipline of good books inevitably softened her heart and improved her disposition. She began to realize, that amidst all her newly acquired knowledge, her own character which she'd believed she knew through and through had emerged as terra incognita—pathless, wild, uncharted. Erringly and strangely she began the task of self-examination. She condemned herself at first. Then, as she weighed her own good qualities anew, she began to balance with fairer scales the shades of good and evil in her life. I who longed beyond words to restore her to the happiness it was still in her power to enjoy, watched with anxiety the result of these internal proceedings.

Here matters stood when, after the lapse of more than a year, Adrian returned from Greece. Only with his arrival did we learn the alarming truth, that he'd been seriously wounded. His mind was unaffected, though, and his story sobered us in our joy at seeing him again.

He and Raymond had arrived in Athens at a time of truce between the Turks and Greeks, one of those truces that treats a ceasefire like a restful nap. Both sides were renewing their energies. From its capital and closest military strongholds, Greece had pushed north, following the Aegean shore, to take back Thrace and Macedonia from Muslim control, actions which had led its armies nearly to the gates of Istanbul. In the meantime, economic diplomacy did its work; the country's extensive commercial relations gave most of Europe an interest in a Greek success. Obviously, the Turks would meet these signs of enemy strength with an immediate resolve to crush that enemy; soon, using a limitless supply of troops from the Muslim east, and all the best weapons, ships, and military means that wealth and power could command, they must try. Our exiles found the Greeks preparing to make a vigorous national resistance. There was universal conscription, and the parents left at home gave their costliest ornaments to fill the war funds; like the Spartan mothers, they sent their children off to conquer or die. Leading the Athenian division, a post that ranked second only to commander-in-chief, was Lord Raymond. His talents and courage were remembered with high esteem by all the Greeks; but Athens had claimed him for her own and awarded him that honor. The Earl of Windsor enlisted as a volunteer under his friend.

"It's fine," said Adrian now, "to chat about war in pleasant surroundings, and fun to stay up past midnight celebrating victories that have caused thousands of our fellow creatures to leave in pain the sweet air of their Mother Earth. No one can deny that I support the Greek cause; I know and feel its necessity; it is beyond doubt or comparison a good cause. I have defended it with my sword, and was willing that my spirit should be breathed out in its defense; life is worth less than freedom, and the Greeks do well to defend their privilege unto death. But let us not deceive ourselves. The Turks are human beings; they feel every wound and spasm in mind or body as keenly as a Greek; our own limbs and hearts are no more sensitive."

He'd last seen action in a victory we'd read of, over a fortified town: the Turks resisted to the last, until the Greek troops entered by assault. The rest, none of the newspapers had told us. Adrian's voice continued, "Every breathing creature within the walls was massacred. Could you think that with the shrieks of violated innocence and helpless infancy coming from every side, I felt in less than every nerve the cries of my fellow beings as they suffered? They were men and women and children, before they were Muslims, and when they rise turbanless and naked from the grave with the rest of us, in what except their good or evil actions will they be better or worse than we?

"I saw two soldiers fighting over a girl, a couple of wretches whose brutal appetites had been excited by her beauty and fine clothes; perhaps good men among their families, they'd been changed to devils by the moment's fury. An old man, decrepit, bald and silver-bearded, he might have been her grandfather, interposed to save her, and got his skull cleaved by a battle axe. Now I rushed to her defense, but rage made the soldiers blind and deaf; they couldn't see that I was in Christian dress, couldn't hear what I was saying—words were weapons too blunt, while war cried havoc, and murder gave fit echo. One of the men, enraged at my interference, struck me with his bayonet in the side, and I fell senseless.

"This wound will probably shorten my life, having shattered a frame already weak. But I am content to die. I have learnt in Greece that one person, more or less, is of small importance, while enough living bodies remain to fill up the ranks of the soldiery when they get thin. An individual's identity may be overlooked, so long as the muster roll maintains its numbers. All this has a different effect upon Raymond. He's able to contemplate the ideal of war, while I am sensible only to its realities. He's a soldier, a general. He can influence the bloodthirsty war-dogs, while I resist their propensities vainly. Of the National Assembly during the French Revolution, Burke wrote this, as I remember: *In all bodies. those who will lead must also, in a considerable degree, follow*. I cannot follow; for I do not sympathize in their dreams of massacre and glory. To follow and to lead in such a career, is the natural bent of Raymond's mind. He's always successful, and all signs point to his being able to acquire high name and station for himself, while at the same time securing liberty and a probably extended empire to the Greeks."

Perdita's state of mind wasn't helped by this account. "Yes!" she cried. "He can be great and happy without me. Would that I had a career of my own! Would that I could load some nice new-built little boat with all my hopes, energies, and desires, and launch it forth into the ocean of life, headed for one attainable point after another, with ambition or pleasure at the helm! But adverse winds detain me on shore; like Ulysses, I sit at the water's edge and weep. Only my boat even remains unbuilt. My nerveless hands can neither fell the trees nor smooth the planks."

As these words show, Adrian's return saw my sister's thoughts take a melancholy plunge. Yet his presence did the immediate good of breaking through our unnatural law of silence. It wasn't long before Perdita got used to the sound of Raymond's name again. Love returned with familiarity, and soon she'd listen avidly to all the accounts of his achievements. Clara too got rid of her restraint. Adrian and she were old play-fellows; and now, as they walked or rode together, he'd yield to her pleas and tell, for the hundredth time, some favorite story of her father's bravery, munificence, or justice.

The daily news from the battlegrounds gushed with optimism. At Windsor, we followed every exhilarating detail of Raymond's heroics, his perpetual rise in the Greeks' estimation. He himself wrote briefly now and then, letters proving how engrossed he was by the interests of his adopted country—which would have been happy, he told us, to keep the territory already won, sign a treaty, and go back to their normal life, making money; but the Turkish invasion roused a patriotic resistance. A string of victories instilled a spirit of conquest. The Greeks had begun to look on Istanbul as their own—Istanbul, which they would call Byzantium again.

The battle of Makri was fought to decide the fate of Islam in the region. The Muslims were defeated and driven entirely from the country west of the river Hebrus. Raymond was conspicuous for his conduct and choice of position in the encounter. First he led the charge of cavalry, then he pursued the fugitives across the plains of Thrace all the way to the banks of the Hebrus—a tranquil river, beside which his favorite horse was found grazing. Makri was a sanguinary battle, the loss of the Turks apparently irreparable. The many Greeks strewed upon the bloody field lay nearly forgotten, a nameless crowd, as far from consideration as the value of a victory that had cost the winning side its second-in-command.

Although his death seemed likely, Raymond was nowhere to be found among the fallen thousands. Had the Turks taken him prisoner? Where was their ransom demand, in that case? Or, finding themselves possessed at one and the same time of so illustrious a captive, and the enemy fighter most hated and feared among the Turkish ranks, had they resolved to satisfy their cruelty rather than their avarice and commit a secretive act of cold-blooded murder?

In England, where Raymond was far from forgotten, his one-time people clung eagerly to every hope that he'd survived. Since his sensational abdication, the narrow views of those in office were constantly contrasted with his political vision's magnificence and boldness—he'd understood how to change the whole system—and the end of his Protectorate was referred to with sorrow. A figure of perpetual interest and excitement, a favorite child of fortune, whose military glory cast his contemporaries in shadow, whose untimely loss eclipsed the world: this picture of Raymond dominated the day. His fate was on every mind.

At last, in May, the results of its inquiries were reported by the British ministry at Istanbul. Raymond had been captured, alive, but grievously wounded, and brought to that city. His present condition was unknown. Should he be found to have survived their notoriously cruel treatment of prisoners, his release would be demanded of the Turks with urgent diplomatic force.

The instant she heard this, my sister—who had never for a moment believed Raymond was dead—resolved to go to Greece immediately; she must arrive before the captive's return. Her duty to help nurse Raymond back to health was absolute. Our counter-reasoning and persuasion were wasted; she would endure no hindrance, no delay. In our little circle, we'd long held it as a truth, that if someone could be turned from a desperate and emotional purpose by the force of argument alone, then it was the right thing to talk them out of it; for if they were so easily dissuaded, neither the motive nor the end were of sufficient force to bear them through the inevitable obstacles. If, on the contrary, they were proof against all expostulation, this very steadiness was an omen of success; and it became the duty of those who loved them to assist in smoothing the bumps from their path. So it was that, finding Perdita immoveable, we set about discussing the best way to get her to Athens.

She couldn't go alone to a country where she had no friends, where she might arrive only to hear dreadful news which must overwhelm her with grief and remorse. Adrian, whose health had always been weak, was suffering more than ever from the effects of his wound and couldn't possibly travel. Idris could not endure to leave her brother in this state; nor was it right either that the two of us should quit or take along a young family for a journey like this. In the end, I resolved to accompany Perdita. The separation from my Idris was painful—but necessity reconciled us to it in some degree: necessity and the hope of saving Raymond and restoring him to my sister, and to happiness.

No delay was to ensue. Within forty-eight hours, we'd set off. The weather was clear for the season; we were promised a fine voyage. Embarked on the open sea, we saw with delight the receding shore of Britain and the well-filled sails above us. Light, curling waves sped us southward, and old Ocean smiled at the freight of love and hope committed to his charge; gentling his tempestuous plains with a fond stroke, he smoothed our path. Day and night a wind right aft gave steady impulse to our keel—nor did rough gale, or treacherous sand, or destructive rock interpose an obstacle between my sister and the land which was to restore her to her cherished first beloved...

Her dear heart's confessor—a heart within that heart.

(20)   LITTLE CLARA accompanied us to Greece. The poor child didn't quite understand what was going on. She'd heard where we were bound, and that she'd see her father; did this mean his name

was allowed again in Perdita's presence? She prattled it tentatively. No more rebukes: her mother smiled and caressed her.

During this voyage, while on calm evenings on deck we watched the changeful sky and the glancing waves surround our conversation with light shows in every direction, I discovered the epochal change that Raymond's disasters had wrought in my sister's mind. Likewise to the glaciers when they melted, set loose from their frozen chains, old waters of love lately cold, cutting, repellent as ice, flowed again and gushed too fast through the regions of her soul; her spirits rose on floods of grateful exuberance. Disbelieving he was dead, she was certain Raymond was in danger, and the hope of assisting in his liberation, and the idea of soothing by tenderness the ills that he might have undergone, re-harmonized the jarring element that had lately returned to her being. Not as something hoped, but securely expected, the thought of seeing the lover she had banished, the husband, friend, heart's companion from whom she had long been alienated, wrapped her senses in delight and her mind in placidity. It was beginning life again; it was leaving barren sands for an abode of fertile beauty; it was a harbor after a tempest, an opiate after sleepless nights, a happy waking from a terrible dream.

I was less sanguine than she as to the result of our voyage; and indeed, on landing at Athens we learned that Raymond's fate was still in doubt. The Turks had released no word of him. No man ever excited so strong an interest in the public mind. This had been apparent even among the phlegmatic English; but in Athens, where women taught their children to lisp his name when saying their thank-you prayers, his manly beauty, his courage, his devotion to their cause, had raised him in the popular regard nearly to the status of a god, one of their Olympian deities come down to defend his ancient soil. Naively almost as Perdita, the Athenians had expected their hero to return in triumph. Now, when they spoke of his probable death and certain captivity, tears streamed from their eyes— Athens was a city in mourning. Naturally, Lord Raymond's wife and child became objects of intense interest. The gates of their abode were besieged by the wives and mothers of Greece, all lamenting our English Raymond; through the windows came the sound of prayers breathed daylong for his restoration.

All these circumstances added to Perdita's growing dismay. From afar, she'd been able to imagine that when she set her foot on Grecian shores, all the news would turn good instantaneously. Raymond would be freed, and her tender attentions would soon entirely obliterate even the memory of his misadventure. As facts stood, she began to fear the worst. Had she risked her soul's hope on a losing chance? I wasn't there to comfort her; my own exertions to find out what I could were unremitting. When Athens yielded no more answers, I traveled to join the army stationed at Kishan in Thrace. From there, closer to Istanbul, a combination of bribery, threats, and espionage soon discovered the secret: Raymond was alive, a prisoner in that city, suffering the most rigorous confinement and wanton cruelties. Now it was a matter of employing every bit of policy and all the funds we could, to redeem him from Turkish hands.

During the two long months these negotiations consumed, my sister suffered the most painful bouts of impatience, uncertainty, repentance, and sorrow. The very beauty of the Grecian climate, Athens in spring, added torture to her sensations. The incomparable loveliness of the flower-clad land—the genial sunshine and generous shade—the melody of the birds—the majesty of the wooded hills—the splendor of the marble ruins—the clear pulsations of the night stars— the combination of all that was exciting and voluptuous in this transcendent land, by inspiring a quicker spirit of life and sensitivity inside and throughout her frame, only gave edge to her grief's poignancy. Raymond: with what eager delight he'd used to make her the partner of his joyful hopes; with what grateful affection he'd received her sympathy in his cares. Now she counted each long hour, thinking every minute, *He is suffering.* She abstained from food, she lay on the bare earth and slept on the floor, and by such mimicry tried to commune with his distant pain. I'd quoted Romantic poetry at her once, telling her that someday she'd regret casting Raymond on the thorns of life. When disappointment had sullied his beauty, when a soldier's hardships had thickened and bent his manly form, and long loneliness made even triumph bitter to him—after all this waste which could have been avoided, I'd said, she would repent; and regret for the irreparable change would *move, in hearts all rocky now, the late remorse of love.*

She remembered answering me scornfully back then. Those storm clouds of her nature were nowhere to be seen by this time. In Athens and its clear immortal light, she discovered where she'd gone wrong. And the stinging remorse of love pierced her heart.

Wasn't she the cause of his going to Greece in the first place, and thus the cause of his dangers—and his imprisonment? She pictured the anguish of his solitary confinement; she knew how much he hated being alone. But she hadn't cared, she'd left him that way. She was haunted by how often she'd heard him declare that solitude was to him the greatest of all evils, and how death itself felt more full of fear and pain when he pictured to himself a lonely grave. "*My best girl* (she could actually quote him) *relieves me from these fantasies. United to her, cherished in her dear heart, never again shall I know the misery of finding myself alone. Even if I die before you, my Perdita, treasure up my ashes till yours may mingle with mine. It is a foolish sentiment for one who is not a materialist, yet, methinks, even in the grave, that dark cell, I may feel that my inanimate dust mingles with yours, and thus have a companion in decay.*" Not long ago, in her resentful mood, she could think of these words with nothing but acrimony and satirical disdain. Here in her softened hour, their recollection took sleep from her eyes and all hope of rest from her uneasy mind.

Finally, we obtained a promise of Raymond's release. The Turks had put him through enough to look upon his recovery as impossible. Threatened with reprisals by Britain should he perish while in their hands, they delivered him up as a dying man, willingly making over to us the rites of burial.

He came by sea from Istanbul. The harbor tower fielded constant inquiries with every new sail that was spotted—until the first of May, when the gallant frigate bore in sight on a favorable wind, freighted with a treasure greater than the wealth of empires.

Before the vessel even cast anchor, the news had spread across Athens, and the whole city started to pour out through the Piraeus Gate, down the roads, through the vineyards and olive groves and plantations of fig trees, down to the harbor to see their hero rowed ashore. Along the way, the noisy joy of the populace in their brightest dress collided with the tumult of carriages and horses and contingents of soldiers; the waving of gaudy banners, and bands playing martial music, added to the high excitement of the scene—while all around us, reposing in solemn majesty and sunlight, stood the relics of ancient time. To our right the Acropolis rose high, that severe spectatress of a thousand changes, of ancient glory, Turkish slavery, and the recent restoration of dear-bought liberty; thickly strewn, adorned by climbing vegetation, lay marble tombs and cenotaphs; and the mighty dead who hovered over their monuments, beheld in our numbers and enthusiasm a renewal of the epic scenes they'd known.

I attended Perdita and Clara's closed carriage on horseback. When we reached the harbor, the entire beach as far as it stretched was covered by a seething multitude that advanced and receded in unison, urged by those behind towards the sea, only to be rushed backward as the heavy waves with sullen roars burst close to those in front. The frigate, wary of approaching nearer in this windy season, had cast anchor by now. Raising my spyglass, I could discern a boat being lowered and a rope ladder unfurled. With a pang, I saw that Raymond was unable to descend the vessel's side; wrapped in cloaks, he was let down in a chair and laid at the bottom of the tender boat.

I dismounted and immediately engaged some sailors who were tied up nearby to take me into their skiff. I heard swift footsteps on the rocky sand, then Perdita seized my arm. "Take me with you!" she cried. She was trembling and pale; Clara clung to her. I told her no: the sea was too rough, and he'd land soon anyhow—didn't she see the tender? But she was already climbing into the skiff, and the sailors assisting Clara to follow. The cheers began, and a loud hurrah echoed from the crowd as we pulled out of the inner harbor.

My sister seated herself in the prow, careless of the spray that broke over her, deaf, sightless to all, except the little speck, just visible on the top of the waves, that we were approaching with all the speed six rowers could give. The sounds of exulting music followed us. I looked back. The eager crowds on the beach, the groups of soldiers in their orderly and picturesque dress, the flags being waved and stirred by breezes, eastern dress, eastern flags, eastern breezes; the sight of temple-crowned rock, sun glittering off the white marble of the buildings set in bright relief against a wedge of far-lofting mountains; the roar of the sea in my ears, the splash of oar blades, and dash of spray, all steeped my soul in a delirium, unfelt, unimagined in the common course of common life. Trembling, I closed the spyglass. Our approach was so rapid, that soon we could make out the occupants of Raymond's boat quite clearly. Its dark sides grew big, and the splash of its oars became audible. Now I saw the languid form of my friend, rising into sight at our approach.

Perdita was panting with emotion as our rowers pulled alongside. With a huge effort, she mustered her all her strength and the last of her firmness. She stepped from one boat to the other. Then, with a shriek, she sprang towards Raymond and knelt at his side. Gluing her lips to the hand she'd seized, her face shrouded by her long hair, she gave herself up to tears.

I watched awestruck, mute. Was this man really Perdita's beloved? Sunken cheeks, hollow eyes; pale and gaunt, he could barely sit up. Then, as he looked at the poor girl sobbing beside him, he smiled at her—no, he smiled *on* her, that was the difference. As when a ray of sunshine strikes a dark valley, the way it illuminates what had been shadowed there, this smile had welcomed the Protectorate; with this same smile he'd betrothed himself to Perdita. Seeing his smile play on the altered countenance, made me feel in my heart's core that this was Raymond.

He stretched out his other hand to me; I saw the trace of manacles on his bared wrist. I heard my sister's sobs, and thought, how fortunate were people who could weep, and with passionate caresses disburden the oppression of their own feelings. I was one of those people who held back out of shame and habitual restraint, but I'd have given worlds to have acted as in boyhood days—strained him to my breast, pressed his hand to my lips, wept over him. Even now my swelling heart choked me. Without my being able to stop them, big rebellious tears gathered in my eyes; I turned aside, and they dropped in the sea—they came fast and faster. Yet I could hardly be ashamed, for the tough-featured sailors were plainly not unmoved. Raymond's eyes alone were dry. He lay in that blessed calm which convalescence always induces; secure in his liberty, reunited with her whom he adored, he basked in tranquil enjoyment.

At length my sister subdued her burst of passion and looked round for Clara. The child, frightened, not recognizing her father, and neglected by us, had crept to the other end of the skiff. We coaxed and helped her across and Perdita, finally able to speak, presented her to Raymond, saying "Beloved, embrace our child!"

But the little girl held back; until her father said, "Come, sweet one—don't you know me?" She knew his voice, and threw herself into his arms.

Perceiving Raymond's weakness, I feared the press of the crowd on our landing. But the Athenians were awed, as I had been, at his changed appearance. The music died away, the shouts went silent. Where the soldiers had cleared a space we found a carriage drawn up: Perdita and Clara followed after Raymond was placed inside, and an escort closed round its wheels. A hollow murmur, not unlike the roaring of the nearby waves, went through the multitude, which fell back as our party advanced. Lest the noisy joy they'd come to share should injure him, the onlookers satisfied themselves with bending in a low salaam as he passed unseen. The carriage went slowly up the Piraeus road, past antique temple and heroic tomb, and rolled beneath the craggy rock of the citadel. The sound of the waves was left behind; that of the multitude continued at intervals, suppressed and hoarse; otherwise, though tapestry and banners decorated every house front, church, and public building in the city, though soldiers in uniform lined the streets whose inhabitants were assembled by the thousand to cheer him, the same solemn silence prevailed. The soldiery presented arms, and the banners were lowered—though many a white hand waved a streamer. Curious eyes sought in vain to discern the hero in the vehicle, which, closed and surrounded by guards on horseback, drew him to the palace allotted for his abode.

(21)　　DESPITE his exhaustion, Raymond took proud pleasure in the interest he could see excited on his account. He was nearly killed with kindness however. True, the populace restrained themselves; but a perpetual hum and bustle rose from the throng round his palace, where, too, jingling soldiers, riders, and carriages wheeled to and fro constantly, to the sound of rifles and cannons or fireworks being set off nearby. This noisy effervescence of which he was the focus, retarded his recovery so much that we moved him out of the city to a place in Vari. Here by the seaside, each day of rest and tender care increased his strength. Perdita's zealous attention was the primary cause of his rapid recovery, followed closely by the delight he felt in the Greeks' affection and good will. We were said, humanity, to love much those whom we greatly benefited. Raymond had fought and conquered for the Athenians; he had suffered, on their account, peril, imprisonment, and hardship; their gratitude, their enthusiastic devotion, affected him deeply. He vowed to himself that their fate and his would be united forever.

All this I witnessed. My own disposition, markedly social and sympathetic, had always drawn me heart and soul into the vortex of every living drama enacted around me. Now I became aware of a difference. I loved, I hoped, I enjoyed; but I also wished to know more. My labors as a writer, a biographer, had changed me. What made the people around me behave as they did? What internal principles? Attempts to read their minds accurately preoccupied my own. Events still held my undiminished interest. But now I seemed to watch them twice; and in my mind's eye, to every person I assigned due place, to every emotion its proper balance. This undercurrent of thought would later come to soothe me amidst distress, even agony. When the soul would have revolted from the naked truth of misery and disease, when despair over deplorable changes threatened, it gave me a mental refuge in picture-making. Those beach villa days roused this faculty, or instinct: I watched my sister's reawakened devotion; little Clara's shy but fierce admiration of her father; and his appetite for renown, and responsiveness to the Athenians. Attentively perusing this animated tale, I was the less surprised at what I read on the next page.

Advancing along the Sea of Marmara, the Greeks had captured a port city they called Rodosto, which the Turks wanted back; their army had it under siege. Athens and the rest of the country had been sending reinforcements every day, and preparations were on for a decisive battle. Should they gain the victory, the Greeks' next move would be a short march east, for an attack and siege on Istanbul.

Stimulated by love of the Greek people, appetite for glory, and hatred of the barbarian government under which he had suffered even to the verge of death, Raymond, somewhat recovered, began preparing to take up his command again.

Far from opposing him, Perdita only stipulated that she be permitted to come along with the army. She trusted that Raymond's high command would exempt them both from danger in battle or siege. One thing alarmed her: as yet, no more than an alarming word—but the word was **PLAGUE**. This enemy to the human race had raised its serpent head early that spring in Egypt, and from the Nile shores had begun to spread. Regions not usually subject to its evil were infected. It was in Istanbul; but they had plague there every year, and small attention was being paid to reports of a death toll already higher than usually seen through the whole of the hotter months. Neither plague nor war could prevent Perdita from following her lord, though, or induce her to do other than acquiesce cheerfully in all his projects. If he wished to repay the kindness of the Athenians, to keep alive the splendid associations connected with his name, and to eradicate from Europe a power which, while every other nation advanced in civilization, stood stock still, a monument of antique barbarism, then she was with him. To be near him, to be loved by him, to feel him again her own, was the limit of her desires. The object of her life was to afford him pleasure. She'd used to please him without thinking, only by being herself; she'd been accustomed, in any question of choice, to consult her own wishes, as being identical to his own. Now she sedulously put herself out of the question, sacrificing even her anxiety for his health and welfare to her resolve not to offer a breath of opposition.

Having reunited my sister's family, I was eager to return to England; but at Raymond's earnest request I agreed to travel east with them and stay until autumn. My curiosity had been awakened, too. I felt an indefinable anxiety to behold the catastrophe, now apparently at hand, in the long-drawn history of warfare between Christian Greek and Muslim Turk.

Our regiments quitted Athens as soon as Raymond's health allowed, on the 2nd of June. He'd lost the gaunt and pallid looks of fever. If I no longer saw the fresh glow of youth on him; if care had acted on him as in Shakespeare's second sonnet, besieged his brow and dug deep trenches in his beauty's field; if the grey streaks in his hair and the consideration in his look, even when zealous, were signs of maturity and past sufferings, yet there was something irresistibly affecting in the sight of someone, lately snatched from the grave, renewing his career, untamed by sickness or disaster.

We had a six-week march ahead of us. All Athens accompanied us for several kilometers. At their hero's landing a month ago, the noisy populace had been hushed by sorrow and fear; but this was a universal festival day. The air resounded with shouts; gaily colored costumes flaunted picturesquely in the sunshine. Everyone was gesturing, talking: Raymond was the theme of every tongue, the hope of every loving heart tied to a husband, wife, child, or lover off fighting in the Greek army, that he'd lead them to victory and home.

Inspired by the intense sensations of recovered health, Raymond discoursed freely. He felt that in commanding the Athenians, he at last filled a post worthy of his ambition; for he'd be leading them in the conquest of Istanbul—a towering landmark event in human history, an exploit unequalled, unprecedented. Byzantium, as the city would again be known, a place of the most venerable associations, a site whose beauty was a wonder of the world, for many hundred years a Muslim stronghold, must be rescued from slavery and barbarism, and given back to its founders—the people of Greece, that is, a people illustrious for genius, civilization, and a spirit of liberty. To all this Perdita listened in delight, resting on his restored society, on his love, his hopes and fame, like a sybarite on a luxurious couch.

Our journey to its hazardous object was full of romantic interest, as we passed through the valleys and over the hills of this divine country. The weather during our journey was serene. Each day before dawn we left our night's encampment, and watched the shadows retreat from the land before the golden splendor of the day star's approach. The troops of soldiers, with Athenian vivacity, derived enthusiastic pleasure from the natural beauty around us. Starting with the triumphant strains that hailed each rising of the sun, music poured from their ranks almost like birdsong as they marched the morning restlessness of spirit away. At noon, our tents pitched in some shady valley or embowering wood among the mountains, a stream prattling over pebbles would induce grateful sleep. Our evening march, less intense, offered more plentiful delights, as the bands played airs of moderated passion—a farewell to love, or lament at absence—before closing on some solemn hymn which harmonized with the tranquil loveliness of evening, and elevated the soul to grand and religious thought. Often all sounds were suspended, that we might listen to the nightingale, while the fireflies danced in bright measure, and the soft cooing of the scops owls (we called them aziolo) spoke of fair weather for travelers. From valleys where mild shades encompassed us, and rocks tinged with beauteous hues, we climbed to heights that showed Greece, a living map, spread beneath us. *Her renowned pinnacles cleave the ether; her silvery rivers thread the fertile land; far off, ever-present, the blue Aegean:* afraid almost to breathe in our ecstasy, we English people surveyed this splendid landscape, so different from the sober hues and melancholy graces of our native scenery.

Descending from Macedonia into Thrace, we found the country folk of its low plains quick to do honor to Lord Raymond. An advanced guard gave word of our approach, and we entered their villages through triumphal arches of greenery or blazing lamplight; tapestry waved from the windows, the ground was strewed with flowers, and the name of Raymond, joined to that of Greece, was echoed in the people's cheers.

We reached the Greek camp ahead of schedule, on the 7th of July. Alert to our approach, the Turks had retreated from the Rodosto siege; but after meeting with reinforcements, they'd turned around to try again. In the meantime, Argyropylo, the Greek commander-in-chief, had advanced so as to be in the Turks' path to Rodosto; a battle, it was said, was inevitable. Raymond offered me a choice. Perdita and their child were to remain in the town nearby, a place called Kishan. Would I prefer to stay with them?

"Now, by the hills of Cumberland," I cried, "by every bit of vagabond and poacher that lives in me, I will stand at your side, draw my sword in the Greek cause, and be hailed as a victor along with you, Raymond!"

My sword, as it turned out, was not required. Every garrison within reach had been emptied to swell our forces; Greek troops filled the entire plain from Kishan to the coast. We met trains of civilian baggage wagons on the way, and many families, of high rank and low, heading out of battle range to await the issue in safety. At Rodosto we found the scheme of the battle arranged. Having taken the field, the armies camped overnight; early the next morning, the sound of firing told us they'd engaged. Now regiment after regiment advanced, colors flying, bands playing.

I could not have counted how many descriptions of battles I'd read by then, in all my years of leisured study and serious research; when I would picture a spot, plain as a table, and soldiers small as chess pieces, and be able to perceive the science and order behind the disposition of forces. In reality, I beheld regiments file off to the left, far out of sight. Fields intervened between my view of the main battalions. I could see almost no fighting.

I decided to keep a close eye on Raymond instead. He showed himself collected, gallant, imperial; his commands were prompt, his intuition of events seemingly miraculous. Early in the day, Argyropylo was wounded, and Raymond assumed command of the whole army. My chance to witness and understand a battle arrived, as I followed him and his aides-de-camp to the observation post, set on the highest mound among a line of tumuli (sites of old burials, their age uncertain) on which the Greek cannon were planted for best advantage, these being the only elevated points on that level plain. The cannon roared; the band music still raised its cheery voice at intervals above the shouts and clamor; Raymond, spyglass raised, issued a series of orders. I wondered at his ability: all I perceived was a thick stew of dust and smoke, from which regimental banners and flagstaffs peeked out now and then. Of the fallen sheaves already gathered into death's storehouse, I could see no sign.

Lord Raymond peered through his glass, and doubt crossed his face like a cloud. Then all at once he turned radiant. Triumph in his voice, he cried:

"The day is ours—the Turks fly from the bayonet!"

And with the swiftness of his command for a cavalry charge, the enemy was routed. The cannon ceased to roar. Pursued on horseback, the remains of the Turkish army made a wholesale retreat across the dreary plain.

In the busy aftermath of victory, Raymond dispersed his staff in various directions to make observations and bear commands. Ordered to climb the northernmost tumulus and see if any enemy detachments might have escaped that way, I found myself spurring my horse towards a distant part of the battlefield, across level ground. Waving lines of mountains ringed long stretches of a far-off horizon. There had been so much fighting in this part of Thrace for so many years, that the land wasn't cultivated, and presented a dreary, barren appearance. From atop the mound, when I reached it, I could see the terrain was unvaried by the least irregularity, only marked by undulations that resembled the figures of waves. The whole Turkish army, followed by the Greek, had poured eastward; none but the dead remained in the direction of my assignment. I looked far round—all was silent and deserted. In the distance, across the glittering Sea of Marmara, the Asiatic coast lay in a low cloud haze.

The last beams of the sinking sun flared across the scene at my feet, as burnished helmets, bayonets, and swords fallen from dead arms, reflected those departing rays; flashes scattered far and near. From the east a band of ravens, old inhabitants of the Turkish cemeteries, came sailing along towards their harvest. The sun disappeared. This hour, melancholy yet sweet, has always seemed to me the time when we are most naturally led to commune with higher powers. Our mortal intransigence departs, and gentle complacency invests the soul. But now, in the midst of this carnage, these dead, how could a thought of heaven or a sense of tranquility touch me, one of the murderers? During that eventful day, my mind had yielded itself a willing slave to the events and the mindset around me; I'd been swayed by a long-standing hatred for an historical enemy, and held fascinated by my first view of real-life battle. Now, from where the soft, calm evening star hung pendulous in the sunset's orange hues, I turned my eyes to the corpse-strewn earth and felt ashamed of my species. So perhaps were the placid skies; for they quickly veiled themselves in mist, hastening the swift extinction of twilight usual in these latitudes. Heavy cloud-masses, their edges shot with red and turbid lightning, rolled up from the southeast; a rushing wind that disturbed the garments of the dead was chilled as it passed across their icy forms. Night gathered round; the objects about me became indistinct. I descended from my station, and with difficulty guided my horse so as to avoid the slain.

With a piercing shriek, a form seemed to rise from the earth and fly at me, then sink to the ground again as it drew near. All this happened so suddenly that I had trouble reining my horse so as not trample on this prostrate being. A soldier, not in body armor; a woman, as her shrieks which kept on told me. I dismounted to her aid. Hand to her side, groaning heavily, she resisted my attentions. In the flurry of the moment I started soothing her not in Greek but English. The sound produced a wild and terrific exclamation from the dying soldier—yes, Evadne. "*Raymond!*" She recognized the language of her lover, but understood nothing I said: the painful effects of her grievous battle wound had deranged her intellect.

I unhooked and lit a small lantern from my saddle. The only time I'd seen her, she'd far surpassed the portrait Adrian carried: eighteen, beautiful as poet's vision, splendid as a Sultana. Twelve years later—twelve years of change, sorrow, hardship—Evadne's brilliant complexion had coarsened; her limbs had lost the roundness of youthful womanhood; her eyes had sunk deep; yet I knew her at once. Who did she mistake me for? Her piteous cries and feeble efforts to escape, penetrated me with compassion. In wild delirium she called out Raymond's name, accused me of keeping him from her, while the Turks could kill him at any moment in their torture chambers. Her voice fell, and I heard her lamenting her hard fate; that she, as a woman, as an artist, should be driven by hopeless love and vacant hopes to take up the trade of arms, and suffer almost beyond endurance so many months of privation, labor, bodily pain. Was it the news of Raymond's capture that caused her to enlist, I asked? Her dry, hot hand pressed mine. I offered water. A fever had set in; her brow and lips burned with consuming fire.

As her strength grew less, I lifted her from the ground; her emaciated form hung over my arm. She rested her sunken cheek on my breast and murmured in a sepulchral voice, "This is the end of love." A few moments passed. Then frenzy lent her strength, and she raised an arm to point at heaven:

"Yet not the end! *There* is the end—there we meet again! Many living deaths have I borne for you, Raymond. And now I die, one final time, your victim to the last.

"Fire, War, Plague—be my instruments! I dared, I conquered you all, till now! I have sold myself to death, with the sole condition that you, Raymond, follow me. Fire, and War, and Plague—unite for his destruction!"

Her arm fell back.

"O my Raymond, there is no safety for you in this life now."

Night advanced and the temperature kept dropping. I made Evadne as comfortable as I could with the cloaks I had about me. Her violence was over. I felt her clammy brow; death was near. Her delirium continued brokenly. She predicted a speedy meeting with her beloved in the grave; his death was nigh, almost at hand—for he'd been summoned, she said. At the last, she bewailed his hard destiny. Her voice grew feebler; a few convulsive movements, and her muscles relaxed, the limbs fell, no more to be sustained; one deep sigh, and life was gone.

I bore this monument of human passion and human misery away from the mass of dead; wrapped in cloaks, I placed her beneath a tree, and heaped over her body all the heavy branches and stones I could find, to guard against scavengers, until I could give her a fitting grave. Sadly and slowly I left the heaps of slain behind, and, guided by the twinkling lights of the town, at length reached Rodosto.

(22)   I FOUND the town full of tumult. The army was already ordered to march on Istanbul, and troops filled every thoroughfare with their steady departure. Argyropylo's wound was severe, and Raymond continued as first in command. Tireless, he spent all night visiting the wounded, seeing to details, and giving orders for the siege he had in mind. The whole army was on the move at daybreak. With no opportunity to speak to Raymond first, I chose one assistant and hurried off to bestow the last offices on Evadne Zaimi. The dazzling sun and glare of daylight deprived the scene of proper solemnity. We dug a deep grave for her at the foot of the tree, and without disturbing her warrior shroud, placed her in it; we heaped the fresh earth with stones. From Evadne's low tomb, I joined Raymond and his staff on

their way to the Pearl of the Bosphorus.

Istanbul under siege. The entire Greek fleet blockades it by sea; the Greeks hold Pera, too, across the Golden Horn. The old city, a crowded peninsula enclosed within walls built by Greek emperors, is all of Europe that the Muslims have left to call their own; they've destroyed the Galata Bridge with explosives to cut off one approach. Our army look on Istanbul as certain prey. Watchers tally the enemy garrison, whose relief is impossible. When even their triumphs do the Turks irreparable damage with every loss of fighters, every skirmish is a victory for Greece. Our manifold siege trenches and engines encircle the whole line of the ancient walls, just as did the armies and cannon of Mehmet the Conqueror, over six centuries ago.

One morning I rode out with Raymond to a piece of high ground not far from the Top Kapi or so-called Cannon Gate, close to the walls' midway point where, in 1453, the Ottoman Turks finally breached and entered Constantinople, and the last Byzantine emperor died. The plain surrounding us was dotted with cemeteries pillared with cypress trees, where Turk, Greek, and Armenian went their separate ways. Camped among woods of more cheerful aspect, squadrons of the Greek army could be seen moving to and fro in drill formations. Raymond's eyes were fixed on the city, whose lofty domes and minarets towered above the ramparts and their mantles of ivy and weeds.

"I have counted the hours of her life," said he. "This so-called Istanbul. One month, and she falls. Remain with me till then, Lionel; wait and see the cross returned to Hagia Sophia; and then go back home to your peaceful glades."

"You," I asked, "remain—in Greece, then?"

"Certainly. Yet believe me when I say this, I look back and regret ever leaving our tranquil life at Windsor. I am but half a soldier; I love the renown, but not the profession of war." He shook his head. "Before Rodosto, I was full of hope and spirit. To win that battle, and then take Istanbul, felt like the ultimate dream, a fulfillment of my highest ambition. But my enthusiasm is gone, I don't know why. I seem to myself to be descending a lightless chasm. The ardent spirit of the army that I loved is irksome to me now, the rapture of triumph, extinct in me."

He stood lost in thought. Perceiving some kind of likeness between their attitudes that called her to mind, I asked him, "From the time you returned to Greece, have you heard anything of the Princess Evadne?" He gave a start and eyed me uneasily. "Or," I continued, "you might have seen someone resembling her—perhaps among the troops?"

"Yes!" he cried. "I knew her name was coming. Long, long I had forgotten her. But since we arrived here, she visits my thoughts daily, hourly. Whenever people speak to me, in every message I receive, I expect her to be mentioned. At last you've broken the spell; tell me what you know of her."

I described our encounter on the battlefield. He asked to hear the details of Evadne's death more than once. His questions concerning her prophetic curse upon him were painfully serious. When I tried to treat her words as the ravings of a maniac—for the Greek had been maddened by pain, at least—he stopped me. "No, no, don't deceive yourself," he said. "Me, you cannot deceive. She has said nothing I didn't already know: you've only provided confirmation. Fire, the sword, and plague! They may all be found in yonder city. On my head alone may they fall."

From this day Raymond's melancholy increased. Whenever his duties allowed, he secluded himself; forced into company, he couldn't keep sadness from stealing over his features, and would sit absent and mute no matter how busy the crowd that thronged about him. Perdita rejoined him around this time, and he forced himself to appear cheerful with her, for she was like a mirror that changed as he changed; when he grew silent or anxious, she'd ask why and start seeking remedies. She and Clara were quartered some distance up the Bosphorus from the siege, in the Sultan's now-unused summer palace. This delightful, scenic spot, undefiled by war, overlooked a pleasure garden known as the Sweet Waters of Asia, where a wide fresh stream flowed into the salt blue strait. Raymond joined them there; but for him could be no pleasure in any sight on heaven or earth. He continued solitary, often taking a little sailboat out alone onto the limpid waters, where he floated idly, musing. Sometimes I joined him. He'd seem relieved to have company at first. I could get him to discuss the affairs of the day with some degree of interest. I could get him to begin upon the subject of his current despondency—but just when he'd seem poised to speak of what was nearest his heart, he'd always turn away; with a sigh, he'd try and fail to consign some painful idea to the winds. Then he'd fall into dejection.

One evening a number of Greek chieftains were invited for supper. The intriguing Palli, the accomplished Karazza, the warlike Ypsilanti, all three were present, talking of the day's events. A skirmish at noon with the Infidels, as they called the Turks, had not only defeated and put them to flight, but also diminished their dwindling numbers. Though still ferocious in appearance, the enemy troops, they thought, had looked wasted, haggard. It couldn't be long now. At first, Raymond played an active part in the discussion, offering lively remarks on the extremities to which Istanbul had been reduced. Famine and pestilence were at work for Greece, he observed, and the infidels would soon be obliged to take refuge in their only hope: "Submission!"

Up went a shout of agreement from the chieftains, who shared lofty dreams about the national prosperity of Greece once Byzantium was reestablished as its eastern capital. The interesting topic of trade gave way to news from Asia, and the ravages plague was making in that continent's chief cities. And in Istanbul, besieged, how far had it progressed? From Raymond came no answer: in the midst of his harangue, he'd suddenly broken off, as if stung by some painful thought; rising uneasily, he'd left the table, then the room. The discussion—and the flow of wine—continued without him.

He didn't return; but soon little Clara crept up and gave my arm an unobtrusive tug. She had a habit of taking me aside when her Papa had gone off alone. "Can we go find him?" she'd say. "He'll be glad to see you." She always knew the fugitive's whereabouts; and so it proved tonight. I took her little hand and let her lead me to the Sultan's dock, where Raymond was just about to embark for a sail. He readily agreed to receive us as companions.

After the hot windless day, a cooling land breeze ruffled the current, filled the canvas, and bore us away from the old city, dark to our south. We drifted up the sweet waters whose reposing banks, lined with lamp-light, appeared to float among sparkling reflections; the night possessed a dower of loveliness that might have characterized a retreat in Paradise. A single deckhand attended to the sail while Raymond steered. Clara, snuggled against him, fell fast asleep. My own drowse was broken by Raymond, who spoke abruptly:

"This, my friend," he said, "could be our last chance to talk. Now that my plans are in full operation, my time will become more and more occupied. So I want to tell you everything now, at once, and then never return to these painful subjects again. First, I must thank you, Lionel, for having remained here at my request. I asked it out of vanity, to be frank; yet even here, I see the hand of fate at work. Your presence will soon be necessary; you will become Perdita's last resource, her protector and consoler. You'll take her back to Windsor—"

"Not without you!" I broke in. "You don't mean to separate again?"

"Don't deceive yourself," Raymond answered. "The separation at hand is one over which I have no control. But near at hand it is; the days are already counted. May I trust you, Lionel? So many times I've longed to tell you about these mysterious presentiments that weigh on me; but I was afraid you'd ridicule them. Please don't, my gentle friend. As childish and unwise as they certainly are, they've become part of what defines me.

"Of course, I can't expect you to sympathize. You are of this world; I am not. Your hand that you hold out is Lionel's hand; not a piece of mortal form divided from your actual self. How then can you understand me? Earth is to me a tomb, the firmament a vault shrouding mere corruption. Time is no more, for I have crossed the threshold of eternity; where I am, each person I meet appears as the corpse they're soon to become, deserted of an animating spark, on the brink of decay and corruption." Mournfully, he quoted the lines ending, "*cada soldado un esqueleto vivo,*" from Calderón's La vida es sueño.

"A dream indeed," he sighed. "Yes, my soldiers appear like living skeletons to me now. A few months ago," he continued, "I was thought to be dying; but life was strong within me. My human affections, hope and love, fueled me like the sun. Now? Our guests tonight, future conquerors of the infidel faith, dream of wearing laurel wreaths; they talk of honorable rewards to come, of titles, power, wealth. All I ask of Greece is a grave. Let them raise a mound above my lifeless body; let it still be standing when the dome of Hagia Sophia has fallen."

It was useless to object or question him. He didn't pretend to account for his mood by any particular event. At his first sight of Istanbul, all joy had begun to depart from his life. My account of Evadne's curse had sealed his death warrant. "Perhaps I've caught the plague," he said lightly. "Disease may be causing my prognostications. Why or wherefore I'm affected doesn't matter. The shadow of Fate's uplifted hand already darkens me—no power can avert the stroke.

"To you, Lionel, I entrust your sister and her child. Never mention to her the fatal name of Evadne Zaimi. It would double her sorrow to know of the strange link that enchains me to that woman, making my spirit obey her dying voice and follow her, as it is about to do, into the unknown country."

I listened with wonder, and was still considering whether to respond with some gentle but bracing derision when Clara broke out crying. Raymond's prophecy of his own death had terrified the poor child. Her father, who'd forgotten her presence, was moved by her violent grief; he took her in his arms and soothed her, but with too much solemnity to calm her fears. "Weep not, sweet child," said he, "the coming death of one you've hardly known. I may die, but in death I can never forget or desert my own Clara. In your sorrows or joys to come, believe that your father's spirit is near, to save or sympathize with you. Be proud of me, and cherish your memories of me. Thus, sweetest, I shall not seem to die. One thing you must promise, never to speak to anyone but your uncle Lionel about the conversation you've just overheard. When I am gone, you will console your mother, and tell her that death was only bitter because it divided me from her; that my last earthly thoughts will be spent on her. But while I live, promise not to betray me; promise, my child."

Clara promised, through her tears, and clung to her father in a transport of sorrow all the way back to shore; while I sought to treat what he'd said lightly and somehow ease her mind. We heard no more of Raymond's fears, in any case. The final days of the siege were about to engage all his time and attention.

The empire of the Muslims in Europe is at its close. With Greek ships blockading every port, no help can reach Istanbul from Asia. By land there's no way out. Each desperate skirmish in the shadow of Constantine's walls only reduces the number of Turks, while making no impression on our lines. Their garrison is now so much diminished that if we stormed it now, we could carry the city with ease. Humanity and policy both dictate a slower mode of proceeding. Who could doubt that in the fury of contending triumph and defeat, its palaces, its mosques and fabled stores of wealth would be destroyed? The defenseless citizens have already suffered enough; why unleash a storm of rampage and massacre in which beauty, infancy, and old age must all be sacrificed alike to the brutal ferocity of soldiers? Famine and blockade are infallible means of conquest; and on these we rest our hopes of victory.

But our advance posts are assaulted every day, and our trench-digging impeded constantly; dozens of fire-boats strike at our naval forces without warning. Our troops sometimes recoil from the devoted courage of fighters who did not seek to live, but to sell their lives dear. The difficulties of combat on such terms are aggravated by the season: high summer. From deserts south, a steady Asiatic wind bears us intolerable heat. Shallow stream beds lie dried up; beyond the Topkapi Palace heights, meanwhile, the vast basin of the sea is one molten glow under the solsticial sun's unmitigated rays. Nor does night refresh the earth. Dew is denied; herbage and flowers there are none; the very trees droop; and summer assumes the blighted appearance of winter, abridging humanity's means of sustenance. In vain does the eye pierce the oppressive and windless atmosphere, and strive to find the wreck of some northern cloud in the stainless empyrean, some hopeful harbinger of moisture. All is serene, burning, annihilating.

For the besiegers, the woods offer shade. Good running sources supply the whole army with water; indeed, one detachment is employed in furnishing it with ice, some of it trekked from the mountains of Macedonia. Refreshing fruits and wholesome food keep up the strength of our forces, and help us stand the unrefreshing air. But things are different inside the walls, where the sun's rays are refracted from acres of pavements and buildings of pale and white stone—where the public fountains have stopped—where the scarceness of the food has turned worse than its quality. For the inhabitants, an extreme state of suffering is further aggravated not only by the scourge of disease, but by the city's own defenders; for the garrison commandeers resources and its soldiers range at will, adding by waste and riot to the necessary evils of the time. Still the Turks won't capitulate.

Then we see a sudden change in the system of warfare. We experience no more assaults; we labor on our works unimpeded. Stranger still, a troop advance finds the city walls apparently vacant, with no cannon pointed in readiness. Everyone by now has heard about what happened overnight at sea. The watch on one of the vessels anchored near the Topkapi's harem walls, roused by a slight splashing sound—muffled oars—raised the alarm. In twelve small boats, a band of Turkish fighters was attempting to sneak through our fleet to the opposite shore at Scutari. Once spotted, they started firing, some giving cover to others whose boats sped off, trying to escape from among the high dark hulls that filled the way. In the end, they were all sunk and their crews drowned, with the exception of a few prisoners. The results of questioning hinted that several similar expeditions had already conveyed persons of rank and importance to safety in Asia. For their own part, when taunted with having abandoned the defense of their city, the captured fighters reacted with disdain. Witnesses heard the younger one cry:

"Take it, Christian dogs! Take the palaces, the gardens, the mosques, the abode of our fathers. And take pestilence with them! Plague is the enemy we flee; if she's a friend to you, go, hug her to your bosoms. Allah's curse is on Istanbul—go share her fate."

A murmur is rising: the city is the prey of pestilence. A mighty power, not ours, has already subjugated its inhabitants. Death has become lord here.

Needless to say, from the first report of the enemy's emptied positions, Raymond had been busy collecting intelligence. He'd even gone to Pera to look for himself through the Galata Tower's high-powered telescope, adding his own minute observations to those of his scouts. The silent city looked desolate. He commanded the army to be drawn out before the walls.

Now we stood again on the height overlooking the Cannon Gate.

The ramparts remained vacant and the massive city gates themselves, though locked and barred, appeared unguarded. No calls to prayer sounded over the countless domes and glittering crescents that pierced heaven within. Their every ivy-crowned tower and weed-tangled buttress a survivor of ages and witness of history, those old walls might as well have been rocks in an uninhabited waste. Neither shout nor cry, nothing but the occasional howling of a dog, broke the high noon stillness; for even our soldiers were awed to silence. The bands had paused their playing; the clang of arms was hushed, though whispers wondering at the meaning of this sudden peace traveled up and down the lines. Suspecting an enemy stratagem, Raymond changed spyglasses. He saw empty house terraces, empty everything. Not a single shadow moved; not even the trees waved, but copied the architecture in a mocking, immobile show. Completely vacant, intact and unharmed, Istanbul was his. He lowered the glass and descended the hill with a face beaming triumphantly.

Had the myriad Muslim troops of Asia been able to come to the city's relief, I am convinced that each and every Greek in the army would have marched against those overwhelming numbers, all fired with patriotic fury for their country and her cause. But here no hedge of bayonets opposed itself, no death-dealing artillery, no formidable array of brave soldiers. The unguarded walls afforded easy entrance, the vacant palaces offered luxurious shelter and spoils; only there, hovering in the sky above it all, the superstitious, awe-struck Greek forces saw Plague, and shrank in trepidation.

Their general, actuated by far other feelings, raised his sword's point at the great gate, commanding his troops to down the barricades—their last obstacle to total victory. At his cheerful words, the soldiers drew back instinctively; they looked aghast. Raymond rode in front of the lines to address them. "By my sword I swear that no ambush awaits you. There is no danger! The enemy is already vanquished. The pleasant and the famous places, the noble dwellings and spoils of the city are already yours. Force the gate; enter and possess the treasured seat of your ancestors—Byzantium, your own inheritance!" An universal shudder and fearful whispering greeted this exhortation. Not one soldier moved.

"Cowards!" cried Raymond. "Give me an axe—I'll go in by myself. I'll plant your flag. Maybe when you see it waving from the highest minaret in there, you'll gain some courage and rally round it!"

One of his officers stepped forward and answered him. "General, we neither fear the Muslims' courage nor their arms; neither an open attack, nor a secret ambush. We are ready to expose our breasts, exposed ten thousand times before, to the infidels' bullets and scimitars, and to fall gloriously for Greece. But we will not die in heaps, like dogs poisoned in summertime, for having breathed the pestilential air of that city—we dare not go against the plague!"

A multitude of people remains feeble and inert, without a voice, a leader; give them that, and they regain the strength belonging to their numbers. Shouts from a thousand voices now tore through the air—applause became universal. Raymond perceived the danger. He was willing to save his troops from the crime of disobedience; for he knew that between commander and army, contention once begun would inexorably weaken the first and empower the latter. This was no time or place to lose control. He gave orders for the retreat to be sounded, and the regiments returned in good order to their camps.

(23)   I HASTENED back to the Küçüksu Palace to tell my sister of these strange events. Raymond, when he joined us, looked gloomy and perturbed. Perdita's greeting did nothing to improve his mood.

"The decrees of heaven," she exclaimed, "are wondrous and inexplicable beyond all our imagining!"

"Foolish girl," he retorted, "are you like my valiant soldiers, then? Panic-struck? What is so inexplicable? Pray, tell me. We know the plague is rampant across Asia; we know it strikes Istanbul every year. To what would have been high numbers anyhow, you add siege, shortage, extreme heat and drought—of course the death toll looks worse than usual. But it's not plague—by the God that lives! It's neither pestilence nor impending danger that makes us abstain from the ready prey, like birds in harvest-time, terrified by a scarecrow. It is only the Greeks' base superstition."

He began pacing the length of the seraglio's marble hall. His very lips were pale with rage and quivered while they shaped his angry words; his eyes shot fire as he went on: "And thus the valiant lose the field to fools, and high-souled worthy ambition is made the plaything of tame rabbits! Istanbul shall be ours yet, though. By my past labors, I swear it; by my torture, by my imprisonment, by my victories, by my sword, I swear; by my hopes of fame, and by whatever I've earned of eternal reward, I deeply vow—with these hands to plant the cross on the first mosque I reach inside those city walls!"

"Dearest Raymond!" Imploringly, my sister tried to interrupt.

"Perdita," he overrode her. "I know what you want to say; I know that you love me, that you are good and gentle; but this is not your field. You have no conception of how strong a hurricane is tearing me to pieces!" Looking half afraid of his own violence, he dashed from the hall. Perdita signaled me to follow.

I found him with his passions in a state of inconceivable turbulence. His dog watched from a crouch nearby. "Will Fortune toy with me forever?" he cried. "Must the individual, the heaven-climber, always fall victim to the crawling reptiles of the human species? When I was young I prayed to become one of those people who make the pages of world history splendid; who exalt the human race, and turn this little globe into a dwelling of the mighty. Alas, for Raymond! the prayer of his youth is wasted—the hopes of his manhood are null."

I kept pace with him as he strode up and down the garden, and listened as he continued: "Were I like you, Lionel, looking forward to many years of life, to unbroken chains of love-enlightened days, to refined enjoyments and fresh-springing hopes, I might yield, and resign my generalship, and come back home with the rest of you to seek repose among Windsor's glades. But I am about to die!—no, don't interrupt me.

"Soon I shall die. From the living earth, from all human sympathy, from the favorite haunts of my youth, from the kindness of my friends, from the affection of my only beloved Perdita, I am about to be removed. Such is the will of fate. This is the decree of the High Ruler from whom there is no appeal: to whom I submit.

"But to lose all—to lose with life and love, glory too! No—it shall not be!

"I, and in a relatively brief time, everyone alive—this panic-struck army included, and the whole population of our fair Greece—will be gone. But other generations will arise in their place, who across the ages and forever will continue to be made happier by what we do today, and to feel glorified by our present valor.

"From my dungeon in yonder city, I swore I'd be its ruler someday. How can I stand before its vanquishment, and not dare call myself a conqueror? I must act! Didn't Alexander the Great, in the Punjab, seize the first ladder and climb the citadel walls alone to meet its defenders' swords, showing his coward troops the way to victory? Even so will I brave the plague—and if no one follows me, I'll still plant the Grecian standard, yes, atop the Hagia Sophia."

Before Raymond was called away to a staff meeting, I reasoned with him in vain. Alexander's death, I reminded him, had been much hastened by his wound from that affray. Why not hold off a while? Winter temperatures, I said, would dissipate the pestilential air, and restore courage to the Greeks.

"Don't talk to me of cold weather!" he cried. "I've lived my last winter. This year's date, 2092, will be carved on my tomb." He gave the sky a long, mournful regard. "Already I perceive," he said, "the bourn of my existence, a precipitate edge over which I will plunge into the gloomy mystery of the life to come. I am prepared, so long as I leave behind a trail of light so radiant that my worst enemies cannot cloud it. I owe this to Greece, to you, to my Perdita—and to myself, Ambition's victim."

Alas! for human reason! Raymond accused the Greeks of superstition: what name did he give to the faith he lent to Evadne's dying words? So ran the thoughts with which I made my way, at his request, from the lawns of Sweet Waters to the scorched precincts of the encampment, my task to observe the soldiers and report to him about their mindset. I found commotion and swirling rumor. Marvelously exaggerated and embroidered, the day-old story about the fleet's latest prisoners had been linked to tales of prophecies from centuries past; fearful accounts of whole regions currently laid waste by pestilence alarmed the troops as well. Discipline was lost. I saw the army begin to disband itself. Each individual, formerly part of a great whole, moving only in unison with others, now reverted to the original, natural unit of one, and thought of self alone. The soldiers stole off at first singly and in pairs, then in larger companies, until, unimpeded by their officers, whole battalions sought the road back through Thrace.

By midnight I was across the Bosphorus again. Raymond met me alone at the palace and received my report calmly. He said, "You know, Verney, my fixed determination not to quit this place until Istanbul is fully ours. If these soldiers shrink from following me, others, more courageous, can be found." Then he handed me some dispatches and ordered me to bring them to Karazza; I must tell the sea chieftain that her help was needed at the city walls. Raymond needed fighters. If just one regiment were seen to follow him, he said, the soldiers who remained would follow along as a matter of course. If I left before daybreak, Karazza's marines might be on their way to him tomorrow; I must return with word of their dispatch by noon.

I left him with assurances of my obedience and zeal; but his plan left me skeptical, and I was weary. I decided to take a few hours rest. With the break of day I rose, dressed to leave, and lingered. I wanted to talk to Perdita first. The sun began to rise outside my window, a golden splendor. Weary nature awoke to suffer yet another day of heat and drought. No dew fell to cool the petals of the wilting flowers; the dry grass had withered on the lawns. No birds braved the burning fields of air with song; only the locusts, children of the sun, began their shrill ear-splitting chorus among the cypresses and olives. I saw Raymond's horse, a superb coal-black charger, brought to the palace gate. A small company of officers arrived soon afterwards, their faces marked by sleeplessness and care and fear.

Surprisingly, I found Raymond and Perdita still together in their chamber. He was watching the sunrise, one arm around her waist; she looked on him, meanwhile, the sun of her life, with an earnest gaze that mingled anxiety and tenderness. Raymond started angrily when he saw me. "Here still?" he cried. "Is this your promised zeal?"

"Pardon me," I said, "but even as you speak, I am gone."

"No, pardon me," he replied. "I have no right to command or reproach you; but my life hangs on your departure and speedy return. Farewell!" His voice had recovered its bland tone, but a dark cloud still hung on his features. I would have delayed; I wanted to tell my sister to keep a watchful eye on him, but his presence restrained me. I had no pretence for further hesitation, and when Raymond said farewell a second time, I clasped his outstretched hand. It was cold and clammy.

"Take care of yourself, my dear Lord," I said.

"Oh no," said Perdita, "that shall my job. Don't be gone too long, Lionel."

Twice I turned back, just to look again on this matchless pair: Raymond, playing absently with his beloved's golden locks, while she leaned against him. My feet felt slow and heavy, even though it had not yet occurred to me that my mission was mostly Raymond's pretext to get me out of his way. My horse had been saddled for me, my escort assembled, and I was nearly mounted when Clara flew out of nowhere and grabbed me, to implore that I hurry back quickly—she'd had terrible dreams, she said, ones she didn't dare tell her mother. At this point I didn't want to leave at all, but as I told Clara, with a promise to return very soon, I had my orders.

They took me to the Marble Tower, furthest point on the city's old land walls. There, with the blue sea at our shoulders, I saw Karazza, who showed surprise at my request. She'd see what could be done, she said; but she'd need time—at least a day. To promise anything by noon was impossible. She welcomed me to wait there, at the tower, or else I could return tomorrow. My choice was easily made. A restlessness, a fear of what might be about to happen, a gnawing doubt as to Raymond's intentions, urged me to find him right away. I rode, keeping in sight of the walls, past our half-deserted camps, until I reached the base of the hill overlooking the Cannon Gate. From this tree-caped height, Mehmet II had studied Constantinople, his prey; Raymond with his spyglass had stood in another conqueror's footprints. It was noon when I reached the top and raised my own spyglass.

I saw Lord Raymond on his charger amid a small company of mounted officers. Gathered at ground level was a promiscuous rabble of soldiers and subalterns, their discipline lost, their arms, their band instruments, their banners thrown aside. The only flag in sight was the one Raymond carried, the flag of Greece. He pointed with it at the gate, and the circle around him fell back. With a great gesture, he leapt from his horse, seized a hatchet hanging from his saddle, and attacked the massive timbers and bolts with silent fury. A few soldiers joined him, then several more. Combined force soon vanquished the obstacle, which fell with a low whisper. Gate, ramparts, portcullis, fence lay demolished. Straight ahead was the wide sunlit way to the city's heart.

The ones who'd helped shrank back, as if fearful of what they'd already done; they might have been expecting some mighty phantom to stalk, in offended majesty, from the opening they'd made. Raymond sprang lightly onto his horse, took up the flag again, and addressed them—how, I couldn't hear, but his gestures seemed to release them, even dismiss them, from the obligation of completing their conquest. Even as he spoke, the crowd backed further away from him. In a transport of indignation and disdain that he made no effort to conceal, he said a few more words. Then, turning from his coward followers, he set himself to enter the city alone. The very horse beneath him appeared to shy from the fatal entrance; his dog, his faithful dog, lay moaning and supplicating in his path—no use. One more moment passed before he plunged the rowels into the charger's sides. The stung animal bounded forward, the dog dashed ahead, and Raymond, through the gate, was galloping up the broad deserted street.

I forgot the distance between us. "Wait, Raymond—I'll go with you!" I cried, taking my eye from the glass. The cloudless sun almost blinded me: I raised one hand for shade and looked again. Half a kilometer away, the wall, the gate, and a surrounding pigmy swarm could be discerned; Raymond's form, no. Stung with impatience, I spurred my horse downhill, my sole thought to arrive at the side of my noble, godlike friend before he met any danger.

My view was lost behind buildings and trees when I reached the plain, but I could make better time. I took off down the city road at a gallop, and hadn't gone very far when there was a huge explosive crash, sharp, thunderous. As it reverberated through the sky, the air grew dark. Moments later I rode into the open. I saw the Cannon Gate walls, dwarfed by the murky cloud rising from the city behind them—a pillar of cloud, hovering, towering, swirling with fragments of buildings half-visible through smoke. Flames burst out beneath, and ongoing explosions filled the air with terrific concussions.

Debris was falling beyond the circuit of the massive walls, whose ivied ramparts tottered. Crowds of soldiers fleeing these perils made for the road by which I came. I was surrounded, hemmed in by them, unable to get forward. Impatient beyond all measure, I stretched out my hands and implored his soldiers to turn back and save their general, the conqueror of Istanbul, the liberator of Greece! Tears, yes, searing tears gushed from my eyes—I would not believe in his destruction; yet every dark mass in the air before me seemed to carry a portion of the martyred Raymond. My struggles to approach the gate offered meager mental relief from the horrible imaginings that turbid cloud inspired.

Yet when I finally got there, all I could see through the opening was a city of fire. The wide street down which Raymond had ridden was enveloped in smoke and flame. The explosions ceased after a while, but the flames still shot up from various quarters. The Hagia Sophia's dome had disappeared. Strange to say (the result perhaps of an atmospheric disturbance produced when the Turks' trip-wired Pearl of the Bosphorus got blown sky-high), a fleet of gigantic white thunderheads arrived on the southern horizon and approached together; amidst this havoc and despair, they were a sight to give pleasure after months without a single blot to break the unforgiving blue expanse. With incredible swiftness, the whole sky turned grey. A lightning flash forked from the bulging clouds, a great cymbal-crash of thunder followed; then the big rain fell. The fires raging across the city bent beneath it, and the smoke and dust slowly returned to the ruins they'd issued from.

As soon as I saw the flames abating, an irresistible impulse drove me to try and penetrate the town. Given the enormous piles of rubble everywhere, I left my horse behind; I could only do this on foot. I'd never visited the old city before and its layout was largely unknown to me. The streets were blocked up anyhow, the ruins smoking. I climbed up one heap only to see a succession of others in prospect, and no way to tell where the center of town might be, or towards what point Raymond might have been heading.

The rain ceased, the sky cleared. I scrambled on, until I came to a street lined with wooden houses. Those that weren't burnt were still standing, and in the street I saw people, the first so far. I hurried forward. Dead, defaced human forms, some hard to distinguish as such: none could be Raymond. I turned my eyes away, while my heart sickened within me. After this I reached an open space; from the mountain of ruin in its midst, a large mosque must have stood there. Scattered about were various articles of luxury and wealth, all destroyed, singed, but recognizable. Ornaments, artworks, jewels, strings of pearls, embroidered robes, rich furs, glittering tapestries: they seemed to have been collected here to make bonfires, only the dousing rain had stopped the havoc midway.

Hours passed, without a sign of Raymond. Evening came. Insurmountable heaps made me retrace my steps sometimes; still-burning fires scorched me. With nightfall, the glare of flames showed the progress of destruction. Fiery flickering made weird living shapes out of the piles around me. I marveled at these sublime beings and their gigantic proportions, and yielded my thoughts to imaginative fiction's soothing power.

The drumbeats of my human heart drew me back to blank reality. *Where are you, my friend, in this wilderness of death? Ornament of England, deliverer of Greece, hero of unwritten history—O Raymond, where in this burning chaos are thy dear relics strewed?* "Raymond!" I called aloud for him.

Through the darkness, over the scorching ruins of fallen Istanbul, his name was heard. No voice replied, not even an echo.

Excitement could sustain my search only so long. The solitude depressed my spirits; and as my enthusiasm and hope faded, I was gradually overcome by weariness, dust, heat, smoke, and a famishing hunger. When my strength failed at last, I'd reached the site of another great edifice. My limbs trembling, I sat on its sole remaining step, huge and magnificent even in its downfall; a few broken colonnades, partially spared by the gunpowder, stood in fantastic groups. A flame glimmered at intervals on the summit of the pile, far overhead. Dazed and weak with hunger, I rested my head on the stone. I watched the constellations reel and then go out. Once or twice I strove to rise, but I yielded to the grateful sensation of utter forgetfulness. In that scene of desolation, on that night of despair—I slept.

(24)   THE STARS still shone brightly when I struggled awake from a torturous nightmare. My first lucid thought was of Perdita; I pictured the wild excesses of my sister's grief. I must get to her. But my disturbing dreams kept a hold on me. With a keen appetite, I'd attended a feast but only got served a plate of hot water; from this Timon of Athens type, my host turned into a furious Raymond. I got up and fled as he began hurling the tableware. The shards released a fetid vapor; behind me, my friend's distorted shape shot up a thousand-fold; I turned when the shadow that it cast enveloped me. Looming there, methought I saw a gigantic phantom Raymond with the sign of Plague emblazoned on its swelling brow. For even still the specter grew, expanding as it rose across the sky, trying to fill and finally burst beyond the sustaining arches of the adamantine, world-enclosing vault.

Taurus high in the southern heaven showed me it was midnight. With the stars as my only guide, I turned to the awful ruin of Istanbul, and, after great exertion, succeeded in leaving. This was by another gate, where a company of soldiers lent me a horse. I raced to retrieve my own mount, then on to my sister, noting along the way how much further the break-up of our encampment had progressed. Relics of the disbanded army met here and there in small companies. Every face I saw was clouded, every gesture an expression of shock and dismay.

I was heartsick as I entered the palace and approached the hall where my sister was waiting, the same in which we'd parted—only yesterday! I kept my resolution before me: I was there to support her, and to help draw such food from despair as might best sustain her wounded heart; I must evoke austere laws of duty, balanced by tenderest regrets, to recall her from the edge of the abyss she'd feel this widowhood to be.

She sat slumped on the floor, wringing her hands. Through her disheveled hair I could see a face pale as the marble she sat on; agony contracted every feature. She looked up enquiringly at my step. Her half-glance of hope was misery, and words died before I could articulate them. I felt a ghastly smile wrinkle my lips. Perdita understood. Again her head fell; again her fingers worked restlessly. When I could finally speak, my voice terrified her; the hapless girl had understood my look, yes, and the last thing she wanted was to hear its translation into hard, irrevocable words. Indeed, wishing to distract my thoughts from the subject, she rose from the floor, whispering, "Quiet—Clara's just stopped crying, she's finally asleep. We mustn't disturb her."

She crossed to sit down on the same ottoman where I'd left her before, resting her head on Raymond's heartbeat. Now, she startled at nothing, made nervous gestures. I dared not approach her, but sat and watched from a distance. She broke the silence abruptly to ask, "Where is he?" I was quiet.

"Don't be afraid," she continued, rising to her feet, "that I have any hope! Just tell me, have you found him? All I want is to have him in my arms once more, to see him, however he looks. I must find him, even if I have to dig up Istanbul to do it. Then you can cover us again, and pile a mountain on top of us for a tomb—I don't care, so long as one grave holds Raymond and his Perdita." Weeping, she clung to me. "Take me to him!" she cried; but I didn't move. "Unkind Lionel, why are we waiting? I can't find the place by myself. You must lead me there." These agonizing plaints filled me with intolerable compassion for my sister.

But I begged her patience to listen to the story of my night's adventures and my disappointed efforts to find our lost one. Turning her thoughts this way, I gave them an object which rescued them from insanity. With apparent calm she discussed the likeliest places to search, and how best to start; responding to my ordeal, she herself brought me food. I seized these favorable moments to try and awaken in her something beyond grief's killing torpor; but as I started to speak, my subject carried me away. Deep admiration, grief of my own, the fruits of truest affection, the overflowing of a heart bursting with sympathy for all that had been great and sublime in my friend's career, inspired me as I poured forth his praises:

"Alas, for us," I cried, "who have lost this latest honor of the world! Beloved Raymond! He is gone to the nations of the dead; become one with the mighty of soul who went before him. When the world was in its infancy, death must have been terrible. The first people left their friends and kindred to dwell as solitary strangers in an unknown country. But the newly dead of our day find many companions at their reception. The great of ages past populate the afterworld, where they welcome our exalted heroes to join them in rendering the grave even more illustrious. Meanwhile this our life becomes more truly a desert and a solitude.

"What a noble creature was Raymond, the foremost personality of our time. By the grandeur of his conceptions, the graceful daring of his actions, by his wit and beauty, he won and ruled the minds of all. One fault he had—maybe—but if so, his death has cancelled it. I've heard him called feckless; after he walked away, for the sake of love, from a probable crown, and again when he abdicated the Protectorship, many people blamed a basic infirmity of purpose. Now his death has crowned his life, and to the end of time it will be remembered that he devoted himself, unflinchingly, a willing victim, to the glory of Greece. Such was his choice: he expected to die. He foresaw that he should leave this cheerful earth, the lightsome sky, and your dear love, Perdita. Yet without hesitation, never turning back, he kept right onward to the mark he aimed to make on history and fame. While the earth endures, his actions will be called praise-worthy; his name will resound in patriotic hymns; in devotion, the youth of Greece will heap flowers on his tomb."

Perdita's agonized features had softened, as grief yielded to tenderness. I went on: "To honor him this way, is the sacred duty of his survivors. To make his name into a spot of holy ground, enclosing it with our praise from all hostile attacks, shedding love and regret on it like blossoms, guarding it from decay, and bequeathing it untainted to posterity—such is the duty of his friends. An even higher one is yours, Perdita, as the mother of his child. Don't you remember how happy you were, when she was a baby, each time you'd recognize some new way Clara seemed to unite you and Raymond in one being? A *living temple*, you used to call her; your eternal love manifested. So she is still. In her, flesh of his flesh, bone of his bone, Raymond yet lives with you. And past the downy cheek and delicate limbs you love to trace, in Clara's enthusiastic affections, and the sweet qualities of her mind—there, indeed, you'll find him living, the good, the great, the beloved. Make it your care to foster their best similarities. Resolve to raise her to be worthy of him, so that she may live to see her own attainments be as glorious as her origins."

Recalled to the duties of life, my sister didn't listen with the same patience as before. She appeared to suspect a plan of consolation on my part, from which she, cherishing her newborn grief, revolted. "You talk about the future," she said, "when the present is everything to me. Let me find my lover's body first—then we'll move on to other thoughts, and my new course of life, or whatever else Fate, in her cruel tyranny, may have planned."

I took a brief rest before going back to try and accomplish her desire. On my way out, later, Clara appeared. She knew all. Grief had made a deep impression on her young mind; she looked pale and scared. I greeted her lovingly and she sprang forward, clasped her hands and begged me to take her along—she wanted to see the gate by which her father had entered the city she too called Byzantium. She promised to be quiet and good, and I could send her back right away. Perdita had no objection and I couldn't refuse; for Clara was not an ordinary child. Her sensibility and intelligence seemed already to have endowed her with an adult's rights.

She fit easily on the front on my saddle, though, and so we arrived at the Cannon Gate. A knot of soldiers was gathered there in a strange sort of quiet; they recognized Raymond's daughter almost absently. I pointed across her shoulder. "That's the opening, and that's the street your father rode up yesterday." Whatever Clara's intention had been in asking to be brought here, the soldiers' presence made her shy. After a long, earnest gaze at the wall of smoldering ruins which was all that could be seen, she told me she'd like to go home. At this moment a melancholy howl struck our ears.

"*There!*" The soldiers cried out all at once. "Human," said one. "A dog," replied another.

Again they bent to catch the regular distant moaning sound that issued from the precincts of the ruined city—again. "It's him!" cried Clara, "He's there, that's Florio, my father's dog!" The crowd by the gate looked up at her. He must be with his master, she insisted. It seemed to me impossible that she could recognize the sound, but the soldiers gave ready credence to her claim. A benevolent action to rescue the sufferer, whether human or brute, was soon organized. Several members of Raymond's personal bodyguard, who had loved him, and sincerely mourned his loss, rode up to accompany me into the desolation. I sent Clara back home with her attendant, and entered Istanbul for the last time.

Through a labyrinth of smoking piles, the mournful voice led us to the most fire-gutted part of the city, a terrible vista, quenched, blackened, cold. Here we found his dog, covered in burns, crouched beside Raymond's mutilated form. At such a time sorrow cannot speak; affliction, tamed by its very vehemence, is mute. The poor animal recognized me, licked my hand, crept close to its lord, and died. He must have been thrown from his horse by some falling ruin, which had crushed his head and defaced his whole person. The soldiers gathered round to see. I bent over the body, which the fire had largely spared, and took in my hand the edge of Raymond's cloak, less altered in appearance than the human frame it clothed. I pressed it to my lips.

How sharply we mourned this worthiest prey of death. Yet not even endless lamentation could relight the extinguished spark or call the liberated spirit back to its shattered jailhouse. Limbs and flesh worth a universe the day before, when they enshrined transcendent power, a being whose goals and achievements deserved recording in letters of gold; now, a day later, only the superstition of affection could see value in this broken mechanism which, incapable and clod-like, defaced and spoiled, no more resembled Raymond than the fallen rain does its former mansion—the high sun-gilded cloud in which it climbed the air and attracted every gaze, satiating the sense by its excess of beauty.

We wrapped our cloaks about the thing that he had now become, lifted the burden on our shoulders, and bore it from this city of the dead. Remembering the Greek cemetery that lay on our road to the palace, I had him laid there, in the gloomy shade of some cypresses, on a tablet of black marble. The funereal trees accorded well with his state of nothingness; we cut branches and placed them over his makeshift shroud, and on these again his sword. I left a guard to protect this treasure of dust, and ordered a circle of perpetual torches.

Perdita, already apprised of my successful undertaking, was in a manic state by the time I reached her, and met me with an outpouring of words. Her sole and eternal beloved was restored to her. So what if his limbs were motionless and his lips could no longer frame the syllables of wisdom and love? Though he lay like a clump of rotting seaweed on the beach—even so, that was the body she'd caressed, whose breath she'd drunk and commingled with her own— a body she'd called hers as much as Raymond's. True, she looked forward to another life; true, love like hers was certainly eternal. But right now, admitting her own human fondness and frailty, she clung to all that her senses could possibly get of his physical self. Just so, to be near his dust, would future generations make his sacred tomb a place of pilgrimage.

Though her features had lost the distortion of grief, my sister's look worried me. As she heard my account of how we'd found Raymond, not just her pupils but her very person seemed dilated; yet far from healthily flushed, she was pale as marble. I described the arrangements I'd made for the much-mutilated body, adding that I certainly thought it should be buried there, in the Greek cemetery. I watched a treacherous calm settle on Perdita's countenance. She didn't agree.

"Where, then?" I asked.

"At Athens," she replied. "You know how he loved Athens ."

"Where in Athens? A church?"

"No, outside the city, on a spot of higher ground. Hymettus, it's called."

"Hymettus is a mountain."

"A low mountain," she said, "with a rocky recess on one slope which he pointed out to me as the spot where he wished to repose."

"In a ravine on a cliff on the side of Mount Hymettus," I summarized. But her wish was of course to be complied with. "Very well. Start packing, please—we'll leave right away."

Behold our melancholy train. With our creeping pace, we are the coda to the siege of Istanbul. Cheated of the rich spoils promised them and their families, the troops barely feel the victory; if each one's empty pack were full of gold ingots they wouldn't march beneath the weight half so slowly as they trudge now across flat, drought-ridden Thrace. To spare our horses, the riders and cavalry also go on foot as we make our winding ascent through the waterless defiles that will, eventually, return us to the mountain streams of Macedonia and the ever more fertile landscapes across which we'll march on our way back to the Athenian plain.

The way is long and feels longer. Rumbling in the midst of our slow-motion cavalcade go Raymond's military hearse and Perdita's closed carriage behind it. The casket's gorgeous pall draws the eye, a perpetual presence casting melancholy on each noon's repose. My sister, when she emerges into company, remains shut up in herself, speaking little, looking pale and cold, staring at the ground, indulging thoughts which refuse communication or sympathy. Day follows night, and our journey seems no closer to the end. The monotony becomes intolerable.

But here we are after all, on Hymettus; within sight of Athens, though not from our position at the head of a ravine on the southern slope. Perdita has led us to where she says Raymond's dear remains should lie. From where they meet, just ahead, the chasm walls soar to the summit—tall, fissured cliffs overgrown on either side with myrtle bushes and wild thyme, the food of many nations of bees. Turn around, for a limitless view: beyond the laughing valley stretched below us floats the blue Aegean, sprinkled with islands, bars of sunlight glancing off its waves. Enormous crags protrude at all angles into the cleft; from the ground, in a central position, one high, solitary, conical rock points at the sky like a natural pyramid. Being limestone, it will be easily hewn into a perfect shape, and a narrow cell scooped out beneath to receive Raymond's body; and a short inscription, carved in the living stone, will record his name and his death.

(25)   THE PROJECT was speedily accomplished under my direction; meanwhile I struck an agreement that turned over the completion and guardianship of Raymond's tomb to the church heads at Athens, which left us free to sail for England. There was a steamship that could take us at the end of October. I'd had bad news from home and by now my very soul was sick with yearning to rejoin my Idris and our surviving babes. I knew it would be a more painful

departure for my sister—painful for me, as well, should I appear to be dragging her from the last scene that spoke of her lost one; but to linger here was useless, I told her. In reply, Perdita asked me to come with her to Raymond's tomb.

It was late afternoon when we reached the spot, which I hadn't visited in some days. I'd seen the path up to it enlarged, the rock steps hewn that made the way to the tomb platform less circuitous. New to me were the foundations someone had dug off to the left side of the platform, or extending from it, in a recess overshadowed by the straggling branches of a wild fig tree. Already framed, with rafters—I guessed some enterprising church faction had hurried to plant a guest cottage in the ravine. A good investment, I reflected, as I stood on the unfinished threshold to admire the view beyond the hero's tomb. Slanting sunlight traced shadow lines along the plow-marked valley, and dyed trees, rocks, waves with beauteous arrays of changeful color. I gazed with rapture on the graces of earth and ocean. In years to come, this spot would be the cynosure of Greece: Perdita was right, I said.

"Yes," she agreed. "And wasn't I right, despite everything, to have Raymond brought here? In a place like this, death loses half its terror, and even the dust possesses a sacred beauty—a Grecian beauty. Lionel, he sleeps there. That's Raymond's grave, he whom in my youth I first loved; whom my heart stayed with, in days of separation and anger; to whom I am now joined forever. Never—listen to me carefully—never will I leave this spot. His spirit is here with what remains of him; though crumbling and mute, the widowed earth clasps nothing more precious to her sorrowing bosom. The rocks, the myrtle leaves, the honeybees among the thyme, are all tied to him; the light here, the sunset purpling the hills, the sky and mountains, sea and valley, are imbued with the presence of his spirit. I will live and die here!

"You go home to England, Lionel. Return to sweet Idris and dearest Adrian; return, and take my orphan girl into your house as your own child. Look on me as dead. Truly, if death be a mere change of state, I am dead. This, where I am, is another world from the one I inhabited before. The present is now your home, not mine. Here I hold communion only with what has been, and what is yet to come. Go back to England, and leave me alone where I can stand to drag out the miserable days still left to me."

I sat in silence through the shower of tears that closed her sad harangue. Though I'd expected some extravagant, fanciful proposition, I still needed several moments to collect my thoughts after hearing this one. "You cherish dreary ideas, my dear sister," I finally said. "Nor is it any wonder that your better reason should still be influenced by grief—and by sublime beauty. Even I am in love with this last home of Raymond's. Nevertheless, we must quit it."

"I expected this!" she cried. "I knew you'd treat me as a mad, foolish girl. But don't deceive yourself, Lionel. This cottage is being built by my orders; and here I shall remain, until the hour arrives when I may share Raymond's happier dwelling-place."

"My dearest girl!"

"Enough! What's so strange about my plan, anyhow? I might have deceived you, I might have talked of remaining here only a few months. In your anxiety to reach Windsor you'd have left me, and without reproach or contention, I might have done exactly as I wanted. But I scorned to lie; or no—rather, in my wretchedness it was my only consolation to pour out my heart to you, my brother, my only friend. And you dispute with me, your poor, misery-stricken sister!

"You know how willful I am. Take my girl with you; wean her from sorrowful sights and thoughts; let childish fun revisit her heart, let her eyes light up again, as they never could were she near me. It's really far better for her, for all of you, never to see me again. For myself, I will not seek death—not, that is, voluntarily, not while I can command myself; and I can, here. But drag me from this country and watch my power of self-control vanish. I can't answer for any violence my agony might drive me to commit."

"You clothe your meaning, Perdita," I replied, "in powerful words, yet that meaning is selfish and unworthy of you. How often have I heard you agree that the only solution to the riddle of life is to improve ourselves, and find ways to contribute to the happiness of others? And now, in the very prime of life, you desert your principles, you shut yourself up in useless solitude. Will you think of Raymond less at Windsor? Will you commune less with his spirit, while you watch over and cultivate the rare excellence of his child? You have been sadly visited; nor do I wonder that you should feel driven to harbor bitter and unreasonable ideas. But a home of love awaits you in England. Your brother will be there—my affection, and the company of Raymond's friends, are bound to be of more solace than these dreary ideas. We will make it our first care, our dearest task, to add to your happiness."

Perdita shook her head. "If what you ask were possible, I'd be wrong to refuse you. But it's not a matter of choice. I can only live here. I'm a part of this scene; everything in it is a part of me. Dear brother, this is no sudden fancy. This is my life now. The knowledge that I am here, when I wake each morning, enables me to endure the daylight; it mingles with my food, which would be poison to me otherwise; it walks and it sleeps with me. Here, alone, I may even stop repining, and begin to accept the way he was taken from me. I know he would rather have died such a death, which will be recorded in history to endless time, than have lived to old age unremarked, unhonored. As for myself, having been the chosen and beloved of his heart, I couldn't desire anything better than to stay here, in my prime, before age has time to tarnish the best feelings of my nature, and watch Raymond's tomb, and speedily rejoin him in his blessed repose.

"That's all, my dearest Lionel, there is to tell you. I stay here. If you want to remove me by force, fine. Drag me away, I'll return; lock me up, jail me, I'll still escape and come back. Or would my brother rather see her lying on the floor of a madhouse, than allow his heart-broken Perdita to spend the rest of her life in a peace and place she's chosen for herself?"

I admit, I thought she was crazed and barely responsible for what she was saying. Grief had done this; so I imagined that it was my imperative duty to take her from scenes so forcibly reminiscent of her loss. Nor did I doubt that in the tranquility of our family circle at Windsor, she'd recover some degree of composure, and in the end, of happiness. My affection for Clara also set me against Perdita's fantasies. The child's mind and senses had already been too overloaded, her innocent light-heartedness too soon exchanged for deep and anxious thought. Her mother's strange and romantic scheme, as much as her abandonment, might confirm and perpetuate the painful view of life which had already marked her prematurely.

Back at my rooms, I was handed a message from the steamship company. Accidental circumstances, it said, had hastened the departure I'd inquired about; if I wanted to sail, passage could be arranged immediately, but our party must come on board at five o'clock the next morning. I sent back a hasty consent, and as hastily formed a plan by which Perdita would have to come along. I believe that most people in my situation would have acted in the same manner. Yet this consideration does not—or rather did not, later—diminish the reproaches of my conscience. At the moment, I felt convinced that I was acting for the best, and that all I did was right and even necessary.

After supper, as we sat alone, I led Perdita to believe that she'd won my assent to her wild scheme. In her happiness she must have thanked her deceiving, deceitful brother a thousand times over. The night drew on. She talked, her spirits regaining an almost forgotten vivacity. Then I pretended to be alarmed by a feverish glow on her cheek and begged her to take a mild sleeping tablet. The one I produced was actually a strong opiate. She accepted it docilely from my hand; I watched her swallow it down. Falsehood and artifice are in themselves so hateful, that, though I still thought I did right, a feeling of shame and guilt stabbed me.

Sleep came fast, and she was unconscious when we carried her on board. The ship weighed anchor and found a favorable wind; under full canvas, with the engine powering at full speed ahead, we were soon far out at sea.

I'd stationed an attendant to watch over Perdita and report to me. Upon waking, late in the day, and gradually taking in her new surroundings, my sister leapt up wildly from her couch and dashed to the cabin window. A blue and troubled sea sped past, with no sign of shore; the racing, cloud-racked sky; the creaking of the masts beneath their weight of sail; the ship's bells, the crew's unhurried footsteps: everything told her truly. She was far from land, far from Greece. She questioned the attendant, who told her we were headed to England.

"And my brother?"

"Is on deck, Madam."

The poor victim turned again to her watery wasteland view and exclaimed, "Unkind! unkind!" Then, without further remark, she threw herself on the couch, closed her eyes and lay motionless; if it weren't for the deep sighs that kept bursting from her, she might have been thought to be asleep.

As soon as I got word that she'd spoken, I brought Clara to her cabin and sent her in before me. I hoped the sight of that lovely innocent might inspire gentle and affectionate thoughts. But Perdita only looked at her child with a face full of woe and didn't speak. She turned away at my entrance. I asked and finally demanded that she say something. She responded: "You don't know what you've done."

Though sullenly, she'd spoken, which I read as a sign that the struggle between her disappointment and her natural affections had begun; and I trusted that in a few days my sister would be reconciled to her fate.

Another attendant was to sleep with her and Clara in the cabin, but Perdita asked for the child to be put to bed somewhere else. Then, around midnight, she woke and sent the night attendant to see whether Clara was resting quietly—she'd had a bad dream and was worried, she said. The attendant obeyed and left her alone.

I was back on deck, enjoying our swift progress. The breeze, which had flagged at sunset, was rising again. Our rate couldn't have been less than eight knots. I filled my ears with the rush of waters as they divided before the steady keel; the murmur of the full, motionless sails; the whistling of the wind among the shrouds; the engine's deep, regular throb. The sky had cleared but the constellations sought their accustomed mirror in vain; for the sea was in a gentle agitation, flashing whitecaps all around.

The sound of a heavy splash startled me. The sailors on watch rushed to the side rails. "*Overboard!*" rose the cry. The helmsman said whatever it was hadn't come from the deck, but been thrown from the aft cabin: my sister's. A call for the boat to be lowered was echoing outside as I rushed below to find her gone.

With the speeding vessel brought arduously to a stop, another hour's search saw my poor Perdita brought on board. No care could revive her, no medicine cause her dear eyes to open or the blood to flow again through her still heart. Clenched in one hand we found a slip of paper; it read:

To Athens.

Intending her body to be found, she'd taken the precaution of tying a long shawl round her waist and fastening the other end to the cabin window. But she'd drifted and been caught beneath the keel, out of sight, which delayed the recovery.

Thus the unlucky girl died a victim to my senseless rashness. Thus, so early, she left us for the company of the dead; to the animated scenes this cheerful earth afforded, and the society of loving friends, she really did prefer a share of Raymond's rocky grave. Thus at twenty-nine she died, having enjoyed the happiness of paradise for some few years before suffering a reversal to which her impatient spirit and affectionate disposition could not submit. As I marked the calm that had settled on her dead face, I felt, in spite of the pangs of remorse, in spite of heart-rending regret, that it was better so—better to die than to drag through long, miserable years of repining and inconsolable grief.

I supposed I must turn back with my sister's body and fulfill her request, though how Clara was to fare meanwhile I couldn't imagine. But at our next port I met an old friend and warm partisan of Raymond's, a vice-admiral of the Greek fleet who was sailing for Athens in a matter of days. I committed the remains of my lost Perdita to his custodianship; he oversaw their transportation to Hymettus and their placement in the cell with Raymond's, beneath the pyramid. All was accomplished as I'd specified. Perdita reposed beside her beloved, her name united to his in the new inscription on their tomb.

Slowly, haltingly, the realization came upon me: the beauteous couple was gone. Their names, blended eternally with the past, must be erased from every anticipation of the future. Raymond I'd always admired—his talents; his noble aspirations; his grand conceptions of the glory and majesty of his own ambition; his utter freedom from mean passions; his fortitude and daring. In Greece I'd learned to love him. His very waywardness, his wild surrender to his own superstitious side, made me doubly fond; he might be weak, but he was the opposite of all that was groveling and selfish. I missed him. And Perdita, dear being, my sole relation, lost through my own accursed self-will and conceit: from tender childhood through the varied paths of life, I'd marked her progress. She'd always been conspicuous for integrity, devotion, and true affection—some might have said, for all that constitutes the peculiar graces of the female character. Finally, still in her youthful prime, I saw her become the victim of too much loving, too constant an attachment to the perishable and lost. Her choice to cast off the pleasant world apparent to her senses for the unreality of the grave, had orphaned poor Clara. I concealed from this beloved child that her mother's death was voluntary, and did everything I could to introduce cheerfulness into her sorrowing spirit.

First, in a willed recovery of composure, we bid farewell to the sea, whose hateful unremitting splash kept recalling my sister's death to my ear, again and again. Its roar was a dirge; the dark hulls of ships it tossed on its inconstant bosom doubled as biers, death-conveyances for all who trusted to its treacherous smiles. So, farewell to the sea...

Hello to the sky! Come, my Clara, sit beside me in this aerial boat. Quickly and gently it cleaves the azure serene; it glides upon air currents with soft undulations. Should a storm shake its fragile mechanism, the green earth is below: we can descend, and take shelter. Here aloft, with swift-winged birds for our companions, we skim through the unresisting element, fleetly and fearlessly. The light boat neither heaves nor breasts crashing waves; the ether opens before the prow. The globe of shadow from the balloon that upholds us, gives shelter from the noonday sun. Behind lie the plains of Italy. Now the vast undulations of the wave-like Apennines are beneath us; a fertility of double harvests reposes in their valley folds, and woods crown the summits—a garden of the world. Ahead, the Alpine peaks. When we emerge from their deep and brawling ravines, we'll be looking down on France.

After an air journey of six days, we landed at Dieppe, furled the feathered wings, and closed the silken globe of our little vessel, which was soon grounded by heavy rain. So we took a steamship for the fairly short passage to Portsmouth.

A strange story was rife here. The previous month, a badly damaged ship had appeared offshore. Hull dried out and cracked, torn sails set in a careless, un-seamanlike manner, the rigging tangled and broken: clearly, disaster had come before the storm that blew her towards land. Drifting near Portsmouth harbor, she got stranded among the sandbanks at the entrance. A crowd of idlers followed the custom-house officers sent to visit the scene. One person from the ship had already climbed to shore, taken a few steps towards town, and fallen dead on the beach. Every sign pointed to a long-protracted misery. The whisper rose: *Plague.* No one dared board the vessel, and no one else emerged; though strange things were said to be seen at night, walking the deck, hanging around the masts. The ship soon went to pieces; I was shown where she'd been. A lot of timbers still tossed on the waves. The stranger's corpse had been buried deep in the sands; and no one could tell me anything more, except that the vessel—the *Fortunatas*—was American-built, and had sailed from Philadelphia, of which no tidings were afterwards received.

(26) AFTER ALL the agitation and sorrow I'd endured in Greece, I viewed Windsor much as a storm-driven bird does the nest where it can finally fold its wings in tranquility. On my return, in the autumn of 2092, I felt sick with the hope and delight of seeing my loved ones again. My heart had been with them all along. In their presence, happiness, love, and peace walked the forest paths and tempered the atmosphere.

How unwise had the wanderers been, who'd deserted the shelter of home, entangled themselves in society's web, and entered on what worldly types called Life—that labyrinth of evil, that scheme of mutual torture. To "live," in their sense, we must not only observe and learn, but also feel; we must not be mere spectators of action, we must act; we must not describe, but be subjects of description. Hilarity and joy, that lap the soul in ecstasy, must at times have possessed us; but deep sorrow must have sheltered in our bosoms, too. Fraud must have lain in wait for us; confidence tricksters must have deceived us; sickening doubt and false hope must have checkered our days. Who, knowing what Life is, would pine for this feverish species of existence?

"I have lived, Idris," I told her. "I've known festivals, ambitions, victories. Now—I say shut the door on the world, and build the wall higher against its troubled scenes. Let's live for each other and for happiness; let us seek peace in our own dear home, near the murmuring streams, the gracious waving trees, the beauteous landscapes and sublime pageantry of the skies. Let us leave 'life,' so that we may live."

Idris, whose native sprightliness needed no encouragement, agreed to my resolution with a smile. Little would change for her, whose pride and blameless ambition was to make each and everyone around her glad. Mainly, besides our children, she was concerned with how to ease the strain on her brother's fragile existence. In spite of her tender nursing, his health perceptibly declined. Walking, riding, the common occupations of life, overcame him: he felt no pain, but seemed to tremble all the time on the verge of annihilation. Yet, as he was still alive after having been like this for months, he didn't inspire us with any immediate fear; and, though he talked familiarly about thoughts of death, he didn't cease to exert himself to render others happy, or to cultivate his own astonishing powers of mind.

Winter passed away and spring, month by month, awakened life throughout nature. The forest was dressed in green; the young calves frisked on the new grass; the wind-winged shadows of light clouds sped over the green cornfields lying in gentle relief along the clear horizon. The hermit cuckoo's monotonous all-hail to the season used up its last notes near sunset. Then, while Venus, the evening star, pulsed in the warm sky, her minion the nightingale, bird of love, began to fill the woods with song.

We and our guests shared the delight of gazing down on this scene from the Castle terrace. But delight was awake in every heart that season, delight and exultation; for there was peace through all the world. The temple of Universal Mars was shut, and no one had died that year by another person's hand.

"Let this last only twelve months," said Adrian, "and our world will become a Paradise. The energies we've aimed at destroying our own species, can now be directed at its liberation and preservation. Humanity cannot repose—we must aspire. Now, finally, our restlessness will bring forth good instead of evil. The resource-rich countries of the global south will throw off the iron yoke of corruption and servitude; poverty will fade away, and sickness with it. Liberty and Peace, their forces united as never before—what lies beyond them to achieve for our lives and our planet?"

Ryland gave a short laugh. "Dreaming, forever dreaming, Windsor!" Raymond's old adversary was a candidate for the Protectorate at the next election. He went on, "Be assured that Earth is not, nor ever can be heaven, while the seeds of hell are native to her soil. When the climate has become equally temperate everywhere; when the environment breeds no disorders; when farmlands are no longer liable to blights and droughts—then sickness will cease. When human passions are dead—then poverty will depart. When love is no longer the flip side of hate—then brotherhood and sisterhood will exist. We are very far from any of these states at present."

"Not so far as you might suppose," observed a little old astronomer, Merrival by name, as he shuffled forward. "The poles precede slowly, but surely. In one hundred thousand years—"

"We shall all be underground," said Ryland.

The astronomer was undaunted. "At that time, Earth's celestial poles will coincide with the pole of the ecliptic. A universal spring will result, and the entire planet become a paradise."

"In a hundred thousand—why should any of us," Ryland had begun contemptuously, when I looked up from the evening news in my hand.

"Here's something strange," I said, "in the paper. It seems that a large contingent of Greeks, relying on the supposition that winter had purified the air, recently worked up the courage to enter Istanbul with the idea of rebuilding it from the ruins. But they say the curse of God is on the place, for everyone who ventured within the city walls has come down with the plague—which is now spreading in Thrace and Macedonia. For fear of a spike in infections during the coming hot season, Thessaly has already shut its borders and imposed a strict quarantine."

So we returned from the prospect of paradise, shimmering in a very close or very distant yet-to-come, to our present time's immediate pain and misery. We talked of how the pestilence had ravaged so much of the world last year, and how dreadful must be the consequences of a second wave. We discussed the best means of preventing infection, and of preserving health and normal activity in a large city at a time of pandemic—London, for instance. Merrival, growing more and more distant from the conversation's practical tone, drew nearer Idris, to whom he carefully explained how the joy he took in picturing the paradise to come was ever-clouded by the knowledge that, in a certain period of time after that first hundred thousand years, an earthly hell or purgatory would occur, when the ecliptic and equator would be at right angles.

My own thoughts also strayed, only to the recent past. The others talked of Thrace and Macedonia as they might of a lunar territory, unknown, indistinct, of no interest to them. I had trod the soil. The faces of many of its inhabitants were familiar to me. On our eastward march the year before, among their towns, plains, hills and valleys, I'd known some of the best times of my life. Romantic villages, cottages, more elegant abodes, inhabited alike by the lovely and the good, rose before my mind's eye; with each one came the haunting question: *Is the plague there, too?* That same invincible monster which hovered over and devoured Istanbul—alas, that fiend more cruel than tornado or tempest, less tame than fire, was unchained in Greece, that beautiful country. I could not reflect without extreme pain on the desolation this evil would cause there.

Our terrace party began to break up. "We're all dreaming anyhow," Ryland said. "It makes about as much sense to discuss the probability of a visitation of the plague in a well-run modern metropolitan area like ours, as to calculate how many centuries must elapse before we can grow pineapples on the open slopes of Hampstead Heath."

He returned to town and an election that was agitating the country's political state more than usual. Should he be chosen as the new Protector, as the eternal populist Ryland was expected to raise, for its first debate before parliament, the question of abolishing hereditary rank and other feudal relics. The topic was so incendiary that it hadn't even been referenced during the present session. Yet this very silence was loaded—overloaded—a sign of the deep weight attached to the question, to which was added both parties' fear of risking an ill-timed attack, and the certainty of a furious fight sometime ahead.

But although the phantom walls of old St. Stephen's echoed nothing of the voice which filled each heart, the newspapers teemed with nothing else; and no matter how remote its beginnings, every private conversation in company soon verged towards this central point. Voices would be lowered, chairs drawn closer. The aristocrats, as they built on their minority base across the kingdom, could be seen appealing to prejudices and old attachments without number; also to perennially fresh hopes and expectations, held by thousands, of someday gaining peerages. And they'd raised that reliable scarecrow, the specter of all that was sordid, mechanical, and base in America and the other commercial republics.

"Shame on the country," Ryland was heard to say, "that lays so much stress on words and frippery—when it's a question of nothing—of repainted carriage-panels, and new embroidery designs for footmen's coats."

Could England really do without her lordly trappings, and be content with the democratic American style? But more—were the pride of ancestry, the patrician spirit, the gentle courtesies and refined pursuits, the splendid attributes of rank, to be erased throughout society? No, we were told, this would never be the case; for we were by nature a poetical people, a nation easily duped by words, ready to dress a cloud in splendor, and bestow honor on the dust. This spirit we could never lose—indeed, we were assured that when the words *British Citizen* became the sole patent of nobility, we should all be noble; when none felt others their superior in rank, then courtesy and refinement would become our common birthright. Let not England be so far disgraced, as to have it imagined that it could ever be without people—nature's true nobility—who show what they are in their face and bearing, who are from their cradles elevated above the rest, because they are better than the rest. Among an independent, generous, and well-educated populace, in a country where the imagination rules, there need be no fear that we should lack a perpetual succession of the high-born and lordly.

At any other time, the arrival of the plague in Athens would have excited society's highest interest and compassion—especially with the British diplomatic corps and hundreds of other people returning from Athens to London. Now the news was almost passed over, lost in the general engagement with the coming controversy. But I, keeping far from the salons and drawing rooms, gathered every report and read each one with anguish. Questions of rank and right dwindled to insignificance in my eyes, when I knew that Raymond's beloved Athenians, the free and noble people of the divinest town in Greece, were falling like ripe corn before the merciless sickle of the adversary. Combing reports of the deaths of only sons, and of wives and husbands most devoted; of friend losing friend, and young mothers mourning their first-born—a merciless rending of ties twisted with the heart's fibers—I could put faces to many names, people I knew and esteemed, people I loved, among the sufferers.

Athens, the city, sounded harder to recognize. Its pleasant places were deserted, its temples and palaces converted into tombs, its sublime and far-reaching energies forced to converge on one point: protection against the innumerable and finally overwhelming arrows of the plague. Friends and fellow soldiers of Raymond's and mine, families that had welcomed Perdita to Greece, admirers who'd helped lament her loss, the builders of the tomb she shared, all alike were swept away, gone to dwell with that ill-fated couple in the formless beyond.

The plague at Athens showed the contagion's spread towards Europe from Asia and the southern hemisphere, where scenes of havoc and death continued to be acted on a scale of fearful magnitude. This year's visitation had also struck North America, where the epidemic's spread showed an unprecedented virulence. The devastation wasn't confined to the populous areas, but spread to rural ones; the hunter died in the woods, the farmer among plantings, the angler knee-deep in the trout stream. The merchant and investor classes, in whose view the present year would see the plague die out, continued to thrive on hopes of improvement. Governments waited to get back on the road to prosperity. But the inhabitants of the stricken countries were driven to despair, or to a resignation which, arising from fanaticism, assumed the same bleak character.

A strange story reached us from overseas. No one would have believed it, if there hadn't been a multitude of witnesses, in various quarters—Asia, the Caucasus and Middle East, much of Africa—all attesting to the identical facts. On June 21st, an hour before noon, another sun rose in the west. Comparable in size to the regular sun, but completely dark, the beams it cast were shadows. This black sun, as people called it, ascended the western sky with unusual speed. An hour brought it to the same meridian where our sun, the day star, was hanging—and where the strange sun eclipsed it entirely. Sudden and total darkness: the stars came out and supplied their ineffectual glimmerings as fear took hold in country after country down below. Daylight soon returned where it belonged, as the dim orb continued its transit in a lingering descent of the eastern sky. But now its lightless rays crossed the other's brilliant ones and deadened or distorted them, so that the shadows of things assumed strange and ghastly shapes. Wild animals took fright and fled in stampedes; birds, strong-winged eagles, suddenly blinded, fell onto marketplaces, while great numbers of owls and bats showed themselves in the premature dusk.

Among human populations the dread and confusion were even greater. When the black sun finally sank beneath the horizon, sending a last shot of shadowy beams high into the otherwise radiant air, panic ruled multitudes. The mosques and temples were full; so were graveyards, as people hastened to their dead relatives' tombs with offerings and propitiations. The plague was forgotten in this new terror spread by a freak celestial event. As the dead bodies multiplied in the streets of Isfahan, Beijing, Delhi, people walked with gazes fixed on the ominous heavens, disregarding corpses at their feet. Believers streamed toward Mecca without fear of being pillaged on the way: the robbers were joining the pilgrim caravans, ready to pray that the general destruction might spare their desert hideouts. Where there were churches, Christian maidens in white shining veils formed long processions and filled the air with hymns. Then a wailing cry would burst from the lips of some poor mourner in the crowd, and the rest, raising their eyes, would fancy they could see fantastic wings sweep the air as angels hovered, looking down and lamenting the disasters about to befall humankind.

I cannot describe the rapturous relief with which I turned from political brawls in London, and the disorders of distant countries, to the peace of my own dear home, that select abode of goodness, love, and every sacred communal sympathy. Had I never left Windsor, these emotions wouldn't have been so intense; but the deplorable changes I'd experienced in Greece, those periods of anxiety and sorrow, loss and fear, magnified my attachment to the domestic circle left to me. Here, though indeed the progress of years brought change—time, as it is wont, stamped the traces of mortality on our pleasures and expectations—I let no such miseries intrude. Secluded in our beloved forest, we lived tranquilly.

Idris, the most affectionate wife, sister, and friend, was a tender and loving mother. The feeling was not with her as with many, a demanding pastime; it was a passion. We'd had three children; one, the second oldest, died while I was in Greece. For Idris, this event had splashed grief and fear across a triumphant and rapturous emotional landscape. Before, her motherhood had beamed upon the little beings, sprung from herself, heirs of her transient life, with lives of their own to come; afterwards, maternity meant a perpetual state of dread that the pitiless destroyer might snatch her remaining darlings, her gems, as it had snatched their brother. She was miserable if she had to be away from them at all. Their slightest illness sent her into throes of terror. Fortunately, she had small cause for fear. Our firstborn, Alfred, was a robust little fellow with radiant features, soft eyes, and a gentle though independent disposition. Elvis, our youngest, was still an infant; but his downy cheeks were sprinkled with the roses of health, and his tireless vivacity filled our halls with innocent laughter.

Having survived the troubling state of mute misery in which she'd returned to her Windsor cousins, Clara had grown dear to all. She displayed so many fine qualities in such perfect balance—intelligence and candor, taste and tolerance, transcendent beauty and endearing simplicity—that she hung like a pearl in our midst, a treasure of wonder and excellence.

At the start of the winter term, our Alfred, now nine years old, entered school at Eton, very happily. We'd lived so long in the neighborhood of the school that its population of young folks was well known to us. Many of them had been Alfred's playmates before they became fellow students. Here, swelling these youthful throngs, were the future governors of England; these Etonians, and others like them, were the beings who'd be tapped to run the vast machine of society when their turn arrived. Signs flashed through of the men and women to come, the future landowners, politicians, generals, stage actors. For Alfred, his school life, the rigors of study and games, developed the best parts of his character—perseverance, well-governed firmness, generosity. By his talents and virtues, he distinguished himself always.

What deep and sacred emotions are excited in a father's breast, when he first realizes that his love for his child is not a mere instinct, but worthily bestowed on someone worth knowing! At this point in their lives, when an animal's love for its offspring ends, the human parent's true affection starts. The younger mind develops, and moral propensities reveal themselves in time as worthy of our hope. There's much they still don't know; and we have our anxieties about their weakness; but we begin to respect the future adult—whom we also start trying to impress as we might some social equal. Indeed, though, what could be more important than to have our children's good opinion? For this reason, our honor must be spotless in all our transactions with them, the integrity of our relations untainted; so that, should fate and circumstance finally separate us, love and honor for their parents, as a comfort in sorrow, an aegis in danger, a consolation in hardship, will remain with our children on life's rough path.

Willingly I step aside for you, dear Alfred! Advance, offspring of tender love, child of our hopes; advance a soldier on the road I've pioneered! I'll make way for you. Look—I've already put aside the carelessness of childhood, youth's unlined brow and springy gait, for you to wear. Advance, and take all I lose, including the graces of maturity. Time shall rob the fire from my eyes and the agility from my limbs; eager expectation and passionate love, the better part of life, stolen from me, shall be showered in double portion on your dear head. Advance! Take these gifts, you and your comrades. Please remember not to disgrace your benefactors. May your progress be uninterrupted and secure. Born during the springtide of human hopes, may you stand at the head of a summer to which no winter may succeed!

So philosophically could we watch the individual pass away, even our own individual self; for the species would remain. Human life, as Edmund Burke put it in his reflections on the French Revolution, was "the mode of existence decreed to a permanent body composed of transitory parts—wherein, by the disposition of a stupendous wisdom—the whole, at one time, is never old, or middle-aged, or young, but, in a condition of unchangeable constancy, moves on—through perpetual decay, fall, renovation, and progression."

(27)   THE WHOLE world asked the wind, *Why? Why do you roar and howl like this, and why won't you stop?*

Day and night, over four long months, raging winds wrapped the planet in ear-splitting havoc. Clouds blown up gigantically deluged the continents with rain; rivers forsook their banks, wild torrents washed away the mountain roads. The seashores were strewn with wrecks, the entire ocean surface had become impassable. Our frail balloons no longer dared the agitated skies. Windswept gardens, plains, wooded parks, forest dells, stripped of leaves, were despoiled of their loveliness. Even our cities seemed to be wasting away beneath this wind. England felt as if a giant wave were being prepared to rise and wrench our island from its roots and cast it like refuse upon the vast wastes of the Atlantic Ocean.

This was more than a crisis of climate, we thought. Sunspots or a like disorder in the heavens must be to blame—or maybe something gone wrong in the very nature of weather itself. How long and how far would humanity be victimized by such destructive powers from outside, beyond our control? Was our survival still secure? In the midst of such questions, Ryland's ascension to the Protectorship was not much noted.

A feeling of awe, a breathless wonder, a painful sense of humanity's degradation, began to grow in every heart. Nature, our mother, our friend, had turned on us with a menacing frown; she showed us plainly, that though she permitted us to systematize her laws and subjugate her powers, she only had to lift a finger and we must quake. Not only England—our whole mountain-fringed globe, girded by the atmosphere in which we and all that lived had our being, could be picked up and pitched like a ball into space, where life would be drunk up, and all humanity's achievements be forever annihilated.

What were we, really, we inhabitants of Earth—one small planet among the hosts of them populating the skies? Our minds could embrace infinity, infinite space; yet the mechanism of our being was subject to merest accident. A scratch disorganized us, an ill-timed infection wiped out our health; subject to the same physical laws, none could call themselves truly safe. Even so, we lorded it over creation, wielding its elements in humanity's service, believing ourselves to have mastered life and death. We could learn to regard dying without terror when, like some family lineage, the continuity of our species looked assured. With the entrance of doubt, however slight for now, all we could see was our own insignificance.

I remember, after having witnessed the destructive effects of a fire, not even being able to look at a lit stove without a sensation of fear. The mounting flames had curled around the building as it fell: that's what flames did—they embraced and insinuated themselves into the substances around them, making any impediment to their progress yield at their touch. Could we take integral parts of this power for our own use and not be subject to its operation and effects? Could we domesticate the cub of a wild beast and not fear its growth and maturity?

So we began to feel with regard to death, lately so manageable, now so multitudinous. As the titanic winds abated, the plague became our greatest alarm. Because it thrived in the heat, we feared summer's approach. A commercial people, we were obliged to regard plans designed to keep out the invisible enemy, in light of our need to maintain our industries, our shipping, our trade, and our endless streams of foreign visitors; consequently the question of contagion took on the highest importance. Other countries could shut their borders, but for England there was no retreating from the outside world.

To face down the plague, we needed answers on these points:

How contagious was it, and how did it travel—that is, how did the plague arise in a certain place and then increase? Unlike some storied predecessors, it showed no proven links to vermin; unlike long-extinct diseases such as smallpox or scarlet fever, it didn't appear to be passed through human contact. We were left with a theory: it must spread through the air. Moreover, some air must be more subject to infection than other air. It was common knowledge that ship crews carrying virulent fevers had been known to leave one port town half in coffins by month's end, and the very next stop's population unscathed; some places were so much more fortunately situated. But how were we to judge of airs as the plague might, and decide, in one city, *Nothing for me here*, and in another city see a banquet set for death's plentiful harvest? Likewise, factors of physique appeared to be in play. Some individuals might escape ninety-nine exposures and receive the death-blow at the hundredth; bodies were sometimes in a state to reject the infection, the sickness, and at other times almost thirsty for it.

Wrestling with these reflections, our legislators were slow to decide on the laws to be put in force. The evil was so wide-spreading, so violent and incurable, that no care, no prevention could be judged superfluous which added any chance to our escape. Yet the immediate necessity for caution was in doubt. England was still secure. France, Germany, Italy, Spain, themselves uncontaminated, stood rampart-like between us and the plague. Safe in our island abode, we could have nothing to fear—and we weren't afraid, not openly. Yes, speculation was rife. We proceeded nonetheless in our daily occupations; we bought things and paid our expenses as usual; we kept making plans whose accomplishment must be many years away. No voice was heard telling us, *Hold back!*

Commerce continued. When foreign distresses came to our notice, we sought to apply creative remedies through all available channels. Charities boomed; funds were established for emigrants newly-arrived and in need, and for British merchants bankrupted by failures of trade. The national spirit awoke to its full splendor of activity, and, as it had ever done, set itself to resist the evil foe, and to stand in the breach which diseased Nature had suffered chaos and death to make in the ordered bounds we'd always known.

By the start of summer, with countless emigrants from plague-struck lands inundating the entirety of western Europe, many thousands had already reached the refuge of our island. A vast proportion were utterly destitute; and their increasing numbers were on course to overwhelm the usual systems and modes of relief. Ryland, who'd pursued the Protectorship so tenaciously, always with the idea of turning the whole force of high office onto the suppression of Britain's privileged orders, tried to minimize the crisis; but from the start he saw his measures thwarted, his schemes interrupted by the new state of things. As trade fell off and slowly failed between us and even our most loyal partners—India, Egypt, Greece, America—the routine of our national life was broken. In vain our Protector and his partisans sought to conceal this truth; in vain, day after day, he appealed for a discussion of the new laws concerning hereditary rank and privilege; in vain he endeavored to represent the evil of the plague as partial and temporary. Its visible and tangible effects came home to so many bosoms, and, through the various channels of commerce, were carried so entirely into every class and community, that of necessity the pandemic became the first question in the state, the chief subject of our most urgent attention.

From the domestic realm, we turned to the rest of the world with wonder and dismay. Could it really be true—cities laid waste, whole countries annihilated by the recent disorders? Quito: destroyed by an earthquake. Mexico: emptied by the combined effects of windstorm, plague, and famine. India's fertile plains, China's megacities: menaced alike with utter ruin. Where late the busy multitudes assembled for pleasure or profit, now only the sound of wailing and misery was heard. In that poisoned air, each human being inhaled death, even those in youth and health, their hopes in flower.

One third of Europe's population, we recalled, died of bubonic plague around 1348. As yet, the western part of the continent was uninfected by this new killer. Would it always be so?

O, yes, you heard people say. Of course it will. Fear not! In the wilds of the fiery, weather-tossed Americas, what wonder that plague should be flourishing? An old native of the East, sister of the tornado, hurricane, earthquake, and typhoon; child of the sun, and nursling of the tropics, this plague can't survive our sun-challenged climate. It drinks the dark blood of the south's inhabitants, but it never feasts on the pale-faced Celt. And should we find some stricken Aztecs or Asians among us, the plague would die with them, unspread, harmless to our kind. Let us weep for our brothers and sisters, though their dire fate cannot be ours. Let us lament over the children of this world's pleasure garden lands, and try to assist them. Not long ago we envied them their airy homes, their spicy groves, their fertile plantations and abundant loveliness of being.

But in this mortal life extremes are always matched; the thorn grows with the rose, the poisonous tree and the cinnamon mingle their boughs. For all its gold-draped wealth, the Arabian Peninsula is now a tomb; even the nomads' tents are fallen in the sands, and their horses begun to run wild in herds. The plague rages up and down the African continent, from Morocco to the Cape of Good Hope. It has desolated far-off Tasmania. Once more, the voices of lamentation fill the valley of Kashmir; its dells and woods and lakesides, cool fountains and gardens of roses, are polluted by the dead. In Georgia and old Circassia, the spirit of Beauty weeps over the ruin of its favorite temple: the physical form of a Black Sea woman. O, for a medicine vial to purge unwholesome Nature, and bring back our world to its accustomed health!

At home, our increasing distress was inversely proportional to British commerce's rapid decline. Despite all Ryland's fictions, bankruptcies skyrocketed among sectors dependent on trade or financial exchanges—banks, retailers, manufacturers. Jobs and products vanished. Such things, when they happen singly or a few at a time, affect only the immediate parties; but the prosperity of the nation was now shaken by frequent and extensive losses. Families bred in opulence were reduced to begging for loans. Ironically, the very state of world peace in which we'd gloried proved injurious, for it limited employment and kept too many idle, surplus young people inside the country.

Ryland came to Windsor to consult with us. He was a man of strong intellect, capable of quick, sound, and decisive action in the usual course of events. He stood aghast at the multitude of disasters that assailed us.; and the solution confronting him—tax the landed interests to save the commercial economy—went entirely against his grain. To have any chance of doing it, he'd first need the chief landholders, the British nobility, his sworn enemies, to agree. That meant he'd have to conciliate them by abandoning his cherished scheme of equalization; confirm them in their manorial rights; act against the permanent good of his country, in exchange for a temporary hand-out. He must throw his weapons aside and sacrifice his paramount goal for present ends. Every day he waited only added to his difficulties; the arrival of fresh emigrants, the total cessation of commerce, the desperate starving multitude that thronged around the palace of the Protectorate, were circumstances not to be trifled with. So the deal was struck. The aristocracy obtained all they wished, and agreed in return to pay a special twenty percent monthly tax on all the rent rolls of the country for the next year.

With the infusions of cash that followed, calm was restored to our markets and streets. At Windsor, we returned to the consideration of distant calamities, wondering if the future would bring any let-up. It was high summer, so there could be small hope of relief around our hemisphere. On the contrary, the disease gained virulence while starvation did its usual work. Thousands died unlamented—for the mourners fell beside the still-warm corpses, mute, dead.

On August 18th, the plague was reported in France and Italy.

Idris and I happened to be in London that day. At first, the news was only whispered around town, too soul-shaking to mention out loud. Friends met in the street; one would say, already hurrying on, "You've heard!" and the other reply, with a gasp of fear and horror, "What will become of us?" At length the news was reported—a single line dropped in an inside corner of the late edition: **We regret to state that there can be no longer any doubt of the plague having been detected at Livorno, Genoa, and Marseilles.** Not a word of comment followed; the readership was left to feel as if they'd heard that their house was on fire, and had rushed home, borne along by a lurking hope of a mistake—*not our house, our house will be there when I turn the corner*—only to arrive in time to see its sheltering roof collapse in flames. Advanced from rumor to definite, undeniable, and indelible publication, the knowledge went forth. Such obscure placement on the page only served to render the item more conspicuous. Its small print assumed gigantic proportions; gradually, to the bewildered and terrified eye, the very universe seemed to disappear behind the letters, as if covered by a billboard sign.

Now, in one great revulsive stream, the British expatriate and tourist classes came pouring back to their own country. Crowds of well-off French and Italian emigrants joined them—with Spaniards soon to follow, as plague was seen there, too. Our little island was filled even to bursting. The foreign newcomers, unlike the earlier crowds from further east and south, could afford to pay their own way at first, and local economies were flooded with cash as a consequence. But the uptick was brief; for these people had no means of replenishing what they spent among us. With the advance of summer, and the plague's spread back home, the rents on the properties they owned went unpaid, and the remittances from their investments and business holdings failed them. Lately so well-versed in modern convenience and luxury, they were soon indistinguishable from the crowds of wretched, perishing creatures who'd proceeded them onto our social care rolls.

At Windsor, we recalled England's history of hospitable refuge. People driven from their foreign homelands by several centuries of wars and political revolutions had found here a generous welcome; our generation could not be backward in rendering aid to the victims of a more wide-spreading calamity. Our own family counted many personal friends among the new arrivals. We sought them out, relieved their immediate wants, and brought many of them home to stay. Our Castle became an asylum for the unhappy. With a small population to support now on his tax-reduced land revenues, Adrian and I imposed some unfamiliar limits on household spending. It wasn't money, though, but basic necessities that became scarce; food, above all. Local livestock shortages turned national; demand could not be met. It was difficult to find an immediate solution. The usual one of imports was entirely cut off. In this emergency, to feed our own resident refugees, we were obliged to convert Windsor's pleasure-grounds and parks into kitchen gardens, grazing pasture, and farmland; along with many trees, even the poor deer—our antlered pets, almost—were obliged to fall for the sake of a worthier cause. As these scenes began repeating themselves around the country, its overcrowded metropolitan areas witnessed an exodus;

the labor required to bring large estates to this sort of culture employed and fed the cast-off workforce of their shuttered businesses, stores, docks, and factories. People followed the food; and another crisis in the cities was averted.

We had Adrian to thank for this fragile progress. Observing the success of our innovations at Windsor, he at once launched himself into a tireless campaign to convince England's wealthiest landowners to emulate him and likewise convert their possessions. He made them direct proposals in Parliament to this effect, in speeches whose eloquence did nothing to ingratiate. None of his listeners really enjoyed the idea of plowing over their best parkland views, or making drastic cutbacks in the national expenditure on horses kept purely for pleasure and sport. Yet the earnestness of his pleas and the sheer benevolence that shone through Adrian's words proved irresistible. To the honor of their nation, let be it recorded that after an initial delay, seeing the misery of their fellow creatures became only more glaring, the landed gentry came through with enthusiastic generosity. Declaring Windsor's solutions very obvious, those with the most luxurious lifestyles were often the first to part with their past self-indulgences. Indeed, as so often happened in communities, a fashion was set. Almost no one of high birth rode in carriages anymore, and they'd have felt disgraced to be seen on horseback for any but urgent reasons. The infirm could be wheeled or carried as of old in chairs; for the rest, it wasn't uncommon to see women of the highest rank going on foot around town, or arriving at some fashionable resort on a bicycle.

Soon, if they possessed landed property, even the most confirmed Londoners had left town for their estates, often accompanied by whole troops of indigents, foreign and native. They'd cut down their woods to build temporary dwellings, and carve up their parks and flower gardens to divide among needy families— many of whom had held high rank in their own nations. Now they were hoeing, weeding. Everyone worked with such a vengeance that Adrian was required to spearhead a new campaign, urging moderation. The spirit of sacrifice must be checked when generosity passed over into lavish waste. Based on earlier pandemics, the plague would probably be gone in a year or two. Better, in that case, not to destroy our fine breeds of horses, or change our most beautifully designed landscapes past recognition.

Winter, the plague cure, wasn't far off. Gratitude welcomed the browning woods and swollen rivers, evening mists, morning frosts. The purifying effects of cold weather were clear and immediate; the mortality rates across Europe dropped every week. Many of our visitors from the south left us, fleeing delightedly from the cold and the tightening rations; even after fearful losses to plague, their native lands were still full of plenty. In England, we breathed again. What next summer would bring, we didn't know; but the present months belonged to us, and our hopes of an end to the plague were high.

(28)   I HAVE lingered all this while beside the stream of life, dallying on its banks—dallying with the shadow of death about to stretch across its waters like a wasting shoal—cradling my heart in retrospection of past happiness, times when hope existed. Why stop? I'm not immortal. I've barely touched on my marriage, my fatherhood; the thread of my narrative might easily be spun out to the limits of my existence. But the same feeling that first made me dredge my tender recollections, now hurries me on; the same yearning of this warm, panting heart, that sent me after the words to record my vagabond youth, and all the pages that followed, makes me now recoil from further delay. I must complete my work.

So here I stand. The year (then) is 2094, the stream of human life still fleet and flowing. And now away! Spread the sail, ply the oars, past dark impending crags and down steep rapids, even to the sea of desolation I have reached.

On June 20th, circumstance called me to London, where I heard the first talk that plague symptoms had been observed at some city hospitals. I cycled back to Windsor with a heavy heart, reaching the shaded road through the Home Park by late afternoon. A great part of the Castle grounds lay under cultivation, here divided into strips of potatoes and corn. Rooks cawed loudly in the immeasurable boughs of the remaining oak trees, but through their hoarse cries came strains of music. On the park green, I found a small country-style fair in progress, local youth—Alfred's fellow Etonians included—playing host to the neighboring public. Tents of flaunting colors speckled the lawns, gaudy flags waved in the sunshine, a makeshift dancing platform was crowded with young figures in motion: a gay scene. Parking my bicycle at a rack, I found a shady tree to lean against and watch the dancers, whose feet were given wings by one of the wild Turkish-style airs popular then. I tapped my toe as unconsciously as the rest of the onlookers; for a few moments, the tripping measure lifted my spirit with it; my eyes followed the mazes of the dance with gladness. Then revulsion—heart-piercing steel.

You're all going to die, I thought.

Already your tomb is built up around you. Gifted with agility and strength, you imagine otherwise: but life's bower of flesh is frail, and the silver cord than binds you to existence very easily dissolved. The joyous soul, charioted from pleasure to pleasure by graceful well-formed limbs, will suddenly feel the axle snap, the wheels dissolve in dust. Not one of you, O! fated crowd, can escape—not one! not my own ones! not my Idris and her babes! Shriek, you church bells! Howl, trumpets! Pile dirge on dirge; pound out funereal chords; let the air ring with dire wailing; let wild discord rush in! Horror and misery!

The blue sky and the merry dancers had vanished. Instead I saw the park green strewn with corpses, the air dimmed and fetid with deathly exhalations. My ears heard no music, only the windy sound of guardian angels, humanity's attendants, hastening away from a finished task. A melancholy tune started up, and I saw the world weeping over the angels' departure. Tearful human faces distorted with sobs began to stream across my gaze, even when I opened my eyes, faster and faster, countless woebegone expressions thronging around my perceptions, faces marked by every type of wretchedness. I recognized a few. Adrian's countenance flitted past, tainted by death. There was Idris with livid lips, about to slide into the wide grave. Ashy pale, Raymond and Perdita sat apart, looking on with sad smiles. Confusion grew: their looks of sorrow changed to mockery; they nodded their heads in time to the music, whose clangor became maddening.

To throw off a feeling of insanity, I leapt from the shelter of the tree and rushed into the midst of the crowd. Idris spotted me and advanced with a light step. I wrapped her in my arms. What made an entire world to me, I felt, Idris in my embrace, was yet frail as a droplet of dew on a lily's petal when the risen sun begins to thirst. Rare tears filled my eyes. Then more: my boys' joyful welcome, Clara's soft hug, Adrian's handshake; it was all too much for me. They were here, I knew; I felt them near and safe—yet no, methought it all a deceitful vision; they were gone. The earth reeled, the old trees danced on their roots.

Overcome by dizziness, I sank to the ground.

It wasn't easy to allay the natural alarm of my beloved family and friends without mentioning plague; but I knew that once the word passed my lips, they'd construe my perturbation for a symptom and see infection in my faintness. I'd scarcely recovered my feet and was trying to pass off the episode with smiles, when I noticed the Lord Protector approaching our little circle.

In his younger days, Ryland had served as Britain's ambassador to the United States, and over several journeys to the far West of that immense continent had gone so far as to choose a site to build on; for many years, he intended to migrate and live on his Wyoming ranch. Ambition turned his thoughts from these designs; ambition, laboring through every setback and hindrance, had now led him to the summit of his hopes. The man might have passed for a rancher even so, or a farmer—someone whose muscles and full-grown stature had been developed under the influence of vigorous exercise and exposure to the elements. This was to a great degree the case. A landed proprietor with an ardent, industrious, and forward-looking disposition, Ryland had given himself up to agricultural labors on his own large estate for some years already.

His countenance was rough but intelligent, his brow ample. Quick grey eyes seemed to be on constant look-out over his own and his enemies' plans. His voice was stentorian; his gigantic hand, stretched out in debate, seemed to warn his hearers that speech was not his only weapon. At the same time, no politician could "crush a butterfly on the wheel" with better effect, and no one excelled him at covering speedy retreats from more powerful foes with the least loss of face—see how he'd conceded that earlier election to Lord Raymond, before any votes could be cast. Beneath his shrewd and imposing exterior lay a cowardly streak and chronic infirmities of purpose that few people, as yet, had discovered—though they might have read them in his unsteady gaze and uneasy glances; in his extreme desire to hear everyone's opinion; even in the feebleness of his handwriting, the failings destined to undo his Protectorship might have been traced. It was a post he'd canvassed for eagerly, intending his term to become historic by its innovative dismantling of the aristocracy. Instead he found each day monopolized by a global pandemic, a ruinous, convulsive force from nature that threatened everyone. As we had already seen, Ryland was incapable of meeting the crisis by any comprehensive system. He'd resorted to expedient after expedient, and could never be induced to put a remedy in effect, until it came too late to be of use.

Certainly the man who advanced towards us now bore small resemblance to the powerful, ironical, seemingly fearless campaigner for preeminence. Our Native Oak, as his partisans called him, appeared to have been stricken by a premature and nipping winter. He looked half his usual height, and moved as if his joints and limbs could hardly support him. His eyes were wandering in his grey, pinched face; his every gesture expressed debility of purpose and dastard fear. I knew what he would say.

"Plague." In the midst of the others' greetings, the single word fell, as if involuntarily, from his convulsed lips. "The plague."

"Where?" gasped Idris.

"Everywhere," Ryland said. "We've got to leave, now—but then what? Where next? No one knows—there might be no refuge on earth. It's coming down on us like a thousand packs of wolves—we must get away, run. Windsor, Verney—what do you think? Where will you go? Where can any of us go?" the iron man finished, trembling.

"Where, indeed," Adrian said. "Where would you run, Ryland? We must all of us remain where we are, and do our best to help our suffering fellow creatures."

"*Help?*" Ryland's voice had turned shrill, almost reedy. "There *is* no help!—great God, who talks of help? The whole world has the plague!"

Adrian gave a gentle smile and observed, "Then to avoid it, we must leave the world."

Ryland, whose forehead was covered in cold sweat, groaned. Some more vigorous soothing on our part was needed before we could get him to explain the grounds for his present alarm. The crisis, it turned out, had come sufficiently home to him, when one of his servants, while waiting on him at table, suddenly dropped dead—from plague, he'd been told by the medical team that responded. We stood there trying to calm him, but our own hearts weren't calm. I saw the anxiety in the look Idris turned from me to our children, whose eyes showed worry. Their Uncle Adrian stood absorbed in meditation. For myself, I echoed Ryland's panic as his words rang in my ears: *The whole world,* yes. In what uncontaminated seclusion could I hide and save my beloved treasures, until this pandemic's death spree had passed? We sank into silence.

All this the crowd saw, though our group had moved aside and soon went off together, up the terrace steps towards the Castle. Our collective change of demeanor had been striking; also, a rumor that Ryland had fled London from fear of plague was making the rounds before his appearance that day, a textbook image of man on the run.

Any spirit of gaiety eclipsed, the fair wound down forlornly. Its attendees broke up into whispering groups. The music stopped. To the young Etonians, looking around, their own light-heartedness—dressing up, decorating tents, creating so much amusement—suddenly felt like a terrible mistake, a sin against, and some kind of provocation to, a calamitous destiny about to paralyze all hope and life; their merriment both unholy and unlucky. Meanwhile, those fairgoers who were foreigners still living in our parts, plague refugees themselves, had caught on that their last asylum was now invaded. Some whom fear made garrulous found an eager local audience for firsthand accounts of the disease's insidious and irremediable nature, and the many miseries they'd witnessed back home.

Overhead in the Castle, Idris stood at a window and looked out at the park with maternal eyes; though Clara and our own children were safe in their playroom, it was clear how many of the other children were being drawn or swept into the audience for these raconteurs of horror. One little girl we watched creeping nearer and nearer until a wild gesture of one speaker's arm accidentally struck her. We both winced, but kept quiet in the silence of the long room. Our reflections were painful. Ryland stood by himself at another window while Adrian, revolving some new and overpowering idea, I could tell, paced the carpet behind us. At length he stopped, turned, and spoke to Ryland:

"I've long expected this. How could we reasonably hope to remain exempt from a universal affliction? This evil is come home to us, even here on our island, and we must not shrink from our fate. What are your plans, my Lord Protector, for the benefit of our country?"

"For heaven's sake, Windsor!" Ryland cried. "Don't mock me with that title. Death and disease level all. I can't pretend to protect anyone, or to govern a hospital—which is what England will quickly become."

"Do you then intend, now, in time of peril, to walk away from your duties?"

"Duties!" The other laughed. "Speak rationally, my Lord! When I am a plague-spotted corpse, where will my duties be? Every man for himself! The devil take the Protectorship, I say, if it exposes me and mine to danger!"

"Faint-hearted man!" returned Adrian indignantly. "Your fellow citizens, your people put their trust in you, and you betray them!"

"You say I betray them," Ryland answered. "I say the plague betrays me. Faint-hearted! It's easy for you, shut up in your castle, out of danger, to scoff at honest fear. Let someone else take the Protectorship—before God I renounce it!" And for the second time, I saw the insignia of my nation's highest office removed by its wearer and tossed onto a tablecloth.

On this occasion, Adrian was ready: "And before God," he replied fervently, "do I receive it: myself. No one else will campaign for this honor now, none envy my danger or labors. Put your powers in my hands, Ryland. I've fought with death for a long time, and much" (he stretched out his thin hand) "much have I suffered in the struggle. This I know: it's not by fleeing, but by facing the enemy, that we can conquer. And if I'm to go down in the fight—so be it."

Ryland would have left immediately, but Adrian was already exhorting him to consider the panic his departure would cause.

"Return to London. Encourage the people by your presence. I'll go with you and incur all the danger. You've always been thought a wise and magnanimous person—would you destroy your own legacy?"

The pair was still talking as twilight deepened, and the last activity dwindled from the park below. A banquet in the downstairs hall for the fairgoers was next on the agenda, and thither Idris and I repaired, after putting on our gala dress, to receive and entertain the small and melancholy numbers who appeared. All the festive touches to the great room only gave it a more solemn and funereal appearance. Idris, framed by looping flower garlands, sat at the top of the half-empty hall, pale, tearful, almost forgetful of her duties as hostess. All her attention was fixed on Alfred and Clara, whose nervous demeanor showed the effects of what they'd overheard in the park; and on Elvis, the only mirthful creature present, whose bursts of laughter at his own infant fingers and thoughts echoed alone off the vaulted roof.

At last, his poor mother, who'd been struggling to suppress any sign of her anguish, burst into tears, folded the baby in her arms, and hurried out, the two children at her heels. In their wake a confused murmur rose from the assembled guests. The hall grew louder as more and more began to voice their fears. Several younger people gathered round my hosting seat, to ask my advice; they were anxious about their friends and family in London. I replied as encouragingly as I could. The death toll reported there was still very small; the metropolitan districts' orderliness, good sanitation, and world-class facilities were all in our favor—on the whole, indeed, the outlook for England's cities might be a very positive one. And as for themselves, living close to Windsor like us, the plague could well have lost its venomous power by the time it crawled so far outside the city limits—where our naturally salubrious air would tend to counteract any remaining harm. The pandemic spread's was powered, I explained, by poor air quality. By now, I realized, my remarks had the whole room listening; so I rose to conclude:

"My friends, our risk is common. Our efforts and precautions shall be common too. If the courage to resist can save us, we will be saved. We will fight the enemy to the last. Plague won't find a ready prey in us; we'll fight over every inch of ground; and, by methodical and inflexible laws, we will raise invincible barriers against our foe. Perhaps in no part of the world has this evil sickness met with so systematic and determined an opposition. Perhaps no country is naturally so well protected against our invader—certainly, nowhere have nature's gifts been better seconded by human ability. We will not despair. We are neither cowards nor fatalists; but, believing that God has placed the means for our preservation in our own hands, we will use those means to our utmost. And, remember, these are our best medicines: cleanliness, sobriety, kindness, generosity and, yes, a good sense of humor."

In a short while my listeners departed with thoughtful steps, to await the events in store for them. Upstairs, I found Idris in fresh tears. Her brother was with her. In regard to the Protectorship he'd won a partial victory: to help reassure its frightened populace, Ryland had agreed to return to London for a period of weeks, time enough for everyone to get used to his leaving. Adrian planned to be with him every step of the way. Terrified at the risk he planned to run, Idris saw the situation in a tragic light; he was trying to convince her to trust his judgment.

Strikingly, the sinking sadness with which he'd heard the plague news earlier that day had vanished. His body radiated purposeful energy—I saw strength, solemn dedication, self-belief. His physical weakness, every trace of the old illness, had passed from him, like the fleshly human disguise of a god. Such was Adrian. Apparently given up to contemplation, listless and averse to excitement, a lowly student, a man of visions—but offer him a worthy theme and watch him spring to the highest pitch of virtuous accomplishment. At such times his eloquence was hard to resist.

"Finally," he told us, "I've encountered a job tailor-made for me, one requiring no gift for intrigue and no affinity for the labyrinths of human passion. Instead, I can bring what is needed: to the sick, patience, sympathy, high standards of care; to the miserable orphan, to the mourner, hope and a hand back up again. And to the great work of keeping the plague within limits, minimizing the misery it's bound to cause, I can bring the necessary restraint, courage, and watchfulness.

"Relieve your minds from fear on my account. I don't plan to overtax my strength or seek out needless danger. I simply feel that I know what ought to be done, and that I need to be there to see it done right—which, if anything, will increase the care I'll take of myself.

"Disappointment and sickness have dominated my life; I've existed, nearly isolated, under a tyranny of prohibitions. Congratulate me, then, that I've found fitting scope for my powers. Many times I've thought to go to France or Italy and offer my help among the plague-stricken towns; but I didn't want to upset you—and, also, I knew this catastrophe was bound to reach us eventually. Now, to England and its people, those mighty spirits, I dedicate myself. If I can save a single one from death; if I can prevent disease in one solitary, smiling cottage, I shall not have lived in vain."

He went to London. With him went enthusiasm, and firm, high-wrought resolve, and the ability to look death in the eye without faltering. With us remained sorrow, anxiety, and unendurable expectations of evil. *He that hath wife and children hath given hostages to fortune,* wrote Francis Bacon long ago. It did no good to philosophize, or to be brave. Any reliance on probable good was equally vain. I could find a set of scales and pile every bit of logic, courage, and resignation in the world onto one side; it only took a single fear for the lives of Idris and our children on the other, to outweigh everything and kick the beam with an ugly clang.

(29)　*THE PLAGUE—in London! Fools that we were, we never foresaw this. We wept over the ruin of the boundless continents to the south and east of us, then mourned the desolation of the western world. The watery barriers between our island and the rest, we fancied, would preserve us, alive, among the planet's dead.*

Methinks Calais lies not so far from Dover. From either shore, the naked eye easily discerns the sister land; they were united once; what runs between them on our maps is but a footway trodden through the high grass of geological time. Yet this runnel was to save us—and the sea, yes, raising adamantine walls around our British Isles. On the other side, disease and misery; inside lay shelter from the foe—a nook of the garden of paradise—a patch of celestial soil, which no evil could invade—truly we were wise in our generation, to imagine all these things!

But we are awake now. The plague is in London, and England's air is tainted; her lost sons and daughters strew the unwholesome earth. And now, the sea that was defending us seems to imprison us instead: hemmed in by its empty gulphs, we'll die like the famished inhabitants of a city under siege. Other nations, with contiguity, have a certain fellowship in death. But we, with no neighbors, must bury our own dead, and little England become a wide, wide tomb.

Though my feelings partook of this universal misery, the thought of danger to my wife and children possessed my whole being with fear. The idols of my soul: how to save and keep them from the plague, obsessed me. The wildest plans, to reach an uninfected spot and build our home there. Maybe a wave-tossed raft at sea. Or some healthy wild beast's den emptied by my hand for the purpose; or else an aerie where a mountain eagle had its nest, but now my family and I would live there, for the next several years, suspended in an inaccessible recess of a cliff overlooking a rocky sea! No labor looked too great, no scheme too outlandish, if it promised life to them. . .O! you heartstrings of mine, if only you could be torn asunder, and my soul kept from spending itself in tears of blood for sorrow!

Idris, after the first shock, recovered her strength of composure. Studiously shutting out all thoughts of the future, cradling her heart in present blessings, she kept the children constantly in sight; as long as they were near, healthy, playful, she could enjoy contentment and hope. I, meanwhile, was troubled by a strange, wild restlessness, all the more intolerable for being kept concealed. My fears for Adrian never abated. August, our hottest month, saw plague fatalities surge rapidly in London. All who had the power of leaving had deserted the city by now; and he, the brother of my soul, was still exposed to the perils from which most everyone we knew had fled. Alongside those poor souls chained there by circumstance, he stayed behind to do combat with the fiend, virtually unaided; infection might even reach him, and he die unattended and alone. By day and night these thoughts pursued me until I made up my mind to visit London, despite the risk. I had to see him, and quiet my agonizing worries somehow—whether by hope's sweet medicine, or the opiate of despair.

About midway there I started seeing a host of changes on the suburban scenery's face. The better sort of houses were boarded up, along with businesses on every side. What commerce there was, looked to be struggling; what people I saw, shared an air of anxiety. I met several funerals but counted few mourners. My bicycle's passage attracted wondering glances—I was the first person they'd seen heading towards London in days.

Adrian's chief effort, I knew, after the immediate care of the sick, had been to disguise the symptoms and progress of the plague in London from the city's own inhabitants. He acted on the principle that fear and melancholy forebodings would aid the pandemic's spread; that in both individuals and groups, desponding, brooding care reduced immunity to infection. No unseemly sights were therefore discernible: the shops were in general open, the major roads and attractions in some degree kept up. But since the third week in June, when I'd last seen it, the city was a different place. Grass had sprung up in the streets deserted by traffic. Row after row of drawn shutters gave a desolate look to the house fronts I cycled past, almost alone in the road. Frightened stares followed me, and strange looks very different from the Londoners' usual business-like glances.

I found the streets of the fashionable neighborhood around the Protectoral Palace almost deserted. Adrian's antechamber within, however, was crowded at this hour with petitioners. Hesitant to interrupt his work, I stood aside and watched several dozen passing in and out. Middle- and working-class people who'd lost the means to support themselves with the stoppage of trade, which had trickled down to paralyze the money-making spirit at every level of society; in general, those waiting to see Adrian displayed an anxious air, and a few showed signs of terror at their plight. What a contrast from their look—calm, resigned, even satisfied—upon leaving his audience chamber. I could read my friend's beneficent influence in their enlivened bearing. Order, comfort, and even health, rose under his influence, as from the touch of a magician's wand.

Two o'clock struck. Those who'd failed to get in this time went sullenly or sorrowfully away, while I entered the audience chamber.

The clear signs of improvement in Adrian 's health struck me at once. Gone was that resemblance to an over-nursed flower of spring, grown tall beyond its strength, weighed down by its own blossoms. Concentrated energy was diffused over his whole formerly languorous person. His eyes bright, his features composed, he sat at a table with several secretaries who were arranging notes and petitions. Adrian was still occupied with a few petitioners who'd lingered. I admired his justice and patience in his remarks to them, and his generosity to one, who needed passage money for his family to get safely to relatives in the Midlands.

"I'm glad you've come," he said, when at last we were alone. "I can only spare a few minutes, and must tell you much in that time. The plague is now in progress—there's no denying the fact—the deaths increase each week. What will come I cannot guess. I look only at the day before me. As yet, thank God, I can handle the government of the town." My impulsive arrival, I learned, was fortuitous. Though Adrian had been able to keep him in town far past the few weeks originally asked, he'd received the Protector's final ultimatum. Ryland would be leaving London before the end of the month. His deputy, an appointee of Parliament, who'd been preparing to undertake the remainder of his term, had died of plague the previous day. Parliament, Adrian explained, must name another deputy Protector at once. "I've advanced my claim," he said, "and I don't expect to have a single competitor. The House is meeting tonight to decide the question. Ryland's too ashamed to show himself near Parliament. But you, Lionel, my friend, you godsend—you can nominate me! You must. Please, won't you do me this service?"

How lovely is devotion! Royally born, bred in luxury, by nature averse to the usual struggles of a public life: now, in this dangerous time, when simply to live was the highest hope of the ambitious, here was my beloved and heroic friend, offering in sweet simplicity to sacrifice himself for the public good. The very idea was generous and noble. Beyond this, his direct and unpretending manner rendered the authentic virtue behind his action ten times more touching. I'd have withstood his request, even so; but I'd seen the good he diffused; and his resolve felt unshakeable. So, with a heavy heart, I consented to do as he asked. He grasped my hand affectionately.

"Thank you, Lionel. You've helped me solve a painful dilemma—and are, as you ever were, my best friend." With that, our interview had to close. Adrian, leaving for his daily round of hospital visits and neighborhood inspections, told me I should go upstairs and talk to Ryland for a few hours. "Though he deserts his post down here, he could render us immense help back home in the north of England. Receiving and assisting new arrivals from London, contributing to the city's food supply—awaken him, I entreat you, to some sense of duty."

I found the present Lord Protector much altered, even from the wreck I'd last observed at Windsor. Perpetual fear had jaundiced and shriveled his whole person. A slight relaxation of the wince in which his face seemed fixed denoted a smile at my news, that Adrian would surely be made deputy that night. He began sorting papers to pack as we talked. Ryland couldn't wait to leave London. Every day since his grudging return, he'd expected to catch plague; every day, he was unable to resist the Earl of Windsor and the gentle violence of his detention. Now, after tonight, he could escape to safety. His spirits rising by the moment, he cheerfully entered into a discussion about what he, as a leader in his home county, should plan to do in aid of the nation at large. Forgotten for the moment, I guessed, was his cherished and well-known resolution to shut himself up in the mansion and grounds of his estate, away from all outside contact.

That evening, Adrian and I headed to Westminster. Along the way he rehearsed me in what I was to say and do. My mind felt strangely blank as we entered Parliament. While Adrian lingered to chat in the coffee-room, I went in and took my seat in old St. Stephen's. The silence was unusual. I hadn't been there since Raymond's protectorate, which had witnessed high water marks in attendance, eloquence, and warmth of debate. Tonight's benches were at least half empty. Those customarily occupied by the hereditary members sat entirely vacant. The city members were there, and members for the commercial towns. I spotted few landed proprietors, and almost none of those who'd entered parliament for the sake of a career.

The announcement broke into the quiet: first subject for the attention of the House, was an address by the Lord Protector, who was requesting the members to appoint a deputy during a necessary absence on his part.

Full silence prevailed. Everyone knew Ryland wasn't there.

His deputy must be chosen next. Now for the first time I saw the full extent of my responsibility and felt overwhelmed by what I'd brought on myself. Through fear of the plague, Ryland deserted his post; through fear of the plague, no one else but Adrian wanted it. And I, the Earl of Windsor's kin by marriage, was to propose his election. I was to thrust this matchless friend of mine into the land's most dangerous position—no! Impossible! The die was cast—I would offer myself as candidate.

The few members present had come more for the sake of settling the business by a quorum, than with any idea of hearing a debate. I'd risen mechanically, my knees trembling, my first words hesitant. "The necessity of choosing a person adequate to the dangerous task at hand" was as far as I'd gotten. But with the decision to take my friend's place, the load of doubt and painful hesitation was lifted from me. My voice was firm now, my eloquence spontaneous. What Adrian had already done, I credited fully, and promised the same vigilance in furthering all his views. I drew a touching picture of his vacillating health, and boasted of my own strength. I prayed them to save, even from himself, this irreplaceable scion of the noblest family in England. My alliance with him was the pledge of my sincerity; my union with his sister, my children, his presumptive heirs, were the hostages of my truth.

This unexpected turn in the debate was quickly communicated to Adrian, who hurried into the chamber just at the peak of my impassioned harangue. With my soul in my words, I didn't see him— only a vision of his form, tainted by pestilence, sinking in death; he seized my hand through the image of his future floating in my eyes, saying, "Unkind friend—you've betrayed me!"

Then, with the air of one who had a right to command, he sprang forward to claim the place of Lord Deputy to the Protector as his own. He had bought it, he said, with danger, and paid for it with toil, during an interval devoted to the interests of his country—was Lionel Verney now to step in, and reap the profit? Let his listeners remember what London had been when he, Windsor, arrived: the panic and attendant famine, the daily loosening of every moral and legal tie. He had restored order—a work requiring perseverance, patience, energy. He had neither slept nor waked but for the good of his country. Would they dare wrong him like this? Would they take away his hard-earned reward, to bestow it on an absolute stranger to public life, who lacked all experience where he himself was a proven adept—and Ryland's own choice for the position?

Adrian went further. From the tone of his appeal, he might have been asking to be made the highest power in England, and not, as was the truth, to be foremost in the ranks of loathsome toil and inevitable death: for he demanded the deputyship as his right. Never before, he reminded us, had he, born the inheritor of England's throne, ever once asked favor or honor of those who were now his equals yet might have been his subjects. Would they refuse him? Could they topple from the path of distinction and worthy ambition, the heir of their ancient kings, and heap another disappointment on a fallen house?

Into the murmur of sympathy that followed Adrian's final words, I shouted, "Don't listen to him! He's lying—lying to himself!" But I wasn't allowed to explain. Silence reestablished, Adrian and I were ordered, by custom, to retire while the House decided. Any hopes I had were mistaken: we'd hardly left the chamber before Adrian was recalled and confirmed in the office.

We returned to the Protectoral Palace together.

Adrian spoke first, through a smile. "Why, Lionel? What did you intend? You couldn't hope to win, and yet you give me the pain of a triumph over my dearest friend."

"Don't mock me," I replied. "You know why. As you, adored brother, uncle, friend, the one being, of all the world contains, who's dearest to our hearts—you devote yourself to an early death, I was trying to prevent it. My death would be a small evil by comparison, and with my ruder health I'm likelier to survive; while you can't hope to escape."

"As to the likelihood of escaping," said Adrian, "ten years from now the cold stars might be shining on all our graves. But as to my peculiar liability to infection, I could easily prove, both logically and physically, that in the midst of contagion I have a better chance of survival than you." I waited for the proof, but he continued in another vein.

"This is my post, Lionel. I was born for this—to rule an England endangered, in anarchy—to devote myself to saving her. The blood of my forbearers cries aloud in my veins and bids me be first among my people. Or, if this mode of speech offend you, let me say this. My mother, the proud Ex-Queen, instilled a love of distinction in me very early on. I might have started struggling for my lost inheritance years ago, had my bodily weakness and peculiar opinions not prevented it. But now my mother, or, if you will, my mother's lessons, awaken within me. I can't lead forces into battle; I won't intrigue to raise again our throne upon the wreck of English public spirit. But I can be the foremost support and guardian of my country, now that terrific disasters and ruin have laid strong hands upon her.

"That country and my beloved sister are all I have. I'll protect one—the other I commit to your charge. If I survive, and Idris be lost, far better I died too. Preserve her. For her own sake I know you will; if you require other incentive, bear in mind that in saving her, you save me. Her faultless nature, a compendium of perfections, is wrapped up in those she loves, their slightest injury hurts her. Already she fears for us; fears for the children she adores; fears for you, their father, her lover, her husband and protector. She needs you near, to support and encourage her. Go back to Windsor then, my brother—for such you are by every tie. Fill my place there along with yours. And let me, in all my sufferings here, turn my thoughts towards you all in that dear seclusion, and say, *There is peace.*"

(30)   MY INTENTION when I left for Windsor was to come straight back. Determined to share his work, and to save him, if necessary, at the expense of my own life, I planned to stay at home only long enough to gain Idris's consent that I return to London, where I would take my place beside my matchless friend. Yet I dreaded to witness the anguish my resolve might cause her— especially now, at the hour of greatest need.

Having begun my journey in anxious haste, I downshifted, and let my route turn circuitous. *If only,* I wished, *I could make the ride last days, weeks, months; if only I could avoid the necessity of action; if only I could escape from thought*—I wished vainly. What was ahead came nearer and nearer, a world clasped in shadow's embrace.

A detour through Bishopsgate took me to Perdita's old cottage, where I stopped and dismounted. This spot of sweetest recollection, with its now deserted dwelling and neglected garden, was well adapted to nurse my melancholy. In our happiest days, my sister had adorned every inch with decorative beauties of art and nature; in that same spirit of excess, after the separation from Raymond she'd caused it to be entirely neglected. Deer had been getting through the broken fence. Grass was sprouting from the threshold. A broken, breeze-swung shutter creaked a signal of utter desertion. The sky, blue; the air, impregnated with fragrance by rare blossoms that survived among the weeds; the trees, making nature's favorite melody with their motion overhead: I saw a gay summer scene dimmed by the meaning of these weed-choked paths and flower beds. The time when in proud and happy security we assembled at this cottage, was gone. Soon the present moments would join those past—and menacing shadows of future hours rose from the womb of Time, their cradle and their coffin.

For the first time in my life, I genuinely envied the dead their sleep. I thought with pleasure of a final bed awaiting me under the sod, where grief and fear have no power. I gave a push to the gate with its broken hinge and felt almost suffocated by tears. To hold them back, I grabbed my bicycle and sped away down the forest road, thinking to myself: *O Death and Change, you rulers of our life—what was there in our tranquility that excited your envy—in our happiness, that you should destroy it? We were happy, loving and beloved; we asked for nothing more, with every blessing already showered upon us. But, alas!*

And I recited an old line of Calderón's: *"La fortuna deidad barbara importuna, oy cadaver y ayer flor, no permanece jamas!"* ("Fortune—barbarous, grasping deity—today a corpse, yesterday a flower—not permanent, ever.")

My ride began to take me past numbers of people from the locality. Everyone looked thoughtful or worried; overhearing a few snatches of conversation, I stopped to ask what went on here. A party of people fleeing London, as many did in those days, had come up the Thames in a boat, my respondents told me. Finding no one at Windsor who'd agree to shelter them, they'd gone a bit further upriver and spent the night in a deserted hut near Boulter's Lock; I knew the place. When they pursued their way the following morning, the Londoners had left one of their company behind, sick with plague. This circumstance becoming known, the deserted wretch was left to fight with disease and death in solitude as best he might— for no one dared approach within half a mile of the infected neighborhood. Urged by compassion, I immediately set off that way, meaning to assess the man's situation and find out what I could do to help.

As I advanced, I met more knots of locals, all talking earnestly of the same thing. Distant as they were from the ghastly hut, terror of contagion showed on every face. One person even stepped into my path to say she guessed I didn't know—an infected person was lying but at a short distance ahead.

"I do know it," I replied, "and I understand he's alone. I'm going there to see what condition he's in." I let a murmur of surprise and horror run through the assembly before continuing: "This poor wretch is deserted, dying, helpless. In these unhappy times, God knows how soon any or all of us may be in his place. I'm going to do as I would be done by."

"But Verney." Here was a man I knew. "You'll never be able to return to the Castle—what about Lady Idris—and the children?"

I shook my head. "My friend, all of you—don't you know the Earl himself, who now fills the place of Lord Protector, makes daily visits to plague cases in homes and hospitals and clinics, going near the infected, even touching the sick? Yet I've never seen him in better health. You labor under entirely mistaken ideas about the plague and its nature. But don't worry, I'm not asking anyone to go with me—or even to believe me, not until I return safe and sound from my patient." So I left them, and hurried on.

At the hut, I found the door ajar and entered. I held up a cloth to my nose and mouth against the stink; the sound of rushing waters filled my ears. Wave-refracted sunbeams bounced through a broken windowpane to play across the walls, illuminating pernicious effluvia in every corner of the room. One glance assured me that the last occupant was no more. Naked, cold and stiff, he lay contorted on a heap of straw. Various stains and marks on and around him showed the virulence of the disorder.

I'd seen those bodies in Istanbul, but had never before beheld a person freshly killed by pestilence. I'd read all I could find about the symptoms and effects. Sensations excited by words, however searing and descriptive of the deaths and misery of thousands, could not compare to what I felt with the reality there before my eyes. Though the buboes, those hard swellings at neck and groin that Defoe describes in A Journal of the Plague Year, weren't to be seen, signs of the "inward gangrene" he writes of were readily apparent—pus, discoloration, a sickening smell.

Stepping closer to the corpse of this unhappy stranger, I bent to raise his rigid limbs. As chill horror began to congeal my blood, I marked the distortion of his face, the stony eyes lost to perception. "So, you've died of plague." Half insanely, I started talking to him. "How did that feel? Painful like torture, from the looks of it." My flesh had started to quiver, my hair was standing on end. From his grey, suppurating lips, the dead man seemed about to answer me. I leapt up and escaped from the hut before he could...

My thoughts in disorder, I pedaled off down the lane. Soon the people I'd left earlier came into sight. They were still stuck in their anxious huddle. They hurried away after spotting the agitation on my face, fearing me contagious.

Conclusions which appear infallible when seen at a distance from facts, often vanish like unreal dreams when put to the test of reality. I'd ridiculed these people's fears, the fears of my fellow citizens, when they related to themselves. I paused in the road, as the fear came home to me and mine now. The Rubicon, I felt, was passed; I'd been exposed to plague. What now? According to the vulgar superstition, my clothes, my body, my breath, carried mortal danger to myself and others. Should I return to the Castle, to my wife and children, with this taint upon me? Not, surely, if I were infected. Though I felt sure I wasn't, a few hours for the appearance of symptoms would settle the question. I'd spend the time in the forest, walking and reflecting on what was to come, and what my future actions were to be.

One immediate effect of my encounter with the dead man, was to drive the last forty-eight hours in London almost from my mind. A misty remainder of those events seemed to clear, and I saw new, more painful prospects before me. My very intentions were altered. Whether I should share Adrian's toils and danger was no longer the question; the prudence and zeal of his government had produced order and plenty in London. My place, these woods, was here. What could I do to imitate my friend's example, in my own neighborhood of Windsor?

Yet another question interposed. Now that plague was spreading, how could I secure my own family's health? Was it even advisable to stay here, so close to London? In my mind, I spread the whole earth before me like a map. There wasn't a single spot on its surface where I could have put my finger and said, *Here is safety*. Human populations across the southern hemisphere had been nearly annihilated by the plague at its most virulent and untreatable; hurricanes and floods, poisonous winds and blights, filled up the measure of suffering for the survivors. In the north, whose sparser residents declined more gradually from plague, famine found the ones yet spared an easy prey.

I contracted my view to England. As I'd just seen, the overgrown metropolis, the great heart of mighty Britain, was pulseless. All resort for ambition or pleasure was cut off—commerce had ceased—the streets were grass-grown—the houses empty—the few Londoners who from necessity remained, wore a doomed aspect. The same tragedy playing out on a smaller yet more disastrous scale had overwhelmed the larger manufacturing towns, where they had no Adrian to superintend and direct the civic sphere, and every week the poor were struck and killed in flocks.

Yet not all of us would die. Though thinned, the human race would continue; one day, the great plague of 2094, like Defoe's of 1665, would be a matter for historians and novelists to make readers wonder at. Doubtless, its spread was the greatest and most global ever known, up to now. All the more cause for us to unite and work hard to dispute its progress; treated so cheaply in the past, when conquerors went out almost in sport to slay their thousands and tens of thousands, a single human life had become more precious than any so-called royal treasure. Look at a human being: the thought-filled countenance, the graceful limbs, the majestic brow, the wondrous mechanism—God's best work was not to be cast aside as a broken vessel. *Homo sapiens* should be preserved, and the generations carry down its name and form to the end of time.

Since some people must survive, my task, above all, must be to guard those people entrusted by nature and fate to my especial care, and ensure that they be among the survivors. My Idris and our babes, the community at Eton, our country neighbors, the migrants already present and those still to come: there, at Windsor Castle, I'd establish a haven for the victims of society's shipwreck. Its forests would encompass our world, its gardens feed us. Within its walls would be Health.

The other hours of my forest mediations, I confess, were filled with thoughts about myself. Once again, life had linked me to Windsor Castle—scene, I knew, of my father's greatest triumphs and regrets. I traced my own life's course, from outcast and vagabond to one exalted by friendship with Adrian, who'd caught me gently in the silver net of love and civilization, and awakened me to human kindness and human excellence. Though I loved wisdom ardently and aspired after good, I'd done nothing of any worth, when Idris, royal born at Windsor Castle like her brother—Idris, who was herself the personification of all that was divine in Woman, she who walked the earth like a poet's dream, as a carved goddess brought to life, or a saint stepping from the canvas of an altarpiece—she, the most worthy, chose me, and gave me herself—a priceless gift. Our children had all been born at Windsor Castle, too.

At the end of the requisite hours for signs of infection to appear, I was still in perfect health, only hungry and fatigued by a walk that had taken me almost to Bracknel and back. The sun was in descent, and I resumed my ride home to Windsor through the flickering of the forest's long shadows on the Long Road. Idris, I realized, having heard nothing from me all day, might well have heard from someone else of my return from London, and my visit to Boulter's Lock—in which case my continued absence could only alarm her. My anxiety on this point increased when I rolled into the town market square below the Castle, and found it in a state of agitation and unrest.

Wrecked hopes birthed superstitions. In a phenomenon observed across the world, with the pandemic's spread, many fanatics arose who prophesied that the end-times were come. They used wild antics and dangerous rhetoric to monopolize the great theatre of public life and proclaim the remaining particle of futurity almost dwindled to zero. The weak-spirited died of fear as they listened to these prophets' denunciations; those of robust form and apparent strength fell into idiocy and madness, racked by the dread of coming eternity.

A man of this kind had found his way to Windsor—where the countryside's present state of alarm made its people fit instruments to be played upon by a maniac. Ragged, emaciated, the poor wretch stood on the top of the town hall steps, and from this elevation, with many frantic gestures, harangued a trembling crowd:

"I come from London, where I lost my wife and our lovely infant child to the plague. We were already starving at the time. Until the work went away, I was a mechanic. But then we starved, and then came plague. And that room where they were lying, my wife and child—though wife and child no more, only dead clay—I left, never to return. I ran outside, no idea where to go, wild with hunger, with watching, with grief. All at once there came a blinding flash of light— *and then I knew!* I knew that I was sent by heaven to preach human extinction to the whole world.

"So I entered the churches, and foretold to the congregations how speedily they'd be removing to the vaults below. I climbed onstage at the theatres to tell the audiences to go home and die. I was arrested, locked up—but I escaped. Now I am a wanderer among you, and a prophet.

"Hear me, you people!" he cried "And Heaven, all-seeing but most pitiless—you listen too. Hear, O my own tempest-tossed heart, which breathes out these words, yet faints beneath their meaning— hear me! Death is among us! The beautiful earth is bedecked with flowers, but she is our grave. The rainclouds weep for us—the stars are candles at our funeral. Grey heads, you hoped for a few more years in your familiar homes; but the lease is up, you must remove. Children, dears, you will never reach maturity. Even now the small grave is dug for you—mothers, clasp them in your arms. One death embraces you!"

As he poured forth his eloquent despair, the maniacal mechanic seemed to unveil each listener's hidden fears and give voice to the thoughts they dared not express. Then he went further. His voice paused, and his eyes looked about to burst from their sockets. Shuddering, hands outstretched, he appeared to follow shapes, invisible to us, in the yielding air above our heads. He gave a cry.

"There they are—the dead! They rise in their shrouds and pass in silent procession. Their bloodless lips are still, even their shadowy limbs are motionless. They glide onwards. *We're coming with you!* I tell them. Because what are we waiting for? Hurry, my friends, and dress yourselves in your best burial clothes. You must prepare to meet royalty: Death, the ruler of all. Why do we tarry? The good, the wise, the beloved, are already gone. Mothers, bestow your last kisses— husbands, protectors no more, lead your partners! Come, O come! while the dear ones are yet in sight. For soon they'll be too far away, and we may never have this chance again to join them."

He passed on to another theme: the horrors of the time, which he painted in minute detail. Heartbreaking tales of the dearest ties being snapped—the gasping horror of despair over the deathbed of the last beloved—the effects of plague upon the human frame, which he described with such unexaggerated but terrific words that groans and even shrieks burst from the crowd. One man in particular, standing rigid and open-mouthed in front, his eyes fixed on the prophet, showed every sign of the most intense fear. The mechanic caught his glance, and I thought of how a cobra's gaze is said to hypnotize its trembling prey. He stood taller, while his frantic features composed themselves into a show of calm authority. The poor man at the foot of the steps trembled harder. The other looked down on him until his knees knocked together and his teeth chattered. At last he fell to the ground in convulsions.

"That man has the plague," said the maniac calmly. A shriek burst from the lips of the poor wretch; then all at once he lay motionless. It was manifest to all that he was dead.

Cries of horror gave place to cries of rage and fear, as everyone in the shoving, desperate crowd tried to escape the town square all at once. In a few minutes, I was alone with the dead man and the maniac; subdued and exhausted, he climbed down to sit on the sidewalk beside the corpse, his gaunt framed bowed. I saw some of the magistrate's people approach, sent to remove the body. The unfortunate being, thinking they'd come to arrest and jail him again, jumped up and fled. I cycled onwards to the Castle.

Death, cruel and relentless, had entered those beloved walls. An old nanny who'd been with Idris since infancy, and who lived with us more on the footing of an elderly relative than a former employee, had gone a few days before to visit her married daughter who lived near London. On the night of her return she sickened of the plague. From the haughty and unbending Countess of Windsor, Idris had received little tenderness; this good woman had been her real source of maternal care. The nanny's very deficiencies of education and knowledge, by rendering her humble and defenseless, endeared her to us, and she was the children's special favorite. I arrived home to find my poor wife literally wild with grief and dread.

She hung over the patient in an agony nowise mitigated by wandering thoughts of her babes, for whom she feared infection. My entrance she greeted as a lighthouse lamp would have been hailed by sailors in the midst of weathering some dangerous rocky point. She deposited her appalling doubts in my hands; she relied on my judgment and was comforted by my participation in her sorrow. Soon our poor nanny expired; and for Idris the anguish of suspense was changed to deepest regret, which though at first more painful, yet yielded more readily to my consolation; until sleep, the sovereign balm, steeped her tearful eyes in forgetfulness.

Idris slept, and quiet prevailed: in the Castle's hushed repose, I was its sole wakeful inhabitant. Through the long night hours, my busy thoughts worked in my brain like ten thousand cogwheels, rapid, acute, unstoppable. All England slept; and from my window, commanding a wide prospect of the starlit country, I saw the land stretched out in placid rest. I was awake, alive, while sleep possessed my race. What if, not sleep, but Death should gain dominion? The silence of midnight, to speak truly, though it seems a paradox, rang in my ears. The solitude became intolerable; returning to Idris in bed, I placed my hand on her beating heart, and bent my head to catch the sound and warmth of her breath, to assure myself that she still existed. For a moment I doubted whether I could really wake her up, so irrational was the horror running through my veins. Great God! Would it be thus—one day I'd walk the earth alone? All humanity extinct, except myself? Inarticulate, oracular, persuasive, such warning voices forced themselves upon me that night as Schiller described in my lost Perdita's favorite translation (Coleridge's, of his Wallenstein):

> *Yet I would not call them*
> *Voices of warning, that announce to us*
> *Only the inevitable. As the sun,*
> *Ere it is risen, sometimes paints its image*
> *In the atmosphere: so often do the spirits*
> *Of great events stride on before the events,*
> *And in to-day already walks to-morrow.*

(31) THE PLAGUE wasn't in London alone, it was everywhere. It came on us, as Ryland had said, like a thousand packs of wolves, howling through the bleak night, gaunt and fierce.

The population of England's suburban and rural counties knew that the plague was in London, in Liverpool, Bristol, Manchester, York; they'd watched the cities' crisis from afar. When it appeared in their midst they were astonished and dismayed, impatient and angry. Driven by terror, they kept senselessly busy, trying anything to throw off the clinging evil; as long as they were in motion, they imagined themselves safer. The inhabitants of smaller towns left their houses and pitched tents in the fields, thinking they avoided the disease by keeping separate from each other; while the farmers and cottagers flocked from their fearful solitude to the towns.

Once plague was introduced into the rural districts, its effects assumed a special horror. In London, for instance, there was a companionship in suffering. Neighbors kept constant watch on each other; and with succor at hand, the path of destruction was smoother. But in the country, among the scattered farmhouses, in lone cottages, in fields and barns, tragedies harrowing to the soul were acted, unseen, unheard, unnoticed. Medical aid was less easily procured, food more difficult to obtain. And human beings, unchecked by shame of being observed, ventured on deeds of greater wickedness, or gave way more readily to abject fears.

Deeds of heroism also occurred: such was human nature, that beauty and deformity were often closely linked. Time and again, our history showed acts of striking generosity and self-sacrifice would follow close on the heels of crime, as our better natures sent redress against the worse. Blood was spilled by murderous hands as the plague advanced; helping hands, meanwhile, extended many lives.

From August, when it first reached England, the plague's ravages peaked a month later and by the end of October had mostly dwindled away—only to be replaced by a typhus epidemic of almost equal virulence. The autumn was warm and rainy. The crops had failed; bad corn and grain, and lack of foreign remedies or wines, added vigor to disease. The chronically ill and infirm died off and were joined in the grave by many young people caught at the peak of health and prosperity.

The rains kept on, and by mid-December had caused flooding over half of England. The windstorms and oceanic tempests of the previous winter were back; but with our shipping already so diminished, we felt fewer effects this year. The floods and storms did more harm to Europe than to us—landing, as it were, the last blow in the string of calamities which destroyed that continent. Across Italy's depopulated countryside, essential riverbanks were left unwatched, untended; monstrously overflowing, Tiber, Arno, and Po rushed upon the golden plains and wiped out their fertility. Whole villages were carried away. Rome and Florence and Pisa were swamped, and the foundations of their marble palaces, so lately mirrored in tranquil streams, sunken, shaken, cracked. In North and Central Europe and Russia the damage was still more momentous.

But winter was coming, and with winter, hope. The first hard frost would bring a renewal of our lease on earth. Frost would calm the furious winds and blunt the plague's arrows; and beneath her garment of snow, which she'd throw off in spring, the land would be purified.

In widespread anticipation of this reprieve, autumn witnessed a travel craze, as people rushed back and forth across England in search of amusement. Throngs filled city theatres, restaurants, and hotels, which had all re-opened; the countryside witnessed dances and music festivals almost every night. Wherever the crowds surged, standards of public safety and behavior dipped dangerously. It would have been useless to try and stop people in transit or curb their habits on arrival; opposition would only have driven them to worse excesses. They had money to spend. Most had known only dependence or poverty, until recent bequests had enriched them; that gain had often meant the loss of parents, moral guardians, mentors and restraints.

Public decorum became a thing of the past, while the evils endemic to our day were doubled. Students left their books, artists their studios. Vocations were gone, but life's amusements remained. Indeed, enjoyment might be prolonged to the very end. All dissembling might stop. Death, its threat, cast a protective nightfall in whose murky shadows the blush of modesty, the reserve of pride, the decorum of prudery would be thrown aside as useless veils.

This wasn't universal. Elsewhere, anguish and dread, fear of eternal partings, and the awful wonder produced by unprecedented calamity, drew closer the ties of kindred and friendship. Philosophers put their principles to work opposing profligacy and despair. Philanthropists multiplied. The religious, close now to their reward, clung fast to their congregations, services, and creeds—the life rafts they counted on to save them from suffering's vexed sea, and bear them in safety to the harbor of the Unknown Continent. And the loving-hearted, obliged to downscale, bestowed their overflow of affection in triple portion on the few that remained to be loved. Yet, even among these more fortunate souls, the present was all the time they dared to hope for; the present, and the winter to come, that is.

Humanity had evolved to expect to be able to count our enjoyments in years, while modern science had extended our prospect of life decade by decade. The long road threaded a vast labyrinth, and its terminus in the Valley of the Shadow of Death was hidden from sight by intervening things—our life's events. But an earthquake had altered the terrain. A chasm yawned right at our feet now; in place of our long outlook was a view of a deep and precipitous drop, yawning wide to receive us; every hour drove us closer to its edge. But winter was at hand, to bring a pause, when months must elapse before we could be hurled from our security.

We became ephemera, to whom the days were years. We'd never see our children grow up, see their downy cheeks roughen, their blithe hearts be subdued by passion or care; but we had them now—they lived, and we lived—what more could we desire? So Idris schooled herself, with some success, to manage her fears. After all, this wasn't like late July or August, when every hour could bring infection; from now until summer came, we were bound to be safe; a necessarily short-lived certainty which yet for a time satisfied her maternal tenderness, and left her calm. Just as a meteor is brighter than a star, so did the felicity of this coming winter promise the extracted and combined delights of a long, long life. I know not how to express or communicate the sense of concentrated, intense, though transitory bliss, that made our present hours a paradise. Our joys were dearer because we saw their end; they were keener because we felt, to its fullest extent, their value; they were purer because their essence was sympathy.

Winter! In our part of England it took until February, but at last we had three straight days of snowfall. The rivers were frozen nearly solid, and the frost-whitened woods crackled with falls of frozen branches snapped by birds in flight.

On the fourth morning, all vanished. A southwest wind brought up rain. Then the sun came out, and at once the weather felt like summer. Unseasonable heat prevailed. We took no consolation, that March, in lanes filled with violets, fruit trees in blossom, the vital corn rising, green leaves coming out. We feared the balmy air—we feared the cloudless sky, the flower-covered earth, and delightful woods, for it was as Calderón put it:

> *Pisando la tierra dura*
> *de continuo el hombre està*
> *y cada passo que dà*
> *es sobre su sepultura.*

Underfoot we felt our future, the scenes we looked on were our tomb, and the fragrant land smelled to our apprehension like a field of open graves.

Yet how lovely the spring! As we gazed from our terrace on the fertile counties spread beneath, speckled by happy cottages and prosperous towns, all looked as in former years, heart-cheering and fair. The plough-furrowed fields, new wheat showing through the dark soil, orchards like tinted cloudbanks of bloom and bud; swallows and martins cut the sunny air with their long, pointed wings; newborn lambs lay safe among the flocks, new leaves fed green into the air, Wordsworth-style, from every treetop. Eventually we humans, too, felt regenerated—maybe too much so. Reason told us that care and sorrow were coming again; but how could we believe an ominous voice, breathed up with pestiferous vapors from the depths of fear, while Nature was laughing, sparkling the waters, scattering fruits and flowers from her green lap, and inviting us to join a party of elastic and warm young life?

I shared the general hope that the pandemic might not revive with the summer, but remained strongly determined that if it did, it should find us prepared. Plague had become a part of our future, our existence; we must develop habits of guarding against it, as we did against floods or violent tides. After long suffering and bitter experience, some cure might be discovered. As it was, the death rate after infection stood at 100%. Those in positions of authority must attempt to fix deep the foundations and raise high the barriers between contagion and the uninfected; we must also aim to establish and maintain such order as would conduce to the well-being of the victims' survivors, and preserve hope along with some portion of happiness in the midst of tragedy. The systems Adrian had introduced in London, while unable to stop the progress of death, yet managed to prevent other public disorders from rendering the city's awful fate still worse.

But try as I might to imitate his example among the inhabitants of the scattered towns and villages near Windsor, I could find no means of leading; my words were forgotten as soon as misheard, and public opinion veered with every rumor. Social class formed a barrier, too. I talked with landlords who were actuated by the purest benevolence, ready to lend the utmost aid for their tenants' welfare. But this was not enough. A true, intimate sympathy generated by similar hopes and fears, similar experience and pursuits, was lacking. The poor could see how many more means of preservation the rich possessed than they did: the rich, who had fewer worries to start with, could also seclude themselves better. Perceiving this, no one trusted their rich landlords' friends, but placed ten times the reliance on the succor and advice of their equals.

Here lay the key to my eventual plan. Each village, I'd observed, however small, usually contained a leader, someone widely venerated, whose advice was sought in difficulty, and whose good opinion was cherished. In the village of Little Marlow, for instance, an old woman ruled the community. In those days her threshold was constantly beset by crowds seeking her advice and listening to her admonitions. She'd been a soldier, and had seen the world. When plague entered the village and rendered the inhabitants almost witless with fright, old Martha stepped forward. She'd once been in a town struck by plague; nor had she escaped it—but she'd recovered. After this revelation, Martha reigned supreme in Little Marlow's every heart and mind. I watched her enter the cottages of the sick; she relieved their wants with her own hand; she betrayed no fear, and inspired all who saw her with some portion of her own native courage. For those too poor to purchase food, she shopped and organized supplies, demonstrating how the well-being of each worked to the benefit of all. She wouldn't permit any gardens to be neglected, nor the flowers in a single window box to droop for want of care. Hope, she told me, was the key to health, and everything that could sustain and enliven people's spirits, had more value than any doctor's prescription.

With Martha in mind, I resolved to seek out her local counterparts; and by systematizing their efforts, and enlightening their views, increase both their power and their use among the other townspeople and villagers. In imagining the reign of peace and happiness on earth, I couldn't help but recall how many writers had placed their utopias in rural settings or small townships, each directed by wise elders—especially when my plan's real success proved so ephemeral. There was the usual ingratitude, watered and fed by vice and folly, which all who ever labored for humanity saw springing from the grain they'd sown. And volatility beset every power structure, however popular. Coups and abdications were frequent. In place of the old and prudent, the ardent youth would step forward, eager for action, indifferent to danger. Often, too, the voice to which everyone listened was suddenly silenced, the helping hand gone cold, the sympathetic eye fallen shut. So it was when we stood at old Martha's graveside. The sun beat down; but with the big heart stilled that had beat for them, the mind forever occupied with projects for their welfare reduced to incommunicable annihilation, the people of Little Marlow shivered again in their fear.

May brought pleasant weather. Where was the plague? *Here—There—Everywhere!* our horror and dismay exclaimed—Plague the Destroyer, forcing the spirit to leave its organic chrysalis and enter upon an untried life. With one mighty sweep of its potency, all caution, all care, all prudence were nullified. Death sat at the tables of the great, made itself at home among the poor, seized the cowards who fled, quelled the brave who resisted.

Constant, wide-ranging activity on the public behalf, permitted my observations of our invisible enemy's virulence to be unusually close and extensive. I watched it destroy a village in one short month. The first person sickened there in May; death had triumphed by June, when I found its streets deformed by unburied corpses, and no one left alive indoors. From such scenes, at other times, I saved deserted infants; sometimes I convinced a grieving lone survivor to come away, for fellowship.

But the powers of love, poetry, and creative fancy will dwell even among sights of woe. At the bedsides of the plague-sickened, among the squalid and the dying, amid anguish and pain: even as they grew familiar, I could endure the despairing moans of age, and the more terrible smiles of infancy in the bosom of horror, without being seized by a sudden frenzy to dash myself from some precipice and so close my eyes forever on the sad end of the world. Instead, feelings of devotion, of duty, of a high and steady purpose, elevated me. A strange joy filled my heart. In the midst of the greatest sadness, while doing good I seemed to walk on air through an ambrosial atmosphere which blunted the sting of sympathetic grief and purified the sound waves of sighs.

Idris, too, at the beginning of our calamity, had devoted herself to the care of the sick and helpless there at Windsor. In my worry over the dangers she faced, I raised selfish objections to what I called her thoughtless enthusiasm. When the knowledge that she was safe strengthened my nerves to endure, constant fears for her well-being only shook my morale, I complained; I also listed several dangers her children incurred when she was absent from home. And she at length submitted, agreeing not to go beyond the forest borders. As it was, within the walls of the Castle we had a colony of the unhappy, mostly destitute of relatives, who could occupy her time and attention; yet she began to languish. Ceaseless anxiety for my welfare and the health of her children, however she strove to curb or conceal it, absorbed all her thoughts and undermined the vital principle.

Still, after the children's safety, her first care was to hide her anguish and tears from me. Each night I returned to the Castle and found repose and love waiting. Many times I attended at a deathbed past midnight, and rode many miles through rain and obscurity, with a single thought to sustain me: the safety and sheltered repose of those I loved. Home, fresh from scenes of tremendous agony, I'd lay my crowded head on Idris's lap, and feel the pounding pulses slow. Her smile could raise me from hopelessness, her embrace bathe my sorrowing heart in calm.

High summer. As the plague went crowned with the sun's burning rays, the nations bowed their heads beneath the advance, and died. Corn sprang up in plenty, to rot on the stalk; the melancholy wretches who'd gone out picking lay stiff and plague-struck in the furrows. The green woods waved majestic boughs above the dying sufferers spread beneath their shade, answering the solemn melody with inharmonious cries. Bright birds flitted close; careless deer reposed unhurt upon the fern; oxen and horses strayed from their unguarded stables, and grazed among the wheat—for death fell on humanity alone.

My poor love and I looked at each other, looked at our babes. "We'll save them, Idris," I said. "And years from now we'll be telling them about these fears we had for a year or two that they barely remember. I intend to save them—even if they're the last ones left alive on earth, still they shall live—healthy, strong, and sweet of voice."

My words were safe from the children's notice, drowned by their laughter at play. At only ten years old, Alfred already understood what a pandemic was, and we'd talked about why so vast a desolation was happening; but at his age, the natural hilarity of youth quickly chased away frowns. Elvis, the gamesome infant shaking back his light curls from his eyes, an hilarious cherub without any notion of pain or sorrow, could make the halls ring and echo with his artless merriment. And Clara laughed happily, too. Our lovely gentle Clara—our stay, our solace, our delight; who flitted through the rooms like a benevolent spirit sent to illumine our dark hour with the alien splendor of her celestial homeland. Always eager to be of help to Idris, she made it her task to share her work around the Castle and attend the sick, comfort the sorrowing, assist the aged, help entertain the young. Gratitude and praise followed wherever she went. Yet with what unassuming simplicity she sat playing with our children on that afternoon of laughter.

July was gone. August must pass, a long tedium, each day eagerly counted that brought us closer to September, when we'd revive our hopes that winter would relive us from plague, at least for the season. That it would vanish altogether was the universal heartfelt hope no one could utter aloud—at least not without crying—so deep were our fears, so small our hopes. With months to go until winter, it was easy to see why some people, who only wanted to leap this dangerous interval, plunged into dissipation, and strove, by riot, and what they wished to imagine to be pleasure, to banish thought and opiate despair.

(32)   RIDING to visit Adrian one day that fall, I had a puncture and stopped to repair it outside a gay pub on the London road. The place was overflowing with uproarious patrons involved in a bellowed sing-along. Among them on the gravel outside, near the threshold, then the window, a small, silent, mournful-looking man hovered, trying to see inside. The sorry state of his clothes combined with his pronounced emaciation to tell of a steep fall into poverty. I watched him recoil from a sudden burst of song and merriment, then take a few steps as if determined to enter; but the barkeep, who must have seen him peeking, came out first. The first man gave a cry and rushed up to ask, "Is my husband here? Can I see George?"

"See George!" the other cried. "Sure you can, if they'll let you in the death house. Last night he came down with plague, so that's where we sent him."

"Ah!" With a cry, the unfortunate questioner staggered against the wall. "Were you really so cruel? Wait!" A confused shouting within had already sent the barkeep hurrying back to the bar; but a more compassionate witness stepped forward with details: George had been taken ill during a night of heavy dissipation; his boon companions, wasting no time, had consigned him to a hospital cart; St B's was the nearest, he was probably there. To which his husband said a fervent thank you, then turned and tottered away.

My tire was quickly patched, and I soon overtook the poor man where he stood almost strengthless, leaning against a signpost, his head sunk on his bosom. He barely raised his eyes at my offer of help, until I added, "You want to get to St. Bartholomew's, is that right?"

"I have to get there," he said. "If I don't die first."

The ride wasn't far, and I persuaded him onto my bicycle's safe passenger seat. He said little at first, but I was able to draw him out with a few more questions. There was a simple, natural earnestness about him that interested me in his fate, especially when he assured me that his husband was the best of men—or had been so, until loss of employment first threw him into bad company. "George couldn't bear to come home," he said, "only to see our business die. Our shop was like our own child to him, his own flesh and blood."

At the hospital I went along inside to help make sure he'd get to see his husband. The poor creature clung closer to me as he saw with what heartless haste they rolled the dead away, and he cried out at the glimpse we caught behind the curtain hung across a holding area stacked with corpses. We made our way to the long, crowded ward on which our patient might be found, if still alive, according to the check-in nurse. My companion, blind to the horrors about him, looked eagerly from bed to bed.

"George!"

There, in the furthest corner, a squalid, haggard creature, writhing under the torture of disease: he rushed towards him, he embraced him, blessing God for his preservation, with radiant smiles.

But to me, unprotected by such strange joy and enthusiasm, the scene inside the death house, truly called, was intolerably agonizing. The countryside offered no horrors like these: solitary wretches died in the open fields, a sole survivor might contend with famine in a vacant village; but the assembly room, the banquet hall of plague, was spread only in London. Though my mouth and nose were covered against the choking effluvia that filled the ward, my heart heaved with painful qualms as I stood among the plague-struck. Some lay in restraints, screaming in pain, others laughing from an even worse delirium; some had weeping, despairing relations at their bedsides, while others, dying alone, called aloud, with thrilling tenderness or reproach, the names of absent friends. The nurses went about their tasks expressionlessly, incarnate images of despair, indifference, and death.

I gave some money to my luckless companion and arranged for his George's removal to a more private room. Then I rode away from St. B's as fast as I could go. Imagination, that tireless tormentor, was showing me pictures of my own loved ones, lying sick and helpless in a place like that, so meanly attended.

Adrian was already out by the time I arrived and wasn't expected back for some hours. As it was a fine afternoon, I left my bicycle there and set out on a leisurely ramble around the depopulated town. Avoiding the frequent funeral processions, I followed my curiosity to observe the state of particular spots—painful wanderings among desolate, neglected landmarks. Amid the general silence and desertion, I met few people; all were woebegone, careworn, and depressed by fear.

Weary at length of empty streets and misery, I headed back towards the Protectoral Palace. Darkness had begun to fall; yet the sky above the buildings ahead grew continually brighter. My ears caught the first grinding, windblown sounds of uproar. The West End had awoken.

No one but Adrian could have governed this night-time London, where fear of plague had united that most diverse of populations in a common public frenzy. Even he was obliged to yield on many points and limit his efforts to keeping the license of the times within bounds. All the usual places of amusement stayed open; but for audiences he introduced measures and modifications designed to reduce over-excitement and with it the misery that so often followed when quiet returned.

On the stage, the deepest, direst tragedies were most popular. People's inner despair made them care less to see comedy played; and sales for those shows weren't helped by their reputation for halting mid-laugh as one or other comedian, struck too hard by incongruity and personal wretchedness, would burst from mimic merriment into sobs and tears. Seized with irresistible sympathy, the poor audience would spent the night weeping after all, and thus wind up feeling cheated.

I wasn't in the mood to try deriving consolation from either kind of scene; buffoon laughter and fictitious tears, their garish and false varnish, held equally little appeal. Its streets festively ablaze with colored lights, Covent Garden rang with enough discordant mirth to awaken and then mock all the heartfelt grief within me. The crowds screaming with laughter on every side were easily recognizable through the disguise: not revelers, but assembled mourners, every one.

Oppressed, distracted by painful emotions, I strode on. Suddenly I found myself outside Drury Lane Theatre. The play was Macbeth, led by the finest actor of the age, who had the power, it was said, to make an audience forget everything but the sound of his voice. Such a medicine I yearned for, so I went in, though the show was half over. Shakespeare's centuries-long popularity was more dominant than ever at this dread period; he was the wizard to rule our hearts and govern our imaginations, and the house was quite full. With the next act yet to start, I had a few moments to study my fellow playgoers. Every corner of society was represented among the aisles, people of all ages drawn in common to seek a few hours' respite from the hells awaiting them elsewhere. No less than the play's first audiences, they sought to escape into this wild but heartily familiar tale of ancient Britain's tangles with the supernatural; above all, they hoped to be entertained.

The curtain rose on Act Four: a pitch dark hollow set among forbidding rocks, where a thick stage mist floated and a single light, fiery red, pulsed beneath the central cauldron. We heard the grim ingredients of the magic charm, but instead of three hag-like witches bent over the pot, we saw a gigantic trio of shadowy, unearthly beings. The entrance of Hecate and the introduction of music in harmony with all witch-like fancies, took us out of our own world entirely: set free of reproof from reason or the heart, returned to a state before fear, our imaginations simply reveled. And Macbeth, entering, far from destroying the illusion, seemed to share our feelings and join us in our enchantment; so that as the displays of magic and prophecy proceeded, we sympathized in his wonder and his daring, and gave ourselves up with our whole souls to the power of the scenic effects. It was too long since my mind had been on any pleasing flights of fancy, and I felt the beneficial result right away, a sense of renewal.

After the incantation scene, the action of the play retained, for a space, its effect of abstract, emblematic power; it took a while to remember that Malcolm and Macduff weren't visions but mere human beings, acted upon by such simple passions as warmed our own breasts; it took longer still to gather what had been excised. By and by, however, our absorption in their encounter was complete. *'Stands Scotland where it did?'* A shudder, as from a shared electric shock, ran through the house, when Ross exclaimed, in answer:

> *Alas, poor country;*
> *Almost afraid to know itself! It cannot*
> *Be called our mother, but our grave: where nothing,*
> *But who knows nothing, is once seen to smile*

The speech was like a bell that tolled our lives away; each word struck. But fearing to look around at one another, we focused our attention on the stage—as if there alone our eyes were safe.

> *Where sighs, and groans, and shrieks that rent the air*
> *Are made, not marked; where violent sorrow seems*
> *A modern ecstasy: the dead man's knell*
> *Is there scarce asked for who; and good men's lives*
> *Expire before the flowers in their caps,*
> *Dying or ere they sicken.*

The actor playing Ross seemed aware of being on dangerous ground by now. Beginning his announcement to Macduff, to tell him about the slaughter of his family, he trembled, stammering, with twisted features, fixed-eyed stares—really afraid to speak the lines and face the outburst of *our* grief, not Macduff's. But falling out of character only made him more effective. Terrified ourselves, we gasped and winced along with him, craning our necks to read every look on his anguished face; until at last Macduff cried out and asked:

> *All my pretty ones?*
> *Did you say all?—O hell kite! All?*
> *What, all my pretty chickens and their dam*
> *At one fell swoop?*

A pang of wild grief wrenched every heart, despair burst past every lip—mine, too—a great outcry echoing the Scotsman's. I'd entered into the universal feeling, been absorbed by the terrors told by Ross. Now I was a witness to how Nature overpowered Art, like a dam-burst flood might sweep away a decorative public fountain in its path.

As if escaping from a hell of torture, I rushed out of the theater to find fresh air, quiet, calm; but the street outside offered none of them. Longing, how much! to be back in the country, amid the dear soothings of maternal Nature, instead I felt my wounded heart stung by the sights, sounds, and smells of London debauched. Roars of heartless merriment from open pub doors, drunkards reeling by, appalling salutations from degraded beings: but then, to how many souls had the name of home become a mockery, something to escape in forgetfulness? So George had fallen.

I set off at a run for a darker part of town, pushing my speed until I finally stopped for breath near Westminster Abbey. The deep, swelling tones of its pipe organ attracted me inside. With a quiet awe that felt soothing, I entered the lighted chancel and stood. A solemn religious chant began, heralding peace and hope to the unhappy. The notes, freighted with prayers, re-echoed through the dim aisles, and the soul's bleeding wounds were staunched by heavenly balm. It seemed to me, that in spite of the world's misery which I deplored, and could not understand; in spite of London's empty sidewalks and England's corpse-strewn fields; in spite of all the variety of agonizing emotions I'd experienced that day—just then, calmed by the music, and by the sight of many other human creatures offering up prayers and submission with me, I thought the Creator looked down in compassion and promised relief in reply to our melodious pleas. A sentiment approaching happiness did follow the total resignation of one's being to the guardianship of the world's ruler.

Alas! When the last note faded, the elevated spirit sank again to earth. Suddenly one of the choristers died. She was lifted from her desk, the vaults below were hastily opened, and she was consigned therein with a few muttered prayers. I went outside again.

Vain for me, these scenes in London showed, to seat myself in a theatre aisle or kneel beneath lofty vaulted arches echoing with praise-song. In the open air alone I'd find relief. Among Nature's beauteous works, her Creator's benevolence grew clear again, and I could once more trust that the same divinity who built up the mountains, planted the forests, and poured out the rivers, would erect another state for lost humankind, where we might awaken again to our affections, our happiness, and our faith.

(33)   FORTUNATELY, I didn't have to visit London very often. While the city dwellers had little left but pastimes, back among the rural districts which our lofty Castle overlooked, everyone not exempted by disease or recent sorrow still had work to occupy them. Native country-folk, displaced Londoners, foreign migrants, many born to wealth: my days were largely taken up with urging them all to ignore the plague and pay attention to the crops. With listless strokes the hay would be scythed, but then no one show up to cart it. Sheepshearers left the wool on the ground for the winds to scatter, rather than collect it to make clothing no one would need. Yet agricultural labor was found very salutary; the sun, the refreshing breezes, the sweet smell of the hay, the rustling leaves, the irrigation water softly gushing in its channels, would reawaken the spirit of life; agitated hearts found some repose, and the apprehensive something like happiness.

Strange to say, 2095 was not without its pleasures. Couples young and old who'd loved long and hopelessly, suddenly found every impediment removed, and wealth pouring in from the death of the very relatives (or spouses) who'd kept them apart. The very danger of the time drew them closer. Immediate peril urged them to seize the day; wildly, passionately, they set out to know each and every delight an existence together afforded—defying plague to try and destroy the life of love and happiness they still had time to create.

In this connection I think of Juliet, a wealthy girl from Windsor, whose heart had belonged to a schoolfellow of her brother's since they were children. He'd always spend part of the holidays at her family's mansion. From playmates they grew into confidantes of each other's little secrets, mutual aids and consolers in difficulty and sorrow. Love crept in almost painlessly; yet by the time each one's life felt completely bound up in the other's, they both knew it was hopeless. Her father the duke would never allow Juliet to marry someone without property. Indeed, he separated the couple—but not before they exchanged a lovers' vow; his, to gain rank and make himself worthy of the match; hers, to preserve her virgin heart, his treasure, until he returned to claim and possess it.

When plague arrived, this same duke was notorious for deriding the idea that proper care couldn't protect a man of his sort, with his family, on his own property. In expensive and cautious seclusion, he proved himself right—until this second pandemic summer, when the destroyer, at one fell stroke, overthrew his precautions, his safety, and his life. Most of the staff on hand fled on the first appearance of disease; those who stayed soon died; once word that plague was there got out, no neighbor, no one local, would go near the mansion. Our poor friend saw father, mother, brothers, sisters, sicken and die, and no help ever came from outside. By a strange fatality, Juliet alone escaped; she to the last waited on her relatives, and smoothed the pillow of death, one by one, until the last blow to her father's house had been delivered.

Finally, the youthful survivor of her race, absorbed in wordless despair, Juliet sat alone among the dead. No living being was near to soothe her or take her away from this hideous company. A rare September night storm of whirlwind, thunder, and hail rattled round the house; in the gusty racket she heard ghastly harmonies, her family's dirge, until they drowned in drumroll-sheets of heavy rain. She looked up from the floor. Someone was calling her: through the windy downpour a familiar voice had cut like diamond—but whose?

Her name again: a voice she loved was calling—but all her loved ones were already present, they lay glaring on her with stony eyes. Was she going mad, or was she dying herself, that she could hear them? As another explanation flashed into her brain, she leapt up and ran to the window—a burst of lightning fulfilled her hope, when it showed Juliet her lover on the lawn beneath. Joy lent her strength to get downstairs and open the door to him; then she fainted in his arms.

Though she reproached herself a thousand times for reviving to happiness instead of grief, the natural clinging of the human mind to life and joy was at full strength in her young heart. She gave herself up to the enchantment: and in the couple's radiant features on their wedding day I saw incarnate, for the last time, the spirit of love, the rapturous sympathy, which once had been the life of the world.

I envied them. My ties in the world had grown too many with the years; I could never imbibe those singular feelings again—optimism, delight, a sense of invulnerability. Above all, the anxious mother, my own beloved, drooping Idris, claimed my thoughts and earnest care. Though I could neither quiet nor reproach her ceaseless, unsleeping anxiety for our family's lives, I exerted myself to distract her attention and keep her from looking too closely at the truth of things. Disease, misery, and death approached steadily. Day after day, some news arrived that seemed to transcend in horror all that had gone before. Wretched beings came to us from everywhere, crawling sometimes, in search of help and shelter; the Castle's population decreased daily, even so. The survivors huddled together in fear, trying to guess who'd be next, watching each other's faces for telltale signs. All this I minimized, concealing whatever I could as I tried to keep Idris from being too much affected by it. As for my own courage, I found it survived even despair: I might be vanquished, but I would not yield.

One day, September 9th, seemed devoted to every disaster, every harrowing incident.

Early that morning, I learned that a grandmother of one of the Castle's staff had arrived in the night, unexpectedly, with a badly bruised wrist and maybe worse. I hurried to pay my respects and learn her condition. This old woman had reached her hundredth year; her skin shriveled, her form bent and lost in extreme decrepitude, she still continued in existence, outliving many younger and stronger; she must have begun to feel as if she'd live forever. Almost everyone else in her village, I knew, was already dead of plague. She was able to tell me what had brought her to us.

When the pandemic reached her neighborhood, she hid from it. Clinging, with the dastard feeling of the aged, to the remnant of her spent life, she barred her door, locked her windows, refused to communicate with anyone. She'd wander out at night to get something to eat, happy to find the village deserted, because it meant she was in no danger from the plague. As the earth became more desolate, her difficulty trying to feed herself increased. At first, her son, who lived nearby, had humored her by placing supplies where she'd find them; at last he died. But even threatened by starvation, her fear of plague was paramount, and her greatest care was to avoid her fellow creatures.

She grew weaker each day, and each day she had further to go to find sustenance. Finally, prowling about one night, far from home, she happened on a bakery. The door was open and the shelves were stocked; no one was around. She gorged herself on bread and pastry, piled all she could into sacks, hurried towards home, and promptly lost her way. The night was cloudy, windless, hot; her load became too heavy for her; and one by one she threw away her loaves, still trying to get along, hobbling more and more lamely, at last too weak to go on. Crawling a little way into a cornfield by the road, she fell fast asleep.

Sounds awoke her in darkness. The tall stalks above her head were rustling. Then, almost beside her ear, came a low, human moan. She wanted to jump up and run but her stiff centenarian joints refused to obey. The rustling grew and she heard a sigh, heaved from the sufferer's heart. Then a smothered voice breathed out, "Water— water!" Shaking with fear, the old woman managed to sit upright. Close, very close, lay a half-naked figure, just discernible in the gloom. She heard it moan and cry again for water. Her ten old teeth chattered, her knees knocked together, she tried to move away—but only managed to attract the attention of her unknown companion. With convulsive violence, her limb was seized; the grasp felt like iron, the fingers like the keen teeth of an animal trap. "Finally! You're here!" came the cry—but these were last words, and a last exertion.

The joints relaxed, the biting clutch fell open; a low, final moan marked the moment of death. Morning broke, and the old woman saw the corpse, marked with the fatal disease, lying next to her. She felt struck by the plague.

And now, believing herself infected, she no longer dreaded the company of other people. With all the speed her aged frame could muster, she'd come straight to her granddaughter at Windsor Castle, there to lament and die. Even as she finished relating these events, the horrible symptoms of plague overtook her. Still she clung to life, and bewailed her bad luck between hideous groans.

The swift advance of the disease suggested, what proved to be the fact, that she could not survive many hours. While I was directing the necessary care to be taken of her, Clara entered, trembling and pale. Alarmed, I asked what was wrong. She started to cry, and threw herself into my arms, weeping: "Uncle, dearest uncle, don't hate me forever! I have to tell you—you have to know, that Elvis, poor little Elvis!"

Sobs choked the rest. The fear of so mighty a calamity as the loss of our adored cherub froze the current of my blood; but the remembrance of his mother restored my presence of mind.

I followed Clara back to my darling's little bed. He had a high fever yet for all my fondness and fears, I detected no symptoms of the plague. He wasn't yet three years old, and his illness appeared only one of those attacks common to infancy.

But Idris must not see him in this state. The fever was violent, the torpor complete; his heavy half-closed lids, his burning cheeks were enough, without the greater fear of pestilence, to awaken alarm. Though so young, only twelve, Clara was so prudent and careful that I knew I could entrust Elvis to her; my task, meanwhile, would be to prevent Idris from noticing their absence. I administered all the appropriate remedies, hoping they'd work fast, and left my sweet niece to watch beside the sickbed, with instructions to come get me right away if she noticed any change.

To my relief, I found Idris with her admirer, Merrival. The astronomer's view of humanity was too telescopic for him to notice its present distress, and he lived in the midst of the pandemic quite unconscious of its existence. This poor man, immensely learned, had the mental competence of a guileless, unforeseeing child. A request to Adrian, for the use of the Castle's private observatory to track certain planetary motions, had introduced him to our clan at Windsor some years back. Despite his renown, it was plain he lived in utter poverty. Indeed, as often as he, his pale wife, and their numerous offspring reached the point of starvation, Merrival—never conscious of hunger—observed nothing wrong. His astronomical theories absorbed him; the walls of the family's inadequate rooms were kept bare for his scrawled calculations; a hard-earned fee, or a coat, he'd trade for a book without thought or remorse; he neither heard his children cry nor recognized the emaciation of the form in bed beside him. His wife was one of those wondrous beings, to be found only among women, whose affections could not be diminished by misfortune. Her mind divided between boundless admiration for her husband, and tender anxiety for her children, she waited on him, worked for them, and never complained, though care rendered her life one long drawn-out, melancholy dream.

Adrian's patronage relieved these distresses for good. The astronomer often thanked us for the books we lent him, and for the use of our instruments, but never spoke of his spacious new home (among other improvements). According to his wife, he hadn't noticed any difference—only remarking about his new private study, that the children were barely in the room anymore; and to her infinite surprise he complained of this unaccustomed quiet.

He'd come now to announce to us (to Idris, really) the completion of his Essay on the Pericyclical Motions of the Earth's Axis, which, he explained, dealt with "the precession of the equinoctial points," and the consequent state of humanity six thousand years hence. A description of the unknown, unimaginable creatures who'd hold our vanished species' leading place by then, might have been of more genuine interest; but we never had the heart to say so to the poor old man, nor to tell him that there were no publishers or readers left. At the moment I came in, he was pointing out a passage to Idris, to ask what she thought of his position—then answered himself without a pause. She couldn't refrain from a smile, which I was glad to see, for it meant she had no idea of our baby's danger. I shuddered to think what would happen if she discovered the truth. Joining the conversation, I did my best to prolong her gentle amusement at the contrast between our present month-by-month views of the future, and Merrival's confident projections of human life at home in eternity.

Too late, I noticed Clara beckon me from the doorway; glimpsing motion in a mirror, Idris had already turned and seen her, seen the girl's grief-stricken face. To spring up—to suspect evil—to perceive that, since Alfred was in the room, her youngest darling faced the danger—to speed, to fly across the castle halls and chambers to his room, was the work of only moments. She beheld her Elvis lying fever-stricken and motionless.

Anguish floored her. Leaving me and Clara to do the nurse's part, Idris sat by the bed, glazed eyes fixed on her babe, holding one little burning hand; so she passed the many hours to follow in this unvaried agony. She could not accept my assurances that Elvis wasn't sick with plague; desperate fear robbed her of judgment and thought. Her whole body shook with terror at every slight convulsion of his features. If he moved, she dreaded a crisis; if he lay still, she saw death in his torpor. One mournful panic followed the next.

The poor little thing's fever increased near sundown. The sensation was dreary, at best, with which anyone looked forward to passing the long hours of night beside a sickbed—especially if the patient was an infant, who could not explain its pain, and whose life could seem to flicker like the *candle in the wind* the old balladeer sang of. Watchers kept casting eager glances towards the eastern view; angry impatience would suck them down further like quicksand with each sight of unbroken dark. The walls and creaky rafters would stir, a slight wail rise from an invisible insect or two: desolation. That night Clara, finally overcome by weariness, lay curled up asleep at the foot of her cousin's bed. Afraid to speak to Idris, who kept her immovable seat, with the child's hand in hers, I paced. I watched the stars from the balcony. I went back to my child. I hovered. I felt his little pulse. I drew near his mother. Again I paced away.

At six in the morning, I heard a gentle sigh from our patient. The fever-burn had faded from his cheeks, his pulse was regular; torpor had yielded to sleep. For a long time I dared not hope, but when all the signs were finally unmistakable, I ventured to whisper to Idris,

"The danger is past." It took a while longer to persuade her that I was telling the truth.

But neither our child's survival nor his speedy convalescence could restore even the partial peace of mind she'd managed to enjoy. Her fear had been too deep, too absorbing, too entire, to be replaced by any sense of security. Idris felt as if she'd awoken from her previous calm, like a passenger on a ship who dreams of being rocked in a cradle—too hard—and wakes up to find the vessel sinking. Before, her placidity had contained and neutralized the occasional pangs of fear; now, she never enjoyed a single interval of hope. No smile from the heart ever beamed across her fair countenance—though sometimes she forced one. Then the tears would flow, and a gushing sea of grief close above the wrecks of former happiness.

Yet while I was near her, she could not be in utter despair. Idris didn't seem to fear my death, or even picture its possibility. To my care she consigned the full freight of her anxieties; like a tiny wind-nipped fawn beside its mother doe's warm flank, she sheltered and reposed against my love. While I, not proudly as in days of joy, but tenderly, and with glad consciousness of the comfort I afforded, drew my trembling girl close to my heart, and tried to shield her sensitive nature from every painful thought or rough circumstance.

One other incident marked the end of that summer. The Countess of Windsor, Ex-Queen of England, returned from Europe. Quitting the vacancy of Vienna and her ancestral home there, she'd delayed the inevitable at Salzburg again for a time, but at last made her way to London among the final wave of refugees. Unable to tame her haughty mind to anything like submission, many weeks elapsed before she gave Adrian notice of her arrival. Though he hadn't heard from his mother in years, he welcomed her with grace and affection, ready to help heal the wounds of pride and sorrow. She responded coldly, and by her total apparent want of sympathy drove him off from further efforts.

Idris heard of their mother's return with pleasure. Her own maternal feelings were so ardent, she imagined the Ex-Queen must now, in this wasteland world, have lost her pride and put aside her harshness. With precious grandchildren to introduce, she pictured a reunion full of delight on both sides. The first check to her elation came with a formal communiqué from the fallen majesty of England. It stated that Lionel Verney, Commoner, was "under no conditions to be intruded upon her presence." She consented to forgive her daughter, and to acknowledge the offspring; larger concessions must not be expected. Idris, writing in return, declined a meeting in that case.

I was left infuriated by the Ex-Queen's message. Now that our dwindling race had lost all distinctions of rank, now that we felt a kindred, fraternal nature with all who bore the human genome, this angry, prideful remainder of times forever past and gone struck me as worse than foolish. Too much taken up by her own dreadful fears to be angry, Idris barely grieved the latest rupture, which she blamed on her mother's basic hard-heartedness. This wasn't altogether true. A domineering will had only disguised itself as callous feeling. The slave of pride, disdaining to exhibit any token of the struggle she endured, the haughty lady fancied that she sacrificed her happiness to a higher and immutable principle.

False! All of it was false—all but our affections, and our natural sympathy with pleasure or pain. There was only one good and one evil in the world—Life, and Death. The pomp of rank, the presumptions of power, the privileges of wealth had vanished like morning mist. One living beggar, or a petty thief, was worth more than a thousand dead aristocrats, more—alas the day!—than the hecatombs of our dead heroes, patriots, men and women of genius. There was severe degradation in this, for humanity. Even vice and virtue had lost their attributes and meaning. Life—life!—the continuation of our animal mechanism—was the Alpha and Omega of the desires, the prayers, the prostrate ambition of the human race.

(34)   THAT SUMMER, the hottest on record, stretched itself into October. On the 18th, the temperature dropped. Plague took its accustomed pause once a winter frost set in. Less than half of England's population was left alive to stand and catch its breath; as if we'd been shipwrecked on a barren rock and now, at the sight of a distant vessel, hardly daring to hope, we fancied salvation first coming

nearer, then again bearing from view. Uncertain as it was, this promise of a renewed lease on life saw rugged natures turn to melting tenderness. The softer-hearted, by contrast, were liable to be filled by harsh and unnatural sentiments. While it appeared that everyone was going to die, we'd grown somewhat reckless of the how and when for ourselves. With the plague in intermission, its virulence so mitigated as to raise the possibility that some might after all be spared, each person was eager to be among the elect, and clung to life with selfish, dastard tenacity. Instances of desertion became more frequent; and even murders, sickening to hear about, where horror of contagion had armed loving blood relations against one another.

But these domestic tragedies were about to yield to a mightier concern. The calm our temporary freedom from infection might have promised was swept away in a tempest born from human passions and nourished by our race's direst, most violent impulses.

A number of people from North America, the relics of that populous continent, abandoning their native cities and plains, had set sail for the east from a mad desire of change. Around the beginning of November, several hundred landed in Ireland, which they found no less afflicted than their own countries. They took possession of such vacant habitations as they could find, seizing upon surplus food and stray cattle; as they exhausted one spot, they went on to another. At length they began to interfere with the inhabitants, whom they ejected from their dwellings and robbed of their winter supplies. Such incidents roused the Irish to attack the invaders. Some they killed, but the major part escaped through quick, well-ordered maneuvers and subsequent care that impressed their attackers; meanwhile the enemy's manner of life, apparently given up to freedom's enjoyment, made many more locals envious. A few gained permission to join the foreign band, and before long the recruits outnumbered the originals, a majority making no attempt to imitate the admirable order which, preserved by the trans-Atlantic chiefs, rendered the strangers so effective. Across the countryside, the Irish followed their adopted track in disorganized multitudes, each day increasing, each day more lawless. Their behavior spread famine.

The North Americans, eager to escape from the monster they'd created, embarked for England as soon as they reached the eastern shore at Drogheda. We'd hardly have felt the incursion, had they come alone; but Ireland united in a collective will to follow.

East and west, the harbors of its desolate seaports were filled with vessels of all sizes, from merchant ships and superyachts to small fishing boats and tugs; some had been rotting there on the lazy deep for two years already. The emigrants embarked by the thousand. Few among them were experienced sailors, and their rude hands made strange havoc of canvas and rope. A surprisingly large number, even among the smaller craft, achieved their watery journey in safety. One contingent, in the true spirit of reckless enterprise, boarded a naval destroyer, and managed to get its vast hull away from the dock. The tide's drift took them outside the bay; then the hapless crew labored for hours to get under sail. But the ship was no longer seaworthy: one fresh breeze, and a hard swell opened cracks on both sides. The bay was crowded with vessels, whose crews, for the most part, had been observing the comedy of the idle destroyer. Now they saw her gradually sink—the waters rising above her lower decks—her upper decks—before they could believe their eyes, she'd utterly disappeared—they couldn't even tell anymore where the yawning jaws of the pitiless ocean had closed around her. A few on board swam to safety, the rest went down clinging to cordage and masts, rising only when death loosened their hold.

Some witnesses of this event and others like it in kind, if not in scale, must have been dissuaded from leaving dry land to make their own attempts. But these were few compared to the numbers who actually crossed. Many went up to Belfast for the shorter route, then journeyed south through Scotland; poor and desperate Scots joined them at every point along their migrant trail; and all streamed with one accord into England.

In towns where enough English people were still alive to feel it, these surprise incursions bred fear. Communication had been so fractured and paralyzed as a result of the pandemic that no one had warning. Truthfully, our hapless country by then held room enough for twice their number, had they been peaceful. But the lawless spirits they let rule them, made these invaders violent. Taking anything they wanted, throwing people out of homes along their way, they delighted most in chances to seize on some luxurious mansion and the well-supplied seclusion of its wealthy, plague-fearing occupants—who'd be forced into servitude or worse while the intruders stayed around. As soon as one place was completely ruined, they removed their locust visitation to another. When unopposed they spread their ravages wide; facing danger they clustered, and by dint of numbers overthrew weaker foes. They moved south; their course appeared aimless, but unquestionably their goal was our unhappy London.

By the time we got our first reports of their presence, they'd already reached Manchester, having swept the country like a conquering army—burning, laying waste, murdering. Vagabonds and others of our underclass joined in. We heard that someone had collected a militia at Derby to try and beat them back; but panic seized its thin ranks at the fight's outset. This brief opposition only served to increase the horde's audacity and cruelty. A hybrid lot united in their fixation on lists of historical injuries, they talked of taking London and conquering England, the oppressor state—they marched to Victory, or Martyrdom.

Waves of terrified people who'd fled their advance began arriving at Windsor. We heard vastly exaggerated accounts of the invading force's numbers, fury, and cruelty—the distortions of rumor and fear, active since human time began. The strange, appalling, impossible attributes assigned to the migrant army marked a final evolution of the Gorgons and Centaurs, of sea monsters, dragons, werewolves. Panic spread, and tumult filled formerly quiet suburbs. Families deserted their homes, escaping with no idea where they might go; those prepared to stay and fight stood trembling, not for themselves, but for their defenseless loved ones. In London, crowded up into the higher buildings around town, anxious watchers imagined they could see distant smoke and flames spread by the enemy.

As Windsor lay squarely in the path of the onslaught, I moved my family into a suite at the Tower of London assigned us by the Protectorate. Once assured that Idris and the children were comfortable and safe, I left to join Adrian, and act as his lieutenant in the coming struggle.

With only two days to prepare, we made good use of every minute. Brought out of storage and into firing condition were ample weapons and ammunition. A general call-up supplied the remnants of enough regiments to muster and put under arms, with that appearance of military discipline which must intimidate the disorganized multitude of our enemies, while encouraging our own side. Banners floated in the air. Even music wasn't wanting: fife and trumpet shrilled and blared forth proper martial airs. The soldiers marched in time. True, a keen ear might have detected many unusually faltering steps breaking their unison; but fear of the adversary wasn't the cause. Our fighters stumbled under burdens of disease, of sorrow—and of those fatal premonitions and prognostications which often weighed most heavily on the bravest hearts.

A careworn Adrian led the troops. Small relief to him that our discipline should gain us victory in this conflict; while plague was still around to equalize conqueror and conquered, it wasn't victory that he desired, but bloodless peace. As we advanced, we encountered bands of civilians coming from the north whose almost naked condition, whose despair and horror, testified at once to the ferocity of the enemy we went to meet: with insane fury, blinded by the senseless spirit of conquest and the greedy thirst for spoil, they'd drowned the country in ruin. The sight of the military restored hope to those who'd fled, and in whom vengefulness now took the place of fear. Their shouts and cheers inspired the faltering soldiers with ardor; our slow march turned speedy. The hollow murmur of the multitude of refugees kept pace and gradually filled the air, a roar of bloodlust drowning out the clang of weaponry and battle tunes. Adrian began to fear it would be difficult to hold back our forces from making a furious attack on the Irish and their allies. He rode through the lines, charging the officers to restrain the troops, exhorting the soldiers, restoring order, and quieting in some degree the violent agitation that swelled every bosom.

We had our first sight of the enemy in the late afternoon, at St. Albans—a few stragglers who retreated at the sight of us. Gathering numbers of their companions on the way, they kept falling back till they reached the main body, where tidings of an armed and regular opposition recalled everyone to a kind of order. Making Buckingham their headquarters, they sent out scouts to ascertain our situation; doing the same, we spent the night at Luton. Our advance movements the next morning were simultaneous.

We converged on the grounds of an abandoned golf course east of Bletchley. It was dawn, and the air, impregnated with the fresh odors of dead leaves and overgrown grass, seemed to toy with our banners in an idle, mocking mood. The same breezes carried our marching band music and heavy boot steps across to the enemy lines, and so inspired surprise not unmingled with dread among our undisciplined foe; for these sounds spoke of other days, days of concord and order, before the present pandemic—a time when humanity lived outside or beyond the shadow of extinction.

The pause was momentary, though. Soon we heard their disorderly clamor, the barbarous shouts, the roil and rattling steps of thousands coming on in disarray. Their troops poured from the woods onto the long, undulating field that lay between us; we advanced across it to a rise and halted, with superior sightlines and position. Those in charge on their side also gave word to halt, and tried to form their chaotic ranks into some imitation of the military discipline they saw facing them. With only stolen guns and horses, they could achieve no uniformity, and little obedience; but their shouts and wild gestures showed the untamed spirit that inspired them. On command, in perfect order, our soldiers started their advance in quick-time. Their mechanical precision, the gleam of their polished bayonets, their rigid silence, and looks of sullen hate, were more appalling than the savage clamor of our far more numerous foe. Both sides came on, the howls and shouts of the Irish increasing. The English proceeded in obedience to their officers, and halted once more on command. But now the first line of infantry were close enough to distinguish the faces of their enemies. The sight provoked them to fury. With a single cry that seemed to tear through heaven, they rushed forward with fixed bayonets, almost disdaining to fire in their zeal to slash and spear. Spotting a gap in the ranks, one of our artillery teams fired a cannon, whose deafening roar and blinding smoke filled up the horror of the scene.

Adrian had ordered the halt a few moments previously. I was nearby, observing his deep meditations as he formed a plan of action to prevent bloodshed. The sudden sounds of battle and cannon fire startled us. Eyes flashing, Adrian exclaimed, "Not one of these people must perish!"

With a plunge of the rowels into his horse's sides, he dashed towards the conflict. He didn't swerve from the bullets that passed near him but rode immediately between the opposing lines. We, his staff, followed to surround and protect him; obeying his signal, however, we fell back somewhat. The English fighters paused in their assault when they saw him there. Silence followed uproar. About fifty men and women lay on the ground, dying or dead. Adrian raised his sword, and turned to address his own troops:

"By whose command," he cried, "do you engage? Who ordered it? Fall back! These misguided people shall not be slaughtered while I am your general. Sheath your weapons. These are your brothers and sisters, do not commit fratricide. Soon the plague won't leave a single life for you to glut your revenge upon: will you be more pitiless than pestilence? As you honor me—as you worship God, in whose image all these too are created—as your children and friends are dear to you—shed not a drop of precious human blood."

Then, turning to our invaders with a threatening scowl, he commanded them to lay down their arms:

"You see us wasted by plague, and think to overcome us? The plague is also among you. Lay down your arms, barbarous and cruel individuals whose hands are already stained with the blood of the innocent, whose souls are weighed down by the orphan's cry! When you've been crushed by famine and disease, the ghosts of those you've murdered will rise to see you dragged to hell. The victory must be ours, for right is on our side—you know it, I can see it in your faces. Lay down your arms, my fellow men! my sisters! Pardon, aid, and fraternal love await your surrender and repentance. You are dear to us, because you wear the frail flesh of humanity; each one among you, I promise you, will find a friend and host among these English forces." He gestured, to ask both armies: "Or shall we continue to wallow in violence, while plague, our common enemy, laughs and triumphs in our butchery, even crueler than its own?"

All was still. On our side the soldiers grasped their weapons firmly, and shot angry looks at the Irish forces—who hadn't thrown down their weapons, either, more from fear than any wish for battle. The two armies eyed each other, stalemated. Adrian threw himself from his horse and approached one of the Irish fighters on the ground.

"This was a man," he cried, "and he is dead!" He waved an arm at the English line.

"Quickly—quickly, bind up the wounds of the fallen—let them not die—let not one more soul escape through your merciless gashes, to tell the story of your sinful fratricide before the throne of God; bind up their wounds—restore them to their friends. Cast away the hearts of tigers that burn in your breasts; throw down those tools of cruelty and hate. Destiny already exterminates us. So then let each living one be guardian and support to the other. Away with those blood-stained blades, and some of you come bind up these wounds."

As he spoke, he knelt on the ground, and raised in his arms a woman from whose chest the warm red tide of life was gushing. The poor wretch gasped—so still had the scene become, that her moans were distinctly heard across the old fairway; and every heart, though just then bent on massacre, now beat anxiously in hope and fear. The fate of the world seemed bound up in the life or death of this one woman. Adrian had torn off his military scarf and pressed it to the wound. It was too late. The woman heaved a deep sigh, her head fell back, her still limbs drooped.

Adrian spoke. "She's dead." As the corpse slipped to the ground, he bowed his head in sorrow and awe.

With that, both sides, deeply repentant, threw down their arms. The English veterans wept. While a gush of love and deepest amity filled every heart, the erstwhile adversaries joined hands. All talked of how the two forces might assist each other. As one body, they obeyed Adrian's order to proceed towards London.

(35)   ADRIAN brought all his considerable diplomatic skills first to forging peace, and then to providing for the invaders' multitudes. London could not support them. Some Irish we sent back to their own island, the rest were marched to various parts of the southern counties, to be quartered in deserted towns. Over the next few months we reinforced our northern border to defend against another migrant surge. Meanwhile, their deputy Lord Protector had a new

plan for England's people. By now, the living were scattered everywhere across the country, many existing alone, or in the most sadly shrunken households. He wanted to congregate what was left in designated population centers; for he was convinced that only through the benevolent and social virtues could the remnant of our race hope for any safety, much less survival.

Our family's Tower sojourn allowed Adrian and Idris to meet after nearly a year. Occupied in fulfilling the laborious and painful tasks of high office, he'd encountered every species of human misery; always, he could do less than he wished; he saw that his aid was of little avail. Yet his purpose of soul, his energy and ardent resolution, shielded Adrian from sorrow. The very excess of his sensitivity made him that much more capable a pilot for a storm-tossed land; while the potency of his virtue endowed him with health and strength. His sister hardly recognized the fragile being, whose form it seemed a summer breeze could bend, in the energetic man before her. He appeared born again.

It was different with Idris. Though never complaining, she wept involuntarily. She'd grown thin and pale; her voice was broken, hushed. Fear possessed her heart. Just as she strove always to hide this fear from me, Idris tried to throw a veil over the change which she knew her beloved brother must observe in her. At last, in a burst of irrepressible grief as they sat alone, she gave vent to her apprehensions and sorrow. I already knew what she must have said when, much later, Adrian told me—I knew it all. The ceaseless, insatiable, corrosive care, a sleepless expectation of evil that gnawed her soul like the vulture did Prometheus; under the influence of this eternal plague-induced excitement, and of the interminable struggles she endured to combat and conceal its effects on her, she felt herself being consumed by her own over-accelerated metabolism. Sleep wasn't sleep, when nightmare trampled the frail control she kept upon waking thoughts evermore transformed into rest-destroying terrors. Worst of all, her state permitted no hope of improvement, no natural alleviation, unless the grave should quickly receive its destined prey, and she be permitted to die, before she experienced a thousand living deaths in the loss of those she loved.

Being in London added to her disquiet, certainly. The plague's ravages were far more visible there than back at home. Great swathes of the city seemed to have returned almost to nature, with streets so grass-grown they looked like thick, frozen lawns. On every side were boarded-up houses, parks overrun with weeds, empty storefronts, lonely intersections. The busiest parts of town felt the most silent and vacant, especially now that all idea of coming to London for pleasure had passed away, along with all London's nightlife. Yet in the midst of desolation, Adrian had preserved order and the law. Secular institutions thus survived certain divine ones—for while a Covenant to preserve our species was broken, human property continued sacred. A melancholy state of things; and though crime rates were kept low, the situation struck the heart as a wretched mockery that Idris felt in full.

She and I had been trying to track down the unworldly Merrival, whose frequent visits to us at Windsor had stopped abruptly; we'd had no word of him, and at this time when no more than a hairsbreadth divided the living from the dead, we'd naturally feared that our friend had become another unrecorded statistic. Being now in London, we'd called at his house to offer any help we could to his surviving family, but no Merrivals at all remained in residence. The place had been used to quarter Irish migrants since after the quelled invasion; we saw expensive astronomical instruments set up as laundry racks, and a celestial chart, dense with abstruse calculations, papering a broken windowpane. The neighbors were uninformative, but from a passing clinic nurse we learned that plague had taken the whole family, except for Merrival himself, who'd "lost his mind," she said, and lived on the streets these days.

It seemed no inquiry could bring us closer to his whereabouts. I encountered him almost by chance. I'd gone to find out whether he'd been spotted near his old home, as the nurse had said he sometimes was. The November afternoon darkened early on my ride there, and I reached Merrival's address amid pattering rain and melancholy wind. Just then, I saw him—or rather his semblance, attenuated and wild— pass me, and sit down on the front doorstep. Wind battered at the grey locks on his temples, the rain drenched his uncovered head. He sat hiding his face in his withered hands. I pressed his shoulder to get his attention, but he didn't move. "Merrival," I said. "Merrival, it's been a long time since we've seen you—here, come with me—Lady Idris wants very much to see you—you won't refuse a request from her, will you? Come—come along with me. We'll bring you home to Windsor with us."

He answered in a hollow voice, "Bring me home? Why deceive a helpless old man, why talk hypocritically to someone half-crazed? Windsor is not my home. I've found my true home, the home that our so-called Creator has prepared for me. But do not tempt me to speak! My words would terrify you." I was amazed at the bitter scorn in his tone as he continued: "For in a universe of cowards, I alone dare use my mind to think—among the graveyards—among the victims of a merciless tyranny, I dare reproach the Supreme Evil. How can He punish me? Let Him bare his arm and transfix me with lightning, like a real god." And the old man laughed. Then he rose to his feet, and I followed him through the rain.

A lost mind, the nurse had called it; yet in reality, poor Merrival was possessed only by the delirium of excessive grief. This very old man, accustomed to looking at prospects of mathematically sound, million-year futures—this visionary who'd overlooked starvation in the wasted forms of his wife and children, and never seen the horrible sights and sounds that surrounded him in plague-time, insensible to any care for self-preservation—this astronomer, apparently dead to life on earth, and existing only in the motion of the spheres—after all, he loved his family. It wasn't just that his absence of mind and almost infantile naïveté made him utterly dependent on them; nor that through long habit they'd become a vital part of himself. His affection for them was undemonstrative, even unapparent, but intense. It wasn't till one of them died that he perceived their danger; one by one the rest were carried off by pestilence; and finally his wife, his helpmate and supporter, more necessary to him than his own body, the kind companion whose voice always spoke peace to him, closed her eyes in death. Merrival felt the system of universal nature which he had so long studied and adored, shift and slide from underneath his feet, and he stood among the dead, and lifted his voice in curses: those harrowing maledictions, bloody with an old man's broken-heartedness, that even a trained professional had misinterpreted as frenzy.

We came to a churchyard. Not far from the gate, he threw himself on the wet earth. "Here they are," he cried, "beautiful creatures—breathing, speaking, loving creatures. She who by day and night cherished the worn-out lover of her youth—they, parts of my flesh, my children—here they are. Call them, scream their names all night long; they won't answer!" He clung to the little heaps that marked the graves. "I ask but one thing, Verney. I do not fear His hell, for I have it here; I do not desire His heaven—no! Only let me die and be laid beside them; let me but only, when I lie dead, feel my flesh as it molders, mingle with theirs. Promise!" He raised himself painfully and seized my arm. "Promise to bury me with them."

I promised readily, but added, "On one condition: return with us to Windsor."

"To Windsor!" he shrieked. "Never! From this place I'll never go. My bones, my flesh, I myself, are already buried here, and what you see of me is nothing but corrupted clay." He stroked the mud that covered him. "I will lie here, and cling here, till rain and winter ruin and dissolve me—I will be made one in substance with them below."

In a few words I must conclude this tragedy. Though Idris and her brother and I undertook to watch over him, our sadder task was soon fulfilled; age, grief, exposure to the worsening elements, all united to hush Merrival's sorrows and bring repose to a heart whose beats were agony. He died embracing the sod that would be piled above his breast, when he was placed among the beings whom he regretted with such wild despair.

Sorrier than ever to be in London after this event, Idris insisted we return home. She had the children's safety in mind as well, she said. In a carriage Adrian supplied, we left for Windsor a day or two later. It was a melancholy thing to go back to this place so dear to our hearts, a scene of such uncommon former happiness, to be on the spot to mark the extinction of our species. Deep, ineradicable footsteps of disease could be traced everywhere across the cherished landscape. Its soil fertile as ever; yet agricultural conditions had so far changed that there'd been no late plantings: too few hands to sow the seeds. The time for such autumnal labors was now gone, and winter had set in with sudden and unusual severity. A cycle of frosts and thaws ended in floods; many roads were already impassable before the first heavy snowfalls of December. The horse team powered us through an arctic scenery. House roofs peeped from white massy cloaks; broken-windowed vacation cottages and stately mansions, equally deserted, no pathways shoveled to their doors. I thought of Adrian's parting words; we'd been talking about what was to come in 2096. He predicted: "Next summer will decide the fate of our species. I won't stop doing everything I can until then. But if plague comes back, the fight must end, so we can begin choosing our graves."

Our little town of Windsor, in which many survivors from the neighboring counties were already assembled, wore a sad appearance. Its streets were blocked up with snow, and the few people to be seen outdoors were shivering, frozen by the prevalent north-east wind of this most uncongenial winter. The altered state of society turned such an accident of nature into a source of real misery and hardship, whose escape must become the focus of all our exertions. It's true that we had sufficient stockpiles of food and all the necessities of life, more than enough to supply the wants of the diminished population; but a great deal of labor was required to arrange these, as it were, raw materials. Families formerly devoted to exalted callings and refined pursuits, accomplished, rich, blooming, young, brought care-fraught hearts to huddle and bicker in their diminished numbers over meager fires, all grown selfish and groveling. Depressed by sickness, and fearful of the future, they suffered in a world without conveniences, cleaning staff, specialists, stores. Regardless of ignorance, inaptitude, or preference for repose, hands unused to household duties must perform them, and knead the bread, and even undertake the butcher's office. Poor and rich were now equal—or rather the poor were superior, since they brought alacrity and experience to the same tasks that wore out the luxurious, humiliated the proud, and disgusted all whose minds, bent on intellectual improvement, held it their dearest privilege to be exempt from attending to mere animal needs.

But goodness and love found ways to emerge from every change. We witnessed sights made for the admirers of the human race to enjoy—acts of self-sacrificial devotion, simultaneously graceful and heroic; to behold them felt like being back in ancient times, amid the patriarchal modes of kinship, friendship, duty. Former young notables of the land worked as servants to their parents or weaker siblings. With amiable cheerfulness, they went to the river to break the ice and draw water; they assembled on foraging expeditions; axes in hand, they went into the woods for fuel. Then the simple and affectionate welcome upon their return—the clean hearth and bright fire—the supper ready, cooked by beloved hands—gratitude for the provision for tomorrow's meal: strange enjoyments for the high-born English, yet now their sole, hard-earned, and dearly prized luxuries.

For graceful submission to circumstances, innate noble humility, and the ingenious fancy to adorn acts of goodness with romantic coloring, no one surpassed our own Clara. She saw my despondency, saw Idris bent beneath aching cares. She made it her full-time employment to save us from trouble, taking on any labor, and managing to spread ease and even elegance over the Castle's altered mode of life. We still had some attendants spared by disease, and warmly attached to us. But Clara regarded their services jealously; she wanted to be Idris's sole handmaid, and sole minister to her little cousins' wants. Nothing gave her so much pleasure as our employing her in this way; she went beyond our desires, earnest, diligent, and unwearied. To adapt an old poem:

> *Clara was ready ere we called her name,*
> *And though we called another, Clara came.*

I had returned to Windsor with a mission; for we were to be among Adrian's first designated population centers. Having taken on myself the guardianship of the district, I wouldn't desert it while a single inhabitant survived. My resolve was intact, but in common with many people at the time, my reserves of energy were stubbornly low. Perhaps, after the past summer's stupendous excitement, the enforced calm of winter made it doubly irksome to rise to the demands of daily toil. I can speak for myself: lack of enthusiasm had never been my failing. Before the plague, I'd dwelt with vigor in the world, engrossed in histories, passionate in my love of family, and like the antique peasant I so resembled, investing nature—the uplands, glades, and streams—with divine attributes. Strange, with the world rushing along an eccentric, untried path, that I should feel this spirit fade. I struggled with despondency, weariness, a choking fog-like depression. Last year's fervor to grasp at life was gone, and over the aching pangs induced by the distresses of the times, a certain numbness was falling. The utter uselessness of even my most successful efforts to improve conditions meant I could take no pleasure in them. Despairing, I longed to return to my old occupations, but of what use, what good were they? Reading was futile—to write, vanity indeed. Where lately had stretched a world-wide gallery for the display of talents and dignified exploits, one vast theatre for a magnificent drama, the earth now showed a vacant space, an empty stage. For neither actor nor spectator was there any longer aught to say or hear.

I spent part of each day paying visits in the town of Windsor, and when the weather permitted, I was glad to ride further out and have some time to muse in solitude. Often, pushing my wide tire bicycle with occasional difficulty through the snow-blocked roads, I crossed the bridge and passed through Eton. No youthful congregation of gallant-hearted youngsters thronged around its gates and doors; sad silence pervaded both classrooms and playgrounds. I met troops of horses, herds of cattle, flocks of sheep that wandered at will, finding food and shelter in haystacks and vacant cottages. Up a hill on a path cut through snow banks, I reached a favorite overlook. But the view I loved, of gentle uplands and picturesque dales, with fields of waving corn, stands of stately trees, and the meandering Thames, was entirely unrecognizable—one sheet of white covered all. I reflected bitterly, that the heart of almost every inhabitant was cold and motionless as the winter-clothed scene itself.

On another frosty day, driven by restless unsatisfying reflections, I rode out to a little wood not far from Salt Hill, and stopped beside a stand of elms, where a bubbling spring flowed and prattled invisibly beneath ice sheets and drifted snow. This spot had a peculiar charm for me. Adrian's favorite resort back when, needing to escape his mother's stately bondage, he'd come to sit on a ledge of rock below the spring and read some beloved book, or simply muse, speculations beyond his years, on morals or metaphysics; back when a distant future was a given in such questions; the place was secluded, and he often said that his happiest boyhood hours had been spent there. Gripped by a melancholy foreboding that I'd never see it again, I set about trying to classify and memorize each tree, along with every winding of the ice-bound streamlet, every stump and irregularity of ground, that I might better call up its idea in absence.

Before my eyes, a robin red-breast dropped heavily from a branch onto an ice patch: not dead but dying, clearly. A hawk appeared in the air; sudden fear seized the little creature; it exerted its last strength, throwing itself on its back, raising its talons in impotent defense against its powerful enemy. Stepping forward, I took the robin up and placed it inside my jacket. Warmed by my body heat, fed with a few crumbs from a biscuit, by degrees it revived; its warm fluttering heart beat against my chest. I don't know why I stop to detail this trifling incident, but the scene is still before me: the birds, the brook, the ice; the leafless trees with their fantastical draperies of hoar frost; snow-covered fields forming distant expanses to be glimpsed through a picket of silvery beech tree trunks; a low clouded sky, drear cold, unbroken silence; while my feathered nursling lay warm and safe, lightly chirping its contentment.

All earth is cold and deathlike as the snowy fields, and misery-stricken the life-tide of its inhabitants. Painful reflections thronged and stirred my brain with wild commotion. *Why should I oppose the avalanche of destruction that sweeps us away? Why steel my nerves and renew my wearied efforts each day—ah, why? So that my firm courage and cheerful exertions might shelter the dear mate, whom I chose in the spring of my life. Though the throbbings of my heart be replete with pain, though my hopes for the future are moribund, as long as your dear head, my gentlest love, can repose in peace on that heart, and while you derive from its fostering care any comfort and hope, my struggles shall not cease, and I won't call myself altogether vanquished.*

Some weeks later, I walked in Windsor Forest with my family, one of those lovely February days whose barrenness could be forgotten in its natural beauty. The deer were turning up the snow in search of hidden grass; the white was made intensely dazzling by the sun's unseasonably genial power. Leafless branches spread the intricate traceries of some delicate seaweed against an azure sky, while the naked tree trunks reared up like columns in a vast, labyrinthine temple. It was impossible not to receive pleasure from the sight of these things. The children, freed from too long indoors, bounded before us like spaniels, chasing the deer, rousing pheasants and partridges from their coverts. As we walked, Idris leant on my arm, smiling: her sadness had yielded to the moment's enjoyment.

All at once, I seemed to wake up. As if it were a heavy blanket, I cast off the clinging sloth of the past months. Earth had a new appearance, and my view of the future was suddenly crystal clear. I gave a cry.

"What is it, dear?"

"Idris," I told her, "We're too far north!"

She frowned. "You think Dorset would be any better?"

"I think the Continent would be better," I said. "Look at our gloomy winter life here—our sordid cares—our menial labors. This northern country is no place for a falling population. When *Homo sapiens* were few, it wasn't here they came—they couldn't have covered the globe with offspring if they had. We need to seek some natural Paradise, some garden of the world, where our simple wants can be easily supplied. For the associations, social pleasures and culture we lose here, the enjoyment of a delicious climate will compensate. If we survive this coming summer, I won't spend next winter in England—nor will any of us."

Still Idris frowned. I heard the question she didn't voice. Would we, any of us, survive the coming summer? As often before, I had the feeling of being chained to a runaway carriage. Our fate was completely out of our control. We could no longer choose what to do or leave undone. A mightier, inhuman power was here to destroy our plans, or demand the work we avoided.

One thing was for sure. To count upon another winter would be madness. This was our last. Our future prospects stretched through the summer to come, and no further; there, instead of more road to travel, lay a yawning gulph into which we must, and would, fall. Humanity's last blessing had been snatched from us, our comfort was dead: for we could no longer hope. Could the hopelessly mad hope? Could a wretch led to the death chamber, feeling the straps tighten, hope? Could a sailor shipwrecked in the Atlantic, exhausted from swimming, who heard the distinctive splash of a shark's fin dividing the waves between them, hope? Such hope as theirs, we had!

(36)   YOU HEAR the rushing sound of the tempest's approach? See the lurid clouds open and pour down dire destruction? Are you deafened by the falling thunderbolts? Can't you feel the blasted earth tremble and crack open with agonized groans, as the air fills with shrieks and wailing—don't you recognize all the expected signs? No? Because none of these things accompanied our end.

A balmy spring, breathed from nature's most ambrosial sources, greens the lovely earth, which wakens and emerges much like a proud young mother leading their beauteous offspring to meet a long absent Papa. Buds deck the trees, flowers adorn the land; thick sap-swollen branches burst into leaf. The variegated foliage of spring, which bends and sings in the breeze, rejoices in the genial warmth. Brooks flow murmuring in the direction of a placid sea whose waters reflect the cliffs and cloudless sky above. Birds awake in the woods to plenty, while abundant food for so-called man and beast springs up from the fertile ground. Where is pain and evil? Not in the calm of air and ocean; not in forests nor in fields, nor among the birds that make the woods resound with song, nor the animals that in the midst of plenty bask in sunshine. Our enemy, our calamity alone, treads human hearts underfoot, and never makes a sound.

Once a royal psalmist sang that God had made human beings to be "a little lower than the angels," and that "crowned. . .with glory and honor," we'd been given dominion over all God's works, the whole world. So, once a favorite with our Creator—but now? Look at us! Plague has invaded the human form, incarnated itself in our flesh, entwined itself with our being, and blinded our eyes from seeking heaven. Man, woman, lie down, and give up all claims to that inheritance you were expecting. You'll never get more than the small piece of blooming earth required for your burial.

Plague comes with spring, with sunshine and plenty. We no longer struggle with it. We've forgotten what we did before plague. That traders plied the gigantic waves of southern oceans with their ships to bring us articles of luxury; that perilous journeys were made after splendid geological trifles like gemstones and gold; that human labor was wasted, and human life ever set at naught—these old facts seem increasingly hard to believe. For now, life is all we covet: that this automaton of flesh should, with joints and springs in order, perform its functions—that this dwelling of the soul should be capable of containing its dweller. Our minds, so recently spread abroad through countless spheres and endless combinations of thought, retrench themselves behind this wall of flesh, eager to preserve its wellbeing alone. Our degradation is sufficient.

Among the notes I remember making that spring, was also this: "In the midst of despair we perform the tasks of hope." Plague cases climbed as the weather got warmer. Such of us who still cared to bestow our time and thoughts on our fellow creatures, were made to toil harder. Going out, day after day, to aid the sick and comfort the sorrowing, we nerved ourselves for the task by picturing ourselves in combat with a deadly foe. Sometimes among the multitudinous dead a rare survivor might be found, and then with our zeal enough to behave like power, we'd bid them: *Rise. Live.* Plague watched us the whole time, laughing its head off.

Still engaged in the attempt to collect a self-sustaining population at Windsor, I went to every corner of the county and beyond. These rides gave me ample opportunity to see how plague had smashed our social order like an anthill; by twos and threes, the dazed survivors struggled from the ruins into daylight. Everywhere stood empty habitations. Law was gone, lost along with its customary curbs on private behavior. On a rising wave of transgressions against the last known rules, the poorest people dared to enter deserted palaces and intrude, no questions asked, into splendid apartments whose very décor represented unknown worlds to them.

Wealth and property no longer circulated. Plague's earlier economic effects had reduced people of every kind to sudden and hideous poverty—yet with the boundaries of private ownership thrown down, the products of human labor at present existing were found to be more, far more, than our thinned-down race could possibly consume. To some among the poor this was cause for celebration. We were all equal now; magnificent dwellings, luxurious carpets, goose down duvets, were given to all. Of carriages, horses, gardens, world-class libraries and art collections, there were more than enough to go around, and nothing to stop anyone from claiming a princely share. We were all equal now; but near at hand was an equality still more leveling, a state where beauty and strength and wisdom would mean as little, finally, as riches, birth, or real estate. Meanwhile the common grave that yawned beneath us posed a prospect so awful, it blotted out any enjoyment of the ease and plenty everywhere at hand.

Still my boys and Clara sprang up in years and growth, unsullied by disease, the bloom on their cheeks unfading. We had no reason to think the site of Windsor Castle peculiarly healthful, for many other families had died out beneath its roof; we lived therefore taking no particular precaution but we lived, it seemed, in safety. If Idris became thin and pale, it was anxiety caused the change, an anxiety I could in no way reduce. She never complained, but sleep and appetite deserted her, a slow fever preyed on her veins and splashed her cheeks with red, and she often wept in secret; the principle of life within her was being eaten up by gloomy prognostications and more agonizing and immediate dread. Of course I saw this—and I often wished that I'd permitted Idris to take her own course, and go to work outside our household for the welfare of others, if such labors might have distracted her thoughts. But it was too late now. With the race nearly extinct, all such toil was almost over; besides, she was too weak. Consumption, as I'd call the hyperactive life within her (Adrian had been the same), deprived her limbs of strength. Nighttimes spent her vital oil; in the early morning hours, without my knowing, she'd wander through our rooms, or lean for hours above our sleeping children's beds. In the daytime, sunk into a doze, she'd twitch and mutter at vexations in unquiet dreams. A confirmed state of wretchedness set in, and her efforts at concealment grew ever more apparent.

As often as I would strive, yet in vain, to awaken her courage and hope, I'd recognize my Idris in her drastic anxieties; for her very soul was tenderness. Trusting that she wouldn't outlive me if I fell prey to the vast calamity, she admitted this thought sometimes relieved her. After traveling the highway of life hand in hand for many years, we might as well take that next step the same way. Her children, though, her lovely, playful, animated children—beings sprung from her own dear side—portions of her own being—depositories of our married love—how often had her motherly imagination pictured their various merits and talents to best effect on life's wide stage! Even if we died, to know that they might reach their golden years would comfort her. But it would not be so. Cut off forever from the hopes of maturity, from the pride of attainments, young and blooming as they were, they would die.

Alas for these latter days! Our world had grown old, and all partook of the decrepitude. Why talk of infancy, adulthood, old age? We were all equal now; arrived at the same point of the world's age together, there was no difference between us. The words *parent* and *child* had lost their meaning; his youngest boy was level now with any father.

Where could we turn, and not find some dire example of the desolation wrought upon humanity? The countryside offered fields left uncultivated, gaudy with wildflowers and weeds—or a few acres of wheat, sign of living hopes; but only sown halfway, the farmer dead in a furrow, his broken plough deserted by the horses. Unattended cattle wandered over the landscape and through the lanes; poultry yard occupants by the thousand, left unfed, had broken out to breed wild; young piglets and lambs were born in the flower gardens, and the donkey bedded down in the hall of pleasure. Sickly and few, people still alive in the country neither went out to sow nor reap, but sauntered about the meadows, or lay around all day in some hedge's shade. Others had secluded themselves, with supplies enough to stay alone inside their homes indefinitely; some had even deserted spouses and children, imagining that only utter solitude would guarantee safety. Such had been Ryland's case, and he was discovered dead and half-devoured by insects, in a house many miles from any other, with piles of food laid up in useless superfluity. Then there were the many instances of people who made long journeys to unite themselves with those they loved, and arrived to find them dead.

London did not contain above a thousand inhabitants, and this number was continually diminishing. Most were country people, come for the sake of change; the actual Londoners had sought the country. East London and its once busy docks were silent, the floors of its looted luxury goods warehouses strewn with bales of jewels and spices, more ransacked than pillaged by crowds motivated as much by curiosity as greed—though the ground before a few barred gates bore signs of how guards or owners had defended them at loss of life. The city's church doors, kept unlocked, creaked wide on their massive hinges to reveal dead bodies ranged up and down the paved aisles within. Wretched women, loveless victims of vulgar brutality, found their way into the homes of our celebrated high-born beauties, where they arrayed themselves in garb of splendor, and died before their own reflections in another's mirror. In the streets below, women whose delicate feet had seldom touched the earth throughout their lives of privilege, had fled in fright and horror from their death-filled homes and lost themselves and their lives in the squalid depths of the metropolis. And what—my soul ached with fear to wonder—might befall my beloved Idris and our babes, if Adrian and I died first, and they found themselves without protectors in this new world? My child of prosperity, the nursling of rank and wealth: so far, her mind alone had suffered. But how much longer, before her delicate frame and shrinking nerves must be assaulted by famine, hardship, disease? Better die at once—better plunge a dagger in her bosom while it was still untouched by the worst adversity—and then sheathe it in my own!

But no. I would not yield in my resolution to defend my dear ones against sorrow and pain, to the last gasp. By my reckoning, in times of misery we must fight against our destinies and strive not to be overcome by them; and if I were vanquished at last, it wouldn't be ingloriously. Our misery's very excess raised our sorrow to the plane of the Sublime, where it might be granted some relief. So I stood in the gap, resisting the enemy—the impalpable, invisible foe who'd so long besieged us—and kept vigilant against its insidious approaches, which might let plague burrow under and burst up through the very threshold of our home, that temple of love at whose altar I daily sacrificed.

With fewer people remaining to die, Death seemed to feed more hungrily; or was it that before, when there were still many survivors, the dead counts affected us less? Now each life, each human breathing form was a gem—though of far, far more worth than any gemstone; and the daily, nay, hourly decrease visible in our numbers sickened the heart. This summer extinguished our hopes and wrecked human society; over the sea of misery, a few tempest-tossed survivors rode their shattered rafts. We existed by twos and threes, specimens of *Homo sapiens* who slept and waked and performed the animal functions. But the human being, individually weak, yet more powerful in congregated numbers than wind or ocean; the human, who'd conquered the elements and reigned over nature, the peer of demigods, existed no longer.

Farewell to the patriotic scene, to the love of liberty and virtuous aspiration's well-earned rewards! Farewell to crowded senate chambers, buzzing with the voices of the wise, whose laws could cut more keenly than Damascus steel—farewell to rulers' pomp and warlike pageantry! The robes and flags are in the dust; the general's hand is cold, and the young soldier's untimely and unhonored grave has been dug among his native fields. Farewell to the desire for office, and the hope of victory; to high vaulting ambition, to the appetite for praise, and the craving for another's vote! The governments and nations are no longer. The marketplace is empty, the candidate for popular favor finds no one to represent—to elections and incumbency farewell! To galas and inaugural balls and all-night revelry—to the panting emulation of beauty, to costly dress and arriviste display, to inheritance and titles bought and born to, farewell!

Farewell to humanity's giant powers—to knowledge that could oppose the ocean waves and pilot ships between unseen opposing shores—to science that directed the silken balloon through the pathless air—to the power that could channel mighty waters, and set the wheels, and beams, and vast machinery of mills in motion; that could split, blast, and harvest blocks of granite or marble, and level the mountains!

Farewell to the arts—to eloquence, the stirring sea wind of the human mind—farewell to poetry and deep philosophy! for imagination is cold, and enquiring minds no longer expatiate on the wonders of life. Whatsoever thy hand findeth to do, do it with thy might; for there is no work, nor device, nor knowledge, nor wisdom in the grave, whither thou goest—*farewell to memory and apt citation of verses from Ecclesiastes! Farewell to graceful buildings whose perfect proportions surpass nature's best; the art of architecture—fair entablatures and peristyles of fluted columns, with their capitals of Corinthian, Ionic, or Doric style; fretted Gothic font and massy Moorish pillar, stupendous arch and glorious dome, forms whose transcendent harmonies are music to the eye!—farewell to sculpture, that made human fleshly shape idealized in marble shine forth god-like!—farewell to painting, the exquisite sensibility or high-wrought sentiment and deep knowledge of the artist's mind, reproduced on canvas, able to encage the wildest uproar of universal nature in a narrow frame; and to those paradisiacal painted scenes, where the ambrosial air rests in perpetual glow upon trees ever-vernal, O farewell! Farewell to music, and the sound of song; to the marriage of instruments, where the concord of soft and harsh unites in sweet harmony and gives wings to the panting listeners whereby to climb heaven, and learn the hidden pleasures of the eternals! Farewell to drama and the well-trod stage—the world's truer tragedy puts mimicked grief to shame; to high-bred comedy and the low buffoon alike, farewell! Laughter is no more.*

Alas! to enumerate these adornments shows, by what we have lost, how supremely great the human race was. It's over now. Solitary, like our first parents expelled from Paradise, each living man and woman looks back towards scenes they've left behind. The high walls of the tomb, and the flaming sword of plague, lie across the view. As it was after Eden, the whole earth before them appears a desert. Unsupported and weak, let them wander through fields where the unreaped corn stands in barren plenty—through the abandoned orchards their own parents planted—through vacant towns built for their generation's use. Posterity is no more; fame, and ambition, and love, are words void of meaning. O deserted ones! Lie down at nightfall like the cattle that graze in the field, unaware of the past, careless of the future; for from such fond ignorance alone can you hope for ease!

Sorrow doubled the load on stooped backs; sorrow planted thorns in a hot hard pillow, and added saltiness to soured water and bitter bread. Onto our basic irremediable distress, every small pelting inconvenience fell with added force; having strung our frames to endure the weight of the world, we sank beneath the added feather tossed at us by chance. Many survivors had been bred in luxury—

others born and raised poor—all by now had suffered various privations; and the idea of another winter like the last one brought terror to our minds. Wasn't it enough that we must die—must we also turn drudge and toil? Must we prepare our own funeral buffets, and carry fuel to heap on our soon-to-be deserted hearths—must we prick our fingers sewing our own shrouds?

No! If we're to die, let's enjoy what remains of our lives to the full. Away with sordid care! Menial labors, inconveniences and pains slight in themselves but too gigantic for our exhausted strength—we'll eliminate them from our ephemeral existences. The first humans on earth, who lived, as we live now, by families, and not by tribes or nations, evolved in a genial climate. Earth fed them freely, without toil; balmy air wrapped them more warmly than feather beds when they slept. The south is humanity's native place, where tree boughs serve for palace roofs; the land of year-round fruits, and roses, and the thirst-appeasing grape. We need not there fear cold and hunger.

Look at England! The meadows that invite with their long grass are dank and cold, no fit bed for us. Our corn is gone, and what grows wild cannot support us. Without heat supplied by fuel fetched from the bowels of the earth, we're subject to maladies and aches. The truth is, the labor of hundreds of thousands of people would be required again to make this inclement island nook into a fit habitation for one single couple. To the south then, to the sun!—where nature is kind and plenteous, and Earth is garden.

England, late birthplace of excellence and school of the wise, your children are gone, your glory faded, your tale of power and liberty at its close! You, England, were the triumph of the human race! Small favor was shown you by your Creator. Isle of the North: a naturally ragged canvas, painted by human hands with alien colors; but the hues we gave are faded, never more to be renewed. So, you marvel of the world, we must leave you—and bid farewell to your clouds, and cold, and scarcity, forever! Bereft of human inhabitants, O little isle! The ocean waves will buffet you, and the raven flap her wings over the land-sea of weeds that overgrows you; your sky will canopy barrenness. You were never famous for your orchids or spice groves or banana plantations; nor for your vineyards and double harvests, nor for your vernal airs and solstitial sun—but for the British people, your children, with their unwearied industry and lofty dreams and goals. They, your fatal glory, are gone, and there you go with them, down the oft-trodden path that leads to oblivion.

(37)   THE SPIRIT of emigration crept in among the few survivors, who, congregating from various parts of England, met in and around London that fall. It existed as a breath, a wish, a far-off thought—until it reached Adrian. Fired by the idea, their Protector instantly and enthusiastically started planning the remaining population's mass departure.

"Our immediate peril of death having passed with September's heat," he said, "we have time to look ahead and think rationally about how we should pass the winter to come. And I can perceive no option more advantageous than this emigration scheme. If nothing else, it draws us away from the immediate scene of our woe. Then, led through pleasant and picturesque countries, we may for a time be amused in our despair."

He'd ridden out to us at Windsor, where the season's renewal of our short-term lease on life had even Idris lifting her head, as a lily after a storm when a sunbeam tinges its silver cup. However she liked this idea no better coming from her brother now than she'd liked it in February, when it came from me. "But Adrian—to leave the country of our ancestors, the land made holy by their graves!"

"Yes!" he cried. "To leave England forever! To turn from its polluted fields and groves, and, placing the sea between us, to quit it, as shipwrecked sailors quit their rock when a ship rides by that might save them. Such is my plan."

But I urged him to consider, as I had done, the real implications of what he proposed. Exiles before us, leaving their native soil voluntarily, for the sake of work or pleasure, remained a part of England, and England part of them. Though divided by thousands of miles from its shores, they heard the daily events of home, each of them knowing that they need only return to resume their place in society—indeed, those with families could surround themselves at once with the associations and habits of childhood. Not so with us, the present day's remnant. "If we leave England, *in vagabond pursuit of dreadful safety*," I said, quoting a phrase from old John Ford, "we leave none to represent us, none to repopulate our desert island. The name of England dies, when we've left her."

He nodded, and replied, "Yet let us go! England is in her shroud—we can't chain ourselves to a corpse. Let's go. The world is our country now, and we'll choose its most fertile spot for our new home. Shall we, in these echoing halls, under this wintry sky, sit with closed eyes and folded hands, awaiting death? Let us rather go out to meet it gallantly: or perhaps—for the entire planet, this fair gem in the solar system's crown, surely can't be plague-stricken—perhaps, in some secluded nook, amidst eternal spring, and waving trees, and rippling streams, we may find Life. The world is vast, and England, though her fields and woods seem interminable, is small. Over on the Continent, at the close of a day's march over high mountains or through snowy valleys, we may happen upon Health. So, committing our loved ones to its charge, may we replant the human race, that up-rooted tree, and leaving to posterity our tales of life before the plague, ourselves become the heroes and sages of the lost state of things.

"Hope beckons and sorrow urges us—the heart pounds with expectation. This eager desire for change must be an omen of success. O, come! Say farewell to the dead! Farewell to the tombs of those we loved—farewell to giant London and the placid Thames, to fair lakes and mountain districts, to birthplaces of the wise and good—to Windsor Forest and its antique castle, farewell! Let them make themes for stories—we must live elsewhere."

Though he dared not give words—not then—to all that was in his heart, we heard hints enough to understand: Adrian felt that the end of time was come. One by one, he knew, we'd dwindle into nothingness. Why await this sad consummation in our native country, when travelling would give us new goals and interests each day, and distract our thoughts from the finale's swift approach? And he believed that if we who still lived went to Italy, to sacred and eternal Rome, we might with greater patience submit to the same law which had laid her mighty towers low, might even lose our selfish grief in the sublime aspect of her desolation.

So he despaired; yet what won us over to Adrian's party, heart and soul, was his appeal to our hopes. At those images of health and life for our children and their posterity, in some place to be found—we knew not where or when—but if never to be found, forever and ever to be sought—Idris smiled her consent. With a smile she agreed to leave her country, which she'd never left before, and abandon Windsor, her birthplace, its forest with its mighty trees, woodland paths, and green recesses where she'd played in childhood and spent her happy youth; she'd leave without regret, for so she hoped to save her children's lives. They were her life, dearer than a spot consecrated to love, dearer than all else the earth contained.

They heard with childish glee of our removal. Yes, we might go to Athens, I told Clara when she asked, and watched her face become radiant with pleasure at the thought of seeing her parents' tomb and the scenes of her father's glory—images whose recollection had filled her mind since infancy with high, restless, over-serious thoughts. Our boys' first concern was for Alfred's dog, and a pet eagle, almost blind with age; these humble beings were dear friends, who'd travel with us. But no such catalogue of favorites could be made without grief over how much we must leave behind. A treasured rose tree, a marble vase beautifully carved: these must come, too, Alfred and Elvis insisted. Tears flooded their mother's eyes as they began exclaiming over other cherished and familiar objects. What a pity, they said, that we couldn't take the Castle and the forest, the deer and the birds along with us. I rebuked them gently, fondly: "We've already lost treasures far more precious than these; and what we desert here is nothing compared to the treasures we seek to preserve—your lives. Let's not for a single moment forget that goal. Let's focus on our hope, and we'll soon stop regretting trifles."

With the children's quick return to their delightful prospects of future amusement, I left them to go in search of Idris, who'd disappeared. I found her below the castle, in the little park to which she'd escaped, there to hide her weakness and indulge her tears in solitude. Her recent smiles erased, she clung to an old oak, pressing its rough trunk with her roseate lips, unable to suppress her tearful sobs and broken cries; with surpassing grief I beheld this loved one of my heart, so lost in sorrow! I drew her towards me; and, as she felt my kisses on her eyelids, as she felt my arms embrace her, she revived enough to speak.

"You're very kind not to reproach me, Lionel. I weep, and a bitter pang of intolerable sorrow grips my heart. And yet I am happy. While mothers lament their children, and wives lose their husbands, you and my children are left to me. Yes, I am happy, most happy, that I can weep like this over imaginary sorrows, and that the loss—the slight loss—of my adored country hasn't been annihilated in some mightier misery. Take me where you will; where you and my children are, there shall be Windsor, and every country will be England to me. Let these tears flow not for myself, happy and ungrateful as I am, but for the dead world—for our lost country—for all of the love, and life, and joy, now choked with dusty death, I'll cry."

The words came quickly, as if spoken to convince herself. Turning her eyes from the trees and forest paths she loved, Idris hid her face against my chest, and we—yes, my masculine firmness dissolved—together we wept consolatory tears. Then, calm, if not almost cheerful, we returned to the Castle.

I thought it best that we should go up to London to make our final preparations for departure. So, one mid-October day I stood with Idris as she took her farewell view of Windsor. For the last time we gazed from the terrace at the countryside spread below. The last rays of sun set alight autumnal tints among the dark masses of the woods. Uncultivated fields and smokeless cottages lay in shadow; the Thames wound through the wide plain, past Eton's venerable, empty walls raised in dark relief. Only the cawing of innumerable rooks, speeding in columns or thick wedges towards their nests in the Home Park, disturbed the evening silence.

Nature was the same, I observed, as when she'd been the kind mother of the human race; now, childless and forlorn, her fertility mocked us; her loveliness masked deformity. I wondered: "Why should the air turn mild and cool, and humanity feel not its refreshment? Why will dark night adorn herself with stars, without human eyes to see? Why are there fruits, or flowers, or streams, when people aren't here to enjoy them?"

I turned to Idris beside me, her dear hand locked in mine, and saw her face radiant with a smile. "The sun is alone," she answered, "but we aren't. A strange star, my Lionel, ruled our birth. Though sadly and with dismay we may look upon humanity's annihilation, we remain here for each other. Did I ever in the wide world seek anyone but you? And since you still exist, why should I complain? You and nature are still true to me. Beneath the shades of night, and through the day whose glare shows up our solitude, you'll still be at my side, and even Windsor won't be missed."

Her words returned to me later, as we were leaving. I'd chosen nighttime for our journey to London, when the change and desolation outside might be less obvious. With bicycles packed behind, our only surviving servant drove us in a carriage, first down the steep hill, then onto the Long Walk's dusky expanse. At times like these, minute circumstances assume gigantic proportions; the very swinging open of the white gate that admitted us into the forest, struck me as hugely significant: this everyday act would never occur again! The moon's setting crescent glittered through the branches overhead. A troop of deer we scared fled bounding away among the forest shades. I turned and looked back at the Castle, whose heavy outline lay in a dark mass against the sky, its windows glistening in the moonlight. The road bent; the Castle vanished; the trees near us waved a solemn dirge with the midnight breeze. Idris leaned back against the seat. Her two hands pressed mine, her countenance was placid; as before, she seemed to lose the sense of what she now left, in the memory of what she still possessed.

I, too, though my thoughts were sad and solemn, felt that I carried with me those dearest to me: I quitted what I loved, not what loved me. After all, neither the castle battlements nor these long familiar trees heard the parting sound of our carriage wheels with regret. I was pleased, after a long separation, to rejoin Adrian, never again to part. And, while I felt Idris to be near, and heard the regular breathing of our two boys, quietly asleep, I couldn't be unhappy. But Clara was greatly moved. With streaming eyes, trying to suppress her sobs, she leaned from the window to catch every last glimpse of her native Windsor.

In the Adrian who welcomed us on our arrival, no trace of sorrowing despair remained; from his look of health, his smile, his animated tones, you couldn't guess that he was about to lead the English nation's shrunken remnant out of their native country, into the tenantless realms of the south—there to die, one by one, till the LAST MAN should remain in a voiceless, empty world.

Impatient to go, he'd advanced far in his preparations. All obeyed the Lord Protector of dying England; all looked up to him. His wisdom guided all. Useless to transport many things, he judged, for we should find abundant provision in every town across the Channel. There would be bicycles or horse and carriage transport enough for everyone. Moving the luckless crowd, who relied wholly on him, Adrian's care was like its soul. His wish was to prevent the need for labor; to bestow a festive appearance on this funeral train.

Our numbers so far amounted to not quite 2,000 persons. Each day witnessed fresh arrivals to London and its suburbs; and small parties had been dispatched to various parts of England in search of stragglers. Though anxious to leave England before winter set in, not until we'd assured ourselves against the possibility of leaving behind a single human being would we actually depart. The plan was for everyone to assemble at one place on the 20th of November. Supervisors and captains had been assigned to various roles. I would be joining the fifty-person council assisting Adrian more closely, its members chosen without regard to station in life, save that given by reputations for benevolence and prudence.

My family repaired as usual to our Hyde Park house. Not far away, the aged Countess of Windsor was residing with her son in the Protectoral Palace. Would the childishness of old age have mingled with her stubborn pride, to make this high-born dame still so inveterate against me? So Idris worried as now, for the first time for many years, she and her mother met. Age and care had furrowed the older woman's cheeks and bent her form; but she remained bright-eyed, her manners—authoritative—unchanged. She received her daughter coldly but displayed more feeling as she enfolded her grandsons in her arms. It was our nature, to wish to pass along our values and beliefs to posterity through our offspring. Perhaps, having failed in this design with regard to her own children, the Countess hoped to find the next generation more tractable.

Idris offered a vivid account of what happened in reply to her first, tentative, deliberately casual mention of my name. Shaken by a convulsive gesture of anger, in a voice trembling with hate, her mother responded immediately:

"I am of little worth in this world, where the young are so impatient to push the old off the scene. But, Idris, if you do not wish to see your mother drop dead at your feet, never mention that person's name to me again. All else I can bear. I have resigned myself to the destruction of every hope I cherished for this family—but it is too much to require that I should love the instrument made by fate to be the most murderous means of my destruction."

(38)   OUR LAST English weather had been temperate; soft rains fell at night, and by day the wintry sun shone out. Our departure was set for November 25th. All those now gathered in London would move forward in separate parties, taking different routes to unite at last at Paris. Adrian and his division—some 500 persons, including our family—would sail by way of Dover and Calais.

On the evening of the 20th, Adrian and I rode for the last time through the streets of London. They were grass-grown, deserted, the sidewalks covered in weeds and piles of filth. The doors of empty mansions creaked back and forth on their big hinges. Voiceless bell towers and church steeples pierced the smokeless air: the churches were open, but no prayer was offered at their altars; mildew and damp had already defaced the carvings and ornaments; birds, and domestic animals, now homeless, had built nests and made their lairs in consecrated spots. Ponderous St. Paul's with its high dome looked not like a temple, but a tomb. *Here Lies England,* I thought, should have been engraved across the portico.

My mind was preoccupied with Idris. We'd now been in London about six weeks. Day by day, during that time, I'd watched her health decline. Not eating, not sleeping, her body wasting away: her heart was broken. To be near her children—or to sit by me, drinking deep the dear persuasion that I remained to her—was all she cared to do. Gone was the forced vivacity, along with those displays of cheerful affection, the springy gait, the light-hearted tone she'd kept up for so long. I could not disguise from myself, nor could she conceal, her life-consuming sorrow. A change of scene, as Adrian said, and reviving hopes, might restore her. All I feared was that plague would catch her first, but so far she was untouched by that menace. Fatigued after a day full of packing and preparations, she'd been resting when I left.

Her brother and I pedaled on through the city, speaking little. All was abandoned, but nowhere in ruins—and this medley of trim, undamaged, valuable real estate ran in discordant contrast to the lonely silence of the streets. No human step was heard, no human form discerned. We saw animals aplenty: troops of dogs; now and then a horse without bridle or saddle; a wide-shouldered ox that lowed at us from the narrow doorway of a feed store.

Night closed in and it began to rain. We'd come as far east as the Minories without seeing anyone and were about to return to Hyde Park, when a voice, a human voice, attracted our attention. Nothing could have been stranger or sadder to hear in that uncanny silence: a child's voice, singing some merry, silly song, laughing now and then; talking—to no one; for we heard no reply as we followed the sound to its source. This proved to be a magnificent private house, the upper rooms brilliantly illuminated as if for a party. The street door stood open. Leaving our bicycles in the darkened high-roofed hall, we followed the ringing voice up a swoop of marble stairs and to a door; it opened on a long brightly-lit suite of splendid rooms containing two inhabitants.

One, the songstress, a laughing little girl about ten years old, we saw dancing wildly, almost in the paws of the other, a large boisterous Newfoundland dog that kept jumping on her. She was dressed to grotesque effect in a nonsensically mismatched assortment of women's undergarments and intimate apparel. Almost toppled to the floor by her gigantic companion, she raised and shook a scolding finger—then, with another laugh, she threw herself down on the plush carpet to play with him. The dog perceived us in the doorway first and jumped up with a loud bark. The child turned: we could see her face lose its gaiety and assume a sullen expression; she leapt to her feet and slunk back, apparently meditating an escape. I walked up and took her hand. She didn't resist, but with a stern unchildlike frown, so different from her former hilarity, she stood still, her eyes fixed on the floor.

I spoke gently. "What are you doing here? Who are you?" A

trembling fit shook her but she was silent. "My poor child," asked Adrian, "are you alone?" There was a winning softness in his voice that went to the young stranger's heart; she looked at him, then snatched her hand from mine and threw herself into his arms. Clinging round his neck, her unfrozen tears flowing, "Save me! save me!" she cried.

"I will save you," he answered. "There's nothing to be afraid of— not this man certainly, he's my friend and will do you no harm. Are you alone?"

"No, I've got Lion with me."

"And your father and mother?"

"I never had those, I'm a social care child. Everybody's gone, they've been gone for days and days. But if they come back and find out I left the property without permission, they'll beat me so hard!"

These few words told her story: an orphan, taken on pretended charity, ill-treated, reviled. Her oppressors had died. Ignorant of everything, she found herself alone. A long time had to pass before she gained the courage to venture out from her solitude; after that, her childish vivacity governed her: she and her playful brute companion enjoyed a long holiday, the girl fearing nothing but the return of her protectors' harsh voices and cruel treatment.

She readily consented to go with Adrian, who soon had her better dressed and installed in his safe passenger seat. With Lion ambling comfortably alongside, we rode away—back to our loved ones. Back through scenes of alien sorrows, a ride through solitude which struck our eyes and not our hearts. While we imagined all the change and suffering that had come upon these streets once thronged with people, now tenanted only by animals—while we rode through the death of the world, and hugged ourselves in the remembrance of what we still possessed—it was all the word to us—all this passing time—in the meanwhile...

Idris had finally closed her eyes for a few minutes. Seated nearby, Clara was reading a storybook to the two boys when she perceived a sudden change in Alfred's appearance. His heavy lids veiled our eldest darling's eyes, an unnatural color burnt in his cheeks, his breath came short. Clara glanced at the mother and saw Idris stir in her sleep at the narration's pause. "Go on!" Elvis urged eagerly, unaware. She started to read again, raising her eyes to look now at Alfred, now at Idris; her voice shaking, she read on till she saw the child about to fall. Starting forward with a cry, she caught him; but Idris sat up, roused. She looked on her son. She saw death stealing across his features; she laid him on a bed, she held drink to his parched lips.

Yet he might be saved. If I were there, Idris thought, he might be saved. Perhaps, like the time before, it wasn't the plague. Without me to tell her, what could she do? Stay and watch him die! Why had I chosen that moment to be absent, and where?

"Look after him, Clara," she burst out. She had to find me. "I'll come right back."

Every room of our house at that moment was occupied by people, future companions of our journey, who'd taken up a temporary residence with us. All anyone could tell her was that I'd gone out with Adrian. Entreating them to try and find me, she returned to her child; he was plunged in a frightful state of torpor. Again she rushed downstairs. She threw open the front door: all was dark, deserted, splashed with rain. The weather had turned with a vengeance. Idris shivered in a blast of piercing cold and then lost all self-possession. She ran into the street and called my name! Only a howling wind replied. Panic gave wings to her feet; she darted forward to seek me, she knew not where; putting all her thoughts, all her energy, all her being into speed alone, most misdirected speed, she neither felt, nor feared, nor paused, but ran right on.

The strength in her legs failed her so suddenly that she had no time to break the fall and landed heavily on the pavement, injuring herself. She lay stunned for a time. When, despite the pain, she got up and started to walk, she was shedding fountains of tears, stumbling every few steps, no idea of direction—only now and then she called to me in a feeble voice; but I was cruel and unkind, she cried heart-piercingly. There was no one to feel or reply: even the city's wandering animals had been driven by the night's inclemency to seek the human habitations they'd usurped. Thin dress drenched with rain, wet hair clinging round her neck, Idris tottered through the dark streets until she tripped on something and fell down again. This time she couldn't get up, she barely tried. Huddling on the ground, she resigned herself to the fury of the elements and her own heart's bitter grief. She breathed an earnest prayer to die speedily, for there was no relief but death. So resigned, she ceased to lament for her dying child but shed kindly, bitter tears over the grief in store for me. While she lay in tears, life almost suspended, she felt a warm, soft hand on her forehead, and heard notes of tender compassion in the gentle voice that asked, "May I help you, my dear lady?"

The presence—the existence—of another human being, sympathetic and kind, galvanized Idris, who sat up, clasped the woman's hands, and begged her through fresh tears to go and find me, and bid me hasten to my dying child, to save him, for the love of heaven, to save him!

Most providentially, the woman endeavoring to help Idris to her feet was our friend Juliet from Windsor, lately married daughter of the late proud duke. She led my darling under shelter, but soon recognized the urgency of getting her home to Hyde Park—where perhaps I'd already returned, or our child revived. Idris agreed and they set off; leaning on her friend's arm, sharing her cloak, she tried to walk at a steady pace, but irresistible faintness made her pause again and again.

By this time, after a parting hastened by the worsening storm, Adrian had turned in at the Protectoral Palace with our little charge— the great dog still loped alongside them—and I was pedaling for home. Soon from the top of the road I spotted an assemblage of persons around our doorstep in whose gestures I instinctively read some heavy change, some new misfortune. Approaching with swift alarm, afraid to ask a single question, I did a running dismount and let the machine clatter down against the curb. The crowd saw me, knew me, and in awful silence divided to make way for me. A groan came from somewhere in the house; and for the second time that night I found myself following a voice—only this time I rushed upstairs without further reflection. Another groan, behind a door I thrust open, my momentum carrying me into a darkened room: where immediately a pernicious smell assailed my senses, producing sickening qualms which made their way to my very heart. At the same time I felt my leg clasped by someone groaning on the floor. I looked down to see a half-naked Black man, his body writhing under the agony of disease. He had me in a convulsive grip; with mixed horror and impatience I strove to disengage myself, slipped, and fell on top of the sufferer, who wound both his naked festering arms around me. His face was close to mine, and his breath, death-laden, entered my vitals. For a moment of aching nausea I was overcome by plague, my head was bowed. Reflection returning all at once, I sprang up, threw the wretch from me, and darted up the staircase to my family's chamber. A dim light showed me Alfred on a couch. A trembling Clara, paler than whitest snow, had raised his body with one arm and held a cup of water to the lips. I saw full well that no spark of life existed in that ruined form. His features were rigid, his eyes glazed, his head had fallen back. I took him from her, I laid him softly down, kissed his cold little mouth. "Clara, where is Idris?" I asked in a whisper. She answered likewise; whispers so vain when the whole world lacked cannon fire loud enough to reach Alfred in his immaterial abode.

(39)   IN THE MIDST of an icy, driving downpour, it came as the worst of news to hear that Idris had gone out to look for me and hadn't returned. The first fearful symptoms of plague were already gaining on me; if I ever wanted to see my love again, there was no time to lose. Without hesitation I returned to the street, mounted my bicycle and rode into the dark and rain. My child lay dead; the seeds of mortal disease had taken root in my bosom; I went to seek Idris, my adored, wandering without me all alone among the labyrinthine streets of a wilderness London while torrents gushed from heaven to bathe her dear head, her treasured limbs, in numbing cold.

I stopped often, for a pounding, feverish headache made me imagine the sound of her voice in every gust that drenched me. Somewhere in Marylebone I heard a woman call out from a doorstep as I passed. Not Idris, though, so I kept pedaling—until in a flash of second sight, I realized there'd been two figures in that doorway, one thin, graceful, clinging to the stronger woman for support. Seconds later I was beside them, taking Idris in my arms. I set her on my handlebars—in her state of total collapse she wasn't strong enough to ride behind—and bound my rain cloak round us both. The well-known face of a good friend, much changed by grief, could at this moment of horror obtain from me no more than a passing glance of compassion for her recent widowhood. Juliet tightened a last strap for us and then stepped back out of the rain, as I started for home.

Dare I admit it? That was the last moment of my happiness; but I was happy. Idris would die: she must, for her heart was broken. I would die, for I must: I'd caught the plague. Earth was a scene of desolation; hope was madness; life had married death, the two were one; but as I rode along with Idris resting against me, sure that our lives were almost at a close, I reveled in the delight of possessing her once more. Again and again I stopped to kiss her and press her to my heart.

Arrived at Hyde Park, I carried Idris upstairs and helped get her out of her wet things; then I left her in Clara's care. After checking in on Elvis where he lay healthily asleep, I changed, went downstairs, returned a brief, reassuring reply to a worried message from Adrian, and then asked of the household at large that my wife and I be left alone to rest. It all felt so time-consuming: with the palsied caution of a miser visiting hoarded gold, I counted every moment and grudged each one not spent with Idris. At last I raced back to the chamber where the life of my life reposed. Just at the door, I paused and took a few seconds to assess my condition. Waves of shuddering nausea; head heavy; chest oppressed; legs watery: the symptoms of my disorder had been worsening fast. But I threw them off resolutely and met Idris with placid, even joyous looks. She was lying on a couch. I locked the door behind me with care and went to sit beside her. We embraced, and our lips met in a kiss long drawn and breathless...

Would that moment had been my last!

"And Alfred?" My poor girl's maternal feelings had awoken.

"Idris, we've been spared for each other, we're together—don't let any other idea intrude." Understanding me, she bowed her head on my shoulder and wept. "I'm happy," I continued. "Even on this fatal night, I declare myself happy beyond all description or conception. What more could we want, sweet one?"

She gave a start. "Why are you trembling like that, Lionel? And your eyes are so bloodshot!"

"I should tremble," I replied, "happy as I am. Our child is dead, and further threats surround us—I should be trembling more! But I'm happy, my own Idris, most happy."

She caressed my face and said, "I understand you, my kind love. Like this, stricken as you are with sorrow at our loss, trembling and aghast, still you try so dearly to assuage my grief. I am not happy." Tears flashed and fell from under downcast lids. "I'm unhappy, Lionel, because we're inmates of a miserable prison and there is no joy for us. But the true love I bear you will render this and every other loss endurable."

"We've been happy together, at least," I said. "No misery to come can take our past from us, the happiness of years. We've been true to each other ever since my sweet princess-love came through the snow to the lowly cottage where I barely existed, the penniless heir of a ruined man. Even now, with eternity before us, only one another's presence hereafter offers hope. Idris," my voice kept musing. "Do you think, when we die, we'll be divided?"

"*Die!*" She stared at me. "*When we die!* What do you mean? We never talk this way—what secret are you hiding from me in these dreadful words?"

"But, won't we all die, dearest?" I asked with a sad smile that failed to calm her.

"Gracious God! Are you ill, Lionel, that you speak of death? My only friend, heart of my heart—speak!"

"I don't think we have, any of us, long to live. So I ask you, Idris, when the curtain drops on this mortal scene, where do you think you and I will find ourselves?"

Reassured by my forthright tone, she fell to considering her answer. "Ever since the plague appeared," she said at last, "like everyone, I've thought a great deal about death. For years now, I've asked myself whether the humanity lost to this life may have been carried or reborn to some other one, and what it might be like there. Dwelling hour after hour on the mystery of a future state, I strove to form a rational conclusion. Think: if indeed, as I believe, we can expect to cast aside the shadow in which we've spent our lives walking, and step forth into the unclouded sunshine of knowledge and love—then how is great Death anything more than a scarecrow, if we're to be revived with the same companions, the same affections, our hopes intact to reach their fulfillment, only our fears left with our bodies in the grave? Alas! the same instinct behind my certainty that I shall not wholly die, makes me refuse to believe that I shall live wholly as I do now. Yet, Lionel, never, never, can I love any but you; through eternity I must desire your society. No, I don't believe that death will tear the two of us asunder; I don't believe the Ruler of the world, who knows my innocence of harm to anyone, would really permit it."

"Your remarks are like you, dear love," replied I. "Gentle and good; let's cherish this belief and dismiss our anxiety. But, sweet, there's no sin, if that same God made our nature, when we yield to what's ordained through its promptings. We are designed to love life and cling to it; we must love the living smile, the sympathetic touch, the voice peculiarly thrilling to our mortal mechanism. Let's not become so secure about the life hereafter that we neglect the present. This present moment, short as it is, represents one part of eternity—the most precious part, since it's all we have and ours alone. You, Idris, the hope of my eternity, are my present joy. So let me look at you! Reading love in your dear eyes, I drink intoxicating pleasure."

In some alarm at my vehemence, Idris returned my gaze—and saw what? My reddened eyes were hot, I felt them starting from my head; every artery beat, methought, audibly, every muscle throbbed, each nerve sent its signal. Her look of wild fear told me that the time for secrecy was past. "Yes, it's true, I'm sick. And this is all the medicine I need." I put my arm around her waist. "So it is, mine own beloved: the last hour of many happy ones. We can no longer shun an inevitable destiny. I can't live long—but, again and again, I say, this moment is ours!"

Idris had already taken in my situation. She felt the burn of fever on the palm she pressed above my heart. "One moment," she murmured almost inaudibly, with lips gone white. "Only one moment." Her features convulsed and paler than marble, she slipped from the couch and knelt there, hiding her face in her hands. While there was hope, the agony had been unendurable; that was all over now; her feelings became solemn and calm. I listened, as she prayed for the strength to fulfill her duty and watch over me until the end.

Suppressing every sigh, every sign of grief, like one of those martyrs in history books who submit, fearless, mute, and uncomplaining, to the instruments of torture, so Idris rose to her feet, and entered upon the endurance of torments of which the rack and the breaking wheel are but faint and metaphysical symbols.

As for me—I'd confessed; and at the moment of knowing that Idris shared my knowledge of our real situation, I was transformed. Every tension relaxed its grip on me. The perturbed and passion-tossed waves of thought subsided and left me rocking on a heavy metronomic swell, limitless and unchanging, till it should break on the remote shore towards which I rapidly advanced. . .

Idris made me lie down on the couch, and drew a low ottoman near at my entreaty. Sitting close to my pillow, she pressed my burning hands between her cold palms and yielded to my feverish restlessness. She let me talk, and talked to me, on strange subjects—strange, that is, between a pair of lovers conscious of catching their last earthly sights and sounds of what was, for each, an only love.

We talked of times past; of our courtship's heights; of Raymond, Perdita, and Evadne. We speculated on what might arise in this deserted planet's future; surely, if even two or three were saved, it might be slowly re-peopled. We talked of the world to be found beyond the tomb, and of our more certain faith that other spirits, other minds, other perceptive beings, so far invisible to us, must populate this beauteous and imperishable universe with their own forms of thought and love.

We talked, I don't know how long. But in the morning I awoke from a painful heavy sleep to find Idris, very pale, sharing my pillow. The large orbs of her watch-wearied eyes had prised the lids apart to show the deep blue lights beneath; the slight murmurs issuing from her parted lips told that, even while asleep, she suffered.

Yet her form was still the temple of a residing deity; those eyes remained the windows of her soul; all grace, love, and intelligence still sat enthroned within that lovely bosom. Once she was dead, where would this mind, the dearer half of my mind, be? And those fair proportions lifeless, deserted, defaced—I pictured a wasteland of sand-choked ruins when I thought of it.

(40)   I SLID from consciousness again. Soon Idris awoke, alas! to misery. She saw the fatal signs on my face and berated herself. How could she have let the whole night pass without trying to find—not cure, that was impossible—but something to ease my sufferings?

She had Adrian called and my couch was quickly surrounded by friends and specialists; I was administered such palliative treatments as were customary by now. It was the singular and dreadful distinction of our 21st-century plague, that no one had ever survived it. The first symptom of the disease was the death warrant: no pardon, no reprieve. My friends had no gleam of hope to cheer them.

Idris never moved from my side. Administering to all my wants, she neither slept nor rested. Resigned to the inevitable, she didn't watch for symptoms of recovery. Her one thought was to nurse me to the last, then lie down and die beside me.

Three nights in, I stopped breathing. I had no pulse. To the eye and the touch, I was dead.

"He's gone, Idris."

Adrian, alone with his sister in this vigil hour, took her shoulder and tried to draw her away. Idris shook her head and wiped another tear from her sunken cheek. He urged, begged, protested, exhausted every argument in favor of her surviving child's welfare and his own; he came near to threatening the use of force. But she insisted on being allowed to watch over me this one more night only—with such affliction behind her sincerity that Adrian yielded. Stepping back, he sank into a chair. Idris stayed where she was, beside the couch, silent and motionless, except when, stung by intolerable remembrance, she kissed my closed eyes and pallid lips, and pressed my stiffening hands to her beating heart.

The dead of night found Idris bent across my body, in bitter mourning for the loss of all the love towards her that my heart had held enshrined. Her hair was disheveled, the long tresses fell on the bed and hung across her face. She noticed one curl gone an ashy grey, in seeming motion, slightly stirred, as if by breath. *But no*, she thought, *for he will never breathe again*. Without emotion, she watched the phenomenon for a minute; till the whole ringlet waved and tumbled, and she thought my chest heaved. Deadly fear gripped her, cold sweat burst from her brow. She watched my eyes, saw me blink. She would have exclaimed, *He's alive!* but the words were choked by a spasm; blood filled her throat and she fell to the floor.

Mine had been initially a torpor of fever. Then came heavy pains to sit like lead on my limbs and make me gasp for breath. Lost to my surroundings, I continued insensible to everything but pain, and at last even to that. Night three I spent in a state of suspended animation; on the fourth morning I awoke as from a dreamless sleep with a nagging thirst, too weak to move. The pain was gone. Across the chamber Adrian gave a cry, and I saw him start up from his chair where he'd been dozing. Our eyes met. From his own shock, her brother understood why Idris lay senseless, weltering in the bright gore that streamed from her mouth. The surprise, the burst of joy, the instantaneous reversal of every sentiment and expectation had been too much for her frame, already worn by long months of worry, lately shattered by every species of woe and toil.

She was now in far greater danger than I, whose life-springs had surged up from their brief suspension. Though for a long time, no one believed I could be healthy again: as if survival so unprecedented must be some kind of trick, people eyed me closely, watching for the dread symptoms to return. I convalesced almost overnight. Health spent her treasures upon me; I felt myself an oak in springtime, fresh green breaking forth from bare gnarled limbs. As the live sap rose and circulated, my frame's renewed vigor, my blood's unblocked currents, inspired me to cheerful endurance and pleasurable thoughts. Indeed, from being the leaden weight that bound me to the tomb, my body had become exuberant with health. Nothing uncommon seemed beyond its reviving strength and the new elasticity of my limbs, nor could anything be missed by senses so refined and susceptible. Methought I could have matched foot speed with a racehorse. Objects appeared visible to me at blinding distances. The hidden processes of nature reached my ears and pulsed there.

Idris, who'd been sunken-cheeked and emaciated even before the ordeal and collapse at my sickbed, offered a more problematical case. The vessel wall in her chest which her extreme agitation had caused to rupture, failed to entirely heal. Drop by drop, the blood to her heart leaked away through the breach. Her appearance was ghastly; her eye sockets were pit-like; her cheekbones, temples, jaws and gums jutted out fearfully; you could see every bone in her skeletal frame. Her hands, mere strings of cartilage set in transparency, hung powerless. It was strange that life could exist in what was wasted and worn into such a close semblance of death.

But I counted hope among my other blessings of those days. If I could only wrap my adored girl in my unwearied attentions; if I could take her away from these heart-breaking scenes and lead her to forget the world's desolation in the simple novelty of travel; if I could get a chance to nurse her failing strength in the mild and sunny climate towards which our journey aimed, I might restore her. All the more eagerly then did I renew the preparations for a departure interrupted and delayed by our joint illnesses.

On November 25th, as planned, two-thirds of our people— England's people—all that remained of us—had quitted London. Adrian delayed to follow with his division until her doctors said Idris could travel, and the first group had already been some weeks in Paris when, on New Year's Day, 2098, some three hundred riders on single and passenger bicycles, Adrian at their head, set out along the Embankment and across Waterloo Bridge in the direction of Dover. The Ex-Queen, Countess of Windsor, an inveterate winter cyclist, rode with her son. The party's ox-cart baggage train had left the week before, to prepare and provision a few rest stops on the way. The remaining horses supplied a number of passenger carriages that followed Adrian's riders; my family occupied one, very commodious for the four of us now and a nurse attendant. I was glad to take a place near the end of the line and spare Idris any hurry, crowding, or clamor; yet I couldn't do much to dispel the sadness of ours being the last human eyes to see London from above the Thames.

But to my surprise, Idris was all smiles. She sat with one arm around Clara's shoulders, the other holding our Elvis in a close embrace; but they'd had to raise her strengthless limbs to place them there themselves. "Don't let my temporary weakness deceive you," she said. "I'm getting better this time—I can actually feel the health return." She told us to expect a full recovery. But she must have read my half-doubtful expression as I eyed her face: it was burning with fever. Her smile deepened. "Trust me, dearest, I shall neither leave you, nor my brother, nor these dear children. My firm determination to remain with you to the last, and to continue contributing to your happiness and welfare, would keep me alive even if grim death were actually at hand."

My hopes excited by her words, I had no fears of an immediate catastrophe; nay, I persuaded myself that she would ultimately recover. *We might even have more children!* The thought crossed my mind as cheerfulness reigned in our roomy carriage. Idris conversed animatedly on a thousand topics. She drew charming pictures of the tranquil, beauteous locale we'd find to settle, and of the simple manners of our little European tribe to come. In her vision, universal and cooperative human love was destined to survive the ruin of nations. Enchanted by her voice, we withdrew our thoughts from the present, just as we turned our eyes from the dreary landscape outside. Winter reigned in all its gloom: brown and grey unrelieved by a colorless sky; unplowed cornfields patched with ice and weeds; the ground snaked with frost, the lanes overgrown; huddling livestock tenanting desolate cottages. The wind turned bleak, and a mix of sleet and snow added to the melancholy of the scene.

One night's shelter was arranged for us at Rochester. But there, alas! a circumstance occurred that changed our plans. While at dinner we were approached by a couple of rain-sodden cyclists from Adrian's division. Delayed by weather during a last nostalgic swing around the Chiltern Hills, they'd missed the group departure by a day and had only now overtaken us. One bowed and spoke somewhat nervously. "Lady Idris, we've got—we bear a letter from someone known to you."

The neighborhood of Windsor lacked many poor families. Lucy Clayton, the eldest and prettiest of five children, came from one of them. Though no scholar, she grew into a bright light: good-humored, sociable, benevolent, beloved as well as honored in her little community. Romantic admirers were never lacking either; but here young Lucy was unfortunate. She loved and married a man who lacked an income; they separated, and she began living with a drunken brute who owned a flourishing hotel in nearby Datchet.

Lucy's motivating care in all things and her strongest human tie was with her mother, a semi-invalid and long-time widow, perennially distressed since Lucy's childhood. My Idris had known the two forever. Before Plague conquered the world, we saw Lucy now and then at the hotel's excellent dining room which she ran very capably. Like her marriage before, the second union was childless. Her mother stayed for free in a junior suite upstairs, an arrangement the hotelier was always threatening to end, saying he'd get rid of her mother—but Lucy was firm here—she would not part with her—if the mother went, she'd go too, and beg bread for both of them—she'd die with her mother, but never desert her. Unable to afford the loss of her management skills, and still strongly attracted, the man would back down. When drunk, though, he beat Lucy more than once. She never left him.

While preparing our removal from Windsor, we'd made sure to visit this ill-starred acquaintance one last time. Much had changed for her by then. The ever-unsuccessful husband who'd kept popping up for years had been among the plague's first English victims. Lucy's four siblings followed one by one. The hotel failed, of course, and its brutish owner ran pleasure-mad to London where he died. We found Lucy destitute and smiling. The mother and her thousand health complaints were still going strong: she was a delightful old woman in her way, fully as kind and devoted to her daughter as Lucy was to her. A perfect confidence and friendship existed between them. Together they were happy but entirely inert, without any idea of going to London for the emigration. Idris helped them decide on a plan, we told them how to arrange everything. With the press of our own plans and our subsequent catastrophes, the pair had slipped from our minds. We'd thought them safe.

"Lucy Clayton!" Having opened the letter, Idris exclaimed at the signature.

"Isn't she in France by now?" I asked sharply. I felt a strange agitation. Idris shook her head, reading. The cyclists explained in quiet tones:

They'd been headed back to London as fast as the worsening weather allowed when a sudden ice storm caught them in the open. They made for the first shelter they spotted, which they described as a pretentious hotel, where to their astonishment and relief they found a log fire blazing in the big lobby fireplace. The woman proprietor who'd admitted them was stranded alongside it with her rheumatic old mother and their luggage; having gotten downstairs, the mother couldn't walk another step; so they'd missed their ride to London. And they were running out of firewood. This the cyclists had replenished from a supply out back; otherwise all they could do was wait out the storm while Lucy penned this plea for help, and agree to deliver it into Idris's hands—hands almost too weak to hold the page she held out to me. I glanced it over: dated 12/31/2097, "Honored Lady," it began. Apparently old Mrs Clayton still expected a "replacement ride" to come. The last part read:

Will you not send someone to us? I am sure we must perish miserably as we are. My mother does not know our state; she is so ill that I have hidden it from her. I can hardly write—I cannot stop my tears—it is not for myself; I could put my trust in God and let the worst come, I think I could bear it, if I were alone. But my mother, my sick, my dear, dear mother, who never, since I was born, spoke a harsh word to me, who has been patient in many sufferings; pity her, dear Lady, she must die a miserable death if you do not pity her. People speak carelessly of her, because she is old and infirm, as if we must not all, if we are spared, become so; and then, when the young are old themselves, they will think that they ought to be taken care of. It is very silly of me to write in this way to you; but, when I hear her trying not to groan, and see her look smiling on me to comfort me, when I know she is in pain; and when I think that she does not know the worst, but she soon must; and then she will not complain; but I shall sit guessing at all she must be dwelling upon, her dear mind full of famine and misery—I feel as if my heart must break, and I do not know what I say or do. My mother— Mother, for whom I have borne much, God preserve you from this fate! Preserve her, Lady, and God will bless you; and I, poor miserable creature that I am, will thank you and pray for you every day of my life.

I was alarmed to find Idris so moved by this letter. She proposed, on the spot, that we get in our carriage, drive off to collect the Claytons, and bring them back with us to Rochester: a nearly 100 km journey either way. I balked, insisting that Adrian would happily send a skilled rescue party; but no, Idris was adamant. Strangers, however instructed, might carry out their duties with coldness or inhumanity. Nor would she hear of my going in her place. What a world of good must it do mother and daughter instead to see friends, to see Idris herself, respond to their call. "Lucy's life," Idris said, "has been one long act of devotion and virtue. Let her now reap the small reward of finding her excellence acknowledged in her hour of need by persons she respects and honors with her trust."

I should never had done it, but Idris always ruled me: as soon as I realized her kind heart was set on it, I agreed that she and I should be the ones to go. Adrian, equally helpless to sway her, could only get his sister to agree that our children were best left safe and warm in Rochester with the nurse and a small colony of attendants he'd leave there to await our return. The carriage we'd arrived in was far too cumbersome for the pace I meant to set, so I'd asked Adrian to requisition and equip us a fast one-horse wagon with a canvas top and leather flaps, along with a groom (Idris wanted no other attendants). We'd travel with three horses, changed out and rested often on those wintery roads; lanterns would enable us to ride by night; I'd sleep an hour or two at a time. This plan had us reaching Datchet in under twenty-four hours, back in Rochester with the Claytons in three days or less. Too much longer and we'd risk delaying the Dover crossing for everyone: fine weather came rarely and unpredictably this time of year.

Joining the inn-yard scene at our dawn hour departure, the Countess of Windsor made a last effort to dissuade her daughter from the trip. "You need nursing, not adventure," she said. "What can be so important about little Lucy Clayton to require this much of you?"

Idris said, "You didn't see her letter."

"So, show me." And Idris handed it over. The Ex-Queen broke off reading with a bitter laugh. "Guilt! Of course! That is what sends you on this crazy mission—the guilt you feel over how you've treated me, how you've rejected me, your own mother."

Idris scoffed angrily and before I could object the Ex-Queen continued: "Yes, that guilt of yours sends you to your death. My only daughter—I feel it, I know it! For God's sake, just look at yourself,

Idris!" Emaciated, faded, pallid: her point was clear for all to see. Idris only kissed her cheek and said farewell.

My own mind misgave me again when Idris had to be lifted into the box seat beside me. I whispered to her, "Please, ignore your mother—but stay here with the children and keep indoors. Let me make this drive alone." But she was in high spirits, full of hope. She declared that she couldn't tolerate even a temporary separation from me; anyhow, the motion of the wheels did her good, and the distance to be covered was trifling.

Which was untrue: we had first to retrace our entire route from London, crossing Hammersmith Bridge this time to reach the Western Road and continue almost to Windsor; one hundred kilometers along roads in general disrepair, at the darkest time of winter, heading west into snowstorms and a northerly wind, was no trifle. As for the good Idris said our excursion was doing her health, I saw no sign of any. Thinking back, I must have observed the fever burning her cheeks and her strength draining away, for I recall these details; death advanced openly, right before my eyes. Was I blind? How could I have kept on risking her safety? But Idris said she was better; and I believed her. Hour by hour, I saw a being still witty and vivacious, whose frame was endowed with an intense and, I fondly thought, a strong and permanent spirit of life—my mind could not accept its possible extinction. Who, after a great disaster, never looked back with wonder at their own inconceivable obtuseness? What we could but vaguely understand and never perceive, were the many minute threads into which fate wove our destinies and caught us; all we knew were the toils of the inextricable nets that enmeshed us completely.

That first day, we were nearing Dartford when the neglected road gave the wagon a series of violent jolts. Hearing Idris gasp, I yanked the horse to a stop: the perishing frame beside me was almost destroyed. We could have turned back—I wanted to, but she wouldn't hear of it. Consequently the groom, a most able one, Worthy by name, was required to ride ahead to find the easiest detours for us, even clearing debris at points; all of which consumed additional time. The formless agitation that had gripped me since the letter's appearance only seemed to increase. At one lengthy stop, the damage to my plans and my nerves drove me to gripe: "Once more, Idris, you observe that Lucy Clayton has made her mother into an excuse for her own passivity and inaction."

"What does that matter now, Lionel?"

I was lost for a reply.

Over a day behind schedule, West London's wastelands weren't behind us until late afternoon. Night closed in quickly, far more quickly than I was prepared to expect. By now there was no mistaking it: my beloved companion grew sensibly worse in health, though her spirits were still light, and she kept trying to cheer me out of my anxiety with comical remarks—to little effect, however. Leaning full yet almost weightlessly against my side, she drew a deep breath and said, "I love the smell of snow." As her words met the air, the first flakes fell. We rode on, our lanterns setting us within a globe of living crystal, through a wonderland. But not for long, as the snow turned steadily heavier and the scene around us less and less transparent. When I urged her to go inside the wagon where we had mattresses and furs, Idris declined: we were amply protected on the driver's box by the leather flaps and canopy; wrapped in an additional layer or two, she declared herself perfectly comfortable. Her liveliness of manner continued. Fixed straight ahead upon the curtain of snow whose churning lamp-lit folds concealed the way before us, her wide gaze glowed. Her fever reached me from the skin of her face in gusts.

Weeks earlier, amid the confusion attendant on my illness, the task of interring our darling Alfred had devolved on his grandmother, the Ex-Queen, and she, true to her ruling passion, had caused his body to be carried to Windsor and placed in the royal family vault beneath St. George's Chapel. I'd visited him there in the first flush of my recovery, cycling out and back on this very road—a journey Idris had been judged too weak to undertake before we left. She was still too weak and sick for it. *Is she dying?* The thought pierced my brain over and over, though I kept driving it away as if it were a symptom of insanity.

Some relief from these painful reflections came when the groom rode up alongside to suggest a new detour. By now we had two horses pulling the wagon; we and they needed food and rest, and a slight swerve from our course would take us to a certain stately home where the stables had once been famous. We agreed, and Worthy rode ahead to try to get a fire going indoors while we followed at our slower pace.

Idris and I knew the house and the family whose deaths from plague had left it vacant. We were trading recollections when a long, ghastly, ragged human scream reached us through muffles of distance and snow. I cracked the reins and shouted, sending us plunging through snow drifts, until the horses reared up at a set of ornamental gates open too narrowly to admit us. I took a lantern, leapt into the snow and staggered off to follow the hoof prints leading up the drive. At a turn past some shrubbery, I saw light ahead: Worthy had carried a lantern. There it was, on a low wall. The screams had stopped but sounds had not. A few steps closer and I saw the dogs, twenty or more, mostly low slung and tawny; the lost family had bred their pedigreed progenitors, and though the past few years had seen some mixing with outsiders, the line ran strong; like corgi jaws. Worthy's blood was steaming on the ground. The starving pack snarled and whined and snapped those jaws as it fed amid horrible tearing noises. I dared not approach closer. The horse Worthy had been riding was nowhere to be seen and must have run off in terror, with canine pursuit; we wouldn't see that horse again. I turned to retrace my steps to the wagon—and found Idris lying in the snow in a faint: she'd followed and seen all.

Miraculously, I thought, she revived in my arms while I was carrying her back to safety, and she resumed her place in the driver's box beside mine as I rushed us away as hastily as we'd arrived—too hastily. Thicker now, and deeper on the ground, snow engulfed us and erased our bearings. A wooded hillside loomed up ahead: I'd lost the road.

Affectionate and unshakably calm—herself, in full—Idris murmured reassurance and pressed a little closer to my side. I could always take heart from her. Putting the wind at our back and keeping the hilly woods on one flank, we covered another unfamiliar mile that ended in another wall of trees, only on level ground; no choice but to turn and ride parallel to it, hoping we might happen on a road cut through the woods. Now the weather pelted us from the side, driving snow into our eyes, coating our scarves and cloaks with ice. I also feared our way might return us to the corgis' territory. Better, perhaps, to stop and take our chances inside the wagon: bundle up together and wait for the sun's sure help. But too much suggested this would be a dangerous experiment. The wind was bleak and piercing; the intense cold I felt myself must be worse for my frailer companion, who'd also been dropped full-length in deep snow by the shock of our tragic adventure; in fact I could add hypothermia to the list of things that might be killing her.

Idris by degrees had sunk into silence. Her head lay heavily on my shoulder, I only knew that she lived by her irregular breathing and frequent sighs. Then methought she slept—hypothermia, surely. A moment passed and then one horse tossed and pulled at the reins. I looked around and saw the heavy outline of a cottage through the trees beside us. I cried out in relief.

"Dearest love, hold on one more moment—here's shelter!"

As I spoke, my heart was transported, and my senses swam with excessive delight and thankfulness. An opening in the trees took us to the back of the property. A narrow drive out front would lead to the main road—later. For now, my single focus was warmth. I brought the wagon to the cottage door, carried Idris into the back and piled her with furs; she remained unconscious. Worthy's death made me our party's groom, and our exhausted horses' needs came next. I unharnessed and got the pair fed and stabled comfortably. Then I returned to the door of this blessed dwelling, which stood open; the snow, drifting in, had blocked up the threshold. My lantern showed me a neat comfortable room with a pile of wood in one corner and no sign of dogs anywhere. I shoved my way in and got a quick fire started in the fireplace before I went back to get Idris. The darkness was thicker since I'd been indoors, at first I felt blinded. When I recovered my sight—eternal God of this lawless world! O supreme Death! I will not disturb thy silent reign, or mar my tale with fruitless exclamations of horror—I saw Idris, who must have been trying to take her seat up front again; she'd fallen to the bottom of the carriage; her head, her long hair hiding her face and most of one arm, hung over the side. Struck by a spasm of horror, I lifted her up; her heart was pulseless, her faded lips unfanned by the slightest breath.

I carried her into the cottage, lay her in front of the fire, and began to chafe her stiffening limbs. For two long hours I sought to restore departed life; and, when hope was as dead as my beloved, with trembling hands I closed her glazed eyes.

There wasn't a doubt in my mind what I should do next. I must proceed to Windsor without delay and place my beloved beside her child in the vault.

I readied the wagon again, harnessing the pair again and lighting the lanterns. I wrapped Idris in furs and placed her across my lap in the driver's box. Then, taking the reins, I sent us forward. Massed on the ground, blinding in its furious descent, snow impeded every centimeter of our way. The hardship and pain occasioned by the angry elements, the iron arrow shafts of cold that pierced my aching flesh—these were a relief to me, blunting my mental suffering. The horses staggered on; the reins hung loosely in my hands. I kept picturing how easy it would be to bend and lay my head close to the sweet, cold face of my lost angel, and never sit up again. But I couldn't leave her prey to the rooks and roaming animals; no, the tomb of her ancestors was where she belonged—and where a merciful God might permit me to rest also.

(41)　　PERSISTENT SNOWFALL caused the horses to drag their load slowly and heavily along the familiar road through Egham, until the wind made a sudden shift to the northwest. A fresh gale cleared the air around us, the dense vapors lifted from the horizon, and the massy dome of clouds, like the columned temple of the Philistines, fell to the south as if toppled by Samson. Night's clear empyrean was disclosed, and the little stars, immeasurably distant in their crystalline fields, showered their small rays on the glittering snow. Even the weary horses were cheered and moved on with new strength.

At Bishopsgate we entered Windsor's silent forest. Our road wound towards, then joined, the Long Walk. At its end rose our destination. Admirable emblem of endurance, nearly as ancient as the rock on which it stands, former abode of kings and queens: I looked with a reverence much mixed with tearful affection at the

Castle; for it was here I'd found asylum to enjoy my long lease of love with the perishable, unmatchable treasure of dust now lying cold across my lap. Now indeed, as one sad association followed the next, I could have yielded to all the softness of my nature, and wept, and cried out for sympathy from her beloved trees, or from the herds of deer who'd fed from her own hands as she passed among them on her fairy feet.

Adrian had long since ordered the removal of the Castle's entrance gates. We rode straight across the snowy quadrangle inside, down through the archway below the feudal tower, and into the Lower Ward. Beneath the tall stone perpendiculars of St. George's Chapel we halted. One door stood open; I entered first to place my lantern and by its light, returning, I carried Idris up the aisle with tender caution. On either side, above the stalls, the ancient Knights of the Garter banners—her family's foremost among them—still displayed their vain emblazonry. Farewell to England's glory and heraldry! With a slight feeling of wonder at how humankind could have ever been interested in such things, I laid her softly down on the altar carpet and bent over the lifeless corpse of my beloved. Looking on her dead bare face, the features already contracted by rigor, I felt as if all the visible universe had grown as soulless, inane, and comfortless as that clay-cold image beneath me. For a moment I was gripped by an intolerable sense of struggle with the world's basic principles and laws; I detested them. Yet the serenity that lingered on my dead love's face, recalled me to a more soothing tone of mind. I was here for a purpose, with a duty to fulfill. As for lamenting her—how could I, when I so envied Idris her happy state of permanent insensibility?

Nothing had changed since my previous visit to the royal vault. In those unceremonious days, the heavy paving stones they'd removed from the entrance for our Alfred's interment had gone unreplaced, and still lay off to one side, a lantern sitting on top where I'd left it. By this second light I descended the steps and followed a turning passage to the large chamber whose walls, behind locked grates, held the coffins of the Windsor line. My little boy's small coffin sat dwarfed on the room's gigantic central plinth. With hasty, trembling hands I constructed a bier beside it of the furs and Indian shawls I'd carried down. Then I bore my lost one to her last bed in this damp abode of death, decently composing her limbs and covering them with a mantle, veiling all except her face, which remained lovely and placid. She appeared to rest like one over-wearied, her beauteous eyes steeped in sweet slumber. Yet not so—she was dead! How intensely I longed to lie down beside her and gaze till I was gathered to the same repose.

But death doesn't come at the bidding of the miserable. My blood had never flowed with such an even current, my limbs had never felt so quick with life since my recent recovery. If I wanted to die, I must choose to. Inside this chamber of mortality, what could be more natural than to take my place beside the lost hope of my life, and give in to famine? Yet even as I looked at Idris, her features' sisterly resemblance to Adrian's brought my thoughts back again to the living, to this dear friend, and to Clara and Elvis, afar off in Rochester, waiting anxiously for our return.

Then I heard a noise upstairs in the chapel—footsteps and clicks combined unmistakably, echoed by the vaulted roof, borne to me through hollow passages—a bicycle being pushed. What sort of ghoul haunted these precincts? I raced up the steps into the dusky chapel and saw a cyclist, spare and elderly, advancing towards the altar alongside one of continental manufacture's top flyweight frames. Notable too were the elite winter cycling outfit, in black, and the tottering step; maybe the bicycle was even being used for support. Hearing me, the intruder looked up. The lamp I held illuminated my own figure, and the moonbeams struggling through the high altar window fell upon the other's face. Wrinkled gauntness, piercing eyes, commanding brow: I recognized the Ex-Queen, Countess of Windsor.

With a hollow voice she asked, "Where is the Princess?" I pointed to the torn-up floor. The vault was too distant for the rays of the small glimmering lamp I'd left behind to be discernible; she walked to the spot and gazed down into the palpable darkness. "Your light," she said. I handed it over and watched her dip it above the precipitous steps, as if calculating how to manage them. Instinctively I made a silent offer of my assistance. She motioned me away with a scornful look, then pointed downwards—a living statue, a study in hate and human, passionate strife—to say, "There at least I may have her undisturbed."

She walked deliberately down, while I, overcome, miserable beyond words, or tears, or groans, threw myself onto the paving stones. Idris was before me, all I could see: her stiffening form, her death-struck countenance hushed in eternal repose underground. That was to me the end of all! Just the day before, I'd been picturing what adventures lay ahead for us and our friends and trying to make plans for our future. Now I'd leapt the interval. Here at the limit and the utmost edge of life, any future was behind me.

Thus wrapped in gloom, enclosed, walled up, vaulted over by the omnipotent present, I was startled by the sound of footsteps. I'd utterly forgotten my angry visitant, whose tall form was ascending from the royal vault in a glow of lantern light. At the top she paused and looked around as if for something she wanted; I wondered what, until, perceiving me on the floor quite close to her, she stooped and placed her wrinkled hand on my arm. Her voice, so harsh before, trembled with tenderness.

"Lionel Verney, my son!"

The way my angel's mother spoke my name raised me to my knees; with more respect than I'd ever felt for this disdainful lady before, I bowed my head and kissed her shriveled hand. She was trembling violently. At once I rose and supported her across the chancel to the steps of the Sovereign's Stall. She leaned back against the wooden carvings; having suffered herself to be led, she kept hold of my hand. Moonbeams variously tinted by the painted glass fell on her glistening eyes, her wet cheeks. Instinctively defending a long-cherished dignity, she dashed them away; yet they fell fast. Through multicolored tears, the Ex-Queen began to explain:

"She is so beautiful and placid, even in death. Animosity never clouded that serene brow. And how did I treat her? All these years, wounding her gentle heart with savage coldness, feeling for her no compassion and refusing hers for me. Could I hope for her forgiveness, even now? How little use in asking—how worthless all talk of repentance to the dead! Had I during her life even one time consulted her gentle wishes, and curbed my savage nature to make her happy, I would not be crying so."

As she continued, I learned for the first time of the extraordinary circumstances which had led to this night's strange meeting of ours at St. George's Chapel. After their bitter parting in Rochester, the idea that she and Idris would never meet again, this premonition had weighed on the Countess's mind, haunting her perpetually. A thousand times she resolved to ride after us, only to be stopped by the angry conceit that enslaved her. Proud of heart as she was, her touring pillow stayed damp from overnight tears, while daytime found her weak and dull and helpless to control her nervous anxiety. The hours may have come as some relief when she gave in to the other feeling that consumed her. This was a boundless hatred of me, the son-in-law and single obstacle to the fulfillment of her dearest wish, that of being present to care for Idris in her last moments.

Their first morning at the Dover encampment, she asked Adrian to walk with her, mother and son. On the beach promenade the wind off the Channel was unexpectedly warm for the time of year, and gusty; inland were storms. The weather spurred the pair to shed their studied mutual reserve and share their secret fears that Idris might not come back to them alive. Indeed, the Countess told her son, this dreaded event was a certainty. Just then her eyes were fixed on a tomblike hollow among the cliffs up ahead—with perfect clarity, she could see Idris pacing slowly towards this cave, through thin air. She had on one of her simple white shift dresses and wore her golden hair loose; only a thin veil covered her from head to foot: a living floating pillar of dim translucent mist, with a posture less docile than dejected, submissive to a commanding power, she entered and was lost in the dark recesses of the chalk.

The Ex-Queen wasn't subject to visionary moods. She lived in the world of reality; yet what she'd just seen, though it resembled a figment, had been too real to doubt. From that moment she couldn't rest, it was worth her whole existence to see her daughter one last time; despite knowing it was too late, she must spare no effort to reach us. Within half an hour she'd left for the hotel in Datchet where she knew Idris and I were headed. Adrian, alarmed, sent a small crew of cyclists to follow his mother's precipitate track; with her long expertise in wintry conditions, she'd outpaced them by hours when night, then snow, began to fall over southeast London—the same quickening storm that found our party on the Western Road. Her projected route had changed; for the previous hours of strenuous thought had convinced her that Idris, if she still lived, would never consent to pass so close to Windsor and not visit her boy in his tomb, she'd insist on saying farewell. . .and after that, what life could be left in her? So reasoning, her mother was bound for the Castle. Cycling into the vicious, icy teeth of the storm, taking wrong turns more than once, her progress felt snail-like.

"And every moment," she said, "still I accused you, and heaped on your head the fiery ashes of my burning impatience. When you pointed at that ghastly hole, her last abode, for all my agonizing pain at that moment, the abhorrence I felt towards you was beyond all expression. You, triumphant Verney—if not for you, she could not have died without me—you I hated. But then I saw Idris, and anger, and hate, and injustice died at her bier. In its place came remorse (great God, that I should feel it!) which must last so long as my powers of memory and feeling endure."

There is a magic power in resemblance. Having lived so long together, it was natural that Idris and her mother shared many gestures and patterns of speech. They were unlike in person: the one's dark hair, deep-set black eyes, and prominent features made an entire contrast with her daughter's soft, blonde, blue-eyed type. Yet illness had lately taken the fullness from my poor girl's face, and in the inflexible shape of the bone beneath—the brow, the oval chin— her mother could be seen. Now Idris was dead, her instrument smashed to pieces, dissolving to dusty nothingness. Though my mind had already formed hopes of an eternity that restored her to my embrace, the painful conscious knowledge that I'd lost her remained. But here, in these similarities, was solace. Seeing Idris in her mother touched a thrilling chord whose sacred harmony I felt in my heart's dearest chamber. Strangely moved, kneeling beside this spectral image, I trembled.

Poor, mistaken Countess! Before, in rare tender moods, she'd let herself believe that long years of severity could be repaid someday with a word or glance of reconciliation; she'd imagined how joyfully Idris would greet this development. Time having run out for the exercise of such power, she fell at once upon the thorny truth of things. Neither smiles nor caresses could reach or influence the happiness of the woman who lay in the vault beneath us now. With this realization came the remembrance of soft replies to bitter speeches, of gentle looks repaying angry ones. Then she perceived the falsehood, paltriness, and futility of her cherished dreams of birth and power; in truth, love and life were our only genuine rulers. All this overpowering knowledge rose like a great tide and flooded her soul with stormy and bewildering confusion—and the fierce tossing of these tumultuous waves, it fell to my lot to allay.

I spoke to her of her daughter, and how happy she'd been; how happy that life in which all her many virtues had found scope and her numerous excellences been properly esteemed. The idol of my heart's dear worship, the height of feminine perfection—I praised Idris in what became an ardent funeral eulogy, feeling my heart's burden start to lift as my words overflowed. I brought Adrian into the picture, alongside little Elvis and Clara: we both had duties, the Countess and I, with regard to these beings most precious to Idris. The best way, I declared, for a melancholy and repentant mother to expiate unkindness towards the dead, must be through redoubled love of the survivors.

So consoling her, my own sorrows were assuaged; my sincerity won her entire conviction. She turned to me, this hard, inflexible, persecuting woman, with a mild expression on her face, the first I'd ever seen there. "If our beloved angel is watching us now," the Ex-Queen said, "it will delight her to see that I finally do you justice. You were worthy of her; and from my heart I am glad that you won her away from me. Pardon, my son, the many wrongs I've done you; forget my bitter words and unkind treatment—take me in hand, and govern me as you will."

The air in the chapel was paler: night was lifting. It was time to be on the road. I agreed with my companion, that we should replace the pavement over the vault. We drew near. "One last look?" I asked.

"I cannot," she replied, "and, I beg you, refrain. We need not torture ourselves by gazing on the soulless body of one whose living spirit is buried in our hearts, and whose loveliness is so deeply carved there, that sleeping or waking she must always be present to us."

For a few moments, we bent our heads and kept a solemn silence.

Consecrating my future life to the preservation of Idris's dear memory, I vowed to serve her brother and her child till death. The Ex-Queen could not suppress a last convulsive sob as, with an ease that surprised me, I dragged the stones over the entrance of the tomb and closed the gulph that contained the life of my life. Then, pushing the bicycle slowly between us, we left the chapel. I felt, as I stepped into the open air, as if I were leaving a happy haven for a dreary wilderness, a tortuous path, a bitter, joyless, hopeless pilgrimage.

(42) THE WELL KNOWN road to Datchet oppressed me with a painful sense of déjà vu. Hadn't I been here before, on an identical mission, drawn by tired horses, a grief-bent form beside me and uncertainties ahead? Everything was familiar in the grey light before dawn. I knew every fence and gate; I'd been inside each cottage; habit guided my hands on the reins at each turn of the road. Though I couldn't see it, I recognized the shallow brook that brawled in spring-time by its ice-bound murmur. All these objects were as well known to me as the cold hearth of my deserted home; every moss-grown wall and plot of orchard ground, alike as twin lambs appear to a stranger's eye, yet to mine bore differences, distinctions, even names—like Falstaff over there. An ancient elm at the Little Park's edge, so-called by our children for its somewhat fanciful appearance, Falstaff was still standing, still atilt, dim light showing through its shattered trunk. So did England remain, though England was dead. It was the ghost of merry England I beheld when I pictured its last generations, wrapped in blue woolen mufflers, sporting in security and ease across the fresh untrodden snow of a winter's morn.

"This land." My companion's voice surprised me. "She could never leave."

"You mean Idris," I said, watching her profile as the Countess nodded.

"It was her birthright. Her duty. Her heart would never permit her to go."

I shook my head and sighed. "We never went abroad, not once. Something always prevented it."

"Even as a child this happened. She became ill every time we planned a voyage."

Such conversation really possessed medicinal properties. I was determined to try and soothe the venerable penitent through any remorseful feelings that might turn into new forms of bitterness; her willingness to talk promised well. My own mind, as my thoughts emerged from hours of numbness and began to grasp at explanations for the fatal tragedy in which I found my life engulfed, was likewise eased. Not only her wish to see our boy in his tomb, but also those native ties too strong for anyone, even Idris herself, to sever—here all along may have lain her motivation in rushing us away to Datchet as she'd done.

We reached the hotel before dawn. In the past, whether noisy with Saturday night revelers or spanking clean and neat again for Sunday brunch, the place had borne testimony to the labors and orderly habits of Lucy Clayton and her staff. This day the snow was high against the front door. The Countess looked around, inhaling proudly. Of the cyclists sent to follow her, no sign: we'd arrived first. The coach yard towards which I directed the horses was at the rear of the property, more sheltered from wind and drifts. I frowned to see the windows uniformly lightless; but there was a faint odor of chimney smoke about. At last I detected a ray of light struggling through the closed drapes at a terrace window, where we found a French door left unlatched.

Lucy Clayton we found amid the luggage and sheet-draped couches that the couriers of her letter had described; two spent logs smoldered in the big lobby fireplace at which she sat staring; between the fingers of one hand she held a threaded needle. A lamp on the table beside her revealed the traces and the toll of care and watching on Lucy's attractive face. The wide eyes were vacant, the attitude desponding, the momentary effect picturesque—until the fearful reality struck me. Beneath that sheet there, a figure lay stretched. Her mother was dead, and Lucy, apart from all the world, deserted and alone, must have been watching beside the corpse this whole dreary night. She seemed unaware of our entrance.

"Lucy Clayton!" The Countess raised her voice and drew a scream from the lone inland survivor of a dead nation; but she recognized us, and recovered herself with the quick exercise of self-control habitual to her, rising to her feet to make a quick bow. "Did you not expect us?" the older woman continued sharply.

"Your Ladyship! You are very good," replied Lucy, "to have come yourself—I can never thank you sufficiently. But it is too late."

"Too late!" I cried, in a strangled voice kept low by the presence of the dead. "What are you talking about? It's not too late to take you from this deserted place, at your own request, and conduct you—" But here my own loss, just briefly forgotten, overwhelmed and made me turn away; unable to speak for the grief that choked me, I crossed the lobby, threw open a window and looked out at that cold, ghastly, misshapen night's last waning. It left a chill white earth behind. Did the spirit of sweet Idris already sail along the moon-frozen crystal air? No, no, a more genial atmosphere, a lovelier habitation was surely hers!

I turned from my meditations at a word from the Countess. "You are much in need of sleep, my son," she said. In truth I welcomed this opening to exit the scene of Lucy's grief. Her expression of resigned despair, of complete misery and its patient endurance, was far more touching than any of the insane ravings or wild gesticulations of untamed sorrow. We'd come upon her sewing the mother's shroud: my heart sickened at such a detail of woe, more painful to the masculine spirit than deadliest struggle or throes of unutterable but transient agony; it was a thing only a female could endure.

So it remained for the Countess of Windsor to engage the mourner in talk, and to turn her thoughts in the direction of the road awaiting us that day. According to Lucy, her mother must have caught sight of the letter to Idris, or else overheard some scrap of conversation between the two cyclists; in any case, she'd become aware of her own and her daughter's appalling situation. Her aged frame could not sustain the anxiety and horror brought on by this discovery. Concealing her knowledge from Lucy, she brooded over it through sleepless nights till fever and delirium disclosed the secret. Her life, which had long been hovering on the brink, yielded to the united effects of misery and sickness; that same morning she'd died.

Lucy wouldn't think of leaving at first. She was one of those people whose imaginations and sensibilities had always been entirely absorbed by the narrow circle immediately in view; people who'd cling to their restricted, often harmful realities with double tenacity from not being able to comprehend anything beyond. Thus Lucy, alone in a dead world, wished to fulfill the demands of custom and give her mother a traditional English country burial. This must not be, the Countess told her. No, the mother's shrouded body could not be kept in the hotel meat freezer to await a ground thaw; no burial could be. Going on to communicate our own recent loss, the Countess painted this as an inducement, giving Lucy to understand that she must come with us for the sake of the son and orphan girl whom Idris's death had deprived of a mother's care. Lucy Clayton never resisted the call of a duty, so she yielded.

Meanwhile, upstairs, I'd sought repose from my various struggles and impatient regrets. For awhile the events of the day floated like a parade of disasters through my brain, until sleep bathed it in forgetfulness. When I awoke a few hours later, it seemed as if I'd slept for years.

My companions had not shared my oblivion. Lucy's eyes remained swollen from weeping. The Countess looked haggard and wan. Her firm spirit had not found relief in tears, and she suffered all the more from her agonizing memories and regrets; yet she remained tirelessly active. The riders sent on her trail had arrived at last, and under her command the wagon was being loaded with such valuable supplies of food and drink as the hotel still offered. We used the rest of the firewood stores to build a funeral pyre for Lucy's mother on her favorite terrace patio; the kind dead woman was eulogized by her former monarch.

With grey smoke still ascending in a thick vertical line at our backs, we left at noon, in fair weather. Lucy rode inside the wagon or up on the driver's box; the rest took turns driving, cycling, or resting within as we returned to the Dover road with speed. Along the way we gathered fresh horses, finding them either in the stables they sought by training, or else where they stood shivering in the bleak fields, ready to surrender their liberty in exchange for some handfuls of corn.

Our party, especially after my reunion with the children at Rochester, was a melancholy one; each was possessed by regret for what was remediless; even Elvis was downcast, his innate infant gaiety shadowed by his mother's absence. The future's uncertainty would assail our thoughts with insistent waves of fantasy and expectation that alternately soothed and frightened us. I myself shuddered to realize that in another day or two we might have crossed the Channel and begun that hopeless, interminable, sad wandering, which but a short time before I'd regarded as the only remedy to our situation's sorrows.

The roaring of a wintry sea announced our approach to Dover when we were still miles inland. Uneasily, we told each other that such sonic phenomena weren't unusual for the season; hadn't we heard such blasts a thousand times before, when we'd seen the wind drive flocks of fleece-crowned waves against that barren coast? But another day's journey brought us to the thunderous show of truth: Dover was flooded. We saw houses ripped from their foundations twirling in its surge-filled streets; hardly less disturbed were the human beings we found assembled at the cliff edge, and with whom we stopped to watch the salt sea's ravings.

During the Ex-Queen's last walk beside it, the Channel had been serene and glassy; the twinkling of its ripples in the sunbeams had cast an added radiance through the clear blue frosty air. At that time, Adrian had already inspected two steamboats which were moored in the harbor; along with this placid appearance of Nature, their evident fitness for our voyage had been hailed as a good omen. The day of his mother's departure, calm still reigned past sunset. But in the dead of night, the emigrants who'd lodged in the town were awakened by shrieks. They heard cries of alarm and warning to wake up or be drowned! and rushed outside, half-dressed, into a tremendous rainstorm, with frightful winds and fusillades of hail, to see what was happening. They discovered the tide already risen past every mark known to history and half the town submerged.

They headed for the cliffs and the safety of higher ground; but the views from the cliff edge drew them. In the darkness, the thunderous waters below stretched unbrokenly white, only the crests of waves showing, as a roaring wind drove the sea at full force before it. The tumult continued at daylight. At ebb tide the town was exposed; hours later, the floodtide rose even higher than it had the first night. Giant ships long abandoned were whirled from their anchorage and driven towards shore. The vessels in harbor, including Adrian's two steamships, might have been seaweed the way they were flung up on land, where the surging breakers battered them to pieces. All this waterlogged ruin was dashed and jammed against the cliffs—which now began to give way in places. An already frightened crowd saw vast fragments of the earth they could have been standing on disappear with a crash into the deep.

These sights operated differently on different persons. The majority thought they were witnessing a judgment of God, sent to prevent or punish our emigration from our native land. However, a good many were doubly eager to quit this sceptered isle that had become their prison, and which appeared unable to withstand the onslaught of the giant waves. So things stood when we arrived at Dover. Though fatigued by our journey, we were drawn to the crowd scene at the edge of the cliff; with the rest, we looked, listened, marveled, and added our own to the thousand conjectures being made. Gradually a cold dense fog narrowed the horizon; sky and sea were enveloped in equal obscurity. Still we loitered there a few hours longer before retiring to Dover Castle, whose roof now sheltered all who breathed English air.

Sleep restored some strength and courage to our worn-out frames and weakened spirits. And early the next morning, Adrian brought welcome news: the wind had changed. Though somewhat increasing the sea's fury, this northeast gale that stripped the sky bare of clouds had turned its mountainous waves a cheerful bright green color. Meanwhile the tide at ebb looked to have receded from the town for good. Our optimism grew steadily.

So did the crowd at the cliff edge; few of us were missing by late afternoon, as if some deep wish to read a promise in the sunset skies had drawn us there with one accord. We watched the mighty day star approach within a few degrees of the tempest-tossed horizon.

Suddenly, a wonder! Three other suns, parhelia equally burning and brilliant, rushed from various quarters of the heavens and began to whirl around the real sun in a glare—to our dazzled eyes all four seemed joined in dance. The sea beneath them glowed like a furnace, like the sides of Vesuvius erupting with lava. Terrified whinnies reached us from the gated fields where our horses were grazing; further off, we heard the frightful yells as a herd of cattle, panic struck, light-blinded, smashing through fences, raced right over the brink of the cliff. Next with great suddenness the three mock suns collided to make one, then plunged into the sea. Seconds later, from the spot where they'd disappeared came a gonging, deafening, awful watery sound.

Meanwhile the sun, freed of those strange satellites, continued its stately progress towards the western maritime horizon. Could we trust our glare-struck eyes? As the sun dropped, we saw the surface of the sea rise to meet it—yes, the sea mounted higher and higher, and soon obscured the fiery orb—and still the wall of water kept climbing the horizon. There appeared to have been a breakdown in the motion of the Earth: the ancient laws no longer applied, we'd been turned adrift in an unknown region of space. Or no: for here were shouts, and assertions that those had been no mere sundogs, nor meteors, but globes of burning matter which had set fire to the planet and caused the English Channel, like a vast cauldron at our feet, to bubble up in tidal waves; obviously, Judgment Day had arrived, and we stood only a few moments away from beholding the awful countenance of the omnipotent judge. Those less given to visionary terrors, watching the waters advance, asked whether the cliff we stood on could resist this new assault. Only wasn't the giant wave far higher than our precipice—so high, indeed, might not our whole little island be deluged? Even as people fled in terror for their lives, they kept stopping now and then to look back at the spectacle.

With that solemn resignation which an unavoidable necessity instills, I stood where I was before the menace, the approach of utter destruction; a sublime sense of awe calmed my pounding heart. In the twilight that the drowned sun had left behind, the towering ocean's aspect grew more terrible by the moment. Cloud rack raced overhead as a fresh west wind blew up. And then, by slow degrees, as it advanced, the tidal wave assumed a milder appearance; the wind, or the Channel currents, or some obstruction in the seabed checked its progress, and it subsided—but not without leaving the surface of the sea uniformly higher than ever before. From fear of an immediate catastrophe, we moved to anxiety over flooding in the near future. All night we watched the furious sea and the driving clouds, through whose openings the rare stars rushed impetuously; the elements warred with a thunder that made sleep impossible.

So it went on without ceasing for three days and nights. The stoutest hearts quailed before the savage enmity of Nature. In vain we told ourselves that these extreme weather conditions were not entirely out of the ordinary, nothing that didn't fit somewhere in the natural order. Our disastrous and overwhelming destiny turned the best of us to cowards. Death had hunted us through the course of many, many months, all the way to the narrow strip of time on which we stood; narrow indeed, our footpath overhanging the great sea of calamity, and buffeted by storms, and eroding under our feet. It required something like superhuman energy to bear up against the menaces of destruction that everywhere surrounded us—especially when, even supplemented by the wagonload from the Datchet hotel, our provisions began to run out, and our foraging parties reported little success in the nearer towns.

But on the fourth morning, the gale died away. Among the storm-ravaged trees, the last yellow leaves left on the topmost branches hung motionless. Seagulls sailed upon the calm bosom of a windless atmosphere, above a sea no longer furious; the massive roaring breakers had made way for the usual long, sweeping swells that burst against the shoreline almost sullenly. Our optimism was back, reinforced by that day's clear, golden sunset. The ships we'd counted on may have been lying in splinters, but to see the Channel turned tranquil enough for crossing gave us hope.

The steep waves were a radiant purple. We watched them from the cliff with pleasure, before noticing a novel sight: popping in and out of view as it rode the peaks and troughs, a dark speck, an object—actually, a boat—was coming towards us.

(43)   WE HURRIED DOWN to shore and hoisted a signal at the only usable landing place. Spyglasses showed us a nine-member

crew, soon recognizable: English, they came from the two divisions that had preceded us to Paris. The general surmise was that our compatriots there, concerned by our extended delay on the opposite side of the Channel, must have sent a party of inquiry: nine fit rowers. What else could have prompted them to brave this return through waves that remained so perilous?

But our joyous greetings received a puzzling welcome, our outstretched hands but cold and limited returns. Our visitors seemed disinclined to even speak to us. They looked angry and resentful; and though we guessed ourselves at fault, they were plainly much more displeased with each other. In loud, contending voices they demanded an escort to Dover Castle for an immediate audience with the Lord Protector of England.

"I'm here with you already, my good friends." As Adrian stepped forward he added, "Yet Lord Protector no longer." He'd long since discarded that empty title, before it became too bitter a mockery of itself. "I am, however, honored to be in a position to welcome all of you at Dover Castle, to enjoy every hospitality we can offer. You must be exhausted. Please, come!"

And he proceeded to lead everyone from the beach via the cliff path to the Castle Road, where the procession spread out and continued uphill. The nine from the boat were tight-lipped; their plans had been upended but their grievances remained, and they mostly frowned at Adrian's attempts at conversation. Though he was all gentility, from time to time he looked at them with the same interest and wonder the rest of us felt; he marveled with us at the strangeness of seeing these human beings the sea had delivered, these unexpected specimens of inestimable rarity, so full of towering passion and furiously discordant spirits.

Adrian opened the castle's large council chamber to the curious, who sat in suspense until the guests, suitably refreshed, took the floor. Eager to discover the secret meaning of this strange visitation, we were confused and dismayed to hear nothing but angry demands to speak first. By degrees, from one's bellowed assertions, another's fierce interruptions, and a slew of bitter scoffs, we ascertained that all nine were deputies from our colony at Paris, one trio from each of three antagonistic factions into which the English emigrants had split.

With almost the sole point of agreement among them being my old friend's unique fitness to act as arbiter, these nine had been selected and dispatched from Paris to Calais and across the storm-rocked Channel—all the while, even when they shared an oar with an opponent, indulging the most violent hatred against each other. Now they stood below Adrian's chair, voices raised to plead their rival causes with unmitigated party spirit. A few random words such as *Tuilleries* and *Hellfire* emerged from the hubbub, but no clarity. Adrian overcame his reluctance to reach for the big wooden gavel and brought it down with a crash.

A firm, careful examination of each deputy in turn showed us the true state of things at Paris. Two separate embarkations, some days apart, had supplied the English population there. Normally loyal and submissive to the Earl of Windsor, they'd been without him for almost two months, time enough for a leadership vacuum to develop into violent schism. One party represented the emigrants of the division that sailed first, landed at Dunkirk, and found France a blank. Vacant towns, desolate countryside: on the way to Paris they encountered not one living person, a painful shock then as now to us. In England, where communication from one part of the island to the other had become extremely slow and rare, we'd gone years without letters or news from the Continent. Melancholy voyagers were no doubt swallowed by the greedy ocean on their way to us from France; plague must have caught and silenced the rest before they could tell of the desolation behind them. Our state of ignorance had helped us hold onto vague hopes that across the Channel we'd find survivors in substantial numbers—companions, society, human existence. But the fearsome disaster that had so diminished us had assumed even greater scope for mischief in our sister land.

In Paris were found a few, perhaps a hundred people, resigned to their approaching fate, who flitted about the beautiful but lifeless streets and gathered to converse of past times with the vivacity and even gaiety that seldom deserted the French. To our emigrants' reasons for being there they listened with shrugs and incredulous looks; how bizarre they thought it, to have traded sea breezes and natural quarantine for their own ill-fated city. "Go back to your island," they counseled; or else exchange any promise of health for certain calamity. Where the plague had claimed a hundred lives in England, a thousand had died there. "Regard how you outnumber us now!" For a long time the capital had offered no diversion from the spectacle of sick Parisians burying their dead; only this past year had been happier for those who were left. "The pang of struggle has passed away," they said, "and the few left here wait patiently for the final blow. But you, who are not content to die—you should breathe no longer the air of France, or soon you will only be a part of her soil."

This prescient warning went unheeded, and the emigrants' swift possession of Paris went uncontested by a native populace that saw itself outnumbered ten-to-one after the second English embarkation had arrived from Calais. Most conspicuously, the first arrivals had occupied the Louvre and appropriated many of its treasures to themselves. The Calais party also moved into the Louvre where they were made to feel like latecomers, given second-best; the upstairs rooms overlooking the Seine were all taken, which seemed most unfair; other examples abounded, resentment grew, and so the second faction was born. A petition it originated against the party of the first arrivals, demanding a fresh apportionment of Louvre treasures, particularly oil paintings, led to angry scenes that ought to have had no place in an expiring world.

But it was the next crisis that had brought our nine guests to Dover—a crisis precipitated by the nature of the third faction. Mingling the first two, it contained the fewest people, but their purpose was more unified, their obedience to their leader more entire, their fortitude and courage more unyielding and active. They followed a self-proclaimed prophet who preached against material-ism and condemned their fellow emigrants to flames eternal; while attributing all power to God's rule, this man had attained complete command over his own private strike force. Their violent midnight raid upon the first party's sumptuous apartments at the Louvre netted him dozens of treasures, Raphaels and Leonardos and the like, which according to the prophet were nothing but pernicious objects of temptation that belonged in a bonfire. He'd ordered a huge pile of old broken chairs to be raised on the Place Vendôme in readiness. Before a match was struck, hundreds of individuals from the other factions descended on the scene to threaten bloodshed. The Elect Body, as the prophet and his followers called themselves, met this development with every show of zeal. With both sides showing weapons, the plague might have been spared much work to come. One syllable would have done it; and there on the Place Vendôme the last humans would have burdened their souls with the crime of murder, and dipped their hands in each other's blood.

Tragedy was averted. A sense of shame entered the breasts of more than one person present who recalled that not only favorite artworks but the existence of the whole human race was at stake. If these ranks were thinned, no fresh recruits could fill them up; each man and woman was like a priceless gem of which the deepest mine on earth could yield no other to compare. Repenting their own part in the day, feeling that all the blood about to be spilled would be on their own heads, these individuals were moved by a common impulse to step between the contending sides and demand a truce. So far they'd been successful. The great majority of emigrants acknowledged the Lord Protector as their head and agreed that he must have a chance to rule on the controversy before further possibly mutinous or treasonous actions were taken. Officially, the Elect Body refused to admit Adrian's authority to arbitrate, since their obedience was only to God and to his delegate on earth, their chief. At Dover, his three fanatical ambassadors proclaimed his cause: purification. The treasures of the Louvre must burn in order to redeem some part of the human race from hellfire. The Elect Body must be allowed to act without interference from idolaters and unbelievers.

All this we were hearing on January 28th—and the truce in Paris was fixed to expire on January 31st. It was of the utmost consequence that Adrian's intervention should arrive in Paris by then. Failing which, on the first day of February all three parties would reconvene to celebrate or contest the promised bonfire of masterpieces; the art could well be saved, but only at the cost of a massacre.

So that very night, Adrian and I packed our bicycles in the delegation's long boat, and along with twelve other people put off from shore. The same furious storms that had delayed their mission at Calais, had beaten to pieces and destroyed every vessel moored near Dover. We all took our turn at the oars. Beneath a serene, starlit sky, the outline of the English coast was continually lifted into view as we rode the broad-backed waves. I looked with sad affection on this last glimpse of my native land and strained my eyes for more, long after losing sight of it. *Tomb of Idris, farewell! Grave, in which my heart lies sepulchered, farewell forever!* When a solitary seagull winged its way above our heads, flying to its nest among the cliffs we'd left behind, I thought, *Yes, you can revisit the land of your birth—but we in this boat never shall.*

The heavy swells obliged us to row with all our strength for the full twelve hours we were at sea. The stars faded with morning's approach, and through a dim grey veil the French coast appeared. Broad and red, the sun had just risen as we walked, exhausted, over the sands into Calais. Our twelve boat mates included all three Elect Body delegates, who had refused to prolong a separation from their head that was already intolerable; they could take no more Godlessness. Without another word, they went to retrieve their bicycles and left for Paris, sixteen hours away. The rest of us sat down and took some refreshment, then made our way to the harbor. Adrian intended for those companions who remained, nine skilled volunteers, to pilot the most seaworthy crafts we could find back to Dover; and so would commence the last emigration. Soon, any uninhabited, unnamed, unmapped rock in the wide Pacific would be of equal account in the world's future history, as desert England.

Adrian and I set off while there was still plenty of daylight. Our recent snowstorms hadn't reached these shores: on clear roads in surprisingly good repair, we crossed the blue-green plain round Calais with impetuous speed. Thereafter, obstacles were frequent, and even with lanterns to guide us, our progress after dark felt too slow for Adrian. My friend had crossed paths with the Elect Body's leader enough times to suspect that the truce in Paris was doomed to a premature end.

In the years after the pandemic reached our shores, England's religious leaders enjoyed great power—a power of good, if rightly directed, or of incalculable mischief, when guided by fanaticism or intolerance. But this one, despite the trappings he employed, never acted from religious motives. He was an impostor in the most determined sense of the term. His father had risen from small parish ministry to become a bishop of the Southern Cone; whatever the moral influence of the bishop's notably harsh doctrines of purity and so-called election, the fact was that his son lacked a conscience. Educated in England and raised in wealth, by early life the future false prophet had done so much to indulge his own vicious propensities that he'd lost all sense of rectitude or self-esteem. When ambition woke in him, unbridled by any scruple, he gave himself up to its indulgence.

He'd pursued various schemes to acquire adherents and power in plague-stricken London, where Adrian had foiled him every time; but in Adrian's absence, the wolf tried on the shepherd's cloak, and the flock allowed the deception. A few weeks in Paris had been enough for this villain to form a party whose members believed that safety and salvation were only possible for those who put their trust in him. True fanatics, eager to show their adherence to the anti-materialistic creed of his divine mission, they'd burn the Louvre's treasures gladly—and Adrian didn't expect their leader would deny himself this awful tribute in the end.

Our journey featured one gruesome delay. Near Abbeville we happened on a fallen rider, one of the Elect Body delegates, who must have been stricken by plague in the hours since leaving Calais. The other two had left their companion to die alone on the cold earth. We arrived in time to offer some small comfort to the sufferer, whose symptoms were the most extremely virulent either of us had ever observed. An hour later we buried her corpse beneath a pile of stones. Was this even worse form of plague already stalking our loved ones in Dover? Our long ride stretched on, burdened by new worries.

Around noon on January 30th, we entered Paris. A first for me; but my friend knew the city well and our pace across its empty arrondissements was rapid. It soon became apparent that we were right to have hurried, as we rode directly towards a rising, roaring sound, a vocal clamor interspersed with what we feared might be the clash of weapons. A knot of French people stood looking off in that direction with murmurs of dismay and disbelief; here we paused and Adrian, identifying himself, pledged to do his best to mitigate the madness of their invaders. Pedaling hard again, we raced round a few more curves before Adrian shouted: "There!" With its tall green bronze column, a fantastical relic of empire in sight, the Place

Vendôme lay just ahead.

And there, in a flood of sunshine, we found a direful scene completely out of place in those days of depopulation. The crowd of hundreds looked huge, oceanic. No less incongruous were the weapons being brandished—the drawn swords and fixed bayonets, the pikestaffs, pole-axes and spears—which must have been looted from antiquities collections; so too the pieces of armor that dozens of people had on. Ornamental breastplates flashed in the sun for the first time in centuries. Other gilding caught the eye, a disturbance of golden stripes popping up amidst the central commotion: these were picture frames. The whole screaming mob seemed close to insanity, ready for bloodshed.

Standing apart was a group of women who'd gathered there to protest the use of violence; mercifully, they recognized Adrian and raised a cry. Some moments of confusion later, we heard cheers for England and the Lord Protector as the throng parted to let us through.

We'd soon learn that Adrian hadn't been alone in his suspicions about the charlatan from London. Close watch had been kept on the Hôtel Ritz where he'd made his headquarters; and when the transport of artworks started up two mornings early, the first and second factions descended on the Place Vendôme in time to overpower the Elect Body and reclaim the Louvre treasures, without loss of life on either side. The bonfire had never even been lit. But when the controversy over right of possession flared up again almost immediately, the victors turned on each other. To many there, Adrian appeared like an angel of peace descended among them. Others took a more practical view. In response to the delegation's appeal, the Lord Protector must have come as an arbitrator. Their voices rising, emigrants of both factions demanded his ruling on the spot: Who should have these treasures now?

Years earlier, watching Lord Raymond among his troops, I'd seen his majestic attitude win their respect and obedience. How different was Adrian, with his slight figure, his obliging gestures; yet multitudes saw him, saw his fervent expression, and recognized a fearless love that won their hearts. They knew he never flinched from danger, nor let himself be actuated by other motives than care for the general welfare. The Earl of Windsor was the one person all were ready to obey. Mildly, now, but with the utmost firmness, he said that the treasures of the Louvre were the property of the French people and must be restored that very day to the gallery walls from which they'd been taken—arms and armor too, every shield, halberd, and battle axe; this was his decree. And so it would be done, without argument.

One faction however remained, its people cut off from the rest, standing apart to wait until they could counterattack with best advantage, after their foes from the Louvre had mutually weakened each other. The Elect Body neither sympathized in the joy evoked by Adrian's arrival, nor imbibed the spirit of peace which fell like dew upon the softened hearts of their fellow emigrants. Behind them, near Napoleon's column, rose an immense pile of broken chairs on which they'd labored for nothing. At their head stood a ponderous man carrying some holy book. He was soberly dressed in an overall show of great care and costliness. The malign look he'd fixed on us flashed into gloating delight when his stern-faced followers decided to make threatening gestures and advance; he stepped forward with them.

Seeing this, the two factions at peace just moments before were warlike again; truly, their mutual anger had been a fire of straw compared to the slow-burning hatred they both entertained for these fanatics, these castaways who'd colonized the world to come, and who'd have listened with delight to their leader shout denunciations against the mere common art-loving children of worldliness, while humankind's immortal legacy was being reduced to ash before their eyes. The Elect Body's forward advance of its little army reawakened all the larger, heavily armed body's animosity; antique weapons grasped, hundreds waited only for Adrian's signal to charge. Instead they heard the clear tones of his voice commanding everyone to fall back. With a confused, clamorous murmur not unlike surf retreating from sand, our side obeyed. The other stood its ground.

Adrian wheeled his bicycle onto the open paving stones. Halfway between the hostile lines he stopped. Rather than joining him there in parley, the other chief advanced with his whole troop. The many women among them seemed more eager and resolute than their male companions; the most devoted, praying aloud, pressed round their leader as if to shield him. When Adrian met them half way again, they halted.

"What," he said, "are you after now? Are you really prepared to risk death for the sake of a bonfire of vanities?" Here the whole Elect Body started shouting about sin and salvation. Adrian looked straight at their scowling leader. "Can you not silence your followers? Mine, you perceive, obey me."

The other took a moment to raise his hand for quiet. "I will make answer to this creature."

Adrian smiled. "What, I again ask, are you after now?"

"Repentance!" thundered the charlatan. "Your repentance from sinful materialism. Your obedience to the will of the Most High, which has been made manifest to these his Elected People. Do we not all die through your sins, O generation of unbelief? And from you, the man whose presumption was to lead us, my Most High Lord of Sin, does not God give us the right to demand acts of repentance and obedience?"

His opponent inquired mildly, "And if we refuse your acts, what then?"

"Beware, Sin Lord!" The words rang off the sides of the Place Vendôme. "Beware and repent. God hears you and will smite your stony heart in his wrath; his poisoned arrows fly, his dogs of death are unleashed! We will not perish unrevenged—and mighty will our Avenger be, when he descends in visible majesty, and scatters destruction among you."

"My good fellow," said Adrian, with quiet scorn. "You don't believe a single word of that—you and I both know it. Threats to public property and order have ever been your stock in trade. Your poor ignorant followers deserve pity: the time will come, however, for them to gain understanding. As for today, it's enough for me to know that you seek nothing of us; and let heaven be our witness, we seek nothing of you. I'd be sorry to embitter by strife the few days that we, any of us, may have left. In the grave, we won't be able to fight; up here we don't have to. Go back to your hotel, or stay and burn your chairs; pray to your God in your own fashion, and let everyone else do the same. My prayers consist in peace and good will, in resignation and hope." He leapt nimbly onto his machine before his angry opponent could reply. "Farewell!"

Calling his friends to follow him, Adrian pedaled off towards the Louvre, where he and I oversaw the return of every treasure to its place. After that, to prevent any fresh outbreaks of theft or violence, he issued orders that everyone willing to follow him should leave the city at once and rendezvous at the Palace of Versailles, our new headquarters.

About two weeks later, the last parties of emigrants began arriving from Dover. Escorts brought them straight from Calais to Versailles, avoiding Paris where the fanatics had remained. The Lord Protector's family found ourselves reunited in apartments prepared for us in the Grand Trianon. There, surrounded by the preserved and reconstructed luxuries of long-departed Bourbons, after the ordeals of the previous weeks, came a time of repose amidst.

(44)   AMIDST all our plans and efforts to quit our wintry native latitude for the luxuries and delights of a southern climate, we'd never fixed on any precise spot as the endpoint of our wanderings. A vague picture of perpetual springtime, of fragrant groves and sparkling streams, floated enticingly in our collective imagination. Versailles saw an inclement mid-winter, yet our diminished numbers could be fed and clothed on what our foraging parties found in the locale, while the palace afforded ample accommodation for what some began to call our colony.

Strictly speaking, it was true. Like a typical colony, we'd been formed overseas and had come to sink our common roots in a new land. But essentials were missing. Where was the bustle and industry characteristic of young colonies? Where were the structures thrown together out of rude materials until bigger, better dwellings could be built? Where were the newly marked fields—the first plantings—the eager curiosity to discover unknown species and herbs—the long treks for the sake of exploring the country? Our habitations were palaces. We found our food ready-to-hand. There was no need for us to labor or investigate, no restless desire to get on—and no enthusiasm, either, for debating the question of where to go next.

If we'd had any assurance that our present numbers were safe, if our thoughts on the subject could have been enlivened by some hope, it would have been otherwise. Beyond our next destination, after all, lay issues more momentous to be discussed and decided. At some period to come, the stores of grain and preserved meat and many manufactured products we relied on for food would run out; the existing herds and flocks would die out or run wild. So what should we eat then? What mode of life should we adopt in general? Our future plans ought to have taken careful account of such questions, productive hours could have been spent in council. But we dared not look ahead, for it meant facing summer and mass death's approach. So it was barely but finally decided: To stay where we were until spring, then head to Switzerland and pass the hot months in its icy valleys. As for destinations further south—Italy, Persia, Egypt— they could wait until the autumn, assuming any of us lived that long.

Surrounded by splendid rooms, gilt-mirrored corridors, and landscaped views designed as the setting for acmes of sensual delight, we last mortals grew heartsick in the mere presence of any amusement. Occasional outbursts of untamed hilarity among the younger set might take the form of dance or song—until they'd suddenly break off, checked by a mournful look or agonizing sigh from one or other friend prevented by sorrows and losses from mingling in the festivity. Their elders could be more determined; yet if laughter sometimes echoed through its halls, that palace was vacant of joy. For my part, whenever I happened to witness such attempts at entertainment, they only increased my sense of woe. In the midst of the pleasure-hunting throng I'd close my eyes and see before me the shadowy tomb where Idris lay among the dead, moldering with them in hushed repose; when my awareness returned to the present hour at Versailles, the sights and sounds of other people's cheerful pastimes would sting like an affront.

So much for life in public—though I remained conscientious about my obligations to the general welfare. The hours most dear to me were the peaceful, private ones I managed to spend at home with my children. Elvis was almost six now; his joyous heart was incapable of sorrow, and he enlivened our wing of the Grand Trianon with innocent mirth.

Children I said, for the tenderest emotions of paternity bound me to my niece Clara. She was then fourteen, a restless, moody time of girlhood—yet she went clothed in a calm that was born of sorrow and sustained by deep insight into what went on around her. That impatience for maturity and its privileges, which almost defined the youthful state for us, had been subdued in her by early experience. Though serious she was not sad. The remembrance of her father whom she idolized, and respect for me and Adrian, had implanted a high sense of duty in her young heart—a heart that was also a fountain overflowing with the love she poured almost equally into veneration of her parents' memory and attention to her living relatives; all else she could spare went to religion. No faith was ever so entire, no hope so fervent, no charity so pure, as that of early youth. And Clara, all love, all tenderness and trust, who from infancy had been storm-tossed upon the seas of passion and misfortune, and now perceived an apparent divinity at work in all of it, in everything—Clara had concluded that her best hope was to make herself acceptable to the power she worshipped. But of this she almost never talked: religion was her heart's hidden law, one she concealed with a child's fierce reserve and cherished the more because it was secret.

Her neglected daughter's dead lips had delivered a lesson to the Countess of Windsor. Shaken, past sixty, from her lifelong dream of power, rank, and grandeur, she was seized with the conviction that love was the one good thing in life, and virtue the only distinction that could ennoble or enrich it. In this regard she was a completely new woman; yet the fiery violence of her former character showed up unchanged as she devoted herself to obtaining the affection of her remaining family, her son first of all. Though he observed a due respect, Adrian had been deeply alienated from his mother for years; the mixed memories of her coldness, his own madness, and their combined disappointments were sometimes enough to make her presence acutely painful to him. The Countess saw this, yet the obstacles made her all the more determined to win his love. Humbling herself to wait, she endured the chill between them until Adrian, servant of love, prince of tender courtesy, opened the gates of his heart and let her in. From that time forth he gave her nothing but warm, grateful tributes of filial affection; well-merited, for the Ex-

Queen's understanding, courage, and presence of mind became powerful allies in his difficult task of ruling the tumultuous crowd. Truthfully, control often swung by a single hair.

The chief source of disturbance was the impostor-prophet. He and his followers continued to reside at Paris, but they sent Versailles a constant stream of missionaries whose claims kept us apprised of the man's intentions. If we'd considered him capable of sincere belief or genuine benevolence, we'd have opened immediate talks and tried with our best arguments to soften and humanize his views; but he was only driven by ambition. Now it appeared that to rule over these last stragglers from death's herds was no longer enough for him. He'd begun telling his followers that their escape from the plague, their children's salvation, and the rise of a new human race from their seed, depended on their making him the object of their faith; he desired their worship. He'd gone so far as to calculate that when, from these crushed remains, a new race should spring up, he might be remembered as its father—if not as a deity, some composite of Jupiter the conqueror, Serapis the lawgiver, and Vishnu the preserver. Greedily imbibed in Paris by his followers, whose overweening credulity made them eager to seek converts to the same beliefs, these doctrines seldom failed to lure a few desperate souls away from our ranks into his, and the palace was in a constant ferment because of it.

Strange, but true: from time immemorial, philanthropists, ardent in their desire to do good, patient, reasonable and gentle, who sought to persuade through truth alone, held less influence over the popular mind than did those grasping, selfish figures who'd stop at nothing— adopt any means, awake any passion, spread any lie—for the advancement of their cause. The contrast was infinitely greater, and the contest that much more uneven, now that the one had few hopes to hold forth, and no cure for the fears he himself was the first to acknowledge; while the other could bring harrowing visions and transcendent hopes into play, then pretend something like godhood, and so rule.

How to reclaim any individual's allegiance from such bonds of fraud, was a frequent subject of Adrian's meditations and discourse. "We must consider," he said, "the miserable state to which we'll be consigning these deluded people when we move on towards Switzerland this spring. Our fellow Britons, fallen into the hands of a dangerous charlatan, left behind to die in torment, the groaning victims of superstition and unrelenting tyranny—can we allow this? Further—can we afford this? With our numbers already dropping, is it not imperative that we start winning some of these poor lost sheep to our own side?" He formed many plans for the purpose, but was given no chance to enact one as the work of maintaining order at Versailles kept him fully employed.

Besides, the preacher was as cautious as he was cruel, inflexible in his authority, and violent in his hatred of outsiders. The missionaries he sent us were brainwashed and organized so as to preclude the possibility of "contamination" by our attempts to reason with them. His three hundred or so followers lived under the strictest control, virtual prisoners at the Hôtel Ritz: primarily women, with about fifty children of all ages and no more than eighty men. The lower classes, including criminal elements, were overrepresented; the exceptions consisted of a few high-born females, who, panic-struck and tamed by sorrow, were in his thrall.

Among these was one whom I resolved to save, a friend from happier days. Idris had loved her, and her excellent nature made it peculiarly lamentable that she should be made a human sacrifice by this merciless cannibal of souls. One of the spies sent by Adrian into the prophet's lair had listed her as an inmate of his inner circle. I'd seen her last on a rain-swept street in London, a woman bereft but still young, lovely, and enthusiastic, whose very goodness would make her an easier mark. There are some beings whom Fate seems to select as targets for limitless wrath that pours down; women and men whom it bathes even to the lips in misery. Such a one was the ill-starred Juliet. I've mentioned her before, the sole survivor of a ducal house near Windsor swept by plague, left surrounded by the corpses of her family. Her Romeo came and rescued her from that place of death; living proof of love's transcendent power, they wed. Then plague killed her young husband—so much I knew, when she saved the life of my Idris from that freezing storm.

Adrian's informant, who'd learned the rest, told how her beloved's death sent the bride insane with grief. Madness killed the pain; but soon, the birth of their child recalled her to the cruel reality of things. While her reason was mostly restored, deep melancholy and angry impatience continued to distort her judgment; she let herself slip into solitude and penury, and would not disclose her distress to friend or stranger. That blessed, tragic night of November 20th, when my love lay fainting in a dark deserted street before Juliet happened by, marked the young mother's first contact with her fellow creatures in weeks. Aware of the plan for universal emigration, she had resolved to remain behind with her child, and alone in wide London to live or die, as her fate might decree, so long as it was near her husband's grave. Idris had fallen near the couple's foreclosed townhouse where Juliet had been hiding. The permanent losses and immediate dangers that were about to overwhelm us, and Idris's subsequent sharp decline, caused us to forget our hapless friend. She was more affected; our encounter revived the forgotten comforts found only in speech, touch, fellowship. Afterwards, a slight illness of her infant proved to her that she was still bound to humanity by an indestructible tie; to preserve this little creature's life must be the object of her being.

She joined the first division of migrants who went over to Paris, where she became an easy prey to the prophet from the Southern Cone. Love for her child made her cling eagerly, acutely fearful and credulous, to the merest straw held out to save it; and her nature, having yielded once before to the narcotic powers of love, inclined her towards the Elect Body's leader—her new rescuer, she imagined. Beautiful as a goddess, with a voice of unrivalled sweetness, she went about in a blaze of enthusiasm for the man and his message, and was often at his side.

And I, remembering her providential rescue of my lost one, reproached myself for neglect and ingratitude, and felt impelled to leave no means untried to recall her to her better self, and rescue her from the fangs of the hypocritical destroyer.

A full account of my stratagems, disappointments, and perseverance would be too tedious to record—at any rate I did at last succeed in penetrating the Hôtel Ritz. Eager to make my search brief, I roamed its common areas and corridors without success. At evening service hour, I contrived to mingle unobserved with the congregation, which assembled in the downstairs ballroom to listen to their prophet's crafty and eloquent harangue. I saw Juliet near him and watched her in a mirror. The shifting glare of madness was fearfully evident in the dark eyes she kept fixed on the man. The child in her arms was less than a year old, and its little shows of restiveness alone could distract her attention from the words of the sermon. When it was over, the congregation followed their master from the ballroom; only Juliet remained. Her babe had fallen asleep, and she'd placed it on a cushioned chair; she sat on the floor beside, watching its tranquil slumber.

I approached quietly. "Juliet, dear friend—it's me—Lionel Verney." For a moment I saw her face light up with gladness. "I've come to take you out of here, you and your child, away from this tyrant's den of superstition and misery. Please, for your own good, and for the sake of one who loved you, our dear Lady Idris—come with me."

But the poor fanatic had already relapsed into her delirium. "No—no—leave me alone—get away, you—!" she snarled and almost swore at me. But her gentle nature prevailed enough for her to continue: "Beware! Get out while you still can, Lionel—right now! It's not safe: I get strange inspirations at times. I hear the Eternal One whisper things." Her words began to come more hurriedly, in a tuneless voice. "He reveals his will to me. Any moment now, he may tell me that to save my child, you must be sacrificed; and so I'll call for the bodyguards; and the one you call a tyrant, he'll have them tear you limb from limb; and no matter how much Idris loved you, I won't shed a single tear at your death," she finished with a wild look. The baby woke up frightened and began to cry. I could see how each sob went to the luckless mother's heart, even as she mingled her soothing endearments with harsh commands addressed to me: "Go now—leave us!" I stood there wondering: could I risk all? Tear her and her child by force from the murderer's den, and trust to the healing balm of time, reason, affection? But the outcome wasn't mine to dictate.

"Juliet! Olá, Juliet!"

I looked around at the familiar voice, heard other footsteps: the preacher was coming back for her, and he wasn't alone. I turned to see Juliet, her child clasped in both arms, in the act of disappearing through a service door. My foe and his bodyguards entered before I could follow.

Surrounded and taken prisoner, I was surprised, after those frantic warnings, to be left unharmed at first. "What brings one of Sin's favorite children to our asylum of the saved?" In this fashion was I questioned. My answers were simple and truthful. "His own mouth condemns him!" exclaimed the impostor finally. "He confesses his intent to seduce from the way of salvation our well-beloved sister in God. Take him away to the lock-up; tomorrow he dies. Brothers and sisters, we are called upon to make a tremendous and appalling example of this man, one that will terrify and frighten away his wicked companions."

"Remember," I said, "who I am; and know that I shall not die unavenged. Remember the Lord Protector, who retains legal authority over all of you—he knows I'm here; my blood will cry to him, and you and your miserable victims will long lament the tragedy you are about to act."

My antagonist turned away and spoke to his guards. "You know your duty. Obey." Now came rough handling as I was thrown to the ballroom floor, tied up, marched to the hotel's former fitness center, and chained to a weight machine; there they left me, alone in the dark. So had ended my attempt to win a good woman away from a man of crime.

I couldn't conceive that he would dare put me to death. Far from dreading the prospect, methought, even at the worst, even from the very scaffold, a man true to himself, courageous and determined, could fight his way through the herd of these misguided maniacs. Yet probably he realized it too, and wouldn't risk a public execution. A private assassination would suit the prophet better. The path of his ambition had ever been devious and cruel. I was in his hands; how much easier to speak the word and have me die, unheard, unseen, in the obscurity of my makeshift dungeon; let me vanish, let the Hôtel Ritz become an object of fear. He was right: Adrian's vengeance might follow less surely if our companions were terrified out of attempting another incursion like mine.

How would it happen? Poison? I'd been given no food or water so far. Did he plan to steal upon me in my sleep? Or would I get the chance to contend to the last with my killers, knowing, even while I struggled, that I must be overcome? Two months ago, in a flickering vault, I'd considered quietly laying me down to die. Death itself I'd despised, believing that I laughed its power to scorn. But now I shook at the approach of fate. To be murdered thus at the midnight hour by cold-blooded assassins, no friendly hand to close my eyes or receive my parting blessing—to die by violence drenched in hate and execration—ah, why, my angel love, when I'd already stepped inside the tomb, did you return me to life—why did you send me away when I'd be coming back again so soon, a mangled corpse!

It would take volumes to give words to the many thoughts which occupied me in endless succession. Hours passed—centuries—in complete silence, pitch darkness. My thirst and hunger grew. The air was dank, the mildewed carpet icy cold. I had until tomorrow to live. When would tomorrow come? Wasn't it already here?

A key turned in the door, the lock was unbolted. Hallway sounds reached me; a clock struck one. *My assassins,* I thought, this being no hour for a public execution. I drew myself up inside my bonds and chains; I collected my forces, I rallied my courage, I would not fall quietly.

The door swung open; the single, slight-figured intruder carried a lamp and a long knife in one trembling hand. But recognition changed at once the temper of my mind—for it was Juliet who stood there, looking at me with a wistful countenance. In a moment, when she regained her self-possession, the warmth in her eyes gave way to the glittery shifting I'd noticed earlier. She said, "I've come to save you, Verney."

"And yourself!" I cried. "Dearest friend, let's both be saved if we can."

She knelt down beside me and found the keys to my chains on her ring. "*Shhh*—don't say a word." The knife took care of my binding cords. When my circulation was restored enough that I could stand, she tugged my arm. "Follow me!"

I obeyed instantly. On light feet we threaded a multitude of corridors and went up and down several flights of stairs; the last one brought us to the end of a long gallery. Set into the wall was a low door that Juliet bent to unlock. A rush of wind blew out the lamp, but in its place we had the blessed moonbeams, the open face of heaven, a set of cast iron steps leading down to a forgotten alleyway—and freedom. I climbed out and turned to help Juliet through the window, when she broke our silence.

"You're safe," she said. "God bless you—farewell!"

"Juliet!" I seized her reluctant hand. "Dear, misguided victim, aren't you coming along? Haven't you risked everything in helping me escape? And could you even think that I'd let you go back alone to suffer the effects of that scoundrel's rage? Never!"

"Don't fear for me," the lovely girl replied. "And don't imagine that you could be where you are now, without the leader's consent. It is he that has saved you; he assigned me to lead you to these stairs."

"But why?"

"Because I am best acquainted with your motives for coming here, and can best appreciate his mercy in permitting you to depart."

"His mercy! Have you forgotten his record of cruel acts and criminal fraud? Juliet, the man dreads me alive as an enemy, and dead he fears my avengers. By setting me loose, he may save his own skin and maintain the esteem of his followers; but mercy is far from his heart." Juliet's hand still trembled in mine. With gentle violence, I began to draw her towards me through the portal, speaking all the time. "Dear friend, as I am free, so are you. Come with me now. Idris's mother will welcome you, her noble brother will rejoice to receive you; you will find peace and love, and better hopes than the Hôtel Ritz has to offer. We can be at Versailles before dawn. Come, sweet Juliet; close the door behind you on this house of crime and hypocrisy; come live among good, loving people"

By now she was outside, standing next to me, listening and yielding to my words, drawn to the thoughts they evoked, the recollections of past scenes of youth and happiness. Suddenly she raised her arms with a piercing shriek.

"My child, my child! He has my child, my darling girl held hostage—no!"

She darted back inside and slammed and locked the door between us; I heard her footsteps hurry off. And so I left her in the imposter's clutches, to remain a prisoner of his crimes and keep inhaling the pestilential atmosphere which his demoniac nature bred.

Beyond the alleyway, a soft breeze swept my cheek, the gracious moon shone upon me, my path was free. Glad to have escaped, yet melancholy in my very joy, I retraced my steps to Versailles.

(45)   TWO MONTHS had passed since we'd had a plague death. But by degrees the winter sun mounted higher, lengthening its daily journey. The long cold nights, respite of our ills, began to shrink. Caught out like the basking flies that congregate on dry rocks at ebb tide, we'd played wantonly with time, allowing our passions, our hopes, our mad desires to rule us; now with a roar like the ocean came hot weather, and our instinct was to flee towards some sheltered crevice before the first wave smashed us when it broke.

We must leave France without delay and get to Switzerland. Among the shadows cast by mighty pine boughs bent motionless beneath their loads of snow; beside icy streams fed by immortal glaciers; amidst frequent storms which might leave the air purified, we should find health—if health were not itself a plague victim by now.

France would be easy to leave. We wouldn't be saying good-bye to our native country, or to the graves of those we loved, or to the flowers, streams, and trees we'd known from infancy. Bidding adieu to Paris would cause us little sorrow. A scene of shame, when we recalled how we emigrants had behaved there, and thought about the flock of miserable, deluded victims we'd be leaving behind to expire under the selfish tyranny of a confidence artist. And we'd feel no heart-pangs at leaving Versailles; not when we feared the gardens, woods, and palace halls of the Bourbons would soon be tainted by the unburied dead—not when we looked forward to Alpine valleys lovelier than any garden, to mighty measureless forests, and walls built not for mortal majesty, but by Nature for itself, out of marble-white peaks roofed with sky.

Yet our preparations for departure, begun so energetically, lost momentum day by day. Our spirits flagged beneath an onslaught of dire visions, bad omens, presentiments of evil that seemed to thicken fog-like around us and make us dread the unseen future. Bats and screech owls circled in noonday sunshine. Muttering thunder startled out of cloudless skies. Sudden and exterminating blight fell randomly on trees and shrubs. Though freakish, such natural phenomena were less disturbing than the sightings of those spectral funeral parades, processions of ghastly faces all begrimed with tears, which flitted through the long avenues of the gardens and passed among our bedsides at dead of night. Or the high wailing cries that came from mid-air: people heard mournful chants stream from the atmosphere, as if spirits above sang the requiem of the human race. What was there in all this, but our own almighty fear taking control of our senses, causing us to see, hear, and feel the presence of non-existent unseen powers? What else but the result of diseased imaginations and childish credulity? So might it be; the fear was real and existed regardless. Real were the staring looks, the stricken complexions, the mute dread that harrowed those among us who were regularly subjected to these phantom horrors—even babies, who could only shriek. At last it was the fear that drove our preparations forward. We must go, and hope to cure what ailed us by a change of scene, by new pastimes amid greater safety.

About fifty French people had joined us, bringing our numbers at Versailles close to 1,400 men, women, and children. Given the troubles so far whenever we'd divided forces, Adrian was determined that as many as possible should travel in one body, most of them by bicycle, with enough horses and carriages to handle the remaining people and baggage. Our route would take us first from Versailles to Fontainebleau and thence to Auxerre, Dijon, and Dole, before winding up through the Jura's mountain passes to arrive at Geneva. At each of these stops our whole tribe would assemble, and a council be held to discuss the general welfare. Otherwise we'd spread out and cover the route in 25 km stages, in bands of fifty or so, foraging constantly, quartering nightly in different towns and villages along the way. I'd be leading an advance force of a hundred cyclists tasked with making those arrangements, according to how many people and animals each place could accommodate. Adrian and some hundred other persons would bring up the rear, along with his mother, under whose protection my Elvis and Clara would remain for now.

On the morning I left Versailles, my friend rode along with me for half an hour. He was sad, and the tone of voice unusually despondent in which he confessed to me, "I wish to God we were in the Alps by now."

"If you really mean that, why not command a quicker ride? You've said yourself it could be done," I answered.

Signaling me to join him where he coasted to a stop, he let the other riders pull away. His fatigue was apparent, an effect of the supernatural choir that kept him up nights. Adrian was one of the sufferers; one who recognized his delusion, yet couldn't shake the terror that clung to it. He told me, "I don't command a quicker march, because it's too late. A month ago we might still have mastered—possibly mastered." His words trailed off and he looked away, I couldn't see his expression as he continued, in a smothered voice, "Lionel, a man in the Pompadour apartments died of plague last night!"

I gave a cry of dismay and Adrian nodded. Though we'd stopped, he gripped the handbrakes; I could see his muscles straining. "More speed won't save us," he said. "We could never outrace what's advancing on us: our last hour is coming that swiftly. Stars vanish with the sun, and so will we all. I've done my best; with these two weak hands I've clung to Plague's chariot wheel, only to be dragged along while the life gets crushed out of everyone in its path. Now I just want this to be over—let the juggernaut achieve its purpose and stop, because we're gone!" Tears streamed from his eyes. "Instead, I must enact the same tragedy again and yet again; hear the groans of the dying again, the wailing of the survivors; again witness the death throes, again watch the last pangs, which, consummating all, envelope an eternity in their evanescent existence. But why me? So sickly, I should have been among the first into the grave—why was I chosen for this?" He hid his face in his hands and confessed, "It's hard, very hard, for one weak mortal to endure all that I endure!"

While Adrian strove to calm himself, I offered words of sympathy and encouragement, reminding him how he'd fulfilled his self-imposed task up to this time, with undaunted spirit and high feelings of duty and worth; always I'd observed him with reverence and wished fruitlessly to imitate him. He sighed deeply and spoke in tones of prayer: "For a few months, only a few months more, O God, keep my resolve from failing; don't let my courage be bowed down. Don't let sights of intolerable misery madden this half-crazed brain or cause this frail heart to beat against its prison bars so violently as to burst."

He went on: "I've believed my destiny has been to guide and rule the last of the human race till death topples my government; and to this destiny I submit. And so—forgive me, Verney, I've upset you, but I've finished complaining. I am myself again; or really better than myself. You know I've been this way since childhood, my diseased nerves always trying, with too much success, to get the better of my aspirations. You know as well, how willingly I placed this wasted feeble hand on the abandoned helm of human government. My energies have flagged at intervals; yet all along I've felt as if a superior and tireless spirit had taken up its abode within me, or even incorporated its own higher powers with my being. A holy visitant, which was sleeping for a time, perhaps to show me how useless I am without its inspiration." He raised his face and cried out in a broken voice: "O Power of goodness and strength! Stay for a while yet—don't disdain this worn-out mortal flesh, O immortal Capability! While one fellow creature remains for me to help, stay by and support your shattered, failing engine!"

Then he straightened up on the saddle, his chest expanding, his countenance beaming—truly I could almost believe that his eloquent appeal had drawn a more-than-mortal spirit down into his frame, exalting him above humanity. His eyes gleamed like two earthly stars. He turned, held out his hand, grasped mine.

"Farewell, Verney! Brother of my love, farewell. The final syllable of weakness has crossed these lips. I am alive again. On to our tasks; on to our combats with a foe we cannot vanquish, though we'll struggle to the last." With a parting look more fervent and animated than any smile, Adrian wheeled into a quick U-turn and was soon lost to sight. His passion and irrepressible sorrow remained sunk in my heart.

And a man last night had died of plague. As the thought returned, I felt a sickness of the soul come over me and send its contagion through my body. My knees knocked together, my teeth chattered; cold clotted my blood and made my heart labor painfully to force the weighted currents through. With no fear for myself, I was overwhelmed by misery to think that even this remnant, we couldn't save—that those I loved might in a few days be as clay-like as Idris in her antique tomb—and that nothing could prevent it, neither strength of body nor energy of mind. A sense of degradation came over me. Was this what human beings had been created for, in the end: only to fall, molder, and fertilize vegetation? In God's eyes, did we represent nothing more than a season's greenery, or a failed crop?

For we were no better than ephemera. It took their Pyramids to finally outlast the pharaohs lying embalmed within; alas! now every sheet-metal hut and cheap plasterboard villa we passed on the road was almost guaranteed greater longevity than the whole human race. Were our proud dreams thus to fade? I'd begun to ask myself how we could ever reconcile this sad change with our former hopes, beliefs, and powers; when an inner voice, articulate and clear, seemed to answer: *Thus from the birth of the universe it was decreed: this hour and this fulfillment. Would you subvert the eternal laws of Necessity?*

Mother of the world! Servant of the Omnipotent! eternal, changeless Necessity, whose busy fingers never stop weaving events into the unbreakable chains that bind us—then as now I said: *No. Subverting nothing, I will not even raise objections. If my human mind can't acknowledge that all that is, is right; yet since what is, must be, I will sit amidst the ruins and smile. Truly we were not born to enjoy, but to submit, and to hope.*

I rode on and rejoined my division. Overgrown fields, desolate towns, wild bands of riderless horses; roads lined with unburied corpses, left there to await collection in government wagons that failed to arrive; whitening bones poked through parched, stained, decaying strips of cloth and flesh. Sights like these had become so tragically familiar that we'd ceased to shudder as we passed them. Several riders had explored this part of France in better days. They described a region which, without rivaling England or sunny Italy, still boasted frequent and lively towns; they recalled cordiality and ready smiles. Now, sunken-eyed beggars no longer asked charity in the language of diplomats; the souvenir shops where old women sat painting the famous and authentic wooden shoes were dark and vacant; no dancing revelers on holiday chased away anyone's sleep. Only silence, the melancholy bride of death, welcomed us.

Reaching Fontainebleau, we speedily set up our quarters and began preparations to receive our friends. Roll call that night found three people missing. When I inquired, the man who stepped up to offer information managed one word—"Plague!"—and fell at my feet in convulsions; he also was infected. My troop was full of hardened characters; they'd known famine and danger in the course of military campaigns, or even during stretches in prison; for some of London's most feared and successful criminals rode with us, men and women bred from their cradle to see the whole machine of society at work against them. I looked around, and saw despair and horror stamped on every face.

Several more people sickened and died during the next week. Arrivals from Versailles should have begun a few days after our own, but no one appeared. My riders were in commotion, if not outright rebellion: to reach Switzerland, to plunge into its freezing rivers, to dwell in ice caves, had become their universal mad desire. We'd promised the Earl we'd wait—yet where was he? The troop demanded I lead the way forward without him, or else they'd go on without a leader. Yet the only chance of safety, the only hope of preservation from every form of indescribable suffering, was our keeping together: I told them this. They scoffed, and their sullen reply, that they could take care of themselves, ended in menaces.

Finally a messenger arrived from Adrian with word that we should proceed to Auxerre, the route's next major stop, and there await his arrival within a few days. A private letter to me left any further arrangements to my own discretion. Though brief, it conveyed the situation at Versailles well enough to show me that perils of the most frightful nature were gathering around him; the messenger was able to supply what my friend had omitted from his account.

That man's death just before our parting, and the reawakening of plague it signaled, had been kept from general knowledge. After more deaths followed, the truth came out; then fear-born rumors arose that the true death toll must be vastly higher. Contemporaneously, emissaries and disciples of that enemy of humankind, the accursed Impostor, were back in the neighborhood and busily at work among the palace occupants, instilling his doctrine that safety and life could only be guaranteed by submission to their chief; their overnight success was such that the surviving majority (*weak-minded women, and dastardly men*, Adrian wrote) favored going back to Paris over moving on to Switzerland. Why flee towards the Alps' uncertain safety, when by returning they could range themselves under the banners of the so-called prophet, worship his evil principles out of cowardice, and so purchase immunity, as they hoped, from certain extinction?

Detained at Versailles by this discord and tumult, Adrian was tested. First to calm and then to channel the energies and thoughts of enough followers as might counterbalance the panic of the rest, required all his patience, powers of leadership, and single-mindedness. While he could no longer hope to join me very soon at Fontainebleau, he deemed it urgent that I get my riders far enough away from Versailles as would prevent any contagious exposure to the rebellion he faced. When the right time came and he was able to withdraw the main body of the emigrants from the evil influence and its threat, then he would race to join me.

My immediate reaction to hearing and reading all this news, was that Adrian needed me. Accordingly, I called the troop together and explained that we must put away thoughts of Switzerland for now and return at once to Versailles. Our leader needed our help, and the oaths of loyalty we'd sworn made this our highest duty.

Their refusal was unanimous. Their duty was to obey—and hadn't the Protector sent orders to keep riding ahead? What was delaying him had to be a plague outbreak; and here I was proposing to hurry them back to the danger zone. On the contrary, they were resolved to continue, with or without me.

Argument and persuasion were lost on them in this defiant mood. Plague had reduced their numbers enough by now to add a sting to their impatience; all my opposition achieved was to make up their minds for them. The next day they left for Auxerre. Keeping pace at the rear of the pack, I went along. My riders may have broken their word, but I'd also sworn myself not to desert them. It appeared to me inevitable that the same spirit which caused them to rebel against my authority would impel them to desert each other; disordered and leaderless, their journey was certain to end in the most dreadful suffering. For now, my chief aim must be to prevent this.

But after we stopped for the night at Villeneuve-la-Guiard, I began to reconsider. When the rest had gone to bed, and I was left alone to think about Adrian's situation, another view of the subject presented itself to me. What was I doing, and what did I hope to accomplish? Apparently I intended to lead this troop of selfish and lawless people towards Switzerland, leaving behind my family and my best friend precisely when chances were I might never see them again. Was this doing my duty? Was this setting a loyal and loving example? Torn between opposing roles, but driven by my deepest feelings, I hit on a compromise. It was a six-hour ride straight back to Versailles. I would go that very night; and if I found things to be less bad than I now expected, I'd rejoin the troop immediately. Almost before I reached the decision I was pedaling away on my bicycle.

Speed was a relief. Half-crazed with worry over what might be happening to Adrian, I set a reckless pace and followed my lantern beam through the night. My mind ran with vague ideas about how my arrival at Versailles would create some kind of sensational jolt strong enough to influence the vacillating multitude. Meanwhile, I was glad to escape from my own rebellious charges; the more ground I covered, I seemed to leave further behind the sad drama of human misery, featuring evil's recent undefeated record in its struggle with good, back there among them in Villeneuve-la-Guiard. The excellent machine beneath me hummed as if with pride. The constellations wheeled overhead, the breathing trees flashed past. I bared my head to the onrushing air which bathed my brow in delightful coolness. Methought it was happiness enough to live and enjoy the beautifully living green earth, the star-spangled sky, and the uncatchable wind that danced between them.

Dawn found me at Versailles, shooting down the long boulevards, swift as an arrow, towards the steps of the Grand Trianon. Hearing sounds of tumult within, I let my bicycle fall to the gravel, threw open the front doors and dashed inside with a cry:

"Adrian!"

Hearing his voice I cried out again, and again, louder, convulsively, even to my own shame. I found him in the Mirror Room, circled by a dense and needlessly refracted crowd towards which I dove; encountering looks of wonder, I was reminded that, even in our end-of-times, when in public a man must repress such girlish ecstasies as had seized me. I'd have given worlds to have embraced him; I dared not—but I threw myself down full-length at his feet. Could it be, that the gentle successors to the world's present solitude will read this and sympathize when I dare to say why? For the truth is, I wanted to kiss the dear and sacred earth he walked on.

The crowd's noise continued as Adrian raised me to my feet. Gradually bringing the scene around us into focus, I asked the cause of the tumult. He showed me the poignard he held, then turned to indicate a man tied up with belts who lay groaning on the parquet floor. This was a disturbed fanatic from Paris and the antique blade he'd wielded in an attempt on the Protector's life, during a packed council meeting. Though my friend was unharmed, they'd had a close call of it. Greater danger soon faced the failed assassin. Largely demoralized by superstition, their worn-out faith and love unhinged by fear, the emigrants who witnessed this detestable crime experienced a rekindling of all their latent affection for their noble chieftain. A phalanx of faithful breasts closed round him. Twenty strong arms restrained the attacker, a poor wretch who kicked and shouted in his madness, fueling that commotion I'd heard at my arrival, vaunting his own righteousness, demanding martyrdom. He would have had his wish and been torn to pieces if his intended victim hadn't interposed. Adrian stepped forward to shield him, and at the moment of my entrance had been ordering his infuriated comrades to stand down. We saw the prisoner led away through the Mirror Room safely under guard.

Now came the longer task of restoring discipline and peace across Versailles. Adrian visited his troops and went from apartment to apartment in the palace, working always to soothe the disturbed minds of his followers and recall them to their former obedience. The shock of their leader's brush with death was a powerful tonic. But when its effects faded a few hours later they feared their own deaths all the more; and each mind's eye turned towards Paris, drawn and beguiled by the guarantees of that ravenous wolf, the Imposter. So could people be so desperate for a prop, they'd lean on the pointed end of a poisoned spear. When Adrian realized what was happening, the ground being lost after all his work and care, it shook even his resolve; the unyielding friend of humanity was almost ready to abandon the struggle, muster his few remaining adherents and go, leaving hundreds more to become miserable prey of the vicious tyrant who'd stoked their delusions. But this brief wavering of purpose passed. Then he resumed his courage and determination, sustained by the untiring spirit of benevolence which glowed at his core.

And at last, luck was with him. One large convoy had left the palace for the capital, another was readying itself to follow. Our despicable enemy chose this moment to pull down destruction on his own head, and destroy with his own hands the dominion he'd erected.

The Imposter's chief hold on people's minds arose from his claim that he alone would guide the remnant to be saved, the Elect Body, who believed in and followed him, while all the rest of the human race was marked out for death; this was the doctrine his disciples spread. It's impossible to say on what foundations the man built his hopes of being able to sustain such a fraud. He must have been fully aware that murderous Nature was likely to contradict his assertions. He might have been tossing the dice: maybe future ages would revere him as an inspired prophet; maybe he'd be found out and despised by his own dying generation. At any rate, he resolved to keep up the drama to the last act. He took to wearing a sword belted over his cassock to signify himself a conquering hero. Over the plague's recurrence at Versailles he preached exultingly: here was proof, he told his congregation, that they alone lived exempt from the universal calamity. Inspired and ecstatic, true believers streamed forth from Paris until the palace grounds seemed full of them; no surprise that their numbers concealed a few dangerous elements. As for the stabber we'd caught, had he really acted alone? Or more like a crazed and deadly tool—the Imposter's personal and secret emissary? Calculating how quickly Adrian's death would deliver all the lives at Versailles into his own hands, our foe might have dared this supreme trespass.

For he was desperate. Plague, which was well-advanced in Paris by this time, had been showering the Hôtel Ritz with promiscuous infection; the death rate climbed daily. This fact, which would have destroyed the illusions that kept them docile, the wicked Imposter set out to conceal from his victims at any cost. Summoning three or four followers he always relied on when it came to executing nefarious designs, he set them to work. Any person showing symptoms was immediately and quietly withdrawn to a secret location, strangled to death, and buried in a midnight grave; plausible excuses were supplied for each new absence. Often, in order to remove one occupant, the killers secretly drugged everyone else in the room with sleeping pills.

At last, one woman's maternal vigilance beside a sickbed outmatched the sedative's effects. Her limbs numb, fighting through grogginess, she managed to follow her daughter's captors to their workshop of death; only arriving in time to witness how easily they killed her darling girl, under the personal direction of the man to whom the mother had given herself, soul and body: the Imposter.

"Murderer! Murder! Murder!"

Maddened, horrified, her shrieking voice rang out as she dashed forward to snatch up the dead child.

Though Juliet (for it was she) ranked high among his favorites, the desperate villain couldn't risk exposure. He drew his sword and ran her through; somehow she got away and took off screaming. They chased her to the downstairs ballroom, which at that hour was filled with the Elect Body joined in silent midnight prayer. Her screams and the appearance of this beautiful young woman and the dead child she carried—her nightgown dripping with blood, her infant strangled—brought the believers to their feet. She was mortally wounded. They heard her denunciation of their leader's wickedness; they saw his sword unsheathed and stained with red and were aghast. The Imposter watched their horror change to fury; they grasped how far and how malignly he'd misled them; he heard the names of those already sacrificed, called out by the duped relatives who'd just been praying for their swift return. He recognized his danger, resolved to evade the worst of it, and chose self-destruction. With that energy of purpose which had brought him this far in his guilty career, he seized a pistol from one of his henchmen's holsters, and died by mingling his loud, derisive laugh with a gunshot.

The survivors left his miserable corpse where it lay on the

ballroom floor. The remains of poor Juliet and her babe, along with others now discovered, they burned in a great funeral pyre on the Place Vendôme. Hearts subdued to saddest regret, they set off for Versailles; soon, their long procession met the crowd of fresh fanatics who'd just left us to join them. The tale of horror at the Hôtel Ritz was told. The Elect Body was finished. The deserters turned back to journey with their new comrades, sanity restored; and thus at last in their hundreds they all appeared before Adrian, and again and forever vowed obedience to his word and fidelity to his cause.

(46)   I NEVER RESUMED my command. Out of loyalty to Adrian, six riders from the troop I'd left at Villeneuve-la-Guiard followed me to Versailles and remained with us; the rest, abandoning their vanguard duties, were on their way to Switzerland. Delayed by the recent crises, we couldn't start to follow until mid-June; we left on the 18th, nearly 1,500 of us. In our long procession could be found represented every close relationship or tie of love that existed in human society; we were a living, traveling network of mutual support. Full of care over their own darlings and dear ones, every man and woman also kept tender, anxious eyes on what seemed a small army of bicycle-mounted children. Under separate guard came a two-horse convict wagon from the historical collections, in which Adrian's failed assassin rode.

People were sad, but not hopeless. It was such a large group, some of them were bound to survive, they believed; and with that pertinacious optimism which to the last characterized our human nature, each person trusted that their beloved kin would be among those finally spared.

Six weeks later we entered Dijon. Only six weeks, strange to realize: a short time, which in actual progress appeared to be drawn out interminably; six weeks of burning days whose baleful heat the balmy evenings cooled too little and too late; six weeks of fatal events and hourly, daily, agonizing sorrow. By then, the end of July, less than two months had passed: but, alas! in that interval ardent youth had gone grey-haired; permanent wrinkles furrowed the once-blooming young mother's cheek; the elastic limbs of junior cyclists were stiff and semi-paralyzed as if by age.

We rode through France and found it uninhabited. Only in the larger towns there might be one or two people left to roam like ghosts who gladly joined us, adding very few to our numbers which death did so much to decrease. As we never deserted any sick person to die alone or unburied, our journey was long, while every day more frightful gaps appeared in the rosters, names crossed out—they died by tens, by fifties, by hundreds. We stopped expecting death to show mercy, and learned to welcome each sunrise with the feeling that we might not see the next.

Far from being left behind with the spring flowers at Versailles, nervous terrors and fearful visions pursued us on our journey. Every night's camp brought its fresh offering of specters, with ghoulish and appalling shapes descried in every shaggy bush and blighted tree. When these common marvels no longer impressed, greater wonders were called into being. The sun was rising unnaturally late; the sun was fading, turning pale, and shadows had a different look: these things, confidently asserted, were widely believed. No one coming from the late 21st century could have imagined the terrible effects produced on unprotected human minds by extravagant delusions of this sort. Though I still saw nothing, I felt the testimony of my own senses coming close to being outweighed by the majority's belief in supernatural events; alone and sane among the mad, I hardly dared express a point of view that said the sun had undergone no change— that night and shadows were no thicker than they should be—that the wind singing in the trees, or whistling round a land of empty homes and stables, was not imbued with the sounds of wailing and despair that curdled other people's blood.

Once, near dusk, a terrible scream broke from the lone prisoner's cage. We stopped and turned to see an enormously tall, naked figure flourishing about the road behind us, now throwing up its arms, now leaping to an astonishing height in the air, then turning round several times successively, then raising itself to its full height and gesticulating violently. Our troop, primed to detect supernatural forces, came to a halt at the sight of this enigmatic performance. As daylight failed and it kept its distance, even my incredulity saw something appalling in the lonely specter, whose strange gambols, so slight in spiritual dignity, were beyond human powers. Now it made a series of leaps straight up in the air, the last of which cleared a high hedge to its left. A moment later it soared back and landed in the road before us. The caged assassin gave another shriek. A few people rode off at full speed but the rest drew closer, as if we were huddling together to watch this ghostly exhibition. Our goblin now perceived us; we drew back recoiling as he stepped forward to make a low bow of such ludicrous politeness that a shout of laughter rang even from our hapless throats. One final upward spring, then the figure sank to the ground where it was lost to sight in the darkness, a denouement which only deepened the onlookers' silent fear.

When we finally advanced and raised up the dying wretch, we beheld this wild scene's tragic explanation. The man had been a principal dancer of the Paris Opera ballet; I recognized him now, he'd ridden with the troop that deserted from Villeneuve-la-Guiard. Falling sick on the road he'd been abandoned by the rest; in his final delirium he'd imagined himself back on stage. The poor fellow died with his senses awash in applause, the last ever bestowed on his grace and agility.

After that, we were haunted for several days by an apparition our people called Silver Ghost. We never saw it except after nightfall, by moonlight, speeding past on a black racing bicycle; hunched and hooded, gleaming like mercury, helmeted and plumed with black feathers, it was a majestic and awe-striking sight; the ghost's face, said someone who'd glimpsed it at close range, was silver, too. At dead of night while we watched the sick, high-speed wheels would be heard making circles through the strange town outside; it was Silver Ghost come to mark one more inevitable death. He was said to be a giant who went surrounded by an icy atmosphere; animals feared and shunned him, and the dying knew their last hour had arrived when he drew near. The most credulous declared Silver Ghost to be none other than Death himself, come in person to seize a conquered world and wipe out all the humans who remained, sole rebels to his law.

One day at noon, a reflective mass was spotted on the road ahead. We rode up to find Silver Ghost fallen from his saddle, writhing in plague agonies inside his metallic bodysuit. He survived for a few hours, barely long enough to disclose the secret of his mysterious conduct with his last words. He was a French athlete of some distinction who'd been left alone, the only plague survivor in his district. For the past many months he'd wandered from town to town, province to province, seeking some survivor for a companion and abhorring the loneliness to which he was condemned. Yet when he discovered our troop, his desire for society was conquered by fear of contagion. He dared not join us and he couldn't bear to lose sight of us, sole human beings who besides himself existed in wide and fertile France. So he accompanied us in the spectral guise I've described, till pestilence restored him: from ghost, to dead man. Once again, we were left to wish that such vain and episodic terrors could distract our thoughts from more tangible evils. But these were too dreadful and too many not to force themselves into every thought, every moment, of our lives.

Our halts sometimes lasted for five or six days, till another and yet another one of us had been consigned as a clod to the vaster clod which was all that remained of our living mother Earth. When plague claimed the cage wagon driver, Adrian ordered the horses out of harness and the prisoner released; this was partly at Clara's behest, she'd befriended the failed assassin and now she vouched for him, a young man named William who indeed seemed saner than before. From now on he rode with the rest of us as we kept moving through the hottest season. Not until August 1st did we enter the gates of Dijon, by which point our emigrant band had been reduced, incredibly, to just eighty people.

We'd survived the worst and dreariest part of our journey; Dijon already felt cooler, and Switzerland was near. Yet how could we congratulate ourselves, we miserable beings, worn and wretched, passing in our meager sorrowful procession, sole remnants of the human race which, like a flood, like a plague, had once overspread and possessed the whole of creation? Streaming clear and unimpeded from its primal source in Africa, it grew into a vast perennial river, generation after generation flowing on ceaselessly, the same but always changing, diversifying, bringing forth power and knowledge, assuming dignity and authority; always growing and forever swept towards the absorbing ocean whose dim shores were just ahead now. The source was dried up. Death's slackening tide would suck away the trickle we'd become.

So all the more tenacious our cling to such rule and order as we thought could save us; if a little colony could be preserved, we always said, it alone would suffice over time to restore our species. We'd surrendered everything else, let go of every attachment to conditions which had seemed eternal, bidding adieu to the arts, to reputation, to enduring fame, to patriotic zeal. Along with all hope of retrieving anything we'd lost, we gave up all expectation of benefit, except the feeble one of saving our individual lives from the wreckage. Even England we gave up. It became a nameless barren island while we sought to preserve ourselves abroad.

But now we looked around us. Slowly, irrevocably, unanimously, we came to the opinion that our utmost efforts would not preserve one human being alive. A gush of grief, a wanton profusion of tears, and vain laments, and overflowing tenderness, and passionate but fruitless clinging to the priceless few that remained, was followed by languor and recklessness.

It's all over. We lost the game. All of us must die, and be survived by no one. We must all die! While the planet keeps revolving round the sun, and the seasons change, and the tides rise and fall; while birds still fly, fishes swim, and beasts still pasture, our species—for so long the possessor, perceiver, and recorder of all these things—must perish and pass away as though it had never been. O, what mockery is this! Surely death is not death, and humanity is not extinct; but merely passed into other shapes our mortal senses can't perceive. Death is a vast portal, the true high road to life: let us hasten through it; let us exist no more in this living death, but die that we may live!

Though our immediate family was spared, Adrian and I knew losses during the disastrous journey. The little London girl discovered during our ride on that memorable November night, rescued by him from utter desertion, died at Auxerre. The poor child had attached herself greatly to us and the suddenness of her death added to our sorrow. In the morning we'd seen her looking healthy—that night near bedtime, Lucy Clayton came to tell us she was dead. Poor Lucy herself only survived till Vincelles. Dear to us as the children's devoted nanny, the former caretaker of an invalid mother volunteered all her free time among our fellow emigrants to nurse the sick and attend the friendless. Overexerting as both numbers rose, she developed a slow fever; it opened the door to the dread disease that soon released her from her trials. Uneducated and unpretending as she was, Lucy was distinguished for the mild acquiescence with which she met every turn of adversity. When we consigned her to a grave beside a willow-bordered canal, we seemed at the same time to bid a final adieu to certain peculiarly feminine virtues that stood out in her. Patience, forbearance, sweetness—these would never again be shown us, not with the peculiarly English way she had of showing them. It was like a second separation from our country to have lost sight of Lucy Clayton forever.

The Countess of Windsor left us at Dijon. My first hour there I was told she wished to see me. We'd hadn't spoken in several days. I'd been back at a previous stop with a small rearguard troop, helping witness eight more hapless comrades' final moments and conduct their burials. One look at her messenger made me suspect that all was not right. As I hurried to her quarters, a trick of my imagination caused me to fear—what else?—that some ill had befallen Elvis or Clara, rather than this elderly lady—for how could it be otherwise? In these days of horror, it seemed too natural an occurrence, too like past times, for the old to die before the young.

I found my Idris's mother lying on a couch, her tall, emaciated figure stretched out, her face—from which the nose stood out in sharp profile—fallen away. Her large dark eyes, hollow and deep, gleamed with the light that sometimes edges thunderclouds at sunset. Save for these lights, she was all shriveled and dried up; her voice too was fearfully changed, and she could only speak to me at intervals in her struggles for breath. I saw no signs of plague, though.

"I am afraid," said she, "that it is selfish in me, to have asked you to visit the old woman again, before she dies. Yet perhaps, it would have been a greater shock, to hear suddenly that I was dead, than to see me first, like this."

I clasped her shriveled hand. "But what is it? Are you really so ill?"

"Do you not perceive death, in my face?" she replied. "Strange. I ought to have expected this, and yet I confess it takes me, by surprise. Never did I cling to life, or enjoy it, before these last months, this time spent among those I, senselessly, deserted. And it is hard, so soon, to be snatched away. I am glad, however, that I do not die of plague. Probably, I think, I should be dying now, at this same hour, even had the world gone on as it did, in my youth."

I perceived how sincerely she regretted having to die, even more than she cared to confess. Of course, she couldn't complain of an undue shortening of existence; her faded person showed that life had naturally spent itself. As I looked for words to say, Clara came in. The Countess turned to her with a smile and took the lovely child's hand, its roseate palm and snowy fingers in such contrast with the discolored knots and loosened fibers of her own. Bending for a kiss, my niece pressed the warm, full lips of youth to her withered mouth.

The Countess turned to me again. "I need not recommend this dear girl to you, Verney. For your own sake, you will preserve her. Were the world as it was, I should have on your minds, a thousand wise precautions, to impress, that one so sensitive, good, and beauteous, might escape the dangers, the traps, that used to lurk for the destruction of the fair, and excellent. This is all nothing now." Her hand on Clara's tightened. "I commit you, my kind nurse, to your uncle's care. And to your care, I entrust the dearest relic of my better self. Be to Adrian, sweet one, what you have been to me. Enliven his sadness with your sprightliness; soothe his anguished hours by your delightful conversation; when he is dying, nurse him as you have nursed me." When Clara burst into tears, the Countess hummed a note of disapproval. "Kind girl," she said, "do not weep for me. Many dear friends are left to you."

"Yes!" cried Clara. "And you talk about my friends dying too! So cruel—how could I live, if they were gone? If it ever came to Adrian dying before me, I couldn't nurse him; I could only try to join him."

The next day, the venerable lady was dead. The last tie binding us to the ancient state of things: it was impossible to look at her familiar profile and not be recalled to a social order whose bearing on our present situation was about equal with the Wars of the Roses, or the Foreign Fish Laws. For some years England's crown had pressed her brow. My father remembered for his misfortunes; the vain struggles of the late king, Adrian's father; images of Raymond, Evadne, and Perdita, who'd lived in the world's final heyday—prime movers of our past rose vividly before us at her graveside. When we turned away, we left them there. Already no one looked ahead; we'd lost our future. Now we stopped looking back.

In a week at Dijon we lost thirty more people. The survivors left the city on the Geneva road and reached the foot of the Jura two days later. Here we halted, fifty people sheltered from the noonday heat under a spreading walnut grove—the whole earth teemed with food for us but only fifty human beings, the only fifty left alive, were there to search each other's looks and try to distinguish plague symptoms from signs of wasting sorrow, or desperation, or base and careless indifference. Outside the shaded grove, a mighty wall of mountain towered; a brawling stream raised rainbows where it crossed the sunlight; grasshoppers chirped among the thyme. We clustered together, a group of fifty wretched sufferers.

Off alone, a mother cradled in her enfeebled arms the child, last of many, whose glazed eyes were about to close forever. Over here a beloved lay striving to paint his plague-distorted features with a thankful smile, as a beauty, formerly glowing in proud youthful luster, now wan and ill-groomed, knelt beside him and fanned his face with weak uncertain strokes. There a hard-featured weather-worn veteran, having prepared his meal, sat with drooped head, the useless knife falling from his grasp, as thoughts of wife and child and dearest relatives, all lost, passed across his memory and paralyzed his limbs. There sat a man who for forty years had basked in fortune's tranquil sunshine, holding the hand of his last hope, all that remained of his prosperity—his beloved daughter, she'd just attained womanhood; while he gazed on her with anxious eyes, she tried to rally her fading spirit to reassure and comfort him. Here a private aide, faithful to the last, though dying, served an employer who shivered, though still uninfected, as she gazed around with gasping fear on the variety of woe.

Adrian stood leaning against a tree. He held a book in his hand, but his eye wandered from the text and sought mine; we exchanged a sympathetic glance, both confessing by it that the scene spread out before us offered pages more pregnant with meaning, more absorbing, than anything in print.

Over by the stream, in the sunshine, apart from all this, in a tranquil soft green nook, Clara and Elvis were making boats of leaves and twigs to launch on the water. Now Elvis jumped up to chase a butterfly—and returned with a flower for his cousin; his laughing-cherub face told of the light heart that beat in his bosom. Though Clara was trying to give herself up to his amusement, her thoughts were too distracted by the scenes within the grove; she kept turning to see what Adrian and I were doing. At fourteen, though tall, she still looked very young. Now our family group's sole female, she acted the part of the tenderest mother to my little orphan boy; to see her caring for him, or attending silently and submissively to our wants, you thought only of her admirable docility and patience. But, in her soft eyes, and the deep-sea colored veins of the eyelids that veiled them, in the marble clearness of her brow, and her lips' tender expression, there was an intelligence and beauty that naturally excited both admiration and love.

Before us lay an arduous climb to the Col de la Faucille, a famous racing route along the mountain pass there. The steep and winding road offered little sun cover so we didn't start till late afternoon. We had only two more graves to dig while waiting. One mule cart we loaded with bicycles. Only a few of us remained fit to cycle the ascent; some could still manage it on horseback, but most we placed in carts. Our animals began to be hard worked as we trailed our way uphill through a series of sharp curves and narrow, rocky views, the late slanting sunbeams blasting us with heat.

At dusk the cyclists pulled ahead; in the lead of our ill-fated party, Adrian had tasked us with preparing two or three abandoned tour chalets near the halfway mark where the sick and weary dozens behind us could rest. This soon turned into one of those times when every minor difficulty seemed to grow gigantic, every annoyance rankling far out of proportion to its cause. And Adrian, usually the first to defy hardship and fatigue, showed little sign of being able to marshal his spirits this evening. He took little part in our grim explorations; head down, soft pedaling in low gear, elbows on his handlebars, he had to make an effort to rouse himself for every fresh turn. Fear and horror engulfed me. Did his languid attitude mean Plague? *Adrian, too?* My thoughts raced without stopping. *How long will those familiar limbs obey the kindly spirit within? How much longer may I look on this matchless specimen of mortality and perceive that his thought answers mine? How long will light and life dwell in the eyes of this my sole remaining friend?* Side by side, we looked back down the mountain at the lamp-lit procession's slow ascent, coming in and out of view between the craggy spurs. Then the whole cavalcade was upon us, calling for water, bread, repose—mendicant voices raised above the cries of pain and the mourners' sobs. Such made the sorrowful accompaniment to the chalet portion of our trip across the Jura.

Adrian appeared to revive when we reached the base of the Col. Again he rode ahead, but now with purpose and speed. Detained by various things, for a time I lost sight of him. The night was passing away. When I finally caught up again I saw his figure silhouetted against the paling sky: straddling his cycle, he'd paused at the top of the pass. And there he seemed to behold something unexpected and wonderful; for he threw back his head and stretched out his arms, as if to hail some ecstatic vision. Curious, I raced to join him and see for myself.

The rooftops of the terraced villa towns covering the downhill slopes ahead made this flank of the Jura resemble a gigantic slate quarry. But their view! Nature's triumph saw lovely Earth's most unrivalled beauties in resplendent, breathtaking display. Far, far below, as if we looked down a yawning abyss, lay the placid azure expanse of Lac Léman, hedged in by vine-covered hills, and further defended by an irregular rampart of mountains dark and conical in shape; and beyond, high, above—as if celestial spirits had suddenly unveiled their bright abodes to human sight, altitudes inconceivable carved in ice upon the stainless sky, heaven-kissing, companions of the unattainable ether—the glorious Alps. Mont Blanc was being dressed in dazzling robes of light by the rising sun. Gradually, as if the world's wonders had set out to prove inexhaustible, the jagged vast immensities outlined in rose and gold appeared again upon the lake below, for their proud heights to be ruffled by waves.

Wonderstruck, I forgot the death of humanity; for a moment I even forgot Adrian. When I turned to this beloved friend beside me, he was aglow with rapturous admiration for the sight before his eyes, but his tears were falling fast. "Why?" he said finally. His thin hands clasped each other against his breast:

"Why, oh heart, do you whisper of grief to me? Drink in the beauty of that scene instead, and let in a delight beyond what any paradise of fable promised."

Slowly, our entire party summited the steep Col and joined us, not a single person failing to express the utmost amazement. "God gives us a sight of heaven—we may die blessed!" cried one. With broken exclamations and extravagant phrases, person after person tried to express the intoxicating effect of the wondrous panorama. So we remained awhile, lightened of fate's pressing burden; forgetful of death, into whose night we were about to plunge; no longer reflecting that ours would be the last human eyes to perceive the divine magnificence of this terrestrial show. An enthusiasm much like happiness burst like a sudden sunbeam on our darkened life. Precious talent of woe-worn humanity! To have been able to snatch ecstatic emotion from off the killing floor of every hope...

With renewed momentum, we continued on our way to Geneva. One incident stands out. Passing through the deserted core of Ferney-Voltaire, to our profound surprise we heard music—the peal of an organ, coming from a church that faced an overgrown public park. Mingling its beauty with the intense green that clothed the trees, the promenades, the statues, the rich swell of notes awoke a new dimension in the air. Music—the language of the immortals, disclosed to us as proof of their existence—Music—

> *Silver key of the fountain of tears*
> *Where the spirit drinks till the brain is wild,*
> *Softest grave of a thousand fears*
> *Where their mother Care, like a drowsy child*
> *Is laid asleep on flowers*

as the poet Shelley wrote of it—*Child of love*, I'd add, *soother of grief, inspirer of heroism and radiant thoughts*: O Music, in this our desolation, we had forgotten you! For so long we'd been without your cheerful pipes, harmonious voices, thrilling strings; you came upon us now like a revelation of alien life. Transported as we'd been by our first view of the Alps into fancying they must be spirit mansions we saw, now we seemed to hear those spirits' melodious communings. Awe held us spellbound; many knelt. I thought of the pale votary of some local saint, on a midnight visit to the holy shrine, if she suddenly beheld the image she'd come to worship smile at her and wave hello. We all stood mute, until William glided up. The failed assassin, upon release, had remade himself into one of Adrian's most devoted lieutenants. Back home in England—in life, that is—he'd directed choirs. "It's Haydn's Creation, sir," he said.

Adrian nodded. "*A new created world springs forth at God's command,* yes. And look how the same world blooms around us. Still fresh as at creation's day, still worthy of celebration in hymns of praise. Only humanity is old and drooping."

A few of us entered the church. Coils of smoke drifted on the reverberating air: frankincense was burning on the altar though the nave was empty. Adrian and I climbed up to the organ loft, as if into the pipes and valves of Haydn's heart. A blind old man sat working the bellows and listening intently, his whole countenance one bright glow of pleasure—a man all ear. At the keys sat a woman perhaps fifty years of age. There was the echo of a stylish beauty in the way her faded hair hung round her straight shoulders; but now the tears she wept soaked and contorted her face. We could see the effort she made to suppress the trembling and sobs that wracked her thin body just the same. Almost overcome by languor—alas! it was sickness that bent and beset her.

We watched until she struck the last sonorous chord. The organ's peal died away; that alien voice, dissolved in air, was gone forever. The organist, turning to help her aged companion, glanced up and saw us. "Ah, *là—mon petit père!*" With a shriek, she rushed forward to embrace Adrian's knees and cry out a plea for him to save her father, there. A brief hysterical collapse followed. The father's old blind face smiled still, her outburst quite disregarded. Deep senility prolonged his musical enchantment. She whispered us her tale:

Too many other losses had stripped the daughter's life bare for her to retain any wish to prolong it; she'd preserved herself for his sake. Now plague had struck her. She was paralyzed with horror at the idea of leaving her helpless father alone in an empty world; for he had no idea that it was so. His blindness had combined with his second-childhood state to make it possible for her to delude him. Every day at vesper hour, as had been their wont in better times, she led him to the organ loft and played while he worked the bellows. She had held out a hope, ever since they'd become the sole survivors in the land, that the music might attract some passing traveler to them. Playing the opening bars of that day's Creation, she knew that she would never play again. She must talk to her father, and bring herself to tell him the truth—she must try to get the fact through to him that when she was gone, soon, it would be a waste of time to cry for help. As it stood, his dementia was bound to make him believe that other people were ignoring him out of human cruelty. Her desperation at the thought of leaving him to such a fate, felt worse than the plague that was killing her. Adrian and I appeared to come from heaven itself. Her exquisite composure fled with the arrival of relief, and the long-shut floodgates of her woe blew open.

Poor woman! She and her father lie side by side in the crypt there, beneath the altar. The blind man gained cognizance of his daughter's peril, and obstinately held her hand long after it turned cold and stiff. He never moved or spoke again; mere hours later, kindly death returned to take him to his infinite repose. The pair rests beneath the altar stones they made ring with the world's last notes of music. The hallowed spot, hemmed in by the craggy Jura and the far, immeasurable Alps, with the church spire pointed valiantly above the crowding trees, is distinct in my memory; and though their mortal bodies molder, the divine strains and harmonies they loved methinks must still be solacing their gentle ghosts.

(47)   WE CROSSED the border into Switzerland. Here it was, after so much time and effort, our goal accomplished, the scenery of snowy crags and glaciers that was our longed-for shelter. Yet the relief we gained was almost nil: for there were no more people alive here than we'd found in empty France. Neither bleak mountaintops nor avalanches nor thunderstorms nor icy rock-torn cascades had availed to tamp down the contagion and preserve the Swiss—why should it be any different for us?

Who were we to be saved, in any case? Did some special fitness of ours stand to aid us in the combat with all-conquering plague? We were a failing remnant, tamed to mere submission to the coming blow, half dead through fear of death; hopeless, unresisting, almost reckless in our resignation. Like a few ears of unpicked corn left behind in a field, their stalks sure to be flattened in the first winter storm—like a straggling pair of swallows caught and struck to earth by one early frost—like clouds with a north wind at their backs, fading and dissolving in the clear ether—Such were we!

Though Lac Léman was beautiful we left its shores behind and climbed up into the Alpine ravines. Sure that its waters were health-promoting, we traced the icy, mineral-laced Arve to its source, through the rock-bound valley of Servox, past mighty waterfalls, through shadows cast by inaccessible mountains. We saw the gradual exchange of luxuriant walnut and chestnut groves for bristling stands of pine, blue-black trees whose trunks had braved a thousand storms, whose branches sang in the wind; higher still, beyond verdant sod scattered with flowery dells, the sweet-smelling shrubby hollows gave place to naked, sky-piercing rock. Strange that we still looked for shelter here! If mild and fertile climates had turned destroyer on us, what improvement did we expect to find in a place where the planet's bones are showing and human life finds no encouragement; for the river water didn't help. We buried our dead under cairns now, one or two each day. In vain we rode to the vast and ever-moving glaciers of Chamonix, where amid strange roars and thunderclaps those great frozen piled-up seas drip avalanche onto half-buried forests. Plague reigned supreme even here. By the equinox, one by one, beneath the ice-caves, beside the gushets springing from the thawed snows of a thousand winters, another and yet another of the remnant of the human race closed their eyes forever to the light.

Though we weren't entirely wrong to seek a scene like this whereon to close the drama. Many sorrows have befallen our race along its checkered course; and many a woe-stricken mourner has found herself the sole survivor of her people. Thus on lovely Earth, many a dark ravine contains a brawling stream, shadowed by romantic rocks, threaded by mossy paths—but they don't have this, the mighty background, the towering, snow-draped Alps that lift our thoughts from our own dim anguish. Nature, true to the last, consoles us in the very heart of sorrow, harmonizing with our desolation; the sublime grandeur before our eyes soothes our hapless hearts and lends our misery its own majestic shape and coloring. All is one vast ruin. We feel a suitable solemn harmony of time and place for our last act on the planet's stage. Majestic gloom and tragic pomp attend the decease of wretched humanity—no monarch of old ever had a funeral procession more transcendently splendid.

One of the Arve's tributaries issues from a massive ice cave in the side of the Glacier de Bois. We were camped nearby when our species count dropped from five to four. Leaving Clara and Elvis asleep in their tent, Adrian and I carried the corpse to this desolate spot and placed it inside the cave, on a shelf of ice beneath the glacier. Faithful William had died with his mind intact, his hand grasped in Adrian's. The cave walls glowed darkly blue around our lamps; the ice, on closer examination, looked dull and spongy—a record of our recent string of hot dry years. The glacier, left fragile, seemed ready to rive and split at the slightest sound and crush all within its clefts, including any bird or beast of prey unwise enough to profane our burial. So we departed on hushed steps, in silence; but even disturbing the air this much was enough: we were hardly outside before vast blocks of ice detached themselves from the roof and fell, covering William's body.

We made our way to the outlook. A crescent moon was sinking low; the snowy mountains and blue glaciers gleamed with their own light. At our feet, white and foaming in a whirr of spray, the glacial stream dashed across its rocky bed, its ceaseless roar so crowd-like in the stillness. Illuminations of yellow lightning played in silence around the vast snow-clad dome of Mont Blanc. Barren, wild, sublime: such the churchyard, such the requiem, such the eternal funeral congregation for our dear companion!

"Something tells me, Verney, that we can stop dreading such a death now. It's over."

Adrian's words accorded with my own thoughts. It seemed to me that a sort of cloud had just passed from over us, that a weight was taken from the air.

And it was true. We'd placed more than a man in that icy and eternal sepulcher. With this last victim, Plague vanished from the earth. Death kept every way to destroy us—except the one which for the past seven years had enjoyed full sway over our world, missing not one nook of our spacious globe, mingling with its atmosphere, leaving humanity lifeless in Europe, Asia, Africa, the Americas, as if beneath one great all-smothering cloak. With solitude and silence made the co-heirs of its kingdom, the last pandemic's barbarous tyranny reached its end here in the rocky vale of Chamonix.

Henceforth Adrian and I breathed more freely and often held our heads as we'd used to, chins upraised. We felt largely liberated. Yet we did not hope. Though plague wouldn't be our destroyer, we knew our race was run.

The coming time was a mighty river on which we mortals plummeted downstream in a charmed boat. Danger was nigh, and the obvious perils wouldn't be the most deadly in these turbid waters. Awestruck, we sped under beetling precipices, in and out of darkness, irresistibly impelled in the direction of those strange new scenes taking shape in the distance. What would become of us? O for some Delphic oracle, some Sibyl with the secrets of futurity!

(48)   "THUS are we left," said Adrian, "two melancholy trees where once a forest waved. With our branches half-bare, we're left to mourn, and waste away, and die."

I answered, "Yet still we have our duties."

"Which we must nerve ourselves to fulfill, yes." He nodded. "First the duty of bestowing pleasure where we can—and, by force of love, casting rainbows across the atmospheric grief. If we're truly able to preserve what we now possess, without fear of plague, our task is already easier. Though strange, it will be sweet to watch my nephew grow to manhood, and I'll enjoy being there to see how Clara's young heart develops. In the midst of an empty world, we are everything to them; if we live, our goal must be to make them happy—able, that is, to be happy in this new mode of life. Easy for now, when their age makes them content with what the present moment brings. Under our protection they feel safe. But when nature asserts her irresistible and sacred powers—when Clara and Elvis start to want more independence, more privacy, more people!—when the two of them are stung by cravings for sympathy, and for new experiences, and for all that love of which the human heart is capable and susceptible—when all this awakens within them—"

"We cannot guess what will happen then," I said. "We could all be cold and dead as William back there long before it does."

"True—very true, Lionel. We need only provide for the present. Which we can spend trying to fill the inexperienced imagination of your lovely niece with pleasant contents—and these vast sublime scenes all around us aren't the kind to best assist this work. Nature here is like our fortunes, grand, but too bare and brutal to afford her the proper delight. And the snows will soon arrive to dress this wilderness in double desolation. I propose we go to Italy. Let's start riding down from the bleak hilltops to the sunny plains, where we can lead Clara to scenes of fertility and beauty—where her path will be adorned with flowers—where a cheery atmosphere inspires pleasure and hope."

Following this plan we rode out of Chamonix the next day and headed back to the valley of Servoz. In that lovely place we loitered, descanting on the charms of nature, drinking in her beauties. Downstream from a bridge across the Arve we'd found a quiet, sunny pool beside the rapids; whole days passed there while we fished or simply lazed around beneath the view of pine-clad heights and higher mountain snows. Then we set off on a leisurely, rambling tour of romantic Switzerland. With no reason to hurry and no mortal event to oppose us, we yielded to every idle whim along the way. But all the time we feared the coming winter and kept on course; October 5th found us twirling down the hairpin turns below Mont Cenis en route to the Italian border.

I can't explain the reluctance we felt at leaving that land of mountains. Perhaps the Alps stood for a boundary zone between our past existence and our future: as we still clung fondly to what we'd loved of old, so we lingered among their slopes and valleys. It might even be that we savored, like a novel luxury, the choice to continue doing what pleased us for as long as we could. With plague off our minds for the first time in years, we began to believe that we could count on being around for each other for some months to come. There was a thrilling, agonizing, heart-pounding delight in the thought that was sometimes enough to make us cry. Snowflakes falling on a flowing stream were not frailer than our tiny band. But we strove to give life and individuality to the meteoric course of our remaining days, and to feel that no moment escaped us unenjoyed. We teetered on a dizzy precipice—happy. Yes! On those sun-warmed rocks beside the Arve, somewhere between two waterfalls, where the wild goats came to drink and the forest squirrels left the fragrant pines to scamper around us like tame creatures—we were, in an empty world, happy. O that we had lived thus forever and ever!

Stay, still, O days of joy—days when eye spoke to eye, and human voices, sweeter than the breeze music of the pine branches or the river's gentle murmur, answered mine—stay, O days replete with beatitude, days of loved society, of meals shared and regrets cheated by light-hearted sallies or learned disquisitions—days unutterably dear to me, me forlorn!—pass, O pass before me. Remembering you makes me forget what I am. Behold how my streaming eyes blot this senseless paper—behold my features convulsed by agonizing throes at your mere recollection, now that, alone, my tears flow, my lips quiver, my cries fill the air, unseen, unmarked, unheard! Yet, O yet, days of delight! Let me dwell on your dawdling hours!

Resolved to pass the ensuing winter at Milan, we entered smiling Italy. Like travelers before us, we found a land of beauty painted in wondrous hues, full of fantastic groupings. Gold and green, the cornfields lay half wild and grass-grown, tasseled ears winnowed to nothing by the spendthrift winds. Unpruned vineyards wrapped the roadside elms in luxuriant riot and shed slicks of fallen grapes onto our path; overhead among the red and yellow foliage, like illuminated glasswork, sun-touched bunches hung ripe, gold, green, purple, brown. Thick carpets of dead leaves lay everywhere. Weed-grown brooks; dusky olive groves spotted with blackened fruit; chestnut trees yielding their annual harvests to wildlife alone; still a land of plenty, and yet, alas! all poverty.

In the towns, in the voiceless towns, we visited the churches and museums; every town had its masterpieces of art. All sorts of animals rambled at liberty through the gorgeous aisles and galleries, hardly fearing our forgotten sort. Dove-colored oxen turned their full eyes on us and paced slowly by, observed by statues of saints. In an antique period bedroom we surprised a bleating throng of silly sheep which started up, huddled past us, and pattered down a marble hallway to rush through the first open door. We no longer wondered at these occurrences, and worse exhibitions no longer alarmed us—as when a palace had become a mere tomb, billowing pregnant with fetid stench, strewn with the dead. Pestilence and fear had played the same tricks we'd seen before, chasing the luxurious rich into dank fields and bare cottages, and gathering among Indian carpets and bed sheets of silk the lifelong rough and poor and wretched.

We'd rise at dawn and spend each day in unhurried sauntering. As the evening star shone out, and an orange sunset marked the direction of the dear homeland we'd never see again, talk made the hours fly—capturing and sharing our thoughts, our memories, our fancies in talk. Why should our four hearts care about being the planet's last remaining fountains of human life? Much better to be united together like this in an empty world, than to have been left alone in a more populous one, a desert of unknown strangers, and wander truly companionless till life's extinction. In this manner we endeavored to console each other; in this manner, true philosophy taught us to reason.

Adrian and I delighted to wait on Clara, the little queen of our world. On arriving at a town, our first care was to select for her its choicest rooms; to make sure that no harrowing relic of the former inhabitants remained nearby; to seek delicious food for her and minister to her every want, as her devoted servants. Clara humored us with childish gaiety. She made it her chief business to attend on Elvis. But it amused her to array herself in splendid robes, adorn herself with flashing gems, and answer to Her Majesty. Deep and pure as her religion was, it didn't teach Clara to refuse this way of blunting the keen sting of regret; her youthful vivacity made her enter heart and soul into our strange masquerades.

We arrived at Milan and installed ourselves in a small sun-filled palazzo with a fine library. Laws of our own device governed us, dividing our day and fixing distinct occupations for each hour. Mornings were for cycling in the countryside; afternoons were spent exploring the city's wealth of pictures and antiquities; evenings we devoted to reading or more usually to conversation. The books we dared read were few. Most everything in print threatened the smiling disguise we'd placed on our solitude, by reminding us of encounters and emotions we could never experience again. Texts of metaphysics would do; or speculation fiction, the kind to wander from all reality and lose itself in audacious self-created errors; poetry from times so far gone by, they might have happened in Atlantis; or such books as referred to nature only, or lit up the workings of one particular mind. But mostly talk, varied and ever new, beguiled our hours all winter into spring 2098.

With summer's approach, we rode north to Lake Como where we made ourselves at home in the beautiful Villa Pliniana, built on the lake shore in the sixteenth century atop an intermittent spring that interested the younger Pliny. Periodically abandoned, across the years the villa was also operated as a heritage hotel; it was restored for the last time when an English aristocrat bought and fitted it up with every luxury, including new modern spas. We found many comforts intact. The large bright formal rooms still dazzled with their carved and painted ceilings, inlaid marble floors, and walls hung with splendid tapestry. Colonnades and terrace lawns overlooked the deep dark water and the exquisite view up the lake towards Belaggio, all silvery vistas set between blue-green mountainsides speckled with church spires. The famous fountain burbled on schedule in a picturesque courtyard on the property's landward side. Here rose a mountain, its steep slopes carpeted in myrtle, where clusters of giant cypresses seemed to pierce the sky; while higher still, as if from among the clouds, an immense waterfall began a descent that the woody cliffs absorbed and broke into a thousand channels.

Our summer residence came with a well-appointed skiff in which we sailed all over Como, now cleaving its midmost waves, now coasting the craggy overhung banks, and visiting the little twinkling bays of translucent darkness where thick stands of evergreens dipped their bright boughs in the reflective waters. Our chief haunt on the opposite shore, an overgrown citrus grove that yielded us limitless harvests of fruit, was at its fragrant best in full sunlight, when snakes emerged from their clefts to bask on the warm stone walls, and the birds and insects rivaled one another in the outpouring of melodious hymns.

Weren't we happy in this paradise of a retreat? Amid delights on land and water, surrounded by nearly impassable mountains that blocked our view of far-off desolation, we might have been happy, if we'd thought the cities were still resonant with popular hum, and the ploughs still being guided through farmland furrows, while we, the world's freest inhabitants, enjoyed a voluntary exile, and not a remediless cutting off from our extinct species. But no kind spirit intervened to grant us such forgetfulness.

None of us enjoyed Lake Como's scenic beauty more than Clara. Lately a change had taken place in her habits and manner. She'd lost her gaiety, laid aside her playful sporting, and assumed an almost severe plainness of dress. She avoided me and Adrian, preferring to retire with Elvis to some distant nook. Then she didn't enter into his pastimes with the same zest as before, she'd sit and watch him with sadly tender smiles, her eyes bright with tears, yet speaking never a word of complaint. She approached us timidly, avoided our caresses, and wouldn't shake off her embarrassment till some serious discussion or lofty theme managed to call her out of herself for a while. As a rose, opening to the summer wind, discloses leaf after leaf till the senses ache with its excess of loveliness, so her beauty grew. A slight and variable color tinged her cheeks, and her motions seemed attuned to some hidden harmony of surpassing sweetness. We redoubled our tenderness and earnest attentions. She received them with grateful smiles that fled swiftly as a sunbeam from a glittering wave in springtime.

Our one fixed point in common with her appeared to be Elvis. The lovable little fellow was a comforter and delight to us beyond all words. His buoyant spirit and his innocent ignorance of our vast calamity were balm to us, whose thoughts and feelings were overwrought and spun out in the immensity of speculative sorrow. To cherish, to caress, to amuse him was the common task of all. Clara, who felt towards him in some degree like a young mother, gratefully acknowledged our shared parenting. To me, O! to me, who saw the clear brows and soft eyes of his mother, my lost Idris, reborn in his gentle face, to me Elvis was almost painfully dear; if I pressed him to my heart, methought I clasped a real and living part of her, my heart's beloved, who'd lain there through long years of youthful happiness.

Adrian and I went out daily in our skiff to forage among Como's lakeside villas, towns, fields, and orchards. Our return from these expeditions, on which Clara and her little charge seldom joined us, was always an hour of hilarity. While Elvis ransacked our stores with all a child's eagerness, we'd surprise our fair companion with some newfound gift, and describe any discoveries of lovely scenes or painted palaces for our full quartet to visit later. Those sailing expeditions were most divine. With a fair wind or transverse course we cut the liquid waves. When the mood grew too thoughtful and talk failed, I played a clarinet I'd found to wake the echoes and relieve our care-ridden minds. Clara very often regained her old playfulness then; the conversation and laughter flowed freely; and though our four hearts alone beat in the world, those four hearts were happy.

Returning one day with a sizeable haul from the port city of Como, Adrian and I were surprised to see the sands in front of Villa Pliniana vacant. It was our expected hour of return and Elvis and Clara usually met us there. I, as was my nature, refused to see anything sinister in what I called a random absence. Not so Adrian. Trembling with apprehension, he cried out to steer quickly for land; nearer shore he suddenly leapt from the boat and ran staggering through the shallows to the beach; he scrambled up the stairs to the villa garden and disappeared, shouting Clara's name. I followed quickly, through the empty garden. Indoors, empty rooms echoed our calls. Then Adrian spotted her from the veranda: Clara was at the other end of the terrace lawn, inside the glass spa building. We rushed there, and arrived as she was opening the door to step outside; we saw her pause and lean against the frame. Without stopping to remark on her blanched cheeks or her posture of utter despondency, Adrian sprang forward with a cry of joy and folded her delightedly in his arms. Clara, her face strangely blank, her lips quivering, withdrew from his embrace, and, without a word, led us inside. Her despairing heart refused her voice enough at first to express our misfortune. My poor Elvis, while they were playing, had been brought down by a sudden hemorrhage and seizure, and now lay torpid and speechless on a spa chaise beside the empty wading pool.

For two weeks we watched and attended the poor child unceasingly, as his life declined under the ravages of what we realized was a virulent cancer of the blood. At six and a half years old, his form and lineaments encaged the embryo of a grown adult's world-spanning mind. A man's nature, brimful of passions and affections, would have inhabited that little heart whose swift pulsations hurried towards their close. With the growth of sinew and muscle, his small hand's fine mechanism would have achieved works of beauty or of strength; manfully his tender rosy feet would have trod the bowers and glades of his inheritance, Earth entire. Useless reflections, now that he lay unresisting, limbs flaccid, consciousness suspended, awaiting the final blow.

We watched at his bedside, and when he was feverish we neither spoke nor looked at each other, marking only his obstructed breath, the sheen of perspiration on his sunken cheeks, the heavy death that weighed on his eyelids. At night, we wondered to find another day gone by when each particular hour had seemed endless. To say that words could not express our prolonged agony sounds like a trite evasion; yet how can words convey sensations whose tormenting keenness threw us back, as it were, on the deep roots and hidden foundations of our nature, sensations that rocked our very being with earthquake force and left us clinging to commonplaces, clutching at vain fantasy or deceitful hope for support before the final shock could bury us in ruins. Two weeks, I've said, which we passed in watching the progress of my sweet child's disease—two weeks more or less—while day and night changed places unremarked and no one counted; we slept hardly at all, and only ever quitted his room when we were seized by such pangs of grief that we had to retire from each other, and go conceal our sobs and tears. Adrian and I tried in vain to separate Clara from this deplorable scene. She sat, hour after hour, looking at him, now softly arranging his pillow, now giving him sips of liquid while he could still swallow. At length the moment of his death came. The blood paused in its flow—his eyes opened, then closed again—without convulsion or sigh, the frail dwelling was left vacant by its spiritual inhabitant.

Materialist philosophers of old claimed to find confirmation of their beliefs in the sight of a dead body. I always felt otherwise. Was that my child—that motionless thing, already decaying? My child wriggled with joy when I hugged him; his head was full of thoughts he was eager to tell in his dear voice; his smile was a ray of the same soul that sat enthroned behind his eyes. I turn from this mockery of what he was. Take, O earth, your debt! freely and forever I consign to you the matter you supplied. But Elvis, sweet child, amiable and beloved boy, unless your spirit has sought a fitter dwelling, you are enshrined in my heart, and you live while it lives.

We placed his remains under a cypress on the mountain. And then Clara said, "If you want me to survive, take me from away from here. Something in this scenery's transcendent beauty, in these trees, these hills, these waves, keeps whispering to me: *Leave your heavy flesh behind*, it says, *and come be part of us*. Please, dear uncle, dear Adrian, I beg you to take me away."

So on August 15th we bade adieu to this abode of beauty, to our villa and its embowering shade trees, its calm bay and noisy waterfall; to my boy's little grave we bade farewell! And then, with heavy hearts, we set out for Rome.

(49)   THIS SLOWLY laying bare of my soul's wounds: this journal of death; this long drawn and tortuous path down to the ocean of countless tears and voiceless solitude, awakens me again to keenest grief. Wait a moment—have I arrived so near the end? Yes! It's all over now—a step or two beyond those new-made graves and the wearisome way is done, my task accomplished. Can I streak my pages with words capacious enough for the grand conclusion?

And who will read them? Beware, tender offspring of the reborn world—beware, fair being, if human, if your heart is yet untamed by care, and your fresh features yet unplowed by time—beware, lest the cheerful current of your blood be checked, your golden locks turn grey, your sweet dimpling smiles be changed to fixed, harsh wrinkles! Don't expose these lines to daylight, lest day itself turn pale and die. Seek a cypress grove, whose moaning boughs will harmonize fittingly; seek some cave bored deep in earth's dark entrails, where the only light that penetrates, red and flickering, has had to struggle through a single fissure.

There is a painful confusion in my brain, which refuses to supply the succeeding events in any distinct sequence. Sometimes the irradiation of my friend's gentle smile comes before me, and methinks its light spans and fills eternity—then, again, I feel the gasping throes. . .

It was Adrian's wish that we detour to Venice on our pilgrimage to Rome. The English always did find something peculiarly attractive in the idea of this wave-encircled city. None of us had ever seen it. So we found a pleasant boat and took it down the River Po. The days were intolerably hot; we spent them docked in shade, asleep, and traveled through the night, when darkness made the bordering banks indistinct and our solitude less remarkable; when the wandering moon lit the waves our slicing prow divided, and the night wind filled our sails, and the sounds of murmuring stream, waving trees, and breeze-snapped canvas were all we had for view.

Clara, long overcome by excessive grief, had largely cast aside her timid, cold reserve, and received our attentions with grateful tenderness. While Adrian, his voice full of poetic fervor, discoursed on the glorious nations of the dead, or the beauteous earth, or the fate of humankind, she crept nearer to drink it all in with silent pleasure. We banished from our talk, and as much as possible from our thoughts, the knowledge of our desolation. And it would be incredible to a city-dweller, or anyone accustomed to a busy throng, how far we succeeded. Picture a prisoner cast into a dungeon cell and seeming pitch darkness; only one vent, more like a rift, barred and set high in the wall, admits a doubtful light—soon enough, the visual orb having assimilated the beam and adapted to its scantiness, the same prisoner finds the same cell lit like clear noonday. So we, a simple triad on an empty planet, were multiplied to each other till we became all in all. We stood like trees whose roots are loosened by the wind, which support one another, leaning and clinging with heightened tenacity while the wintry storms howl. Thus we floated down the Po's expanding stream, sleeping when the cicadas sang, awake with the stars.

Where the river delta met the Adriatic Sea at Po della Pila, we returned to our bicycles to take the coastal road north. That afternoon, September 6th, we reached the long bridge from the mainland; across waters glassy and blue where dolphins frolicked we rode towards the cupolas and towers of rose-hued Venice. The mouth of the Grand Canal was almost choked with wrecked and sunken watercraft; since Clara had enjoyed our sail more than she'd liked returning to her bicycle, we found a gondola in good enough repair to take us to the city's other end. Violated palazzos lined our route: the tide sloshed sullenly through broken doors and across drowned thresholds; seaweed and monstrous decay blackened their marble facades, while salt ooze defaced the matchless works of art that adorned their interiors. Seagulls flew in and out of shattered windows at the Gritti Palace.

Rowing lightly along the edge of the Lagoon, we came to the Piazza San Marco, where we climbed the campanile to its highest platform and looked down on the sweeping, heart-sickening views of this hapless city. It was a relief to turn and face the sea, which, though it could become a grave, kept its surface free of monuments and ruins. Offshore from that appalling spectacle of human power at an end, triumphant Nature shone even more beauteous by contrast. The Lagoon's radiant waters trembled while the sun made many-sided mirrors of its rippling waves; the sea's blue immensity, seen beyond the Lido, stretched far, far, unspecked by boat, so tranquil, so lovely, that it seemed to invite us to quit derelict land and seek refuge from sorrow and fear on its own placid expanses.

Evening started to fall. As the sun set in calm majesty behind the misty summits of the Apennines, its golden and roseate hues tinged the mountains of the Adriatic's opposite shore with the last glories of the day. "Beyond that land across there," said Adrian, pointing south, "is Greece."

"Greece!" The word struck a responsive chord in Clara. "Don't you two remember? You promised to take me back to Greece so I could see my parents' tomb. Why not now? Why go to Rome? What would we do at Rome? What if it's like this, like Venice? Think— there are so many boats down there, we could launch one and steer right for those mountains."

"Very dangerous," I objected. "And realize, those mountains are in Albania, still a considerable distance from Athens, across savage, uncultivated, almost impassable country."

Adrian said, "Not true at all!" He was delighted with Clara's proposal. The season was favorable for sailing, he said. The currents and the northwest wind would combine to send us across the gulf to the Albanian coast where, in some abandoned port, we might find one of those light skiffs so well adapted to the navigation of the Greek peninsula's waters. Run it down to Patras and the Gulf of Corinth, where the public canal should let us prolong our sail as far as Piraeus on the other side, which meant Athens; thus could we reach our goal with virtually no overland travel and minimal fatigue.

This appeared to me wild talk; but the sea, glowing with a thousand purple hues, looked so brilliant and safe, and my beloved companions were so earnest, so determined, that, when Adrian said, "Well, though it's not exactly what you wish, consent anyhow, to please me"—I could no longer refuse. The vessel we selected when we reached the ground again seemed ideally suited to our enterprise. We bent the sails and put the rigging in order. That night we reposed in one of the city's thousand heritage hotels. We'd sail at dawn.

Our moods were cheerful as we shared the work of paddling and steering across the shallow lagoon, and, when out at sea, unfurling our sails to catch the favorable morning breeze. Air like laughter filled the canvas while sunlight bathed earth, sky, and ocean. Placid waves divided to receive our keel and playfully kissed the sleek sides of our little craft, murmuring a welcome; when land receded, a level blue expanse, mirror of an azure empyrean, afforded us smooth conduct. As tranquil and balmy were the air and waters, so were our minds steeped in quiet.

Farewell to desolate towns—to fields with their miscegenation of corn and weeds—to ever multiplying relics of our lost species! Compared to the unstained deep, dry land is a grave. Its craggy heights and stately mountains are only cemetery monuments; its trees, the plumes of a state funeral hearse; its brooks and rivers run brackish with tears for the departed. Ocean, we commit ourselves to you. Just as old Noah and his kin floated above the drowned world, let us be saved, as we betake ourselves to your never-ending flood.

Adrian sat at the helm, Clara and I attended to the rigging. We ran before a breeze right aft over the untroubled deep. At noon the wind died away to puffs that only just permitted us to hold our course. As lazy, fair-weather sailors, careless of the coming hour, we talked gaily of our coasting voyage; after visiting Athens, we thought we'd make our permanent home on one of the Aegean isles, probably among the Cyclades. On Mykonos or Santorini, amidst myrtle groves and perpetual spring, fanned by the wholesome sea breezes, we'd live long years in beatific union. Was there such a thing as death in the world?

The sun passed its zenith and slid lingeringly down heaven's stainless floor. Lying in the boat, my face turned up to the blue sky, I thought I saw a few white, marbled streaks, so slight, so immaterial, surely they must be mere imagination. But a sudden fear stung me as I continued to gaze; jumping up, I ran to the prow. A cool headwind ruffled my hair—a dark line of ripples had appeared in the east and was gaining rapidly on us—I had to shout my breathless warning to Adrian over the flapping of the canvas as the adverse wind struck it— our boat lurched—swift as speech, the web of the storm thickened above us. Now, to our horror, we learned that there were neither life jackets nor preserver rings on board. We'd forgotten them.

Behold us now in our frail bark, hemmed in by hungry, roaring waves, buffeted by high wind. The sun goes down red, the dark sea is strewed with foam, our craft rises and falls in the waves' yawning furrows. In the inky east two vast clouds collide, lightning leaps forth, and the hoarse thunder mutters. Again, in the south, the clouds reply, and another forked stream of fire shows us the appalling piles of thunderheads that seem to meet and be obliterated by the heaving waves. Great God! And we alone—we three—alone—alone—sole dwellers on the sea and on the earth, we three must perish!

Smoothly, the vast universe, its myriad worlds, the plains of boundless land behind us, the whole shoreless sea around us, contracted to my view. They and all they contained shrank to a single point: our tossing vessel with its freight of glorious humanity.

Despair convulsed Adrian's face, still beaming with love. I saw him set his teeth, heard him murmur, "Yet they shall be saved!" Clara, visited by a human pang, pale and trembling, crept near him. He looked on her with an encouraging smile. "Do you fear, sweet girl? O, do not fear, we'll soon be safe on shore!"

The darkness prevented me from seeing the expression on her face; but her voice as she replied was clear and sweet. "Why should I fear? Unless mighty destiny—or the ruler of destiny—permits it, neither sea nor storm can harm us. And my worst fear is nowhere to be found, the fear I've had of surviving either one of you. If we die now, one death will clasp us undivided."

We took in all our sails save for a jib and changed our course, as soon as we safely could, to run with the wind for the Italian shore. It was so dark, the white crests of the murderous surges were hardly discernable, except during the brief lightning-made high noons that showed us all our danger before restoring us to double night. On the boat we were silent save for when Adrian would make an encouraging observation. The craft obeyed his rudder miraculously well and ran along on the tops of the waves, as if the angry sea were somehow trying to lift her endangered child out of harm.

I watched our course from the prow. All at once I heard the waters roar with redoubled fury: the sound of breakers. We were certainly near a shore. "About there!" I cried, just as a thick bolt of lightning almost directly overhead showed us the waves pounding past huge rocks to reach the level sands—we were close enough to glimpse some stunted, oozy beds of reeds being inundated at the high-water mark. Again darkness; and we drew in our breath with the same relief as people before us might have felt during volcanic eruptions, with the sky raining down red-hot debris, at the moment when some vast fragment cratered the ground directly in front of them. What to do we didn't know—breakers here, there, everywhere, encompassed us—they roared, and dashed, and flung their hateful spray in our faces. With considerable difficulty and danger we managed at length to alter our course and pull off from shore. I urged my companions to prepare for shipwreck by binding themselves to an oar or spar which might suffice to float them. My niece was only an intermediate-level swimmer; Adrian could swim, but had always been prevented by bodily weakness from taking any pleasure in the exercise or becoming even as expert as Clara. I was myself an excellent swimmer, and enjoyed few things more than swimming in an angry sea; I loved to feel the waves wrap me and strive to overpower me, while I, lord of myself, moved this way or that as I pleased. But what could even the strongest swimmer oppose to the overpowering violence of such a storm?

My efforts to prepare my companions were rendered nearly futile, as the roaring breakers made it impossible for them to hear me. The continual waves poured their excess upon us, obliging me to put all my strength into bailing the water out of our boat as fast as it came in. Meanwhile darkness hemmed us round, relieved only by the lightning; once or twice we saw thunderbolts, fiery red, fall into the sea. Vast spouts stooped from the clouds to churn the wild swells which rose to meet them; then the fierce gale bore the rack onwards and all was lost in the chaotic mingling of sky and ocean. Our gunwales had been torn away, our single sail had been shredded and carried off by the wind. We'd cut away our mast and lightened the boat of all she contained. Clara knelt down to help me empty water from the hold. As she turned her eyes to look at the fresh lightning, I could tell by that momentary gleam: resignation had conquered every fear. We, all people, had a power given us in any worst extremity, which propped up our otherwise feeble, timid minds and enabled us to endure the most savage tortures with a stillness of soul which in hours of happiness we could not have imagined. A calm, more dreadful in truth than the tempest, allayed the wild beating of my heart; a calm like that of the gambler, the suicide, the murderer, when the last card was about to be played—while the poison was nearing the lips—as the death-blow was about to be landed.

Hours passed like this, hours which might have scuffed old age into the face of beardless youth and grizzled the silky hair of infancy; hours, while the chaotic uproar continued, while each new gust transcended in dreadful fury the one before; and our craft hung on the breaking wave, then rushed into the cold valley below where it trembled and spun between watery cliffs which seemed about to meet and close around us. At one point the gale paused. Ocean sank down to comparative silence. In this breathless interval, the wind seemed to gather itself like a practiced hurdler in the blocks. Now with a terrific roar it rushed over the sea, and the waves struck our stern. "The rudder's gone!" cried Adrian.

"We're gone," came Clara's voice. "Save yourselves—O save yourselves!" More lightning showed me the poor girl half sunk in the water at the bottom of the boat, until Adrian caught her up and kept her in his arms. Rudderless, we rushed prow-first into the vast billows piled up ahead; the first in line broke upon and filled the tiny craft. One scream I heard, one cry I gave before I found myself in the water, darkness all around. Lightning flashed: the keel of our upset boat was nearby. I clung to it with my fingernails while using each new flash to try and discover any sign of my companions. I thought I saw Adrian not too far away, his arms around an oar; I sprang from my hold and dashed aside the waters with an energy beyond my human strength, as I strove to reach and lay hold of him. No one was there now.

As that hope failed, instinctive love of life reanimated me, along with feelings of contention, as if a hostile will had challenged mine to combat. Determined to reach the shore, I breasted the surges and flung them from me—they might have been the fangs and claws of a lion about to rip open my bosom. When I had been beaten down by one wave, I rose on another. Bitter pride curled my lip.

With every flash I saw the coastline: it was near, yet the progress I made was small. Each receding wave carried me back towards ocean's far abysses. At one moment I felt my foot touch the sand, and then again I was in deep water. Strength drained from my arms, my breath began to fail under the influence of the strangling waters. A thousand wild and delirious thoughts crossed my mind. My chief feeling, as well as I can recall now, was a wish for relief. How sweet it would be to lay my head on the quiet earth, where the surges would no longer strike my weakened frame, nor the sound of waters ring in my ears. Out of longing to attain this repose—not to save my life—I made a last effort. The shelving shore suddenly offered a footing. Before the breakers could throw me down I managed to get my arms around a point of rock and cling, which earned me a moment's respite; and then, on the waves' next ebb, I rushed forward, gained the dry sands, and fell down senseless.

When, with a sickening feeling, I unclosed my eyes, the first great change was that the light of morning met them. Grey dawn dappled the cloud cover as it sped off in squadrons, leaving lakes of pure ether to form in their place. A fountain of light streamed in from the east, across the Adriatic waves; greys turned to roseate hues; then sky and sea were flooded with aerial gold.

A kind of fainting stupor still held me. My senses were alive, but memory was extinct. The blessed respite was short.

Scattered, the fierceness
Of knowledge comes flocking down again—

as the American poet said in Paterson. At the first dawn of recollection I would have started up, but my limbs refused to obey me, the muscles had lost all power. Believing that I might find one of my beloved companions cast like me, half alive, on the beach, I strove in every way to restore my frame to the use of its animal functions so that I might begin the search. I wrung the brine from my hair. The genial rays of the risen sun touched me with warmth. The first moment I was able, I ran to the water's edge, calling the beloved names. Ocean drank in and absorbed my feeble voice, and replied with a low, pitiless roar.

My mind became by slow degrees aware of the universe of misery henceforth to be its dwelling. I climbed a dead tree for a survey that showed only flat sands bounded by scrub pine forest, and the sea clipped round by the horizon. In vain I kept looking further up and down the beach; I found the mast we'd thrown overboard, some tangled cordage, remnants of a sail, nothing else from our wreck. Sometimes I stood still and wrung my hands. I accused earth and sky, the universal machine and the Almighty power that misdirected it. I threw myself on the ground. Then the sighing wind, mimicking a human cry, roused me to false, bitter hope. Assuredly, if any little dinghy or canoe had been there to find, I would have paddled back out to sea; I'd have searched until I discovered the dear remains of my lost ones; clinging round them, I'd have shared their grave.

So the day passed. Each moment contained eternity, though when hour after hour had gone by, I wondered at how speedily time flew. Yet even now I had not drunk the bitter potion to the dregs; I was not yet persuaded of my loss; I did not yet feel in every pulsation, in every nerve, in every thought, that I remained alone of my race— that I was the LAST MAN.

The day clouded over and a drizzling rain set in at sunset. *Even the eternal skies weep,* I thought. Was there any shame then, that mortal me should spend myself in tears? Human beings in the ancient fables could be dissolved away through weeping and transformed into ever-gushing fountains. Ah! that it were so! Then my destiny would bring me close to Adrian and Clara's watery death.

Grief is a fantastic creature. It weaves a web on which to fatten the history of its woe from every form and change around; it incorporates all living nature into itself; it finds sustenance in every object.

Grief, as light, fills all things and like light gives them its own colors.

When my wandering search had taken me some distance from the spot on which I'd been cast, I came to one of those watchtowers which line the Italian shore at regular intervals. I went in, glad of shelter, glad to find a work of human hands after gazing so long on nature's drear barrenness. A rough winding staircase led me up to the guardroom. Fate was kind: no harrowing vestige remained of its former inhabitants. The sight of an open crate containing some stale half-moldy biscuit awakened an appetite of which I'd been completely unaware till now. Thirst, violent and parching, the result of the seawater I'd swallowed, tormented me, too; so did the exhaustion of my frame. Kind Nature designs the remedy of such wants to give pleasurable sensations, so that I—even I!—was refreshed and calmed as I ate of this sorry fare, and drank a little of the sour wine left abandoned in a half-filled flask. The bed, not to be disdained by a victim of shipwreck, consisted of a few planks laid across two iron trestles, with a heap of dried corn husks for mattress. I stretched out upon it. The earthy smell of the Indian corn was balm to my nostrils after the hateful odor of seaweed. I forgot my state of loneliness. I neither looked backward nor forward; my senses were hushed to repose; I fell asleep and dreamed of dear inland scenes— fields and hay-makers—a shepherd whistling to his dog, the sheep driven to fold—sights and sounds peculiar to my boyhood's mountain life, which I had long forgotten.

I awoke in a painful agony from nightmare: Ocean, breaking its bounds, had come to carry away the fixed continent and deep-rooted mountains, together with the streams I loved, the woods, the flocks— it raged around, keeping up that continual and dreadful roar which had accompanied the last wreck of surviving humanity. As my waking senses returned, the bare walls of the guard room closed round me. Rain pattered against the single window.

How dreadful it is to emerge from the oblivion of slumber, and be greeted good morning by the mute wailing of one's own hapless heart—from the land of deceptive dreams, to return to the heavy knowledge of unchanged and inalterable disaster! Thus was it with me now—and forever. The sting of other griefs might be blunted by time; even mine yields occasionally during the day to some pleasure inspired by the imagination or the senses. But I never take my first look at the morning light without my fingers pressed tight against my bursting heart, my soul deluged with the interminable flood of hopeless misery. That morning I awoke for the first time in the dead world—I awoke alone—and the sea's dull dirge, still audible above the rain, recalled me to thoughts of the wretch I'd become. Low, almost crooning, the sound came like a reproach, a scoff; like the sting of the soul's remorse. I gasped: the veins and muscles of my throat were swelling, suffocating me. I put my fingers in my ears, I buried my head in an armful of husks: I would have dived to the planet's core to escape that hideous moan.

But I had work to do. Again I walked the detested beach—again, far and wide, I looked in vain—again I raised unanswered cries, cupping my hands to my mouth, trying to amplify the only voice that could ever again force the mute air to carry syllables of human thought.

What a pitiable, forlorn, disconsolate being I was! One look at me would have told the tale of my despair. My hair was matted and wild, my limbs soiled with salt ooze. Most of my garments I'd lost or discarded in my struggles at sea, so the rain drenched the set of thin summer underclothes I'd retained. My feet were bare and the spiky clumps of reeds and broken shells made them bleed. I kept hurrying to and fro: now peering out, momentarily deceived, at some distant rock; now with flashing eyes reproaching the murderous ocean for its unutterable cruelty.

With time I compared myself to that monarch of the solitudes, Robinson Crusoe. We'd both been thrown overboard and washed up companionless: the novel's hero on the shore of a desolate island; I on that of a desolate world. I was rich in the so-called goods of life. If I turned my steps from this nearly barren scene and entered any of a million different cities, I should find their wealth stored up for my accommodation. Clothes, food, books; while I could take my pick of dwellings beyond the reach of wealth and royalty in former times. Crusoe, deprived of all luxuries, was obliged to toil in the acquirement of every necessity or bit of shelter. I had my choice of climate, latitude, season; he was trapped on a tropical island with small recourse from its heats and storms. Viewing the question like this, who wouldn't have preferred the sybaritic existence I could muster, the philosophic leisure, and ample intellectual resources, to his castaway's life of labor and peril? Yet he was far happier than I, for he could hope—and not in vain. A proper ship arrives at last; he goes back to country, home, and kindred, for whom his ordeal becomes a fireside tale. I could never relate the story of my adversity to anyone. I had no hope. Robinson Crusoe on his lonely island always knew that when the sun shone on him, it shone too on thousands upon thousands of other people living on the shores of the same ocean. But of all creatures beneath sun and moon, I alone bore human features; I alone could express thought in words; and, when I slept, nobody else beheld the day or night. He was transported with terror at the sight of a human footprint. I would have knelt down and worshipped one. A cruel and vengeful Turk, a merciless cannibal—or worse than either, an uncouth, brute, remorseless veteran in the vices of civilization, would have been to me a beloved companion, a treasure dearly prized. Any stranger's nature would be kin to mine; their form cast in the same mould; human blood would flow in their veins; a human sympathy must link us forever.

It cannot be that I shall never behold a fellow human being again!—never!—never!—not if I wait years! Tell me, my soul: Shall I wake, and speak to no one? Pass the interminable hours alone in the world, a solitary point surrounded by vacuum? Will day follow day endlessly thus? No! no! A God rules the world, after all, not a poisoner. So away! let me fly from the ocean-grave, let me leave behind this barren spot, inaccessible by its sheer desolation; let me tread once again the paved town streets, step over the thresholds of shops and dwellings, and no doubt these thoughts will prove to have been only a horrible vision—a maddening but passing dream.

A guard had left a bicycle behind. The next day I entered the nearest city, Ravenna. I saw many living creatures, many oxen, horses, dogs, but no living people. I entered marble palaces, vacant save for the bats and the owls nestled in the tapestry upstairs. I stepped softly, not to awaken the town; I rebuked a dog that by yelping disturbed the sacred stillness.

In part of my mind, I refused to believe that all was as it seemed. The world was not dead, but I'd gone mad—or else I was laboring under a spell which let me see everything else in the world except for its human inhabitants. They were pursuing their ordinary lives, but somehow I was deaf and blind to them; every house had occupants, but I couldn't touch them or feel their touch, I couldn't perceive them. If it had been possible to delude myself into fully believing this, I'd have been far more contented. But my brain, tenaciously rational, refused to lend itself to such fantasies; and though I tried not to, I knew—I knew—that I, the offspring of a man and woman, one among many during most of my life, now remained the sole survivor of my species.

The sun sank behind the western hills; while yet a ray of light remained, I continued to pace the lonely streets. I had no appetite, though I was faint and weary, and hadn't eaten since the evening before. Eventually darkness sent every living creature but me to the bosom of its mate. It was my solace, to blunt my mental agony by embracing personal hardship: of the thousand beds around, I wouldn't seek the luxury of one. I lay down on the pavement; as once before, a cold marble step served me for a pillow. Midnight came; and then, though not before, did my wearied lids shut out the sight of the twinkling stars and their reflections on the stones. Thus I passed the second night of my desolation.

(50)   I AWOKE just as the upper windows of some tall housing blocks caught the first beams of the rising sun. The birds were chirping from their perches on the architecture. I awoke, and my first thought was, *Adrian and Clara are dead.*

I was an untaught shepherd-boy when Adrian honored me with

his friendship. I spent the best years of my life with him nearby. All I ever possessed of this world's true goods—of happiness, knowledge, or virtue—I owed to him. In his personality, his presence, his intellect and rare qualities, he gave a glory to my life which without him it would never have known. Beyond all other beings, Adrian taught me that men could aspire to pure and single-minded goodness; because he showed it in action. Angels must have jostled for a view of him leading, governing, and solacing the last days of the human race.

Along with my bosom friend, my lovely Clara was lost to me—she who as the last of her sex displayed all those feminine and maiden virtues which poets, painters, and sculptors had striven to express in their various languages from time immemorial. Yet, as far as she was concerned, could I lament that she was taken in early youth and spared the misery that was coming? Pure she was of soul, and all her intentions were holy. But her heart was the throne of love, and the sensibility written on her lovely countenance foretold many woes made all the more deep and drear for being kept forever concealed.

These two wondrously endowed beings had been spared from the universal wreck to be my companions during the last year of our solitude. I had felt, while they were with me, all their worth. I was also conscious that every other sentiment, regret, or passion had by degrees merged into a yearning, clinging affection for them. I hadn't forgotten the sweet partner of my youth, mother of my children, my adored Idris. By Elvis's death I had lost what most dearly recalled her to me; but since her spirit remained visible and alive in her brother, I'd gradually enshrined her memory in Adrian's form, thus making him almost more than doubly dear to me. Upon Clara her child, beloved as niece, daughter, friend, I'd further settled a repentant brother's love for my lost Perdita. Today I probe the depths of my heart and try in vain to express how measureless my love for these remnants of my race. If regret and sorrow sometimes assailed me, as well it might in our bereaved, solitary, and uncertain state, one of Adrian's fervent looks, or the clear tones of his voice, dissipated the gloom; or Clara's cloudless brow and deep blue eyes, with their look of mild contentment and sweet resignation, would cheer me up before I knew it. She and Adrian were all to me—the shining suns of my benighted soul—repose in my weariness—slumber in my sleepless woe. Poorly, most poorly have I expressed, with bare, weak, disjointed words, the feeling with which I clung to them. I would have wrapped myself round and round them like ivy, so that the same blow might destroy us; dematerialized, I'd have entered and been so inextricably part of them, that they could never have gone to their new and unreachable abode without me.

Adrian and Clara are dead. I won't be hailed by their good mornings or pass the long day in their company. Never shall I see them more. The ocean has robbed me of them—stolen their hearts of love from their breasts and given over to decomposition and corruption what was dearer to me than light, or life, or hope. Dead! I am bereft of their dear conversation, bereft of the sight of them. I am a tree split by lightning; never will the bark close over the naked fibers of my being, never will their quivering life, torn and harassed by the winds, receive the balm of one moment's relief.

I am alone in the world—

but the misery behind that last complaint had only begun to reveal itself. The tide of thought and feeling rolls on forever the same; the banks and obstacles which govern its course are what vary, along with the sights reflected in its waves. Thus the sensation of immediate loss slowly decayed, while that of utter, irremediable loneliness grew on me with time.

For three days I wandered through Ravenna: now thinking only of the beloved beings who slept in ocean's oozy caves, now looking ahead at the dreadful blank before me; shuddering to make an onward step, writhing when I marked the passing hours. Three days I wandered to and fro in that melancholy town where Dante wrote in exile, going from house to house, listening whether I could detect some lurking sign of human existence. Sometimes I rang a front doorbell; the sound tinkled through unseen vaulted rooms and died away in silence. I called myself hopeless; yet still I hoped and thus remained subject, almost hourly, to the disappointment which plunged its dagger straight into one big aching, festering wound. I fed myself like a wild hunted beast, seizing or snatching up something to eat only when stung by intolerable hunger. I didn't put on new clothes, didn't seek the shelter of a roof; exposed nights sleepless; days a blur of frenzied agitation, burning heat, nervous irritation, a ceaseless but confused flow of thought.

When my fever peaked, a desire to wander came upon me. It was the fifth day after my wreck, just past sunset, when, without purpose or aim, I rode a lightweight bicycle out of Ravenna. I must have been very ill. A little delirium more or less, and that night had surely been my last. I have a clear memory of a place on the banks of the Montone, the river whose course I was following. I stopped to look wistfully on the stream, admitting to myself that its pellucid waves could be a permanent cure for what ailed me; yet unable to account for whatever held me back from seeking their shelter, even while my thoughts' poisoned arrows continued to rain down and pierce me through and through.

I rode a considerable part of the night, and exhaustion finally conquered my repugnance to availing myself of the habitations my species had deserted. The waning moon, before it set, showed me a cottage with a neat entrance and trim garden that reminded me of the England I knew. The front door was unlocked; inside, a single large room, kitchen against one wall. Still guided by moonbeams, I started a fire in the stone hearth with the wood piled beside it. A folding couch became a bed ready-made with sheets of snowy whiteness; a meal had been prepared on the kitchen counter. I might almost have been deceived into believing that I'd found, here, the object of my long search—one survivor, a companion for my loneliness, a solace to my despair. I steeled myself against the delusion; the cottage was vacant. I sat down at the table and examined the meal before me. In truth it was a death feast! The bread was blue and moldy; the cheese lay in a heap of dust. I didn't dare examine the other dishes. A troop of ants passed in double-file across the tablecloth; every utensil was covered with dust, with cobwebs, and myriads of dead flies. No one had been here in ages.

Tears flooded my eyes. Surely this was a wanton display of power on the destroyer's part! What had I done, that each sensitive nerve was thus to be dissected? Yet why complain now, in particular? This vacant cottage revealed no new sorrow—the world was empty, humanity dead, this was fact—I knew it well—so why quarrel with a stale truth? Yet, as I've said, I had hoped in the very heart of despair, so that my soul felt fresh pangs with every new impression made on it by sharp-edged reality. For I had yet to learn the lesson by heart, that neither time nor change of place could bring alleviation to my misery; as I now was, I must continue, day after day, month after month, year after year, while I lived. I hardly dared conjecture how long that might be. I'd just turned thirty-seven. No longer the first blush of manhood, true; but men before me had accounted my age the prime of life. And ever since my miraculous recovery from plague my limbs were as strong and well-knit, my muscles' every articulation as true, as when I'd shepherded flocks back in Cumberland. As I commenced a life of utter solitude, could I really think of these things as advantages? Such were my reflections when I lay down to sleep that night.

The combined effects of warmth, shelter, and less disturbed repose left me restored to a greater portion of health and strength than I'd experienced since my fatal shipwreck. Among the stores I'd found on the cottage shelves was a quantity of raisins, my breakfast as I pedaled away into the morning sun. The next large town was Forli. I entered with pleasure its wide, grassy streets. All desolate, true; yet I loved to find myself in those spots where my fellow creatures had long established themselves. I delighted to ride down street after street, between tall rows of houses; I liked to remind myself that they'd contained beings like me, once. I wasn't always the wretch I'd become. The light and pleasant aspect of Forli's wide central square and the arcades around it cheered me. I was pleased with the idea, that if the earth should ever be populated again, we, the lost race, through such relics, would have left behind an impressive exhibition of our powers for the newcomers.

I entered one of the palaces, opened the door of a magnificent drawing room, and gave a violent start. What wild-looking, unkempt, half-naked savage was here? The surprise was momentary. I stared with growing wonder at the large gilt-framed mirror that faced me. Anyone could see why the lover of the princess Idris should fail to recognize himself in the miserable object there portrayed, in my tattered underclothes in which I'd crawled half alive from the tempestuous sea; my long tangled half-matted hair; my wild eyes gleaming from their dark hollows; my sunken cheeks, burnt by the sun, yellowed by a jaundice brought on by misery and self-neglect, and almost hidden behind a beard of many days' growth.

Why not remain like this, I wondered? The world was dead, and my squalid attire was fitter mourning garb than the foppery of a black suit. And thus, methinks, I should have remained, had not hope, without which I do not believe any mortal could exist, whispered advice to me. Looking as I did, I was bound to be an object of fear and aversion to that long-sought man or woman, preserved I knew not where, whom I fondly trusted I would find someday. Will my readers scorn the vanity that made me start dressing myself with some care for the sake of this hypothetical being? Or will they forgive the freaks of a half-crazed imagination? I can easily forgive myself: for hope, however vague, was so dear to me, and a sentiment of pleasure of so rare occurrence, that I yielded readily to any idea that cherished or promoted either one.

Afterwards I visited every street, alley, and nook of Forli. These Italian towns presented an appearance of still greater desolation than those of England or France. Striking here earlier, plague had run its course and achieved its work much sooner than with us. Probably the previous summer had found no human being alive in all the land between the shores of Calabria and the northern Alps. My search was utterly vain, yet I did not despair. Reason methought was on my side; for though improbable, the chances were by no means nil that there should exist in some part of Italy a survivor like myself. Rambling through the empty town, I formed my plan of future operations. I would continue to journey on towards Rome. After close searching had satisfied me that I left behind no human being in any of the towns through which I passed, I would write up in a conspicuous part of each one, with white paint, in three languages, that Verney, the last of the English race, had gone to live in Rome.

Decided on this scheme, I found a shop where I procured the paint and brushes. It's strange that so trivial an occupation should have consoled and even enlivened me. But if grief rendered us childish, despair made us fantastical. I painted my simple inscription across the base of the Risorgimento monument in the central square, merely adding:

FRIEND, COME! I WAIT FOR YOU!–DEH, VIENI! TI ASPETTO!

The next morning, accompanied by something like hope, I left

Forli behind. Until now, agonizing retrospection had tormented my waking hours, already oppressed by dreary future prospects. Many times I had delivered myself up to the tyranny of anguish—the riverbank outside Ravenna wasn't the only place I'd been tempted to put a speedy end to my woes. The act of suicide was a remedy whose practicability was even cheering to me, an easy, speedy, certain end of my deplorable tragedy. What could I fear in the other world? If hell existed, and I were doomed to it, I'd be arriving well prepared by the past months to suffer its tortures. But dire thoughts like these faded before the bright new expectations. I went on my way, no longer feeling each hour, each minute, to be an eternity saturated with incalculable pain.

To cross the Apennines, I followed one of ancient Rome's great roads through their valleys and over their bleak summits: the Via Flaminia cycling path led me through country which had been trodden by singular heroes and visited by tourists in their countless thousands. Like a tide, all these others had receded, leaving me blank and bare in the midst. But why complain? Didn't I have hope? So I schooled myself, even after the enlivening spirit had really deserted me. Then I was obliged to call up all the fortitude I could command, and that was not much, to prevent a recurrence of the chaotic and intolerable despair I'd been gripped by during those first horrible days after the damnable shipwreck had consummated every fear of mine, and dashed to annihilation every joy.

I rose each day with the morning sun and left the night's desolate refuge. As my wheels took me across the empty landscape, my thoughts rambled through the universe; I was least miserable when, absorbed in reverie, I could forget the passage of the hours. Each evening, despite my weariness, I detested to enter any dwelling and lie down there. I have sat, hour after hour, at the door of the cottage I'd already selected, unable to lift the latch again and face the blank desertion within. Many nights, though autumnal mists were spreading, I stretched out under a holly tree; many times I chose to dine on arbutus berries and campfire-roasted chestnuts in the woods, because wild natural scenery reminded me less acutely of my hopeless state of loneliness. I counted the days by notching them into a peeled willow-wand I carried with me; each night I added another unit to the melancholy sum.

One late afternoon, I'd toiled up a hill which led to Spoleto. At a scenic overlook I stopped and sat down on a boulder, with the view before me of a spreading plain encircled by the chestnut-sided Apennines. A dark ravine that split the nearer hills was spanned by a celebrated bridge aqueduct; though crumbling in spots, its soaring limestone arches testified that humanity had once deigned to bestow labor and thought here, to adorn and civilize nature—savage, ungrateful Nature, which with an overgrowth of climbing wild flowers and parasitic plants was bidding to pull down what remained into the dell below.

To the west, the sun had bathed the atmosphere in gold; the clouds in the east caught its radiance and budded into transient hothouse hues: sunset on a world that contained me alone for its inhabitant. I took out my wand. I counted the marks. Twenty-five days had elapsed since my wreck. Twenty-five days since human voice had gladdened my ears or other human features met my gaze. Twenty-five long, weary days, succeeded by dark and lonesome nights, had entered and become a part of the past, mingling with the years gone by, and equally inalterable. A real, undeniable portion of my life: twenty-five long, long days.

Not even a month! But why talk of days or weeks or months? To give myself a true picture of the future, I must grasp years in my imagination. Three, five, ten, twenty, fifty anniversaries of that fatal shipwreck might elapse; with twelve months in every year, and every one of them longer than the twenty-five days gone by. But how many will it be? Like other people, I'd held death in terror, so much about it was obscure and unknown. More terrible, and far more obscure, was the lonely future I faced now. I broke my wand; I threw it from me. I needed no record of my life inching longer. My unquiet thoughts demanded other ways of dividing time than by the planets' old rules; looking back on the age that had elapsed since I was left alone, I refused to call them days and hours which had more truly been the throes of agony, which accumulated on a different plane.

I hid my face in my hands. The twitter of the young birds going to rest, their rustling among the trees, disturbed the still evening air. The crickets chirped, the scops owls cooed at intervals. My thoughts had been of death—these sounds spoke to me of life. I lifted up my eyes. A bat fluttered past them. The sun had sunk behind the jagged mountains, leaving a band of orange light to follow down the lower sky; accompanied by one bright star, a silvery-pale crescent moon helped prolong the twilight. A herd of cattle crossed a clearing below, untended, bound for their watering place. The grass was rustled by a gentle breeze, and the olive groves, mellowed into soft sea-green masses by the moonlight, were like rippling water to the dry land of the chestnuts' dark foliage.

Yes, I thought, this is Earth; there is no change—no ruin—no rip in its verdant fabric; alternating night and day, it continues to wheel round and round through the sky despite being unadorned with human inhabitants. Bird, bat, cow: why can't I forget myself like one of them, and no longer suffer the wild tumult of misery that I endure?

Yet, ah! what a deadly chasm yawns between their state and mine! Haven't the animals companions? Haven't they each other, mates and cherished young, and homes, doubtless endeared and enriched in their eyes, however foreign to mine, by the society created for them by kind Nature? It is I only that am alone—I, on this little hilltop, gazing on plain and mountainside, on sky and its starry population—I, listening to the moving air raise murmurs from the earth—I only cannot express my thoughts to any companion, nor lay my throbbing head on a loved one's bosom, nor drink from any meeting of the eyes that intoxicating dew, better than the fabulous nectar of the gods. Shall I not complain, then? Shall I not curse the murderous engine which has mowed down my offspring, my mate, my brothers and sisters? Not curse Nature, for driving my species extinct? And shall I not bestow a further malediction on all the rest of nature's offspring, which dares live and enjoy while I live and suffer?

No! I will discipline my sorrowing heart to sympathy in your joys, my fellow creatures; I will be happy, because you are so. Live on, you innocents, Nature's choice darlings. I'm not so unlike you, composed of nerves, pulse, brain, joints, flesh; we're organized by the same laws. I have something beyond this, but I will call it a defect, not an endowment, if it leads me to misery, while you lead happy lives.

Just then, some goats emerged from the bushes near me, two adults and a tiny kid; in the fading light they began to browse the sloping hillside. I approached them without their perceiving me, gathered up a handful of fresh grass, and held it out. The little one nestled close to its mother while she timidly withdrew. The male stepped forward, fixing his eyes on me. I drew nearer, still holding out my lure. He dropped his head and charged at me with his horns. I knew it was idiocy, yet I yielded to my rage: I snatched up a huge stone that would have crushed my rash foe's skull—I readied it— aimed it—then my heart failed me. I hurled my missile well wide and marked its rolling, clattering, crashing progress out of earshot. My little visitants, all aghast, galloped back into the cover of the woods; while I, my very heart bleeding and torn, raced back to my bicycle and pedaled off as fast as my legs would take me, and by violent bodily exertion sought to escape from my miserable self.

(51)   *NO, NATURE, enemy of all that lives: no, I will not stay among your wild scenes, where my race is everywhere forgotten, its memory trampled on, its works defaced; where everything proclaims, from hill to hill and vale to vale—by the torrents freed from the boundaries that we imposed, by the vegetation liberated from the laws which we enforced, by our habitations abandoned to mildew and weeds—that our power is lost, and we are annihilated forever. No, I'll seek the towns; I want storied streets, hallowed ruins, stupendous public works, sacred monuments. Leaving nature behind, I'll go to the capital of the world, humanity's crowning achievement.*

I entered Eternal Rome and saluted with awe its time-honored space. The preserves of the wild Campagna; the grey-green Tiber; the Porta del Popolo: in my passage I hailed each one, these sites of fame, the unalienable possessions of humanity. At the last I gazed around the wide piazza. Twin churches, framing the Corso's shop-lined length; a green prospect up towards the Borghese Gardens; chiseled hieroglyphics on the obelisk beside me: all appeared like fairy work, they were so silent, so peaceful, and so lovely. It was evening, and the larger part of the city's animal population had gone to rest; there was no sound save the murmur of the many fountains, whose soft monotony was harmony to my soul. The knowledge that I was in Rome soothed me; that wondrous city, hardly more illustrious for its heroes and sages than for the power it exercised over human imagination. I lay down to rest that night with my heart's eternal burning quenched, my senses tranquil.

The next day began my rambles in search of oblivion. I endeavored to quiet the sorrows of my aching heart by even now taking an interest in the sights I'd once, in my youth, longed most ardently to see. I set one thought to ring in my brain: *I am in Rome!* Beholding, breathing in, somehow familiarly conversing with this wonder of the world, titan of the mind, majestic and eternal survivor of history! Every part of Rome is replete with its own ancient past. The walls of half the old dwellings enclose a fluted pillar or ponderous stone which once made part of an emperor's palace; the meanest streets are strewed with truncated columns, broken Corinthian capitals, sparkling fragments of granite or porphyry. And the voice of dead time rises like breath from this voiceless matter, animated still by human hopes of glory and permanence.

The famous ruins in my mind's eye were sometimes hard to recognize in their untended state, all green and overgrown—even the Coliseum, which lay entirely concealed behind veils of shimmering verdure. Making my way through the Forum, I recognized the Temple of Saturn; I climbed the base, tore a mass of creeping vines from one of the vast columns, and laid my burning cheek against its cold durability. There I sat for hours. Halls of state and triumphal arches, broken and tumbled, ivy-smothered: I forced myself to see the naked stones, then tried to restore them to their rightful places. So full was the haunted cell of my brain with vivid pictures of antiquity that I soon rejoiced at my success. For there I could see Cato, Camillus, the Gracchi—through their words, that is, and the history they'd made—my old heroes of the Republic whose meteor-light still glowed during the Empire's murky ages. My view expanded: the Forum held multitudes; I saw plebeians and lofty patricians mingling in quiet rows to hear Horatian odes, and courtesans listening to verse recitations by Virgil himself. These very stones had witnessed their wives and mothers, along with great nameless crowds, come to applaud or honor or weep for the matchless specimens of antique humanity. Now I felt myself exalted by long forgotten enthusiasm, as the glowing cadences of Cicero thronged into the opened gates of my mind. So at last I'd found a consolation. The awful journey hadn't been in vain—I had discovered in Rome a medicine for my many and vital wounds.

Then, as if this were a diorama show, the scene shifted. A thousand years had passed; the noonday light had changed to dusky brown and red. Rome in the Romantic era was a place of intrigue, scandal, and song, all ripening to be baked into grand opera. This was the Rome of imperial spies and papal splendor; of dark-eyed ingénues pining in convent seclusion, and rustic tenors leading their cattle to the Campo Vaccino. Yet another shift took me to the years of my own lifetime, before the plague, in the century of mass travel. Innumerable human figures swayed by its Enchantress Spirit had come from every land to marvel at Eternal Rome, they'd thronged the Forum daily. Now only I was left, the wondrous city's sole remaining spectator.

I stayed wrapped in such ideas for a long time. But ceaseless flight wearies the soul; eventually it must dip from its wheeling circuits round and round one spot into a sudden fall, ten thousand fathom deep, into the abyss of the present—into self-knowledge—into tenfold sadness. I roused myself, cast off my waking dreams. Where I'd almost felt my shoulders hustled by a shouting throng, now I beheld the deserted ruins of Rome, a city asleep under its own blue sky. Shadows lay tranquilly. On the Palatine Hill, sheep were grazing. A water buffalo clopped over the travertine paving stones of the Sacra Via. I was alone in the Forum, alone in the world.

Wouldn't one living man or woman, one companion in my weary solitude, be worth all Rome's remembered power and glory?

Double sorrow robed my soul in mourning. The generations I'd conjured to mind had left me all the more alone by contrast. I sat at the topmost point of a pyramid; fallen away on every side, the mighty fabric of society was no more, while I, on the giddy height, saw vacant space around me.

How could I resign myself to such a situation? How cease to repine, since there was no hand near to extract the barbed spear that had entered my heart of hearts? I stretched out my hand, and it touched none whose sensations were responsive to mine. I was girded, walled in, vaulted over, by seven-fold barriers of loneliness. Without love, without sympathy, without communication, how could I meet the morning sun each day or face the evening shades? Why did I continue to live? Why not throw off the weary weight of time, and with my own hand let out the fluttering prisoner from my agonized breast? The very sound of *Death* enticed me. It wasn't cowardice that held me back, when true fortitude was to endure. Could I have seen the hand of an insentient power, or even seen nothing at all, behind the continuing change of the seasons on this empty earth, most willingly would I have lain me down and closed my eyes upon its loveliness forever.

But this I would not do. That stormy night in London, seized on by plague as its prey, Fate had dragged me by the hair from out the strangling waves and administered life to me. By such miracles she'd bought me for her own; admitting her authority, I bowed to her decrees. A willing subject to Fate and servant of Necessity, bound by the visible laws of the invisible God, I was sustained in my belief that my obedience was the result of sound reasoning, pure feeling, and an exalted sense of the true excellence and nobility of my nature.

I turned to contemplating the minutiae of my situation. So far, I hadn't succeeded in the sole object of my desires: to find a companion for my desolation. Yet rather than despair, I looked for cause to hope. True, my inscriptions for the most part were painted on the walls of insignificant towns and villages. Even without them, though, anyone else who'd wound up alone on this depopulated continent just might, like me, come to Rome. The more slender the chance, the more I chose to build on it and accommodate my actions to this vague possibility—one which made it necessary that for a time I should make Rome my abode, at least for some months. Meanwhile, keeping occupied, if I could deliver myself up to the effort, would be the one thing capable of acting as an opiate to my nagging, sleepless sense of woe.

I'd already selected my accommodations. Once I'd emptied and purged its luxurious private rooms of their dead, the Colonna Palace was well adapted for my purpose. I found its grandeur—its treasure of paintings, its magnificent halls—to be soothing and even exhilarating. Its kitchen pantries were also fully stocked with the dried legumes and corn meal out of which I made my principal diet. For other, fresher fare, the hardships and lawlessness of my youth could be turned to good account. A man cannot throw off the habits of sixteen years. Since that age, it's true, I'd lived luxuriously, or at least surrounded by all the conveniences civilization afforded. But now my champion poacher propensities would work to the advantage of meals at my table for one.

I did my hunting in the Campagna preserves. Most mornings I spent cycling around the Borghese Gardens. I passed the long afternoons among various art museums, where I gazed at each statue of a human figure and lost myself in reverie before many a fair Madonna or beauteous nymph. I haunted the Vatican Collections, where I could stand surrounded by marble forms of divine beauty— gods and goddess in stone, each possessed by sacred gladness and love's eternal fruition. Their gazes of unsympathizing complacency drove me to wild outbursts; I'd fling reproaches at them for their supreme indifference. *"Say something! Speak to me! Aren't you human?"* For they were human shapes, the human form divine was manifest in each fairest limb and lineament, in perfect contours so suggestive of color and motion. Often, half in bitter mockery, half in self-delusion, I clasped some set of icy proportions, and, coming between Cupid and his Psyche, pressed my own lips to the blank bare marble.

I endeavored to read. I visited Rome's bookstores and libraries. I'd select a volume and choose some shady nook near the Protestant Cemetery, or on the banks of the Tiber, where I'd attempt to conceal me from myself through immersion in its pages. My mind strayed continually, drifting through the past, returning over many a ruin and through many a flowery glade, all the way back to the mountain hollows from which in early youth I'd first emerged. When I could manage to concentrate, words fit to feed radiant meditation helped only my grief find sustenance and growth, from what otherwise had been divine manna...

While I mark this paper with the tale of my so-called occupations—while I reconstruct the skeleton of my days—Ah! my hands tremble, my heart pants, and my brain rebels, refusing to supply sufficient phrases to express or describe the veil of unutterable woe that clothed these bare realities. O, worn and beating heart, let me dissect your fibers and transcribe what they record of each unmitigable misery, sadness dire, repining, and despair! Then I'll add my many ravings, the wild curses I hurled at torturing Nature. And how I've passed days shut out from light and food, from all except the burning hell alive in my own bosom.

I've made wholehearted endeavors to brave the storm, school myself to fortitude, imbue myself with the lessons of wisdom. It will not do. My hair is nearly grey. My voice strikes strangely on my ears through lack of use. With its human powers and features, my very person seems to me a monstrous excrescence, an accident of flesh. How can I express a woe that no human being until this hour ever knew—how give intelligible expression to a pang none but I could ever understand! No one has entered Rome. None will ever come. I smile bitterly at the delusion I've nourished so long; and still more when I reflect that I've exchanged it for another just as false, but to which I now cling with the same fond trust.

At some point, an additional occupation was presented to me, the one best fitted to rein in my melancholy thoughts. During one of my explorations of Rome's residential neighborhoods, I came upon an author's study; there was a writing machine on a table, along with pencils and bottles of ink, beautiful pens, fine linen paper. Parts of a manuscript lay scattered about. A scholarly work of Italian linguistics; on the desk, one page held an unfinished dedication to Posterity, for whose profit the writer had sifted and selected the niceties of that harmonious language, and to whose everlasting benefit he herewith bequeathed his labors.

"I'll write a book!" I cried.

Questions echoed back: *For whom to read? To whom dedicated?* But the idea persisted against calls to hopelessness. Won't this world be repopulated somehow? In spots unknown to me, pairs of lovers preserved here and there, whose children will wander from their seclusion out onto the Roman roads; happening at journey's end on these prodigious relics of the ante-pestilential race, won't they seek to learn how beings so wondrous in their achievements, with imaginations infinite, and powers godlike, had departed from their home to an unknown country? My decision was made: in this most ancient city, monument of the world, I'd write and leave my record of the last pandemic, a monument marking the existence of Lionel Verney. And then with a silly flourish (what is so capricious and childish as despair?) I snatched up a pencil and wrote,

DEDICATION
TO THE ILLUSTRIOUS DEAD.
SHADOWS, ARISE, AND READ YOUR FALL!
BEHOLD THE HISTORY OF THE
LAST MAN.

At first I thought only to speak of plague, of death, and at last of desertion and solitude; but I lingered fondly on my early years, and recorded with sacred zeal the virtues of my companions, those wondrous human beings I knew and loved. They have been with me during the fulfillment of my task. I have brought it to an end—I lift my eyes from my paper—again they are lost to me. Again I feel that I am alone.

Winter has come again, and the gardens of Rome have lost their leaves. A biting wind drives the city's animal inhabitants indoors. Frost has stopped the gushing fountains—even Trevi has stilled her eternal music. While I've been occupied with authorship, a year has passed. The circling seasons have supplied a changeful backdrop of surpassing beauty. After a year, I no longer guess at my state or my prospects. Loneliness is my familiar, sorrow my inseparable twin. Though I have a companion: a shaggy fellow, a waterdog-shepherd mix, whom I found tending sheep by the Campagna preserves. Probably two years had passed, maybe more; nevertheless he continued fulfilling his duties in expectation of his dead master's return. If a sheep strayed from the other half dozen he forced it back to the flock, while staying on the lookout for any intruder—though his delight was excessive when he saw me. He raced forward to throw himself against my knees, then capered round and round, wagging his tail, letting out short, quick barks of pleasure. From that day the dog has never neglected to watch by and attend on me, showing boisterous gratitude whenever I caress or talk to him. He followed me back to the Colonna Palace, bringing his fold which we graze on the lawns here and shelter in the old stables.

Aided by sundial observations and the stars, I'd made a rough calculation to ascertain the last day of the year. In the old, out-worn age, Rome's bishops made this a great occasion, marking each new year's arrival with a pomp-filled service at their basilica. On the afternoon of December 31, 2099, the dog's pattering steps and mine alongside were the only sound as we crossed the magnificent nave of St. Peter's, leaving our prints to shine in the dust. I carried paint and climbing ropes. We ascended myriad stairways together and finally reached an apartment in the great façade, above the Loggia of the Blessings. From a window ledge I rappelled my way alone to the midpoint of the mighty pediment, where the Latinized name of the Borgia pope who banned Copernicus is carved. Across it I painted four gigantic numerals, to welcome the morrow: *2 1 0 0*.

Last year of the world!

I had long determined to quit Rome, though it was a magnificent abode. But every summer, with no human health campaigns left to prevent it, the risk must increase of catching that fatal malaria for which Rome was once famous; I'd been a fool to stay, really. A solitary being is by instinct a wanderer, and that I would become. The burden of my life should even be lightened by the hope of amelioration which always attends on change of place. And it was still possible that if I looked long and far enough across Earth's surface, I could find another survivor. Methought the coasts were the likeliest finding places: if left alone in an inland district, who wouldn't choose to journey on from the spot where their last hopes had been extinguished, and travel, like me, in search of a partner for their solitude, till the seaside stopped their further progress with a watery barrier? To that water—cause of my woes, perhaps now to be their cure—I would betake myself.

Farewell, Italy! Farewell, you ornament of the world, matchless Rome, for long months the retreat of this solitary one! To civilized life—to a settled home and succession of monotonous days, farewell! Peril will now be mine; I'll hail it as a friend. Death will perpetually cross my path; I'll welcome it as a benefactor. Let hardship, hail, and deadly tempest be my shipmates. Spirits of storm, receive me! Powers of destruction, open wide your arms and clasp me forever! That is, if a kinder power hasn't decreed another end, so that after long endurance I may reap my reward, and again feel my heart beat near the heart of another like to me.

My meditations on method and route begin with selecting a boat from the many tied up there on the Tiber, and embarking with a few books, provisions, and my dog. We float down the current of the river to the sea; then, keeping near land, coast the blue Mediterranean's beauteous shores and sunny promontories. From Naples and Capri, south to Calabria, then Sicily, having dared the perils of Scylla and Charybdis in the shoals between them; emboldened, with fearless aim (for what have I to lose?) I skim Ocean's surface towards Malta and Crete. To Istanbul half in ruins I won't return; instead I'll visit Rhodes, Antalya, Cyprus, Beirut, Alexandria; and make a few journeys inland, to see Jerusalem, to see the Pyramids.

A soundless, oozy sea cave may be my dwelling before I accomplish this years-long voyage; unless the arrow of disease finds my heart first when I'm afloat somewhere on weltering shallows. Or, on the other hand, in some place I touch at, I may find what I seek—a human companion. Or if that is not to be—then to endless time, decrepit and grey-headed, my youth in the grave with those I love, the lone wanderer will still unfurl his sail and clasp the tiller—still obey the breezes of heaven and sail forever round another and another promontory, anchoring in another and another bay. I can picture leaving verdant Europe far behind: I make my way down the Suez Canal, and follow the tawny Arabian shores into the Red Sea. I see my worn skiff moored in a creek shaded by sweet-smelling spice trees, on an far eastern island in the Indian Ocean.

These are wild dreams. Yet for days they've ruled my imagination. By now I've chosen my boat and laid in my scant stores. I've selected a few books, principally Homer and Shakespeare. But the libraries of the world are thrown open to me, and in any port I can renew my stock. I have no expectation that things will be better this way; but the monotonous present is intolerable to me, I must have change. Neither hope nor joy guide me—it's restless despair and fierce impatience leading me on. I long to grapple with danger, to be excited by fear, to have some task, however slight or self-imposed, for each day's fulfillment. I shall witness all the variety of appearance that the elements can assume; I'll read fair augury in the rainbow, menace in the cloud, and some lesson or reminder dear to my heart in everything. Thus afloat around the shores of a deserted world, while the sun is high and the moon waxes or wanes, angels, the spirits of the dead, and the Supreme Being's ever-open eye will behold the tiny bark, freighted with Verney—the LAST MAN.

THE END.